THE MUM WHO'D HAD ENOUGH

Fiona was born in a youth hostel in Yorkshire. She started working on teen magazine *Jackie* at age 17, then went on to join *Just Seventeen* and *More!* where she invented the infamous 'Position of the Fortnight'. Fiona now lives in Scotland with her husband Jimmy, their teenage daughter and a wayward rescue collie cross called Jack.

For more info, visit www.fionagibson.com. You can follow Fiona on Twitter @fionagibson.

By the same author:

Mum On The Run
The Great Escape
Pedigree Mum
Take Mum Out
How the In-Laws Wrecked Christmas: a short story
As Good As It Gets?
The Woman Who Upped and Left
The Woman Who Met Her Match

FIONA GIBSON

The Mum Who'd Had Enough

avon.

Published by AVON
A division of HarperCollins*Publishers*
1 London Bridge Street,
London SE1 9GF
www.harpercollins.co.uk

A Paperback Original 2018

3

First published in Great Britain by
HarperCollins*Publishers* 2018

Copyright © Fiona Gibson 2018

Fiona Gibson asserts the moral right to
be identified as the author of this work

A catalogue record for this book is
available from the British Library

ISBN-13: 978-0-00-815704-3

This novel is entirely a work of fiction.
The names, characters and incidents portrayed in it are
the work of the author's imagination. Any resemblance to
actual persons, living or dead, events or localities is
entirely coincidental.

Set in Sabon LT Std by Palimpsest Book Production Ltd,
Falkirk, Stirlingshire

Printed and bound in Great Britain by
CPI Group (UK) Ltd, Croydon CR0 4YY

MIX
Paper from
responsible sources
FSC™ C007454

This book is produced from independently certified FSC™ paper
to ensure responsible forest management.

For more information visit: www.harpercollins.co.uk/green

Acknowledgements

Thanks to Caroline Sheldon, my brilliant agent, and to Rachel Faulkner-Willcocks, Katie Loughnane, Sabah Khan and all of the fantastic Avon team. Much love and thanks to Tania Cheston, for huge help with – and copious checking of – this novel; to Mary Fine for hilarious anecdotes that I had to steal; and to my dear anonymous buddy who gave me an insight into the mysterious world of the driving examiner. Huge thanks as ever to my beloved friends Jen, Kath, Cathy, Marie, Michelle, Wendy R and Wendy V, for encouragement every step of the way. Finally, love to Jimmy, Sam, Dexter and Erin for putting up with me, and for making everything worthwhile.

To the wonderful carers at McClymont House

'Your partner may not be the best person to teach you how to drive. It can be hard to take criticism from someone you love'

From *How to be a Confident Driver* by
Dawn Campion, Motoring Books

Chapter One

Nate

It's Scout who wakes me by licking my face. Scout, the fox terrier we would only adopt as long as he wasn't allowed on the furniture, and who is now luxuriating, sultan-like, on the king-sized bed.

'Christ, boy, get *off* me . . .' I flip over to joke with Sinead about waking up being snogged.

The joke will have to wait. Sinead isn't lying beside me.

Strange; it's unusual for me to not hear my wife getting up, and these days she's been getting up all times of the night. She is easily disturbed by nocturnal noises – I really should have set those mousetraps last night – and has been suffering from, I don't know . . . anxiety, I guess. Often, I wake up at some ungodly hour and she's lying there with her eyes wide open, looking tense and afraid. Perhaps it's hormonal? At forty-three, I *think* she's a bit young for the menopause – not that I'm any kind of expert.

I just try to help. Really, I do. I gently suggested she might try herbal supplements – I'd heard Liv at work enthusing about the soothing properties of sage – but

Sinead just snapped, 'I appreciate your handy hints, Nate, but I'm *fine*, thank-you-very-much!' Even so, it had been pretty shocking when she announced, a few weeks ago, that she was planning to see a therapist. All I could think of were Woody Allen films and everyone talking about their emotionally abusive mothers, and by all accounts Sinead's childhood was extremely happy.

Did that mean she wanted to see a therapist because of *me*?

Having manoeuvred Scout to one side, I check the time on my phone: 6.43 a.m. I climb out of bed and pad quietly out of our bedroom and across the landing, past Flynn's room.

No need to wake him yet. Our son's school is on the other side of town and most days Sinead drives him there, even though he can manage the bus no problem and thinks it's ludicrous that we want to ferry him anywhere at sixteen years old. Flynn has cerebral palsy. While most kids think nothing of it, you get the odd little arsehole who wants to start something, and there were a few bullying incidents on the bus when he was younger. Understandably, his mum still likes to deliver him safely to the door (or at least, around the corner from school, which is the closest he'll allow). He comes home with his mate Max, who lives two streets away, so that's fine.

Of course it's fine. Flynn is virtually an adult. I need to stop thinking of him as our little boy.

More urgently right now, I have a strong desire to find out where my wife is. I check the bathroom – no Sinead – and head downstairs with Scout trotting along at my side.

In the living room, last weekend's newspapers are still

strewn messily across the coffee table. 'Honey?' I call out. 'Where are you?'

No reply. I go through to the kitchen, expecting to find her there, sipping coffee and explaining that she just woke up stupidly early and couldn't get back to sleep. But there's only Bella, my mother's sleek and regal collie, whom we are dog-sitting while Mum scales some Cumbrian mountains with her new bloke. Still dozing in her own basket, Bella wouldn't dream of jumping onto anyone's bed. Mum thinks it's appalling that Scout is allowed onto ours. Judging by her reaction, you'd think we allowed him to sit on the table and lap at our soup.

'Sinead?' I call her more loudly this time, then place a hand on the kettle. It's cold. *Detective Nate Turner surmises that his wife has not yet made coffee.* I fill it and, as I switch it on, I spot a sheet of lined A4 paper lying on the worktop.

It is entirely covered with my wife's rather charming, elegant handwriting – albeit a little scrawlier than usual – and looks like some sort of list. A to-do list, I assume, giving it a cursory glance. Sinead is fanatical about writing things down; she reckons it's the only way she can 'keep on top of this family'.

I look at the list again, properly this time. At the top of the sheet, she's written a heading and underlined it several times:

Everything That's Wrong With You

I frown and stare at it. She can't mean me. As far as I know, she sat up pretty late last night, probably working her way through that second bottle of Blossom Hill, judging by the empty sitting by the bin. It must be some

3

kind of stream-of-consciousness thing, maybe triggered by yesterday's session with Rachel, her therapist. Although Sinead is loath to tell me what goes on between them, I'd imagine Rachel gives her various mental exercises to do. She probably told Sinead to list all the things she thinks are wrong with *herself*.

I look down at Scout, who is staring up at me with unblinking brown eyes. 'Is that what she pays all that money for?' I ask him, at which he tilts his head. As far as I'm concerned, Sinead is pretty much all-round-brilliant just as she is. I have always believed this, from the night I first spotted her at the All Saints gig in Leeds (we often joke that we wish we could say it was Oasis or Blur) and she was dancing in her vest top and combats, long blonde hair swooshing around her finely boned face. My belief in her wondrousness has only increased over the years.

I look back at the list, suspecting now that I probably shouldn't even read it, if it's meant to be part of her therapy . . .

Unable to resist, I start to read:

You don't listen to me.

You take me for granted.

You don't consider my needs . . .

I frown. Who *is* this 'you' she's talking about? Surely, it's not me. Could it be Flynn? No, of course not. The most she ever complains about is the state of his room and his lackadaisical attitude towards homework. So who else could she mean?

I continue to read:

No effort made re us as a couple . . .

Christ, so it *is* me! I glance around, half-expecting her to be standing there in the doorway with her arms folded and a bemused look on her face. *It's just a joke, Nate!*

Can't you take a joke? Of course she's not there. I can't even start to wonder where she is right now. On a walk, probably, although that would be weird at this time in the morning – and doubly weird that she hasn't taken the dogs with her. She probably just needed to clear her head, I decide. Maybe she had a restless night.

Okay, so this is far from ideal, this list of my apparent shortcomings – but perhaps there's a positive side to it. At least now I can start to understand why she's been unhappy lately, and what made her start seeing that Rachel woman in the first place. If it's about me making more of an effort – well, that's something I can easily put right.

Trying to ignore the tight ball of anxiety that's growing inside me, I read on:

You leave too much to me.

You belittle my job and show no interest in it.

No spontaneity in our lives . . .

Well, this seems a pretty spontaneous gesture, this summary of my crapness, but perhaps she's been planning to write it for weeks?

Your bloody record collection . . .

What the hell!? Okay, I have a *lot*, probably something like a thousand or more, I don't know – I haven't counted them since about 1992 – with a definite bias towards Bruce Springsteen, his influencers and contemporaries. However, they are neatly stored in alphabetical order. Is *that* it? Is she sick of being married to 'the kind of man who alphabetises his albums' (as I once heard her remark to her friend Michelle in a somewhat scathing tone, followed by gales of derisive laughter)? No – it can't be that. No one could object to a superb collection housed on custom-built shelves . . .

Your terrible attempts at DIY . . .

. . . If I say so myself, I'm pretty handy with my Black and Decker Combi cordless drill!

. . . and your blank refusal to get the professionals in. Yes, to save us a fortune!

Handing me a wodge of tenners to buy my own Christmas present . . .

. . . I had no idea she was mad about that. I'd just assumed it was the most practical solution, given that I'd apparently ballsed it up on her last birthday with what she termed 'that terrible skirt' (i.e., the leopard print one I'd thought she'd look wonderful in).

Woolly boundaries re Flynn . . .

Ah, so now we're getting to the nub of things: my ineffectiveness as a father. Clearly, I am a disaster as a human being—

'Dad.'

I mean, what kind of boundaries is she talking about?

'DAD!'

My head flicks round. 'Flynn! Hi.' I scrunch the note in my fist, like a teenager caught in class with an obscene drawing of his naked French teacher.

'What's that?' Flynn peers at me through uncombed, wavy light brown hair. He is wearing the baggy grey T-shirt and black tracksuit bottoms he insists on for bed (proper PJs having long been deemed unacceptable).

'What's what?' I ask in a weirdly high voice.

'That thing there.'

'Oh, just a bit of scrap paper . . .' I sense myself sweating and tighten my grip.

'Can I see it?' His gaze seems to bore into my skull.

'No!' I shout, cheeks blazing.

'All right! God, Dad . . .' He blows out air and shakes his head in bafflement.

'Sorry,' I mutter. 'Sorry, Flynn. I'm just a bit, um . . .' I tail off as he opens the fridge.

'Something smells bad in here,' he observes, taking out the orange juice carton and swigging from it.

I clear my throat, deciding I must dispose of Sinead's note while our son's back is turned, which probably gives me about three seconds. My immediate options appear to be a) eat it or b) conceal it. I opt for stuffing it into my pyjama pocket.

'Dad, I said something smells.' He bangs the fridge door shut and glowers at me, as if I might be the source.

'I think it's Scout,' I say quickly. 'If that's the smell you mean, it's been happening more often since we bought the liver-flavoured food. I think we should go back to chicken . . .'

Flynn nods, and for a brief moment I think, well, I can't be a *complete* disaster as, somehow, I have managed to resume an air of relative normality despite Sinead's note and apparent disappearance.

'Where's Mum?' he asks, pulling the lid off the cookie jar and grabbing a fistful of biscuits.

'Er . . .' I look around, as if it has only just occurred to me to ponder her whereabouts. 'She must've popped out.'

'Popped out? Popped out *where*?'

'Er, to the shop, probably. Maybe for bread.'

Flynn eyes me suspiciously. I have always been a terribly unconvincing liar. 'So, is she taking me to school?'

'Erm, I'm not sure, but don't worry. If she's not back in time, I'll do it.'

He frowns. 'Aren't you going to work?'

'It doesn't matter if I'm a bit late,' I fib. In fact, I'm due to start at 8.30 a.m., and my timekeeping is normally impeccable – because no one wants to be kept waiting for their driving test. That's my job. I am a driving examiner, possibly one of the most derided professions on earth, which requires me to be on high alert for the minor and major faults of the general public. Right now, *my* alleged faults are causing a curious bulge in the breast pocket of my pyjamas.

'I'll just get the bus,' Flynn remarks, posting an entire Oreo into his mouth.

'No, no, I'll drive you.'

He munches his substandard breakfast, his attention caught by my lumpy pocket. I clamp a hand over it. 'Dad . . . are you . . . *all right*?'

'Of course I am. Why?'

'Have you got, like, a pain or something?'

'No . . .'

'It's just, you're clutching at your heart like that . . .'

I whip my hand away. 'I'm fine. Absolutely *fine*. Anyway, we'd better get ready,' I add briskly, establishing a *firm boundary* right there, 'or we're going to be late. You have a shower first . . .'

'Yeah, okay, Dad,' Flynn says carefully, addressing me now as if I am a confused and vulnerable adult he's found wandering about in his nightwear.

With Sinead missing, and her bizarre note stuffed in my pocket, it feels like a pretty accurate description right now.

Chapter Two

The trouble with being left a note like that is that you need time to figure out what the hell's going on. Ideally, you also want access to the person who wrote it to see if they really meant it, or just lost their mind temporarily.

I mean, my record collection! Is it Springsteen that's tipped her over the edge? One too many playings of *Born to Run*? I need to know as a matter of urgency, but it seems that Sinead's phone is turned off.

The other trouble with this whole list business is that real life must continue, which means putting on a great show of everything being normal. It's 7.46 on a bleary Thursday morning, and our son must still go to school, even if he does have a selfish incompetent father, and I need to go to work – plus, obviously, track down my wife.

While Flynn showers, I try to keep calm and not over-react, and only call her mobile eleven times.

Hi, you've reached Sinead. Please leave your number and I'll call you right back . . .

Such a warm, cheery voice, husky with a soft Yorkshire lilt; the voice of a woman who has always embraced life, who has reams of friends – from childhood and her art school days, and even more through being Flynn's mum. Everyone knows her as being supremely capable, great fun, delightful company and, of course, a fantastic mother. We'd have had more babies – a whole gang – if we'd managed to conceive after having Flynn, but it only happened once. Sinead miscarried at ten weeks, when Flynn was three, and after that it just didn't happen at all. We're not really into 'signs', the two of us, but we consoled ourselves that this was probably nature's way of urging us to count our blessings and focus fully on our son. So we didn't go down the IVF route. Our friend Abby did, and she reckons the stress and disappointment killed off her marriage. Plus, with Flynn's condition, Sinead and I spent enough time in clinics and hospitals as it was.

I hear Flynn emerging from the bathroom. Once he's back in his room, I dive in, turn on the shower and take another look at the list, as apparently I hadn't quite got to the end.

You treat me like an idiot (i.e., always texting to remind me not to leave things on trains)
Don't make me feel special
Keep referring to Rachel as 'your shrink' (i.e., making a joke of it and so belittling the issue)
Constant untidiness
Mouse issue (traps!!!)
YOUR MOTHER!
Refusal to pick up Scout's poos in garden!!!

The exclamation marks are coming thick and fast now, pinging into my face like air rifle pellets.

'Dad?' Flynn raps on the bathroom door.

'Yes?'

'It's ten past eight. I can just get the bus if it's easier?'

'No, it's okay.'

'Why are you insisting on driving me? I don't get it . . .'

Because it's imperative that you go to school under the impression that everything is normal, as indeed it will be by the time you come home this afternoon, because I fully intend to sort everything out.

'I'm nearly ready, okay?' I shout back. Through the door, I hear him muttering about my weirdness – the word 'mental' is clearly audible – then wandering back to his bedroom and firmly closing the door.

I drop the note on the floor, pull off my pyjamas and kick them, rebelliously, into the corner by the bin. In the shower I use Sinead's posh Penhaligon's 'Juniper Sling' shower gel rather than the cheap blue stuff – another devil-may-care gesture – and mentally run through as many of her complaints as I can remember whilst sluicing myself down.

The big ones – about being an uncaring, selfish arse-hole – all swirl into one terrible, heady mess, and I find myself fixating instead on the more tangible matter of Scout's poos. Okay, maybe I have missed the odd tiny deposit in our garden, down in the long grass by the shed. Or at least, *they have been missed* (clearly, and without my knowledge, this has become my responsibility). This matter can be easily rectified. From now on I will never again let Scout – or, specifically, Scout's arse – out of my sight.

With a wave of petulance, I dry off briskly and check my phone in case Sinead called while I was showering. Nothing. I'm tempted to phone around her closest friends, but I don't want to alarm anyone and, anyway, what would I say? *'Hello, it's Nate. Sinead seems to have gone missing'*? No need for any of that.

It also occurs to me now that, because she's gone AWOL, I'll have to walk Scout and Bella before Flynn and I can set off. Sinead usually takes Scout around the block first thing, before driving Flynn to school, then she parks back by our house and walks to the gift shop a few streets away, where she works. On top of all that, she also pops home at lunchtime to let Scout into our back garden (naturally, she never fails to pick up his poos). Oh, God, the colossal amount of stuff she does! No wonder she's hacked off. All this perpetual nipping back and forth, plus taking care of most of the shopping, cooking, laundry and homework supervision – and that's just for starters. But then, she's never complained about anything specifically before now . . . At least, I don't think she has (admittedly, I find it hard to keep up with everything sometimes). Instead of harbouring all of these resentments, couldn't she just have let me know?

In our bedroom now I pull on my white shirt and smart dark grey trousers: pretty standard driving examiners' attire. I also text Liv, the manager at one of the three test centres I work from: *Sorry Liv, running slightly late, bit of a family situation, be in asap.* It sounds terrible to say this, but all three managers – and Liv in particular – are aware of the situation with Flynn, and are extremely understanding whenever something unexpected happens.

Suddenly remembering that Sinead's thorough character assassination of me is still lying on our bathroom floor, I rush to retrieve it, shove it into my trouser pocket and call out to Flynn: 'Just taking the dogs out. Make sure you're ready for when I get back, okay?'

His bedroom door flies open. 'I *am* ready.' Indeed, he is kitted out in the faded sweatshirt and skinny black jeans

12

he manages to pass off as school uniform. 'It's you who's making us late,' he adds, not incorrectly. 'Where's Mum?'

'I told you, she must've nipped out . . .' To escape his suspicious gaze, I head downstairs, and search the entire ground floor for my specs, eventually spotting them by the kettle, where I found the note. Jamming them onto my face, I summon my canine charges with a stern command – no woolly boundaries there! – and step out into our well-tended terraced street.

The sky is a clear pale blue and streaked with gauzy clouds, the air cool on this bright May morning. We live on the edge of Hesslevale, a thriving and popular West Yorkshire town nestling in a lush green valley. There are numerous charming restaurants, pubs and a cinema, and the former textile mills now house artists' studios and craft workshops. We are lucky to live here . . . aren't we? At least, I always believed we were pretty happy and sorted, and that my wife thought so too.

I peer hopefully up and down our street, willing an only slightly miffed (or perhaps even *contrite*) Sinead to be walking towards me. There's just Howard from next door, striding out in baggy chinos and a faded peach rugby top with Monty, their enormous labradoodle, who has a tendency to try and hump everything in sight, hence my family's nickname for him: *Mounty*. While he splatters Betty Ratcliffe's wheelie bin in a seemingly never-ending arc of pee, Howard catches my eye and waves.

Clearly, he expects us to catch up with them for a circuit around the block. He and his wife Katrina are terribly cheery and gung-ho, and we often chat over the fence that divides our adjoining back gardens. I shouldn't moan about having friendly neighbours. However, thankfully, there's no time for neighbourly chit-chat now, not when there's school and work to get to, not to mention about eighty-five personality defects for me to address. I raise a hand in greeting, noticing with relief that Sinead's silver Skoda is parked on the corner – suggesting that she hasn't gone far – and start walking briskly in the opposite direction to where Howard is waiting. Unfriendly, perhaps, but preferable to keeping up the *everything-is-normal* facade.

The dogs and I trudge on. As Bella stops to pee, I glance down at Scout. He keeps looking up at me, intently, as if he *knows*. 'How can she stand being married to me if I'm so awful?' I ask him, consumed by a wave of self-pity. Scout just hunches his back in that familiar way, and squats to do his business. I've snatched a bag from my pocket and bagged up his deposit before it's barely hit the ground.

As we recommence our walk, I try Sinead's number again. Still voicemail. *Where are you?* I text her. *What's going on?* Right now, I don't know what else to say. I just need to get home and cajole Flynn into having a proper breakfast (i.e., not just Oreos), but then, should we really be policing these things now? Of course, if Sinead had been there, he'd have had a bowl of cornflakes, some granary toast, fresh fruit salad and his orange juice in a glass and not just slugged straight from the carton.

In a driving test, you are allowed up to fifteen faults (what we call 'minors'). One serious fault – a 'major' – and you'll fail. I'd consider the woolly boundaries thing – in fact, *most* of the points on her list – to be minors, but who am I to know? The main thing, I decide as the dogs and I troop back to the house, is not to panic. Sinead probably just needs some space, in order to think things over, so I won't call her again until her break. On the rare occasions I've popped into the gift shop where she works – Tawny Owl, or whatever it's called – it's been serene and peaceful, so hopefully she'll be in a better mood by lunchtime. In the meantime, I'll drive Flynn to school – he doesn't need to know anything about this – and then onwards to work.

Once I'm there, I'll act normal and be the conscientious examiner I am paid to be, just as I have for the past decade, after a couple of years of working as a driving instructor, when it had become apparent that my playing in bands, and teaching kids to play guitar, just wasn't bringing in enough regular cash. That was okay; I'd given music a decent shot and prolonged my adolescence more than most people manage to get away with. Flynn was just four, and I was thirty-one, and it was high time I grew up. It had always made sense for Sinead to be at home full-time to give Flynn the time and attention he needed.

Plus, I'd enjoyed driving various bands around over the years. I'd loved the banter and camaraderie and, yes, even the farty vans and interminable all-night journeys punctuated with bleary service-station stops. Gallons of bad coffee and oily sausages and eggs: it had all been huge fun, but I was ready for a change, and Sinead had often commented about what a courteous, unruffleable driver I was (looking back, could that now be perceived as a fault? Would she have preferred a screaming maniac with scant respect for The Highway Code?).

It was her encouragement that had prompted me to sign up for driving examiner training. 'You'd be perfect for it,' she'd insisted. 'You're so polite, so well behaved and law-abiding.'

Is *that* what's wrong, a vital point she omitted from her list – the fact that I'm a tedious bore, lacking the nerve to break speed limits or negotiate a junction without indicating at the appropriate time? Would I seem more desirable – sexier, I suppose – if I drastically reduced my mirror usage and constantly lambasted other road users with the horn?

I pause at the privet hedge a few doors down from our house. While Scout and Bella are tinkling in tandem, I pull that wretched note out of my pocket. I read it all again, every damn word, feeling sicker at every line. As I shove it back into my pocket, I reach for my phone for the umpteenth time. But there's no reply to my text; no 'Sorry, I just went a bit mad there but don't worry – I'll be back home very soon.'

Out of habit, I tap my email icon. As the messages roll in, I spot one from her, sent less than an hour ago at 7.40 a.m:

Nate, I assume you've found my note by now. At least, I hope it's you who found it and not Flynn. I'm sorry if it's shocking but I had to tell you how I felt. I didn't know what else to do. It's just got so bad and you're not hearing me. I have tried to talk to you but you won't listen. I'll be in touch soon, and of course I'll spend time with Flynn and talk things through with him. It's important that he understands that none of this is his fault.

I know we'll be okay eventually. We'll still be Flynn's parents together and do the job as well as we possibly can, just as we have always done. He knows we love him and that's never going to change. In time, I'm sure the three of us can work out the practical issues. I know it might seem alarming right now, but when you look at Flynn's friends, it's hardly unusual to have divorced parents—

'What the fuck?' I blurt out loud.

16

So now you have read all my reasons, my wife concludes, *I hope you'll understand why I have been so unhappy lately, and why I am leaving you.*
I'm sorry, Nate.
Sinead

Chapter Three

Sinead

I have done an unspeakable thing. I have left my child. It hadn't been my plan to do this; at least not last night after a shitload of cheap white wine. But then, something had to happen.

Installed at my friend Abby's across town now, I just wish I could erase the image in my mind of Nate's horrified face when he discovered my list this morning. He had no idea how bad things were. The only person who really knew was Rachel, my therapist.

Yesterday, after work, I sat in her small, sparse room with its brown nylon carpet, trying to figure out whether my marriage was definitely over. Was it really that bad? Or, after nineteen years together, was this just what being married was *like*? Rachel – or 'that Rachel woman', as Nate tends to refer to her – tucked her shiny black hair behind her ears and clasped her hands primly. 'You might find it helpful to write down all the aspects you're unhappy with,' she suggested, 'and then all the good things too.'

'The aspects of what?' I asked.

'Well, of Nate and you. Of your relationship.'

I'd first come to see her six weeks ago, having googled 'therapist' and booked an appointment simply because I was sort of unravelling and the voice on her answerphone sounded kind. I'd deliberately chosen someone based in Solworth, rather than Hesslevale – I didn't want to keep running into her in our local Sainsbury's. And so I went along, dry-mouthed and nervous, anticipating an older woman full of wisdom, with an instruction book for life. I hadn't expected to be greeted by a chic young thing in red lipstick and a short black shift with a Peter Pan collar, who probably considered Britpop to be 'history'.

'Writing a list is like talking to a friend,' she explained. 'It can help to clarify your thoughts and work through complex emotions. It's a way of distilling the very essence of your togetherness with Nate.'

'I'm not sure there's anything left to distil,' I murmured.

'Of course there is,' she insisted, 'and this exercise will help you to identify what's still there, and worth saving, underneath the pressures and resentments that clutter up our lives.'

I nodded, trying to process this. I'd been feeling awful for the past year or so: lost and alone, as if I was just going through the motions of getting through each day. Friends had listened as I'd tried to explain how I felt – but there's only so much you can go on before you start to imagine they're glazing over. Anxiety, depression or whatever it was; these things happened to other people, I'd always thought. As a younger woman, I'd always been pretty happy and optimistic, the last person I'd have imagined to end up feeling this way. And so I'd seen my GP, a kindly woman who knew all about the stresses we'd been through with Flynn over the years, who said, 'I think you need a helping hand, Sinead, just to ease you through

19

this rough patch.' She prescribed an antidepressant that had made me feel as if I was viewing the world through net curtains, and killed off my libido stone dead. I'd swapped pills for therapy – and so there I was, blinking back tears in front of a woman who probably has a Snapchat account.

'So, what should I do with this list, once I've made it?' I asked. 'I mean, should I show it to Nate?'

Rachel tipped her head to one side. 'What do *you* think?'

She often does this, batting a question straight back at me.

'I don't know,' I murmured. *Sixty pounds an hour, I paid her. Couldn't she tell me what to think?*

She cleared her throat; my time was nearly up. Age-wise, I'd put her at thirty tops. What could she possibly know about marriage and love? 'The important part is putting it all down,' she replied, 'in writing.'

And that was that. As far as Rachel was concerned, as long as I'd written the darn thing, it didn't matter what I did with it: I could use it to line a budgie's cage – if we had one – or set it on fire. I handed her my debit card, which she popped into the slot of her little machine. In went my pin number, as if I'd just done a grocery shop. I almost expected her to ask if I had a Nectar card.

That was hard-earned money I'd just spent. A whole day's earnings in the shop, come to think of it. It could have bought new trainers for Flynn, the ingredients for a week's worth of dinners or – what the hell – several bottles of industrial cheap white wine from Londis, the kind Nate calls 'lady petrol'. 'Fancy a fine vintage from *L'Ondice* tonight, darling?' he used to ask in a faux-plummy voice, in the days when we still joked around . . .

When we still laughed and had fun . . .

When I still loved him madly and regarded him as my best friend in the world. Nate Turner, my soulmate: the brightest, kindest, funniest – and *sweetest* – man I had ever met.

And now?

I know he's a hardworking man, and a good dad; we function together, but that no longer feels like enough. How can I be expected to love him when he barely registers my feelings?

Rachel had turned to her laptop and tapped something quickly. 'Gosh, I'm busy next week. Could you do Thursday, Sinead? Same time?'

'That'd be great,' I replied, flashing a smile as I trotted out of the therapy room in her warehouse flat, as if we'd just got together for our regular coffee and it was the highlight of my week.

It was Flynn I was thinking about on my drive home, and what he'd make of me seeing a therapist (I still can't quite believe I have one. It feels as bizarre as if I were to say 'my butler'). I've been vague about it, muttering about staying late at the shop to help out Vicky, my boss – not that he's particularly interested in what I get up to. But I know he'd be shocked if he knew where I'd really been going.

I realise it's indulgent, and that when I describe my life, it seems like I have everything I could possibly want. I am forty-three years old, with a husband, a son and a job that doesn't stress me terribly – and of course people have it far worse than I do. Hesslevale is a popular, family-oriented town – the kind of place where people get together and create vegetable gardens on waste ground, for anyone to enjoy. You can barely move for artisan roasted coffee and poetry readings, and I've found myself being wrestled into screen-printing workshops and giant community knitting projects, virtually against my will. Thankfully, our town still retains a slightly shabby edge, which prevents it from toppling into unbearable tweeness; there's a couple of burger joints, and a noodle bar ('Canoodles') that no one I know has ever ventured into. It's been a wonderful, supportive and friendly place in which to raise our son.

The trouble is, somewhere along the way I have stopped loving his dad.

Write down all the aspects you're unhappy with . . .

Did Rachel really mean all of them, or just the big stuff? I'd switched on the car radio in my temperamental Skoda, trying to decide whether the whole therapy business was a colossal waste of time and money. I'd spent £360 so far, and she'd basically told me to make a list. The whole drive home, I started to think of specific reasons why I was unhappy, and where on earth I'd start if it came to writing it all down.

As I'd parked up, another disturbing thought had hit me: my mother-in-law, Judy, was dropping by that evening. The realisation caused me to leap out of my car, hurry to *L'Ondice* at the end of our road, and virtually hurl myself at the wine fridge at the back.

'Oh, you're lucky to have caught me,' Judy announced, eyeing my clinking carrier bag as I strode into our hallway five minutes later. 'I'm just leaving, love. What a pity . . .'

'Such a shame,' I agreed. 'I'm so sorry!' We hugged briefly, and my gaze met Nate's over her shoulder. He was wearing the nervy expression I'd become accustomed to seeing after I'd had a session with Rachel. I caught him scanning my face for clues. 'I thought you were staying for dinner?' I added, greeting Scout as he hurtled towards me.

22

Judy shook her head. She wears her silvery hair in a pixie crop, and was kitted out in her go-to attire of chambray shirt and navy chinos. As rangy as a racehorse, she exuded no-nonsense chic. 'I'd love to, but I really don't have the time. Still so much to do before the trip.' She frowned. 'Shame I've missed seeing Flynn . . .'

'Yes, he's out at the cinema with friends.' I paused. 'I hope you have a fantastic trip. Has Raymond been hill-walking before?'

'No – but he'll be fine,' she said firmly. Having divorced Nate's late father when Nate was a teenager, Judy is partial to setting tough physical tests whenever she starts seeing anyone new. You'd never guess she is seventy-two; her face is virtually unlined, her blue eyes bright, her figure enviable. 'Anyway, how was your . . . *appointment*?' she asked as she pulled on her jacket.

'Appointment?' I frowned, confused. Surely Nate hadn't told her about Rachel?

'Nate said you had an appointment after work.' She studied me, unblinking. 'Nothing . . . worrying, I hope?'

'Oh, no, not at all!' I felt the blush whoosh up my face.

'Not . . . *ill* are you?' She tried, unsuccessfully, to hide a glimmer of hope.

'No, no – I'm absolutely fine.'

Her stare was piercing. Right up to retirement, Judy was a science teacher, and I bet no one lit their farts with a Bunsen burner in *her* classes.

'I, er, just had a massage,' I fibbed.

'A massage?' she gasped, as if I'd said 'colonic irrigation'.

'Yes, just a little treat for myself . . .'

'Oh, I do admire you, Sinead. I really do . . .'

'Why's that?' I asked, genuinely perplexed.

Her mouth flickered with amusement. 'Putting yourself first like that. It's very commendable, I have to say . . .'

'Well, er, I—'

'. . . Although I could never justify spending that sort of money on myself. I'd feel so guilty, so *decadent*, that it would cancel out any enjoyment I'd gained from the massage . . .'

What would she have thought if she knew I've been forking out – *weekly* – to have my head examined?

'Er, Mum,' Nate cut in belatedly, 'a massage isn't that big a deal, you know.'

'Ha. Isn't it? I wouldn't know. Never gone in for those pampering scenarios myself – but each to their own.' She flashed a bemused smile. 'Anyway, I'd really better go. Bye, Bella, darling!' But Bella was far too interested in gnawing Scout's disgusting fluorescent rubber hamburger to even glance in her owner's direction.

A stillness settled over us after Judy had gone.

'Well, that was nice, as usual,' I muttered.

'Oh, you know what she's like.' Nate adjusted his wire-framed specs. At forty-three, with wavy caramel hair and intensely brown eyes, my husband still manages to fall into the 'cute' category. Due to his height and long, long legs – he's six-foot-four – there's something endearingly gangly about him. If he were in a film, he'd be the kindly teacher who helps a colleague carry her unruly heap of books and box files – and bingo, they'd fall in love.

While he started to make dinner, I went to investigate the bathroom, which I meant to tackle the previous night. As expected, it had still been strewn with socks, pants and several T-shirts belonging to Nate and Flynn. Both of them are phenomenally untidy. Nate's music magazines were piled messily on the bathroom scales, and the washbasin was daubed with toothpaste and shaving gel. Of course, none of that needed to be dealt with there and then. What I should have been doing was hanging out with Nate, chopping parsley and chatting companionably, instead of moving on to hoover our bedroom and prickling over a massage I'd never had.

'Ready, love!' he called from the kitchen.

I trotted downstairs to see he'd poured our wine and set out our bowls of pasta very prettily, with salad in a glass bowl and a fresh loaf. Although I have always done the lion's share of the cooking, Nate had started to make dinner on Rachel days. It was as if he was trying to make things right.

'This looks great,' I said, at which he muttered something I didn't catch. We started to eat in silence. I heard the front door fly open; Flynn was home. I jumped up and bounded over to hug him as if he'd just traversed the Himalayas, rather than sat in the Odeon for two hours.

'Hey, Mum.' He laughed and bobbed down to greet Scout and our visiting hound. 'Hi, Bella-baby. You always smell so good! No anchovy breath on you. Not like our stinky old Scout. You look blow-dried as well. Does Gran blow-dry you?' Flynn adores animals and nagged for a dog until we finally gave in. Scout is our second, acquired to help us over the heartache when Larry, our beloved lurcher, died last year.

'So, how was it?' I asked eagerly.

Flynn's lazy grin stretched across his face as he straightened up. He has inherited his dad's features: the full, wide mouth and dark-chocolate eyes, plus the light brown hair with a defiant wave. 'I was only at the cinema, Mum. Not sitting an exam.'

'No, I know that. What was the film again?'

25

He mumbled the name of an action thriller I'd never heard of. Nate and I haven't been to the cinema since something like 1926.

'Was it good?' I enquired.

'Uh, yeah?' He shrugged.

'What was it about?'

He peered at me as I sat back down at the table. 'You don't want to know the whole plot, do you?'

I laughed. 'No, of course not . . . so, have you eaten?'

'Yeah, we got pizza . . .'

'School okay today?' Nate asked stiffly.

Flynn threw him a baffled look. 'Have my real mum and dad been abducted?'

'What d'you mean?' Nate frowned.

'The two of you, grilling me like you're distant relatives instead of my parents. Shall we sit down and talk about what I'd like to be when I grow up?'

Nate and I laughed uncomfortably, and Flynn sniggered and escaped to his room, away from his weird, quizzing parents.

I tried to tuck into the pasta I'd barely touched. 'You're not upset about Mum, are you?' Nate ventured.

'No, it's fine,' I said quickly, gaze fixed on my bowl.

'You know what she's like. So bloody sanctimonious. God forbid anyone should enjoy themselves—'

'It's *fine*, Nate.' I looked up. Tension flickered in his eyes.

'You don't mind having Bella to stay, do you?'

'Of course not,' I exclaimed. 'Why would I?'

'I've no idea,' he replied. 'I just wish I knew what you and Rachel talked about, that's all—'

'It's not about a well-behaved collie coming to stay!' I blurted out.

'What *is* it, then? Why can't you just tell me what's wrong?'

Pink patches had sprung up on his cheeks. What did he *think* was wrong? He knew about my visit to the GP, and the antidepressants – although he hadn't taken the trouble to talk to me then, to try and find out why I was so down, so close to tears much of the time. Depression: a taboo word, as far as Nate's concerned. Brush it under the carpet, that's his stock response to anything remotely uncomfortable. Three-point turns, emergency stops: he's fine with that kind of stuff. But emotions are messy and scary and he prefers not to have to deal with them. It was clearly bothering him that I'd been sharing my own feelings with someone else. It happened every week, this post-Rachel probing.

He *still* wouldn't let it drop, even as we cleared up after dinner. 'How long d'you think you'll carry on with this?' he asked, washing up with unnecessary vigour.

'I don't know,' I replied. 'I mean, there's no grand plan—'

'And you won't share any of it with me? The stuff you discuss with this stranger, I mean?'

'Well, it's kind of private.' I was doing my best to remain calm.

'So private you can't even tell *me*?'

'Nate, the whole point is that it's *not* you . . .'

'Whoah, great, thanks a lot!'

I stared at him, almost laughing in disbelief. 'If it was you I needed to talk to I'd just, well – talk to *you* . . .'

'At least that'd be free,' he thundered. 'You wouldn't have to drive over Solworth either—'

'Oh, right, so I'd save the petrol money as well!'

'Yes, you would. Have you checked our bank balance lately?'

27

'Oh, for Christ's sake . . .' I stared at the man I'd once loved to distraction, and who was now glaring at me, his face mottled red, his T-shirt splashed with dishwater. 'You begrudge me the four pounds fifty or whatever it costs to get there and back?'

'Of course I don't—'

'What's *wrong* with you two tonight?' We both swung around to see Flynn standing in the doorway.

'Sorry, son,' Nate blustered, looking away.

Flynn snorted. 'What were you shouting about?'

'We weren't shouting, honey,' I said quickly.

He blinked at us. 'Yes, you were. And what's four pounds fifty?'

'Nothing,' I exclaimed, looking at Nate for confirmation.

'*Nothing's* four pounds fifty,' he said with an exaggerated shrug, while our son exhaled loudly and strode away, as if concluding that his parents really had lost it this time.

Nate and I fell into a sullen silence, and only much later, when we were watching TV, did he attempt to make conversation with me.

'I meant to tell you, I got her again today,' he remarked.

'Which one?' I asked.

'*You* know. The one with a tiny fringe that stops above the eyebrows, like your old college mates used to have?'

Ah, the art-school-mini-fringe. 'You mean Tanzie? The one who's failed, what, ten times now?'

'Yeah, that's the one. And it's eleven, actually.'

'Poor thing,' I murmured. 'I can't believe she hasn't given up by now. If I were her, I'd resign myself to a life of blagging lifts and using public transport—'

'No, you wouldn't,' he insisted. 'Anyway, that would never happen to you. You passed first time! You're so capable, nothing fazes you—'

'That's right,' I said bitterly. 'I just soldier on, never needing any care or looking after—' Without warning, my eyes welled up. I turned away before Nate could see.

'Tanzie usually just accepts that she's failed,' he went on, as if I hadn't spoken. 'Nadira and Eric say the same – we've all had her, over and over. But this time there were floods of tears. Inconsolable, she was . . .' He sighed loudly and shook his head. 'Anyway, I'm shattered. Coming up to bed?'

'In a little while,' I replied. 'Could you set the mousetraps before you go up? I saw another one this morning . . .'

'That'll be the same one as before,' Nate remarked.

'How can you be so sure?'

'Well, what did it look like?'

I shrugged. 'Small, furry, greyish-brown . . .'

'Yeah, that's the one *I* saw.'

I stared at him, aware of my anger starting to bubble up again. I suspect it's permanently there, simmering just below the surface. 'I didn't spot any distinguishing features,' I retorted, 'and it wasn't wearing a T-shirt with its name on. I think we must have quite a problem – an infestation, actually – seeing as they're appearing pretty much every day . . .'

'No, what I mean is, it's probably just the same one that keeps *reappearing*,' Nate declared, with a trace of smugness.

My chest was tightening, and I was aware of veering dangerously close towards what's commonly known as 'overreacting'. At least, that's what it's called when it's a woman. When it's a man, he is merely 'making a point'. 'I'd say it's more likely that we have dozens,' I went on, 'and they're all shagging away behind the fridge . . .'

'Now you're being ridiculous,' he snapped.

'Am I? Shut up for a minute and listen.' I put a finger to my lips.

'I do *not* want to hear mouse-sex happening . . .'

'Neither do I! And I've told you I can't bear to deal with mousetraps. I know it's silly, but I just can't bring myself to do it—'

Nate stifled a yawn. 'I'll sort it tomorrow, all right, love? It's been one hell of a day. Did I tell you my last candidate of the day called me a wanker?'

'Really?' I looked at him. 'That's terrible. I can't imagine why anyone would do that. Now, could you *please* just set those traps?'

Chapter Four

Nate

Somehow, I manage to drive our son to school as if I am just a normal bloke, fully in charge of his faculties.

'What are you doing?' Flynn barks as I pull up outside the main school gate.

'Dropping you off,' I reply, affecting a cheery tone.

His eyes narrow, beaming displeasure. 'Mum never stops here. She always parks round the corner, by the church.'

'God, yes, of course – sorry. Don't know what I was thinking—'

'*God . . .*' Swivelling only his eyes, Flynn scans the vicinity to assess whether any of his associates have spotted us. Luckily, we appear to be too late for that. Muttering something I don't catch, he grabs his beloved but terribly shabby leather rucksack from by his feet and clambers out of the car, banging the door behind him.

With the engine still running I watch him loping up the wide stone steps. Skinny and tall – he's well over six feet – he still walks with a slight twist to his hips. His left side is weaker than the right, although these days you can barely tell, as years of therapy have helped immeasurably.

31

He tires easily, that's the main thing – although he'd rather carry on regardless, out and about with his mates, than admit it.

He glances back, looking appalled that I am still sitting there, as if I am wearing a fluorescent green comedy wig. What would he make of that terrible email, which effectively signals the end of family life as we know it? Although I'm not quite sure why, I have brought his mother's list out with me; I can sense it, glowing radioactively in my trouser pocket, virtually burning a hole in my hip. Perhaps it's in the hope that I've merely imagined this morning's events, and when I check it later it'll read:

Ketchup
Loo roll
Milk

Outside school, a couple of other latecomers are shambling up the wide stone steps behind Flynn. It's a proud and well-kept Victorian building, a state school with a broad cultural mix. Flynn has always gone to mainstream school, with extra support when needed, all closely monitored by Sinead; she's fought his corner all the way. 'She's a powerhouse,' her old college friend Michelle reminded me once, and of course I agreed. There was a pause, and Michelle added, rather belated, 'And you are too, of course!'

I watch as the other boys scamper up the last few steps to catch up with my son. How carefree they look, how breezy and laid-back, unencumbered as they are by tax returns and remembering to put the bins out. Sure, they might have flunked the odd maths test – but they haven't yet failed at anything terribly important, anything that might mark them out as poor excuses for human beings. The boys stop and laugh loudly at something (thank God Flynn can still laugh – *for now*) and disappear into the building together.

I should have been a better, more proactive and useful man, I realise now. Sinead has deserved more from me. No matter how challenging it's been bringing up Flynn, she has never once moaned or expressed a jot of self-pity. She adores being his mother – considers it an absolute privilege – and has often said that, where our boy is concerned, she would not change a single thing—

Bang-bang!

My heart lurches.

'Nate?' A thin blonde woman, whom I vaguely recognise, is rapping sharply on the driver's side window. 'Nate,' she repeats, leaning closer, 'are you okay?'

I fumble to lower the window. 'Erm, yes – I'm fine, thank you.' I assume she is something to do with school, but I can't remember her name. Sinead is so much better at that stuff than I am, efficiently filing the names of every teacher and medical practitioner, every cub leader and all the parents and their children and their pets that we have ever encountered in her colossal brain. *A powerhouse.*

'It's just . . . you shouldn't really be parked here.' The woman winces apologetically. 'You know. The yellow zigzags . . .'

'Oh God, yes. I'm so sorry!'

Still bending at the open window, she is smiling now. 'I'd have thought, being the driving test guy . . .'

'Yes, I should know better, shouldn't I?' I laugh stiffly.

'I'll forgive you. In fact, I should thank you really.'

'For committing a parking offence?' I gawp at her.

'No,' she laughs, exposing large, bright white teeth. 'For finally passing my mum . . .'

I blink at her, uncomprehending for a moment.

'Her driving test. Her third go, it was. She was lucky to get you—'

'Oh, if she passed, then it was on her own merit,' I say quickly.

'No, seriously. You're my mum's hero—'

'Ha, well, just doing my job,' I say, aware of the tension in my jaw building to critical levels as I bid her goodbye and pull away, trying to focus on the road ahead and what the heck I am supposed to be doing next.

Oh, yes – going to work. Despite everything that's happened this morning I need to conduct seven driving tests today, virtually back to back, because life must go on, and most of these candidates will be in a severely nervous state. Today, I am working in Solworth, a bigger and scruffier town than Hesslevale, a twenty-minute drive away over the hills. Liv has replied to my text: *No worries hope all okay, take care, Lx.* People are extraordinarily kind – yes, even driving examiners. We are not heroes, as that woman suggested, and nor are we mean-spirited arseholes, trying to 'catch people out'. We are just decent people, doing our job. *Passive observers,* is the way I tend to describe our role. Maybe I've been too bloody passive in my marriage too?

I drive on through open countryside on this bright and sunny May morning, then into the outskirts of Solworth, where I pull up at the test centre car park.

Okay, here goes. I climb out of my car, adjust my specs and smooth down the front of my trousers as if that'll make me appear in control of my life. The centre is an unprepossessing, single-storey modern block with a

34

motorway-service-centre vibe, minus the delights of cinnamon lattes and slot machines. People show up, do what they need to do and leave, with no desire to hang around. Well, of course they do. It hardly has a party atmosphere.

I stride into the office and greet Liv, the manager, and Eric, one of the other examiners, who's also a good friend.

'Hey, Nate. Everything all right?' He peers expectantly over a chipped Liverpool FC mug.

'Yeah, fine, thanks,' I say briskly and turn to Liv. 'Sorry about this morning . . .'

Concern flickers in her green eyes. Liv is a glamorous Canadian with big, bouncy chocolate-coloured hair and a youthful face that belies the fact that her fiftieth birthday is approaching. 'Don't worry,' she says. 'We had a cancellation, so Nadira's taken your first candidate. They should be back any minute now.' As she studies my face, I am conscious of Eric going through the motions of organising paperwork at his desk, all the while wondering what the hell's wrong because *I am never late for anything*. That's one thing Sinead could never accuse me of.

'Nothing serious, was it?' Eric asks.

'No, not at all.' I sit down to prepare my own paperwork, aware that an explanation is required. 'Just a bit of a situation at home,' I add. Liv frowns in my direction and gets up to click on the kettle. They are behaving as if I have come to work minus my trousers, and no one quite knows how to bring it up.

'Is Flynn okay?' Liv asks.

'Yeah, he's great, thanks,' I reply.

'Did he get on all right with that assessment the other day?' Eric wants to know.

'Yeah, everyone was really pleased . . .' I catch him

35

studying me whilst sipping his coffee. 'Just one of those mornings,' I add. 'Annoying domestic stuff, y'know . . .' I clear my throat and turn my attention back to my forms, hoping they'll assume I've been delayed due to heroically attending to a blocked drain, or a malfunctioning hairdryer, rather than marital disaster.

'Okay, well, your 9.45's here,' Liv remarks brightly.

'Great. I'll get to it, then.'

I catch her giving me another worried look as I stride towards our office door. 'You know, Nate, if you're feeling a bit off colour—'

'No, honestly, I'm good, thanks,' I say with exaggerated chirpiness. *Apart from being a shabby excuse for a husband and father, I'm just dandy!*

I pause for a moment, trying to gather myself together in order to exude calmness and capability. Through the glass panel in the door between our office and the waiting room, I can see my candidate, whom I have tested before. The weasly young man with straggly blond hair is sitting, deep in muttered conversation, with his instructor.

We know most of the instructors by name as we see them regularly. This one, Karl, looks as if he is trying to calm the lad down, but perhaps failing as, when I push open the door, my candidate barks, 'Hope I'm not getting that lanky fucker with the glasses again. I *know* he's got it in for me.'

*

In fact, he drives extremely competently this time, and remarks, 'So, I did all right today, did I?' with a distinct sneer as we part company (*yes, and that's why you damn well passed!*). Somehow, I manage to cobble together a

36

facade of normality and work my way through the rest of the morning's tests. However, a particular point on Sinead's list keeps pulsing away in my brain:

You don't make me feel special.

Was she referring to a lack of meals out? I wonder, as my current candidate collides with the kerb whilst reversing around a corner. The way things appear at the moment, I suspect it'd take more than dinner for two on Steak Night at the Wheatsheaf to rectify my numerous short-comings.

Having explained to my candidate why she failed, I make my way back to the office. At least Sinead has now texted – twice – which surely indicates that she still loves me? Okay, the first time was to say, *Please stop bombarding me with calls, will phone when I can.* The other one was equally devoid of sentiment: *Don't worry, will let dogs out at lunchtime as usual.* But it did suggest she still cares, I decide, as I pace the shabby streets around the test centre in lieu of eating any lunch.

With just five minutes left of my break, I finally manage to get her on the phone.

'Nate,' she says distractedly, 'I'm in the shop.'

'I know, I know. But we need to talk—'

'Excuse me,' says a shrill voice in the background, 'will you be stocking those pomegranate-scented candles again?'

'I have a customer here,' Sinead hisses, then clicks neatly into her shop lady voice: 'Erm, they were just in for Christmas, but there's a new bergamot and lime fragrance coming in next week. It's lovely and fresh for early summer—'

'Ah, yes, but I was really hoping for something fruitier . . .'

'Sinead!' I bark. 'Could we *please* talk, just for a minute?'

'I'm-at-work.' There's a pause, then the shop voice again: 'Sorry about that. I could call our supplier, if you like?'

Sure – go ahead! Call the candle people and chat away to your customer as if you haven't just pulled the plug on our marriage. I stomp past a car wash where two young men are hosing down a BMW, with tinny music blaring. Alarmingly, tears appear to be falling out of my eyes. I haven't cried properly since I took Flynn to see *Cloudy With a Chance of Meatballs*, and that wasn't because of the film; it was the fact that my dad had died a few days before.

'Nate?' Ah, she's remembered I'm here, that I still exist.

'Where are you staying?' I ask, frowning. 'I mean, where were you last night?'

'At Abby's . . .'

'Cosy!'

'Don't be like that . . .'

'Did that Rachel woman put you up to this?'

'Nate, *stop* this, stop saying that-Rachel-woman . . .'

'I need to see you,' I exclaim. 'You can't just send me an email like that and then be unavailable—'

'Yes, I know, and I'm sorry. But I can't see you today, okay? I just need time—'

'Why?'

'Stop shouting—'

'I'M NOT SHOUTING.'

'You are! Look, I've got to go, okay?' How can she sound so calm and neutral? *How?*

'All right,' I growl, stomping back towards the test centre now. 'Can I just ask, what about Flynn? I mean, does he know anything about this?'

I hear her inhaling deeply. 'No, I haven't told him yet . . .'

'Are you intending to?'

'You're shouting again. Yes, of course I am. Look, I'm going now . . .'

'I'm demented here! Can you imagine what it was like for me to find that note? I mean, a bloody note! Why couldn't we just talk, like normal people?'

'Hang on,' she murmurs.

'It really *is* the pomegranate fragrance I'd like,' her customer explains, as if her world will crumble if she doesn't get one.

'Yes, it is a lovely homely scent,' Sinead agrees. Then, back to me: 'I'll come over tomorrow evening, okay? But I want the three of us to sit down together and talk – not just you and me—'

'But we need to talk things through on our own,' I protest, despite being aware that arguing is futile right now.

'Not tomorrow,' she murmurs. 'You'll try to persuade me to come back, Nate, and I can't handle that right now. I want Flynn to be there . . .'

'But he's only sixteen!'

'Yes, and he's a smart boy. He deserves to know everything. There's nothing I'm going to say to you that I can't say in front of him. So, I'll see you at the house about eightish, okay?' And with that, she's gone.

So it's already 'the house'. Not *our house* anymore. But at least she's agreed to see me, I remind myself over and over as the afternoon crawls on. Not today, but tomorrow – and I'll just have to make do with that.

And now, as I drive home, I picture her sitting next to me on our sofa and explaining that she just lost her mind temporarily and, okay, I have been a bit crap, but I'll try much harder and everything will be all right. In my vision of her, she is wearing one of her vintage frocks covered in spriggy patterns ('you're the only man I've ever known who calls them frocks,' she once remarked with a smile), with a snug-fitting cardigan in perhaps light blue or pink. She is quirky, I suppose: delightfully unique. Sinead knows her own style, favouring flat shoes with a strap across the front – Mary Janes, I think they're called – and wears her fair hair quite long and not especially groomed, just flowing and natural and soft to the touch. In short, she is a ravishing natural beauty – a blue-eyed blonde, with a strong nose, a wide, sensuous mouth and an absolutely knockout body.

God, I love her so much.

I park up and let myself into the house.

'Dad?' Flynn calls through from the living room. I stride in, fearing the worst: i.e., he knows already. His mum did call him after all – or he's simply figured it out for himself.

'Hi, son. How was your day?' My heart is pounding as I take in the sight of him lying flat out on the sofa, phone in hand, schoolbag spewing books and crumpled papers all over the floor. His brown eyes fix on mine. He is growing up into such a handsome young man, his jaw more defined now, his boyish softness remoulding into sharper angles.

'All right, I s'pose. Miss Beazley said to remind you not to park on the zigzags again?'

'Oh!' I almost laugh. 'God, yes. I definitely won't—'

'So, when's Mum coming home?'

Instinctively, I check my watch. It seems so old-fashioned to wear one, but I'm terribly attached to mine. It was left to me when my father died.

'Erm, she won't be around till tomorrow, actually,' I mumble.

Flynn scowls. 'Why not? What's going on? She's not answering her phone—'

'She's, um, staying at Abby's,' I reply quickly.

I fiddle awkwardly with my watch as he stares at me. Dad wore it for as long as I can remember: dependable and unflashy, like its owner. I always suspected that was why Mum divorced him when I reached my teens – because Dad was just too quiet, too normal, working for an accountancy firm and tinkering away in his shed. Perhaps he was ultimately disappointing to her. I'd never found him disappointing. As a shy kid, with a brother five years younger who was the apple of Mum's eye, I could have been bored out of my brains in our bleak suburb of Huddersfield. However, while Joe commanded our mother's attentions, I could always find plenty to discover in Dad's shed. It was a grotto to me where *dreams* could be made from a few screws, some offcuts of timber and a tin of Humbrol enamel paint. I'd always assumed I inherited at least some of my father's DIY talents – but Sinead clearly thinks otherwise.

'Dad, are you listening to me?'

I flinch and look at Flynn. 'Sorry? What were you saying?'

He sits up and regards me with the penetrating stare of a particularly astute lawyer. 'Can you *please* just tell me what's going on with you and Mum?'

I sense the blood surging to my cheeks, and feel rather sick as I perch gingerly on the sofa beside him. Both dogs are standing in the living room doorway and gazing at me, as if blocking my escape.

I clear my throat. 'She, erm . . . wants some time away

from me,' I murmur. 'She hasn't been very happy, so we're trying to sort things out. I'm sorry, Flynn, I really am. I don't know what else to tell you . . .'

His expression is unreadable. 'Why didn't you say?'

'I am. I'm saying now.'

'Yeah, 'cause I asked,' he says sharply. ''Cause I *forced it out of you—*'

I exhale slowly. 'Look, I didn't say anything this morning because, well, I didn't know what was going to happen. I still don't, really. Mum's staying at Abby's – that's all I know. It's all come as a total shock . . .'

Flynn gets up from the sofa, which I take as a signal that it's okay to hug him – that he wants to be held. However, I must have misread the signs as, when I scramble up and try to pull him towards me, he stands there, rigid as an ironing board, arms jammed to his sides.

'So, what's going to happen now?' He disentangles himself and peers at me as if I have gone quite mad.

'I have no idea. All I know is, she's coming over tomorrow evening so we can all have a chat.'

'A chat?' he repeats bitterly.

'Well, yeah.' I shrug. 'I'm sorry. I don't really know what else to call it.'

'Huh,' he grunts. We look at each other in silence. As I can't fathom out what to say next, I call Scout to me, and ruffle his head. It's almost a relief when Flynn slopes off to his room.

Normally, during any kind of tense situation involving our son, I have always tried to be resolutely – possibly irritatingly – cheerful:

Don't worry, Flynn. It's school policy to report any bullying, so I really have to go in . . .

There are loads of ways to play every chord. If that

42

inversion of the G seventh is tricky, we can easily find another one . . .

It's okay, son. Hopefully it'll be Margot again, that nice physio lady with the sticker sheets . . .

Only he's sixteen now, and this isn't something that can be sorted with a Superman sticker or a Freddo bar. There's no point in following him upstairs, as anything I say will be deemed patronising. These days I seem to patronise him simply by inhabiting the same room. It's a miracle he still allows me to teach him anything on guitar.

Should *I* be the one moving out?

Ridiculously, my brain fast-forwards to the weekend, when Mum is due back from her climbing expedition and is coming round to pick up Bella.

'Has everything gone okay?'

'Apart from Sinead leaving me, yes, it's all been absolutely tickety-boo!'

Only, that's not going to happen. This is just a blip, and somehow I'll convince Sinead that I'm not the selfish, uncaring arsehole that she seems to think I am.

I simply love my wife too much to just let her go.

Chapter Five

Never before have I been so grateful to reach the end of a Friday afternoon. Although this has been one of the shittiest weeks of my life – up there along with Sinead's miscarriage and Dad dying – I have somehow managed to muster a smudge of optimism, because tonight is my opportunity to put everything right.

'Bye, then,' I say, pulling on my jacket and already propelling myself towards the door.

'See you, Nate,' says Liv, still emitting an air of concern. 'Try and rest up this weekend, love, will you?'

'Yeah – you look awfully tired and pale,' Nadira remarks.

'Just been a bit of a week . . .'

'Sarah was saying we hadn't seen you and Sinead for ages,' remarks Eric. 'You should come over for dinner sometime soon.'

'Sounds great!' My hand is clamped on the door handle now.

'This weekend? Or maybe next?'

'Um, this weekend's not so good,' I mutter. *Something of an understatement . . .*

'And next Saturday's my barbecue,' Liv reminds us. 'I hope you haven't forgotten that!'

'Oh, yeah, the big half-century!' Eric beams at her, then turns back to me. 'So you'll check with the boss, will you?'

'Huh?'

He frowns bemusedly. 'Sinead. *Your wife.* So we can arrange a night?'

'Oh yes, of course,' I reply as I leave the building, flanked by Nadira, who's by far the youngest examiner in our team.

'Well, have a good weekend, Nate,' she says with a smile.

'Thanks. You too.'

'Got much on?'

'Just playing it by ear,' I mutter, then turn and make straight for my car and climb straight in. When I glance back, Nadira is standing next to her own car, and giving me a worried look. We're a friendly team, and usually there's a bit of chat about our plans for the weekend ahead. Sometimes we even socialise together – Eric and I especially. We often go for a few beers, just the two of us, or get together as couples over dinner.

How am I going to explain that Sinead's left me?

I won't need to, I decide as I drive through the gently undulating hills. Somehow, I'll convince her to give me – and our marriage – another chance. Hell, she has to, really. She can't just throw in the towel on almost two decades together because she's suddenly taken exception to my DIY efforts and I didn't set the bloody mousetraps.

As I near Hesslevale, I make a few firm decisions. Whatever happens tonight, no matter how upset and defensive I feel, I must not let any of that out. I'll *listen* to my wife, and show that I don't intend to take her for granted ever again – not that I ever have! Why does she even think this when I love her madly? WHY? Maybe it's sex: i.e., we've not been having enough lately. Perhaps she thinks I don't fancy her anymore, which patently isn't true. In fact, we actually did it a few nights ago, which seemed to surprise us both – and it was lovely, as it always is. But all too often, we're too knackered to do anything other than fall asleep when we climb into bed. Should we just forget our 'meeting' this evening and go straight upstairs, tell Flynn we're tired? Would that fix everything?

Stopping at red lights on the edge of town, I try to disentangle my racing thoughts. A new restaurant has opened, called Elliot's. I know it's eye-wateringly expensive, but Eric and his wife Sarah have raved about how lovely it is. Maybe I should suggest dinner here sometime?

By the time I pull up in our street, I've almost managed to convince myself that Sinead just needs a damn good rant – then she'll feel much better. However, the very fact that she is coming around at a specified time – 8 p.m. – makes it feel less like a 'chat' and more like court.

Your honour, I only decided to build the shelves myself because the quote that joiner gave was frankly astronomical . . .

I find Flynn in his room, emitting distinct 'do not disturb' vibes. We eat dinner together at the kitchen table, in a rather stilted atmosphere, my slimy noodles and ageing babycorn clearly failing to delight him, even with a liberal dousing of oyster sauce. In fact, Flynn seems to be merely *combing* his noodles with his fork. Given the circumstances – and the fact that he is virtually a fully grown man – it doesn't feel right to tell him to stop playing with his food.

We clear up together, although it hardly seems worth the effort with just two bowls and one wok. As Flynn disappears back to his room, I try to occupy myself in our Sinead-less home by shining up the cooker hob and emptying the kitchen bin and then, when I can think of no other tasks to attend to, pacing randomly around the ground floor.

Finally – FINALLY! – here she comes, knocking lightly on the door (why is she knocking? This is her house too!). 'Hi?' she calls out, stepping into the hallway now, as if she were a neighbour popping in to ask to borrow a cup of sugar. No one borrows sugar anymore, I realise as I hurry through to greet her. Everyone has plenty of sugar of their own . . . 'Hi, Nate,' she says as Scout scrambles past me in order to throw himself at her. *You can't move out. Look how much he loves you!*

'Hi, love,' I say. I look at her, standing there in our hallway, taken aback by how normal she seems. But then, what was I expecting? That she'd blunder in with swollen eyes and smeared mascara, swigging a bottle of Jacob's Creek?

While I wonder whether or not to hug her, she bobs down to fuss over Scout. 'Hello, little man! You'll soon be on your own again, ruling the roost.' She looks up at me. 'Is it Sunday your mum's picking up Bella?'

'Yeah that's right,' I mutter, as if it matters.

She straightens up, strides into the living room and arranges herself at one end of the sofa, where Scout jumps up and snuggles close, and Bella settles at her feet. My wife is a magnet to dogs. Larry, our lurcher who died last year, was the same with her. She'd only have to pop out to the shops and he'd sit at the front door, alternately whining and licking his genitals until she came home. At least I haven't descended to *that* . . .

I perch next to her. For a few moments, neither of us says anything. The mood is so awful, so tense and awkward, we could be strangers sitting side by side in an STI clinic waiting room.

So, what are you in for?

'So, how was work today?' I ask stiffly, showing an interest in her job.

'Okay, I suppose,' she replies flatly.

Well, I'm not okay, I want to shout. *I'm not fucking okay at all.* I rake back my hair from my clammy forehead.

'Where's Flynn?' she asks.

'Upstairs. I thought maybe we could have a chat first, just so we can work out what we're going to say—'

'Nate, I told you already, I really want him to be here too. I think that's fairer. Don't you?'

'Yes, all right.' *Just agree to everything she says and maybe this'll blow over.*

She turns towards the living room door. 'Flynn?' she calls out pleasantly. 'Could you come downstairs please, love?'

'Darling, I just want to say, we don't have to do this,' I say quickly. 'I mean, I know you're upset, and I'm sorry for, well, whatever it is, but—' I break off. Flynn's footsteps are audible on the stairs, and he appears, hair rumpled, eyes rather sore-looking and pink. Oh, God, he's been crying. No one likes seeing a small child upset – but it's worse when they're older, as it's generally rarer and suggests something more serious.

Flynn and his mum fling their arms around each other and hold each other tightly. 'Oh, darling,' she murmurs.

48

'Mum,' he croaks. 'Are you all right?'

'Yes, sweetheart, as long as *you* are . . .' There's no awkward ironing-board hug this time.

After what feels like a week they peel apart, and both settle on the sofa, jammed together, while I perch on the far end and stare at my shoes. And out it all comes:

'The thing is, Flynn, love, I've decided me and Dad aren't right together anymore. I know this is so hard for you to hear, but I want you to understand that it's nothing to do with you. It's about me and Dad . . .'

Flynn nods mutely. He is actually letting her hold his hand. I haven't been allowed to do that since he was about eight years old.

'We've, I don't know – grown apart over the years, I suppose,' she continues, with only the slightest tremor in her voice, 'and I haven't been happy for quite a long time. I've thought about it long and hard, and I *could* stay, pretending everything's fine, until you leave home and have your own independent adult life.' She stops, blinking rapidly, and clears her throat. 'But that would be dishonest, wouldn't it? To you, me and Dad?'

She addresses Flynn throughout all of this. I might as well not be here. I am just a *passive observer*.

'Yeah,' Flynn murmurs, 'I s'pose it would.'

'So I need to be true to myself,' she goes on, 'which means I'll be staying at Abby's for a while, then I'll probably look around for a flat of my own . . .'

Oh, Jesus God. My heart is banging so hard it feels as if it could burst out of my chest.

'. . . which of course you'll be welcome to stay at any time. You'll have your own room there, it'll be your home too . . .'

49

Our son nods, lips pressed together, as Sinead continues: 'I hope you understand why I'm doing this, honey. I'm sorry I won't be here with you all the time, but this is your home, it's where you belong – with Dad and Scout.'

'Yeah,' Flynn says in a gravelly voice. He's being brave, so bloody brave it rips at my insides. Even braver than when he went for surgery when he was nine, to improve his gait, and lay there with one hand tightly clutching mine (maybe that's the last time we held hands?), the other stuffed into his beloved Mr Fox glove puppet, just before he was given the general anaesthetic. Although he'd long since given up on taking Mr Fox everywhere, on this occasion I'd suggested the puppet might like to come along too. Flynn had agreed that that was an excellent idea. I knew he was scared about 'going to sleep', although he was determined not to show it. His jaw was set firm, the small hand gripping mine slick with sweat. Sinead had waited outside the operating theatre as she couldn't face seeing him go under.

'Nothing's going to change, Flynn,' she explains now. 'You can still phone or text me any time, and come over every day if you like – after school, maybe? Or pop into the shop and we'll get a milkshake from that cafe across the road?'

'That'd be nice,' he mumbles.

A milkshake! If I'd suggested that, he'd have laughed in my face. I try to rub at my eyes surreptitiously. Actually, the two of them are so locked in their exchange, his tousled head resting on her shoulder now, I could probably have a cardiac arrest without worrying either of them unduly.

Then before I know it she is gathering herself up to leave, and Flynn has given her one last hug and shot off back to his room. I have said virtually nothing to her, and, quite rightly, she addressed her entire spiel to our son.

'What about your stuff?' I ask as I see her out.

'Erm, I took some clothes and a few other bits and pieces when I came over at lunchtime,' she replies, 'and I'll deal with the rest some other time, probably when you're both out.' I catch her swallowing hard. 'It might be easier that way.'

'Yes, you're probably right,' I reply dully.

'You're okay with me hanging onto a key for now?'

'Of course, yes.'

She looks around for Scout, who trots towards her. 'I'll need one anyway, while I'm still walking Scout . . .'

'Yeah, I guess so . . .'

'Okay, then . . .' A sense of awkwardness hangs between us.

'Um, I could get a dog walker,' I suggest, 'if it's easier for you?'

She touches my arm in a way that is utterly devoid of affection. 'Let's say I'll just do it for now, okay? Bye, Nate.'

'Bye, love,' I croak.

She opens the door and steps outside. I have to say, I'm almost impressed by the speed and efficiency of tonight's proceedings, but then, that's Sinead all over: *a powerhouse.* She neatly summed up my flaws on a sheet of A4 and is ready now to get on with the rest of her life, without me in it.

Incredibly, it seems that nineteen years of being together can all be undone in a little under twenty-five minutes. I stand at our front door, watching Sinead as she marches along our street, willing her to look back or, better still, to turn and run to me and throw herself into my arms, like she would if this were a film with any kind of decent end.

Instead, she climbs into her silver car, with a casualness that suggests she's just nipping out to the supermarket, and drives away.

Chapter Six

Sinead

'So, how did it go?' Abby has arrived home from her shift as manager of the Lamb and Flag, one of Hesslevale's most popular pubs.

'Bloody awful.' I pour a glass of wine from the bottle I picked up on my way home, and hand it to her. We settle on the sofa in her immaculate newly built home.

'Oh, love,' she murmurs. 'It was never going to be easy, explaining it all face-to-face. But at least you've done it now, and he knows exactly how you feel. So maybe the worst part's over.'

I grimace. *Was* that the worst part? I have no idea. All I know is that, two nights ago, it felt as if I had no choice but to leave him. With my heart rattling furiously, I'd glared at the packet of three wooden mousetraps I'd bought a week previously, knowing it would happen soon.

Flynn's music had stopped upstairs, and all was quiet at 83 Allison Street. I poured myself a huge glass of wine and sat sipping it at the kitchen table, then refilled it. Drinking alone, on a Wednesday night – but no wonder. I sipped, and I waited, on high alert now – just like Nate

53

must be every time he conducts a driving test. Then out one popped from under the microwave – a grey blur. I leapt up and screamed, knocking over my glass as the mouse darted across the worktop, skirting the packet of traps and disappearing behind the toaster.

Shaking, I snatched a ring-bound notebook from the cookbook shelf and hurried through to the living room. I'd bought the notebook for collecting recipes that both Nate and Flynn would appreciate because, God knows, it's hard to please both of them. It even had divided sections for soups, mains, desserts. However, food was the last thing on my mind right then.

You might find it helpful to write down all the aspects you're unhappy with . . .

I grabbed a pen, and opened the notebook which I'd bought with the intention of being a good wife and mother; a provider of wholesome fare.

Well, fuck that.

I started to write, and out it all poured, fuelled by *L'Ondice* lady petrol: all the minor faults, the major faults and everything in between. Of course, this wasn't really about mousetraps, the occasional dog poo left on the lawn or any of that. It was years' worth of stuff, tumbling out – about how Nate, who was supposed to love me, viewed me now. I used to be a *person*, supposedly with talent and an identity of my own, way back in some previous life. Jewellery was my passion; I was a silversmith. Things had taken off quickly after I'd graduated from art college; I'd been featured in glossy magazines and my pieces were being stocked by several major stores. I was, as one journalist put it, 'a shining star of the jewellery world'. But not anymore. I was just *there*, keeping things going, invisible to the man I'd once loved.

'How was Flynn, when you explained everything?' Abby asks now.

'On the surface, he took it pretty well,' I reply. 'I just sort of rattled it all out and he sat there in silence, taking it in. You know how he is, Abs. He puts a brave face on everything. And as for Nate . . .'

'He'll be okay eventually,' she says gently, squeezing my hand. 'But it's going to take time. It'll be tough on all of you, but you did what felt right.'

I nod. 'Yes, but I'm a bloody idiot . . .'

'What d'you mean?'

'The way I tried to make things seem better for Flynn, you know? With promises of a room in the home I have yet to find—'

'He's always welcome here, you know that . . .'

'Thank you. I do know, and I appreciate it so much.' I pause and sip my wine. 'I suggested we could get together over a milkshake. A milkshake!' I repeat, sensing my cheeks burning. 'What was I thinking? He's sixteen years old!'

'Hey,' Abby says gently. 'I bet he won't mind what you do as long as you spend time together.'

'That is, if he doesn't hate me . . .'

'Of course he won't hate you,' she exclaims. 'Flynn adores you. Come on, this isn't making you feel any better . . .'

'I'm sorry, I just seem to offload to you all the time . . .'

'Offload away,' Abby says, smiling now. 'You've done the same for me, plenty of times.'

I muster a smile too. 'Well, I'm so grateful, Abs. You are brilliant, you know that?'

She shrugs off the compliment and pushes back her long blonde hair. Dressed in a simple black shift, with

55

minimal make-up, her brand of pub manager is sleekly groomed rather than OTT glamour. Although she is very much my friend – the one she confided in during those failed rounds of IVF, and then her divorce – I first got to know her through Nate, when he and a big bunch of mates shared a house.

We channel-hop now, finally settling on a soothing nature documentary about seals. We share the rest of the bottle of wine and, by the time we say goodnight at around 1 a.m., I am slightly light-headed – yet again.

What kind of mother am I? I reflect as I climb into bed in Abby's spare room. I drink too much. Worse still, I have abandoned my lovely boy who needs me. And I can't even bring myself to set a mousetrap, for goodness' sake! How can that be, when I've dealt with the numerous challenges of raising Flynn? But that's just me. Recently, I seem to have become fearful of quite a few silly things. I don't know whether it's age, or hormones, or what. Maybe Rachel might have some ideas?

At our last session, I'd told her how I'd tried to keep my business going as a new mum. However, Flynn was a terrible sleeper and my determination to graft away into the night soon proved impossible. Even when he finally learnt to distinguish night from day, his early years were filled with medical and therapeutic appointments. Although Nate and I never discussed it, the person to take charge of such matters – and accompany him on virtually all of these – was me.

And so orders fell away, and Sinead Hogan, so-called shining star, was replaced by Sinead Turner in ratty old jeans and a faded sweatshirt, fringe home-cut, face devoid of make-up and frankly knackered. I once went to apply some mascara for a party and discovered that it had entirely solidified. My jewellery equipment and materials were either sold or packed away in boxes and stashed in the attic. My old filing cabinet, in which I'd stored years' worth of magazine clippings, scribbled notes and designs, was shunted into what we have always referred to, optimistically, as our 'guest room', and which is now entirely filled with junk.

It wasn't as if Nate pushed me into any of that. It was my choice to put my business on hold; I *wanted* to be a full-time mum, and no other job was as thrilling and rewarding – or downright terrifying when it was suggested that Flynn's development wasn't following the expected curves. Weren't all babies different? I insisted, belligerently. What did health visitors and GPs know? What could paediatric neurologists and behavioural development specialists actually tell us, with their decades of study and experience in impaired muscle coordination and control?

'They just want to label him,' I protested to Nate – as if there was a 'them' and 'us'. Like these kindly professionals were trying to put our baby into some kind of box, just to be difficult. There were numerous scans, examinations and tests. We joked, rather bleakly, that we should be issued with hospital loyalty cards.

Eventually, a grey-bearded consultant explained that Flynn – who was by then nine months old – had cerebral palsy. No, we didn't 'cause' it, he insisted. It had nothing to do with the wine I'd drunk at our friends' wedding, plus tequila shots, ill-advised gin jellies and God knows what else I'd tipped down my throat before we'd realised I was pregnant.

Eventually, Nate insisted that I had to stop beating myself up or I'd go mad. It took a long time for me to trust these unfailingly kind professionals and not assume everyone was lying to us. If someone had said, 'Your son has this condition because you've worn thongs/took ecstasy – once, in 1992, *and nothing actually happened*' – then they're the ones I'd have believed. Our consultant suggested that I wanted someone, or something, to blame. As our baby's carrier for forty weeks, it seemed that had to be me.

I tried to explain this to Nate, but he brushed me off, implying that I was being silly and even hysterical. Eventually I stopped talking about it as it just seemed to cause rows. Meanwhile, we threw everything into being Flynn's parents. He was our little hero, and our entire life, and when one aspect of life is all-consuming, other things tend to be forgotten. Like paying parking fines on time and sending Nate's mother a birthday present (somehow, since I'd let my business slide, attending to such matters had become *my* job). We forgot about wedding anniversaries, and rarely had nights out, despite numerous offers of babysitting. For the most part, we even forgot about having sex. Let's just say our cars had oil changes more regularly than Nate and I were getting it together. And somewhere along the way, we lost ourselves.

For a while, I assumed the real problem was money, and it was certainly tight. I knew this was partially my fault. All through Flynn's primary school years I was a non-working person, which sometimes seemed to tip into being a non-*person*. But I accepted that, because Flynn was surpassing all expectations and growing up into the sunniest, most determined and delightful boy. CP was just a part of him, like his love of dogs and fascination with his dad's vast record collection.

By the time Flynn was twelve I had an overwhelming urge to return to work. Jewellery was far too precarious an option, and by then I was lamentably out of touch with trends and potential retail outlets. Plus, as Nate often pointed out – quite rightly – our debts were mounting and we needed another regular income. Pre-parenthood he'd scraped a living through teaching guitar, playing in bands and driving musicians, plus their gear, the length and breadth of Britain. He'd enjoyed the driving part so much, he'd eventually trained as a driving instructor, and then the examiner he is now.

Reliable, hard-grafting Nate: willing to swap his life in music for one of tests and minutiae, because he loves us and wanted to take care of us. Meanwhile, I took on some part-time admin work, until last year, when a card in a local shop window caught my eye: *Full-time sales assistant required. Please enquire within.*

'Would it seem ridiculous,' I asked Nate, 'for me to apply for a shop job?'

'What kind of shop?' He started to rearrange the contents of our dishwasher, as he always reckons I stack it incorrectly.

'A new gift shop called Little Owl. It's by that bistro in Stoker Road. You probably haven't noticed it . . .'

There was a clink of crockery as he repositioned the top shelf's contents to ensure effective cleansing. As my friend Michelle once put it, 'A man who criticises your dishwasher-loading technique risks being shoved into it with the intensive setting whacked on.'

'So, what d'you think?' I prompted him.

He removed the forks from the appliance's holder and put them back *properly*, with prongs facing upwards.

I jammed my back teeth together. People have committed murder over less. 'Nate? Did you actually hear what I said?'

'Yeah, sorry, darling.' He turned and smiled. 'Yeah. I think a little shop job would be really good for you.'

Little shop job!

I was replaying all of this as I scribbled that list two nights ago. I hardly knew what I was doing as I placed it by the kettle, then called Abby in a state. Of course I could stay with her, she assured me. She would come and get me, and would I please stop apologising? She met me in her car at 1.40 a.m. at the end of our road.

So here I am now – trying, unsuccessfully, to sleep in her spare room. The plump pillow is wet with my tears, and although somehow it's better than being with Nate, I can't help thinking: *What the hell have I done?*

Chapter Seven

Nate

Weekends are usually an opportunity to kick back, read the papers, walk Scout, maybe meet up with Eric and Sarah. Or Sinead and I would just go out for a drink ourselves: all the ordinary (but now, I realise, intensely *pleasurable*) stuff I've taken for granted all these years. Without Sinead here on Saturday morning – and with no work to go to – I simply don't know what to do with myself.

Still, I can't fall apart. I'm still Flynn's dad and, if nothing else, I'm going to prove that I can run this home, this family, by myself.

Things start off pretty well, considering. Flynn emerges from his room a little before 10 a.m. There are no visible signs of tears or anger; on the contrary, he utters a gruff, 'Morning' as we pass on the stairs. I even dish up a proper breakfast – not that I'm expecting some kind of World's Best Dad accolade for scrambling some eggs. However, we *are* coping, in that we are dressed, and nourished, and I have only checked my phone a handful of times to see if Sinead has been trying to contact me.

Of course she hasn't. *Idiot*, I chastise myself.

Aware of behaving a little manically – in order to prove just how fucking *fine* I am – I suggest to Flynn that he fetches his guitar and we have a go at some new techniques. 'Okay,' he says warily. Minutes later, we're sitting together in the living room while I show him a new take on the traditional twelve-bar blues he knows already.

He's strumming away, albeit rather mechanically, as if he's keen to get on with something else.

'Hang on,' I say, motioning him to stop. 'It'd be good to change your emphasis, give it some whack on the second and fourth beat . . .'

'What?' he asks crossly, brow furrowing.

'Let me show you.' On my own guitar, I start to play a riff, aware of Flynn's gradually flattening expression, his mouth setting in a firm line. I stop and look at him. 'That was Chuck Berry. You can hear how he played about with the timing, the emphasis – that's what gave him that unique sound—'

'Dad,' Flynn interrupts, placing his own guitar carefully on the sofa beside him.

'Hang on, Flynn . . .' I start playing some more. It's helping a little, focusing on the music. Helping me to not fixate on Sinead, just for a few moments . . .

'Dad!' he barks. I stop, taken aback by his abruptness. 'Look, um . . .' He shuffles uneasily. 'D'you mind if we don't do this?'

I look at him. 'You mean, try out this Chuck Berry riff?'

Flynn's eyes seem to harden. 'Well, yeah. I mean, why would I want to play like Chuck Berry?'

'Because he's one of the greats,' I reply with a frown. 'A big influence on Springsteen, actually. He even covered some of his songs. Hang on a sec . . .' I place my guitar to one side, and get up with the intention of fetching my laptop.

'Dad, please,' Flynn cries after me. 'No YouTube clips of old dead guys!'

I swing round to face him. 'He not just *any* old dead guy. He was a major innovator—'

'Yeah, I know who he is. I mean, *was*. Max's dad's got a record of his, that awful song . . . what's it called again?'

I shrug, genuinely confused.

Flynn smirks. '*I* remember. "My Ding-a-Ling" . . .'

'Oh, that,' I retort. 'That was just a stupid comedy record—'

'Yeah, about his dick—'

'Flynn!'

My son's gaze meets mine, challenging me. Was he ever so belligerent when Sinead was here? I'm sure there were occasions, but I can't recall any right now.

'What's up with saying "dick"?' he asks, clearly *pushing boundaries*.

'Nothing, I suppose,' I mutter. 'But it's a bit unnecessary. Okay, shall we try that Stones riff instead—'

'Well, that's what the song's about, isn't it?' he rants on. 'Max's dad was playing it when he was drunk one night. He was a pervert. He put spy cameras in women's loos—'

'Max's dad?' I exclaim.

'No, Chuck-fucking-Berry!'

'Okay, okay,' I exclaim, deciding not to tick him off about unnecessary language on this occasion, although it's definitely out of order, coming straight after 'dick' a few seconds ago. I have a swearing limit and he's definitely topped it. However, things are heated enough as it is. Pick

63

your battles, I've always believed, and I know everyone swears these days. The c-word seems to be as commonly used as 'hello' or, 'how are you?', not that I'm a fan of it being tossed about like confetti. But I try to be easy-going and liberal, often thinking, *Christ – hasn't my son had enough to deal with in life without me lambasting him over trivialities?*

'C'mon,' I add, 'we can play something else. This is supposed to be fun, not an ordeal for you.' He wrinkles his nose at me, as if I have suggested a game of Ludo. 'How about trying that finger picking again?' I soldier on. 'You were doing really well with that . . .' He was too, by which I mean no onlooker would even guess he had any issues with his fine motor movements.

Flynn gets up and grabs his guitar by the neck, and for one split-second I wonder if he is going to bash me on the head with it. 'Look, Dad, what I'm trying to tell you is – if you'd *listen* – I don't want to do this anymore.'

You don't listen to me. Will I soon be presented with a list of my faults from my son, too? Well, why not? Might as well make it a family game.

'What are you saying?' I ask hollowly. 'You can't just give up, Flynn. You're so good!'

'No, I mean—'

'I know it gets frustrating,' I barge in, 'and you can feel like you're not making much progress. But honestly, you have *real* talent—'

'Dad,' he says firmly, shaking his head, 'what I mean is, I want to stop playing guitar with *you*.'

I blink at Flynn. Something cold and hard seems to clamp itself around my heart. He stands there, glaring at me in disdain, as if he can hardly believe I was fifty per cent responsible for his existence. He is gripping his favourite instrument, the one that cost us a fortune for his fifteenth birthday, after I'd managed to persuade Sinead that it really was the best choice for him. *But he only tried it out for ten minutes,* she hissed, as the three of us left the music store in Leeds.

Sometimes, I told her, *it's instant. You just know.*

Love at first sight? she said with a laugh.

I clear my throat and try to pull myself together. 'So, you, uh, don't want me to teach you anymore?'

'Yeah,' he says, with a tone that borders on the callous. 'I mean, no. No, I don't. Is that all right, Dad?'

'Er, yes, of course it is,' I reply, 'if that's what you've decided. So, er, d'you want to learn from someone else?'

'No, I just want to *play*,' Flynn says emphatically. 'I just want to do my own thing with Max, Luke and Si and the others, know what I mean?'

'But you do your own thing now . . .'

Flynn's nostrils seem to flare. 'Yeah, but that's *all* I want to do. I don't want to sit here, learning your things . . .'

'They're not *my* things!'

'Dad, you know what I mean. It's not a big deal, is it? C'mon.' He hoists a small smile, as if I am a child whose balloon has just slipped from his hand and floated away. Then he shrugs and saunters off to his room.

I know I should leave it at that. I should accept that, at sixteen years old – with his mother recently departed from our home – he is fully entitled to continue to progress, or *not* progress, however he pleases. He can never learn another damn thing, if that's what he wants! But instead, I follow him upstairs and loom in his bedroom doorway.

'What is it?' he asks.

I clear my parched throat. 'So, er, you really don't want me to teach you anymore? Is that what you're saying?'

'Yeah. I explained that already, Dad.'

I shrug, feeling ridiculous. 'But I mean . . . isn't it quite handy that I'm here, and available, and we can just do stuff whenever you're in the mood?' *And I can adapt techniques according to your abilities?* I want to add, but of course, I don't.

'I don't really want to anymore.'

'But why not? I thought you enjoyed it. I thought, you know, it was *our thing* . . .' My voice wavers. Oh, God. How needy do I sound now?

'Just leave it, would you?' Flynn mumbles, picking at his fingernails.

And then I must really lose it, as I snap at my beloved boy: 'Suit your bloody self then. *But don't come running to me when you can't figure out a G minor seventh!*'

What a jerk.

Only a prize arsehole would flounce downstairs like a twelve-year-old, summon Scout and Bella for a walk, and march furiously down the street. The sky is drab grey, the colour of a white T-shirt that's been washed with the darks. The dogs plod along at my side, seemingly picking up on my gloom. There's no excitable pulling on the leads, no reaction whatsoever when a scrawny black cat crosses our path. On a positive note, there's no sighting of our neighbour Howard with Monty either.

My phone rings, and I snatch it from my jacket pocket, willing it to be Sinead, or even Flynn, apologising – but it's only my mate Paolo. He lives just outside town, and is happily married to Bea, with three impossibly cute children. He leaves a voicemail message, which I don't play. I can't face telling him what's happened just yet.

Back home, I apologise to Flynn through his closed bedroom door.

'S'all right,' he growls. Instead of pestering him any further, I head downstairs and deal with the dishes I dumped in the sink last night – not because I'm some hapless male, unfamiliar with domestic cleansing rituals, but because I couldn't even face stacking the dishwasher after Sinead had been here and delivered her speech. And now, as I sweep the kitchen floor unnecessarily, I am aware of being poised for a call, or the sound of her coming home; I don't think the enormity of what's happened has truly sunk in yet. I can only liken it to when Dad died. He and his friend, Nick, would often sit together, drinking tea and chatting, on the peeling bench in front of Dad's rented cottage. It was Nick who found Dad; he'd died of a heart attack while gardening. The reality only really hit me when I cleared out his shed.

By the time lunchtime rolls around, I busy myself by making some hearty lentil soup. Never mind that Flynn only manages half a bowlful. So chuffed am I that it's a) edible and b) 'balanced' (unlike its creator right now), I call Sinead to tell her all about it.

'Look, Nate,' she says as I pause for breath, 'd'you mind if we leave any contact for a few days?'

'Er, no, of course not,' I say, clearing my throat. 'Whatever feels best for you, I'm happy with . . .' Happy! Now there's an interesting choice of word.

'I really need some time to get my head around things. I'm sorry.'

'Yes, I understand that . . .'

'Are *you* all right?' she asks, rather belatedly.

'Getting there,' I fib, in a silly jovial tone as I tip the remains of Flynn's soup down the sink.

'I spoke to Flynn this morning,' she adds. 'He seems okay, I think . . . don't you?'

Oh, right, so they've been having cosy chats without my knowledge? 'Yes, I suppose so,' I croak.

'I'm relieved about that.'

'Mmm, me too.'

'Bye then, Nate. I'd better go. Abby's just made us some lunch . . .'

'Great. Bye, love.' I sense the backs of my eyeballs tingling alarmingly as we finish the call.

Once I've cleared up our lunch stuff, I find myself wondering what to do next that doesn't involve standing in the kitchen, staring into a vat of soup on the hob. So this is what the weekends will feel like now: endless, stretching to infinity.

I walk the dogs again, trudging from street to street for a whole two hours, wondering if Scout is exhibiting signs of weight loss from all this exercise, or if Flynn will start to worry that I've hurled myself into the canal. Probably not.

Shortly after I return home, Flynn announces that he's off to Max's, and will stay there for dinner. Later, I am spooning in another bowl of soup, without bothering to heat it up, when my phone rings. Paolo again. I let it ring out. Then a text: *Answer your phone mate. Saw Sinead in town so I know what's happened. U okay? Want a pint?*

Oh Lord, so the news is out there. I try to formulate a reply in my mind, but it's useless; anything I come up with sounds either overly breezy ('*Don't worry about me!*'), or patently untrue ('*am fine*').

Twenty minutes later there's a sharp knock at the front door.

'Hi,' I say dully as I let Paolo in.

He blows out air and shakes his head, looking around the hallway as if the decorators have been and made a real arse job of painting. 'Bloody hell, mate, I am sorry. Some fucking situation this is.'

I nod and shrug. 'Yeah. Well, there it is. She's gone.'

'Jesus.' He rakes at his hair. 'How's Flynn taking it?'

'Better than me, probably, but it's hard to tell. He's in his room most of the time, or out. He's at Max's right now.'

We stand and look at each other, clearly unsure of what to say next. Paolo shoves his hands in his pockets and inhales deeply; I wonder now if Bea insisted he came over to check on my mental state. 'No pub quiz for you tonight then,' he adds in a lame attempt to lighten the mood.

'Oh, God. I'd forgotten that's tonight. The final as well . . .'

'Ah, sod it,' he says. 'They'll have to rope in a couple of substitutes – though God knows they'll be stuffed without us two. You know what Bazza's like with his obscure sixties music questions . . .'

I raise a smile, wishing Paulo would come to the conclusion that he really should go and leave me alone now.

'So, that rules out the Lamb and Flag for us tonight,' he continues, while I try to figure out how to break it to him that I'm not really in the mood for going anywhere. 'We'll go to the Wheatsheaf instead,' he adds.

'No thanks,' I say quickly. 'It's great of you to come over – I appreciate that – but, really, I'm not up to—'

'So you'd rather stay here,' he interrupts, 'on your own, feeling like shit?'

Well, yes.

'C'mon, get your jacket,' Paolo says firmly. 'We're going out.'

Chapter Eight

For a man who once tried to cook a potato waffle in a Corby trouser press, Paolo is actually pretty smart. He was right to drag me out of the house, to force me to drink beer and tell him exactly what had happened. And when I extract Sinead's list from my pocket and hand it to him, it's actually a relief to have it out there, and not just looping endlessly in my brain like some kind of torture technique.

'Christ,' he murmurs as he scans the lines. 'So she actually *gave* this to you?'

'Well, no – not exactly. She left it for me to find in the kitchen, after she'd gone.'

'Bloody hell. What made her do that?'

I shrug. 'So I'd know exactly why she's been so unhappy, I guess. It must have all poured out. Look at her writing. It's so messy. She's usually much neater—'

'Never mind the handwriting analysis,' Paolo says brusquely. 'You poor bugger. Jesus . . .' He shakes his head and exhales.

Most of Sinead's friends – and, I've always suspected,

Sinead herself – fancy Paolo, and anyone can see why. He's a tall, charming and handsome bastard, not to put too fine a point on it; of Italian parentage, which serves only to boost his appeal. We were friends in secondary school in Huddersfield, and he and his wife Bea settled here when they started their family.

'So, where did you see her today?' I ask.

'Just on the high street. She'd been shopping. She didn't say much. Just that she'd left, she was sure you'd tell me, and that she's staying at Abby's . . .' Looking back at the list, he starts to read aloud: '"You don't listen to me. You take me for granted".'

'Yes, okay,' I say quickly, glancing around the pub. At just after 8 p.m., it's already bustling; we were lucky to nab the quiet booth right at the back.

'"You don't consider my needs",' he continues. '"No effort made re us as a couple . . ."'

'There's no need to read it all out,' I murmur. 'I've read it so many times, I could probably recite it by heart.'

Paolo sips his beer and frowns. 'Did you really give her the money to buy her own Christmas present?'

'Well, yes,' I reply hotly, 'because I'd bought her a skirt for her birthday, which I thought she'd look sensational in. But she just gave it this withering look—'

'So you thought it was more practical to just give her cash instead,' Paolo concludes.

I nod. 'Exactly.'

'But she found it unromantic.'

'Yeah, *okay*,' I say, prickling with defensiveness now.

Paolo fixes me with a look across the table. 'Right. So, you're looking at this list as your P45? I mean, you reckon it really is over?'

'Yeah.' I nod. 'It's not just that. There was an email as

well, and then she came over last night and spelled it all out really.'

Paolo sighs. 'Yeah, but I don't think it's like that at all. What I mean is, I don't think she thought it all through, you know? I bet it just all came out in a splurge, after a few wines. She was probably feeling a bit pissed off, and then, before she knew it, she'd worked herself up into a right old froth about being unappreciated, about life being all drudge and no fun . . .'

'Okay!' I cut in.

'. . . and convinced herself that she really had no option but to leave you,' he concludes, stopping to sip his pint.

'Right. Doesn't really help, though, does it?'

'It does, actually . . .'

'I don't see how.'

'Well, look – first thing, stop panicking . . .'

'I'd say it's a pretty normal human reaction,' I remark.

'Yeah, but it won't help you in this situation because you're going to need a clear head.'

I frown at him. 'A clear head for what?'

Paolo slides the list to me across the table. 'Listen, mate – it seems to me like she's written down your instructions right here.'

I pick it up and study it again. 'What d'you mean?'

'Oh, come on. Can't you see that's *exactly* why she's done this? What she wants you to do is work your way through all the points on the list and put them right.' He pauses. 'She's giving you a chance, mate.'

I almost laugh. Paolo isn't a therapist or a psychologist; he's an electrician ('Bea's so lucky, having such a handy husband!' Sinead has crooned more than once). However, as his own marriage seems to be extremely happy, perhaps he does know a thing or two about the workings of the female mind.

'Rectify all my faults, you mean?' I ask.

'Yeah,' he says brightly.

'But . . .' I stare down at it. 'There's a hell of a lot of points on here . . .'

'Oh, come *on*,' he exclaims, draining his glass. 'You want her back, don't you?'

'Yeah, of course I do!'

'Isn't she worth it, then?' he asks with a maddening glint in his eye.

I twiddle with my glass. 'Yes, she is,' I say quietly. 'But some of them . . .' I pause. 'I mean, the DIY thing, that's easy – I'll just get a joiner in next time, not even *bother* trying to save us money . . .' I catch Paolo's warning look and try to erase the bitterness from my voice. 'But what about where she's just written, "YOUR MOTHER!!!"? I mean, I love Sinead – I'd do pretty much anything for her – but I'm not sure I'd have my mum assassinated.'

Paolo snorts. 'I'm sure you can figure something out. It's going to be a test of your ingenuity and, when you've got to the end, you won't even recognise yourself . . .'

I chuckle dryly. 'Is that supposed to be a good thing?'

He smiles and gets up to go to the bar, adding, 'Just get to it, starting tonight. Look at it this way – you really don't have anything to lose.'

He's right, of course – and after another couple of beers I find myself heading home feeling, okay, a little pissed, but also in a far more positive frame of mind. My friend's enthusiasm for life is infectious, I decide. Maybe I should try to be more like Paolo: charming, positive, Italian. I catch sight of Howard apparently swatting a fly at his living room window and wave quickly, then hurry into my house.

Flynn is home, and greets me with a rather subdued, 'Hey, Dad.' We sit together and watch some trash on the TV, which he enjoys from time to time: young people on their first dates. It all seems terribly contrived and awkward, and I start to feel as if I'm there on the dates with them, at least double their age, a sort of chaperone, stiff and uncomfortable with my hands bunched into tight fists.

'Sorry about all that,' I murmur, during an ad break. 'The guitar thing, I mean. I was upset, but that was no reason to act that way. I just meant—'

'It's okay,' he says lightly.

I glance at my son as he pops strong-smelling cheesy Doritos from a family packet into his mouth. If Sinead were here, the Doritos would be in a bowl. As the dating programme resumes, I find myself spinning off, thinking now of the little things she hates, mostly food-related: people licking their fingers and running them around the inside of a Doritos packet in order to collect the orangey powder residue; witnessing anyone piercing a fried egg yolk with a fork.

The programme ends, and Flynn and I say a companionable goodnight. Leaving him strumming his acoustic guitar on the sofa, I manage not to comment or even compliment his technique. Instead, I escape to our bedroom (no, *my* bedroom now – Christ!) where I change into pyjamas and sit up in bed with Sinead's list to my side and my laptop in front of me.

The list is becoming rather raggedy now from being carted around in various pockets and re-folded numerous times. So I open a new document and start to type it out, line by line, each and every one of my heinous shortcomings.

Only now, bolstered by Paolo, the sight of it no longer triggers a great wave of panic and dismay. I glance up for a moment, my gaze resting upon Sinead's red and white spotty dressing gown hanging from the hook on our bedroom door. I look back down quickly and resume typing, taking care to copy the list exactly, even her flamboyant usage of exclamation marks. And when I've finished, and it's all there in a Word document, I can see that Paolo was right.

It's not really a list. At least, that's not all it is. It's a challenge to be a better person; my instruction manual on how to be the sort of husband Sinead needs me to be. I *will* be that person – for her, for my family – and I will win her back.

Chapter Nine

'She's *left* you? You mean, she's just walked out on you
– and Flynn?'

'No, not on Flynn, it's not like that . . .'

'She's gone and left her own son, with everything he
has to deal with in life?'

I jab a finger at the kitchen ceiling. 'Shhh! He's upstairs
in bed. He'll *hear* you . . .'

My mother shakes her head and looks pointedly around
the room, as if it has fallen into terrible disrepair since
Sinead's departure. In fact, it is gleaming. I was up two
hours ago, at 7 a.m., scrubbing and shining, eager to get
started on working my way through the list.

You leave too much to me, she'd written. Perhaps I did.
But not anymore. The bathroom dazzles; the kitchen bin
smells like a summer rose; even the fridge has been wiped
out and reorganised, with Sinead's wilting spinach disposed
of and all the jar labels facing the right way. It's just a
pity my wife isn't here to see it.

Mindful, too, of Sinead's YOUR MOTHER!!! point, I
also decided to tell Mum precisely what had happened

as soon as she arrived, rather than staggering through some terrible, 'Oh, Sinead's just popped out' kind of charade.

'I have to say, you seem remarkably . . . calm,' she acknowledges now.

'Well, I can't just fall to pieces,' I say, as if I have been the epitome of composure since my wife left me.

'This must be terribly tough for you, though. Humiliating, too . . .' Mum perches on a kitchen chair, and I hand her a coffee. Sunshine streams in through the newly-cleaned kitchen window on this bright Sunday morning.

'Hmmm,' I reply non-committally.

She sips her coffee. 'This is very milky, Nate.'

Yes, because I have sloshed in extra cold milk so it's drinkable right away. 'Is it? I'll make you another . . .'

'No, no, it's fine.' Her mouth curls into a frown, and I am aware of her gaze following me as I potter about the kitchen. 'So, where is she then?'

'Just staying at a friend's for the moment.'

Mum sniffs. 'So, she thinks that's okay? To just leave Flynn, at this crucial stage—'

'Please stop this,' I cut in. 'That's *not* what this is about . . .'

'Well, what am I supposed to say?' she asks.

'You're not supposed to say anything, actually.'

'But I think I'm entitled, when it affects my grandchild . . .'

'Mum, Flynn's *fine*,' I say firmly. 'I'm sorry, I can't go into all the details about this now. I'm only just trying to figure out things for myself.' I inhale deeply and lean against the fridge.

'Is there someone else?' she asks, arching a brow.

'No, of course not.' I stare at her, aghast.

A wash of sanctimoniousness settles over her face. 'I

don't mean with *you*. God knows, Nate, with that job of yours and everything else you have on your plate, I can't imagine you'd have the time . . .'

'Mum, *please*—'

'I'm only trying to help,' she points out, as if *she's* the one who's been wronged. She pushes back her chair with a loud scrape, and makes a great show of searching around the kitchen for Bella's feeding bowl, lead and plastic poo bag dispenser, sighing in irritation that I haven't had everything packed and ready in her oilskin bag.

'Okay, if you don't want to talk about it,' she remarks coolly. 'So, any idea where Bella's pigs' ears might be?'

Ah, those gnarly treats – 'They're actual ears of pig!' Flynn once announced with fascination – that Sinead always hides away at the bottom of our veg rack. I unearth the packet and hand them to Mum. 'Here you go.'

'Thank you.' She packs them into the bag and makes a point of wiping out Bella's bowl with a piece of kitchen roll. 'So, where do you and Sinead go from here, if you don't mind me asking?'

'I really have no idea,' I reply, even keener for her to leave, now that she's raised the possibility of my wife seeing someone else. *Could* she have met someone? I'm wondering now. Have I been an idiot to not even consider that this is the real reason, as opposed to my apparent incompetence with a spirit level and drill?

Flynn appears in the doorway, rubbing at his face. 'Hey, Grandma,' he drawls with a bleary smile.

'Oh, Flynn,' she exclaims, instantly adopting a 'darling baby, abandoned by his mother!' voice. 'How *are* you, love?'

'I'm okay.' He hugs her briefly before grabbing a loaf from the bread bin and shoving a slice into his mouth.

Mum peers at him and scowls in concern. 'Couldn't you toast that, darling?' she suggests.

'Nah, s'okay . . .' He shrugs.

'Or at least put butter or jam on it?' I ask, trying to lighten the mood.

He grimaces at me. 'Thanks, Dad. I'm aware of the options regarding toppings, but it's fine.' He crams another slice into his mouth, fills a half-pint glass to the brim with milk and takes a hearty swig.

'Well, Flynn, Bella and I are off now,' Mum announces.

'Okay. See you soon, Grandma.' He gives her a brief kiss on the cheek.

We leave him alternating between chomping on bread and swigging milk as I carry out Bella's basket and see Mum to her car.

She frowns at me as Bella jumps obligingly into the boot. 'Oh, Nate. That poor, *poor* boy, with a broken home now . . .'

'He's all right, Mum. Really . . .'

'He didn't look all right, stuffing dry bread into his mouth!'

Despite everything, I can't help laughing. 'That's not because of Sinead leaving.'

'How can you be so sure?' She bangs the boot shut.

'Because,' I say, in an overly patient voice, 'he has dry bread all the time. It's not a broken-home thing – it's a teenage thing. Toasting or buttering it is just too much effort—'

'That's because of his condition—'

'No, it's not,' I exclaim. 'You know Flynn, what he's capable of. Of course he can make toast. He can cook an entire dinner, actually. Peel spuds, roast a chicken, make one of those terrible microwave cakes—'

'If you say so . . .'

Christ, is she always as maddening as this? Probably, I decide as she climbs into her car. Until now, I've allowed her to breeze in and say pretty much whatever she likes without challenging her. On and on she went, about Sinead's non-existent massage, and all I said in her defence was, 'A massage isn't *that* big a deal', effectively putting my mother's feelings before my wife's. It wasn't just that, either. There was the, 'Your turkey's always quite dry, isn't it?' comment last Christmas, when Sinead had been up at 6 a.m. to cram the damned bird into the oven, and then that remark about the shimmery red dress my wife chose – and looked sensational in – for Flynn's solo guitar performance at the school concert. 'It looks quite nice,' Mum had remarked tersely, *'from the back.'* Years and years of spiky comments, which Sinead has remarked upon now and again, only for me to try and placate her with an, *Oh, you know what Mum's like . . .*

She winds down her driver's side window and peers at me. 'Well, you take care, Nate.'

'Thanks, Mum. You too.'

She pauses, her lips set in a thin line, her hands gripping the steering wheel unnecessarily, seeing as she hasn't even turned on the engine yet. And then out it comes: 'You know, I don't think Sinead has ever appreciated all you've done for this family.'

I gawp at her, unable to respond for a moment.

'All those years,' she continues, 'not having to go out to work while you gave up your career in music—'

'Career in music?' I retort. 'It was just a few crappy bands . . .'

'. . . and went through that gruelling driving examiner training, just to ensure she had the lifestyle she wanted . . .'

81

'Mum!' I snap. 'What on earth are you talking about? What "lifestyle"?'

She blinks at me, clearly startled by my response. 'Well, Sinead's never wanted for anything, as far as I can see.'

I look at my mother, fury rising in my chest now, but knowing there's no point in explaining that Sinead buys most of her clothes from charity shops, drives a car that's on its last legs and probably has her hair done around twice a year. There's no point, because Mum would never listen. 'I won't have you running her down,' is all I say, taken aback by the calm but firm voice that seems to be coming out of my mouth.

Mum's eyes widen. 'I'm only saying—'

'Well, just *don't*, okay? I mean that, Mum. That's my wife you're talking about. I know we've separated, but I won't have it, all right? And I don't want to hear anything like that again—'

'Joe never speaks to me like this!'

Ah: the spectre of my perfect younger brother rears its head. We stare at each other, invisible horns locked. 'No, well, you don't have a go at his wife, do you?'

'No, because Lorraine would *never* walk out on their kids . . .'

'*Stop* this, Mum. Stop it right now—'

'Stop what? I haven't done anything!' She looks aghast, then clamps her mouth shut and closes the window. With just a quick backwards glance towards Bella, who is sitting demurely in the rear – and who we look after *every time Mum goes away* – she switches on the engine.

There's no goodbye, and no wave; just a jutted-out chin and her cool gaze fixed determinedly ahead. But I know she's rattled as she pulls away, as her failure to mirror-signal-manoeuvre correctly causes an oncoming taxi driver to toot at her. Guilt snags at me as she gestures angrily, then disappears from sight.

*

Despite his Victorian-street-urchin diet, Flynn does seem okay as the day progresses. Max and Luke come over, and they all hang out in the living room, chatting away and playing guitars. Understanding that I am required to keep out of their way, I tackle the laundry, then head out to the back garden to mow the lawn and gouge out weeds from between the patio paving stones. Whilst not exactly joy-making, these tasks at least prove useful in stopping me pacing about, obsessively trying to work out who Sinead's new boyfriend might be, not that I think *for one second* that she is sleeping with someone else. But then, even if she isn't yet, at some point in the future she will be, unless I can make myself truly worthy of her.

As I empty the mower's grass container, a particularly unsettling image forms in my brain: of some dashing bloke – Hugh Grant at his peak – sauntering into the gift shop and being overwhelmed by the confusing array of candles on offer. Gosh, he really can't decide! He glances over at the woman sitting at the till, registers her gorgeousness and falls instantly in love.

Meanwhile, at *my* work, I have people referring to me as 'that lanky fucker with the glasses'.

Back indoors, as I wipe down the entire upstairs' skirting boards – so much dust! How come I'd never noticed before? – it occurs to me that I really should have stood up to Mum years ago, whenever she was offhand or downright rude to my wife. Mum was never like that with Kate Whickham, the girl I was seeing just before I met

83

Sinead. Kate who'd been to Oxford and whose family 'owned land', and was working as a consultant, which seemed to impress Mum hugely, even though she didn't fully understand what a consultant actually did. Meanwhile Sinead, who was awash with orders for her jewellery, was regarded with suspicion right from the start. 'She seems nice enough,' Mum said coolly, after their first meeting.

Frozen pizza and oven chips aren't exactly top-quality fare, but it's what the boys want for dinner and, anyway, we can eat whatever we want now and to hell with it. I walk Scout in the rain, which seems to suit the new weekend mood. Back home, soaked to the bones, I run a bath and clamber into it, convincing myself that of course Sinead isn't out on a date right now, canoodling in some bar with her tongue in someone's mouth, but merely watching a box set with Abby.

I mean, she left me on Wednesday night and it's only Sunday evening. Surely no one could meet someone that quickly, unless . . . *she's been seeing someone else all along?*

I eye my phone, which I have placed on the side of the bath in case she wants to talk to me. A text pings in from my mother: *Very upset after the way you snapped at me today. Spoke to Joe. We are both v worried. He thinks you might be having some kind of breakdown?*

Let them think what they want, I decide, placing my phone back on the side of the bath and reclining into the warm water. Let them discuss my mental health and the fact that I was a little offish with Mum today. However, I know the truth. My first weekend without my wife is, thankfully, almost over and – whilst hardly brimming with joie de vivre – I have at least survived it.

'I'm not going to fall apart,' I say aloud.

And now, when I run through Sinead's list in my head,

another idea starts to form in my mind. Never mind all this cleaning and weeding and snapping at Mum. A kind, loving gesture is what's needed: something to prove to Sinead that I'm capable of making everything right. I'll get onto it tomorrow and choose her something thoughtful. But right now, I sense myself drifting, lulled by comforting thoughts of Sinead's surprised but delighted expression as I turn up at Abby's with . . . well, I don't know what exactly. But I'm sure I'll think of something.

It's my wife's heart-lifting smile I'm thinking of as I stretch out and knock my iPhone with my elbow so it plummets, with a small splash, to the bottom of the bath.

Chapter Ten

Sinead

It's 7.45 a.m. when my mobile rings. Wrapped in a towel, I race from Abby's bathroom to my bedroom in order to retrieve it. HOME is displayed on the screen.

'Hello?' I bark in panic. No one ever uses our house phone.

'Hi,' Nate says.

'Nate? What is it? What's wrong?' It comes out more sharply than I'd intended.

'Erm, nothing. I just . . .'

'Why are you calling me on the landline?'

'Er, my mobile's a bit damp. It's drying out in a dish of rice . . .'

'I'm sorry but that never works . . .'

He grunts. 'Yeah, well, worth a try. So, um—'

'Nate,' I cut in, 'I'm just out of the shower. I'm standing here wrapped in a towel and I really need to get ready for work.'

'Yeah, yeah, I know,' he says quickly. 'I won't keep you. All I wanted to say was, could we meet up after work?'

I frown and perch on the edge of the bed. 'Um . . . I can't tonight, Nate. I'm sorry. Why, is there something—'

'Oh, I just thought we could have a drink,' he says lightly. 'Or dinner, maybe? Would you like that?'

'Sorry, but I really don't think we're at that stage yet where we can sit together and have a nice chat over a bottle of wine, do you?'

'Er . . . I don't know,' he mutters.

A fresh wave of guilt washes over me. 'I'm not saying we can't *ever* see each other like that,' I add. 'It's just . . . a bit too soon, isn't it? I hope you understand.'

'Of course I do,' he says, more brusquely now. 'It's only been, what, five days since—'

'Yes, and I need time, you know. It's all been so intense and upsetting . . .'

He clears his throat. 'So you're not up for dinner tonight?'

'No, Nate, because as I've just explained—'

'I get that. I do listen to you, you know . . .'

A silence hangs in the air between us.

'How about tomorrow, then?' he asks.

'No!' I reply, more emphatically now.

'Okay, okay! So not dinner just yet. What about a coffee tomorrow – or just a walk, or a drive—'

'I can't,' I say quickly.

I can sense him frowning. 'Why not? Are you . . . doing something else?'

'Er, yes,' I reply. 'I'm doing something tonight and tomorrow.'

'Oh, right! So, where are you going? Or should I say, who are you seeing?'

'Nate!' I exclaim. 'What are you implying here?'

'I don't know. You tell me! Although I suppose there's

no need, is there? Not now we're apart and can do whatever the hell we want . . .'

'Could you just listen a minute?' Now it's my turn to snap. 'You can imply what you want, and it's up to you whether you believe me or not – but I can tell you right now I'm not seeing anyone else. It's the last thing I'm looking for . . .'

'Okay,' he murmurs. 'Sorry, sorry . . .'

My heart is hammering now as I pull the towel tighter around myself. 'Look, I'm just seeing Rachel tonight, okay?'

'Rachel? On a *Monday*?'

'Yes, Nate. I just felt I needed an urgent appointment, after everything that's happened. She had a cancellation so she could fit me in—'

'So, you're having *emergency* therapy now?'

'It's only one extra session . . .'

'You'll be moving in with her next!' Christ, does he really think this is helping? Actually, it is – because at least it's clear now what I've been living with all these years. I replay what Abby said last night, over a bottle of wine: *I know you'd never have done this on a whim. So you know in your heart that you've probably done the right thing . . .*

'I really must get ready,' I murmur.

'So, how about tomorrow night? What are you doing then?'

'Actually, Flynn's coming over for the evening.'

'Is he? That's nice!' he says facetiously.

I exhale loudly. 'Hasn't he mentioned it?'

'Um, no,' Nate retorts. 'He did say he's going to start getting the bus to school now, though. I suppose that's okay, isn't it?'

88

'Er, I guess so,' I reply. 'I mean, of course it is, if that's what he wants.'

'Maybe he's just worried I'll park on the zigzags again . . .'

'*You* parked on the zigzags?' I gasp.

'Yeah. I wasn't thinking. So, this evening you're having together . . .'

'I just want to spend time with him. I'm sure you understand that . . .'

'Yeah, that's great,' he mutters.

I stand up and delve into the dressing table drawer where I have stashed my underwear. 'We're just going to hang out here,' I go on. 'Watch a movie, order in a pizza . . .'

'Oh!' he crows. 'Will there be popcorn too?'

I grab at a tangle of knickers and tights and let them fall to the floor. 'There's no need to be like that. I'm not taking him to Florida for two weeks. We're just going to sit and watch a silly comedy . . .'

'Yes, okay,' he mutters, sounding ashamed now.

Another silence falls. 'I'm still happy to drop round at lunchtimes on work days and let Scout into the garden, if that makes things easier . . .'

'Erm, yeah, that'd be great. I'll have to sort out a dog walker at some point . . .'

'Well, until you do, I'll hang onto my key and take care of it.' I pause. 'Don't worry, I won't just let myself in at other times. When you're there, I mean—'

'You can come round whenever you want!' he exclaims.

I clear my throat. 'I just thought you might feel uncomfortable about it.'

'Why? What d'you think I'll be doing? Having an orgy or something?'

This stuns me for a moment. 'For God's sake, I wasn't implying that. But, you know, if that's what you *want* . . .'

'Oh, right! So that would be okay, would it?'

'Can we stop this please?' I snap at him. 'Do whatever you want. I'm going now, okay? I really need to get ready for work.'

We finish the call in a fug of ill humour. As I dress quickly, an unsettling image forms in my mind, of Nate being cajoled into taking part in some kind of driving examiners' orgy, with everyone clutching their official clipboards with those mysterious checklists and forms they have to fill in. There'd be someone nominated, I guess, to mark down careless manoeuvres and incorrect signalling, which I imagine would kill the fun somewhat.

Ready for work now, I find Abby in the kitchen. We perch on high stools at her kitchen island, where she has set out croissants, a bowl of scrambled eggs and another of fat, gleaming strawberries. It's like a mini hotel breakfast buffet here, although most mornings all I can face is a strong coffee and a bite of croissant. 'Just had Nate on the phone,' I tell her, 'wanting to meet up.'

'Really? What did you say?'

'I told him I'm just not ready for that. God, he sounded so . . . agitated, Abs. Going on about whether it's okay for him to have orgies now . . .'

'Nate?' she exclaims. 'Having *orgies*?'

'Oh, he was just being ridiculous, you know. Of course he's upset—'

'He'll be okay, given time,' she says. 'At least, he'll accept it eventually.'

I nod wordlessly.

'I know you hate hurting him,' she adds gently.

'Yes, I really do.'

Tears fuzz my vision, and anxiety gathers deep in my gut as I sip my coffee and try to eat. Abby hugs me tightly, and I set off to work on this bright-skied May morning. I just wish the day hadn't started with Nate's call. Now I'm picturing him and Flynn having breakfast together, trying to behave as if everything's normal; then our boy shambling off, with that wrecked old bag he refuses to throw away, to catch the bus to school.

I rub at my eyes as I stride down Abby's road, through her new-build estate towards the town centre. It's a brisk twenty-minute walk to the gift shop. I could have opted to drive, but am hoping that walking will help to clear my head. As I reach town, the bus passes me. Maybe Flynn's on it; I can't bear to look. I miss him so much, and I've only been gone for five days. Flynn's been on numerous week-long trips with school and the Scouts, and I managed fine then – although of course, that was different. Now, I feel hollow with longing. That's just being a parent, I suppose. You have that bond, like no other, from the moment you first hold them in your arms.

Our baby boy was born during a stormy February night when Nate and I were twenty-seven years old. Although that's not super-young, the pregnancy had been unplanned, and this was way before any of our friends had babies. I don't think any of us possessed more than two sets of bed linen. The nappy aisle in Asda might as well have been the Kalahari Desert, it was that mysterious to us.

The pregnancy was the result of a condom mishap in a B&B in Barry Island in Wales after our friends Dave and Di's wedding. But we were thrilled. We'd been together for two years, and talked about having a baby 'one day', and now it was happening – just a little sooner than anticipated.

91

Flynn was born after a terribly long and painful labour, which I'd intended to get through with some gentle acoustic guitar music – entitled 'happy birth day, darling' – which Nate, my clever musician boyfriend, had written and recorded especially for the occasion. However, in the event, it involved every drug available, an awful lot of yelling and, at one point, my protesting that there was no way this baby was going to come out; he or she would just have to stay inside me, forever. When Flynn finally emerged, wailing his little lungs out, we fell in love with him immediately.

Having decided to formalise things like the proper grown-ups we were now, Nate and I got married at Hesslevale registry office when Flynn was five months old. Nate looked terribly dashing in a smart but second-hand navy blue suit, while I'd chosen a simple vintage shift dress to wear with flat DMs, a cropped black leather jacket and an intricate fine silver necklace I'd made myself. I was a mother and a bride, but I still looked like a student. In those days I fiercely avoided anything that could be termed as 'mum-wear' (i.e., leggings, big sweaters, voluminous T-shirts) and clung to the belief that if I could manage to slap on a coat of lipstick, then everything would be okay.

When we'd met, Nate had been living in a shared house, perched on the bank of the canal in Hesslevale. I'd been happy to give up my ropey studio flat in Leeds and settle in Hesslevale with him, as it was a town I'd always liked; we moved into a rented flat above a coffee shop, then to the Victorian terrace where we've lived for seventeen years. We were the first among our friends to get a mortgage – hurtling into a proper adult existence. But it felt right. We were crazily in love, and I thought our life was perfect.

We even managed to come to terms with Flynn's diagnosis eventually. Having being warned that Flynn might never walk or talk – it was too early to tell, the specialists said – Nate and I launched ourselves into devouring every scrap of info we could possibly get hold of. We were a team back then, a rock-solid duo, and refused to think of CP as a disability at all. In fact, we despised the word.

By three and a half, after copious speech and physical therapy, Flynn was both walking *and* talking. Although his particular gait and indistinct speech attracted attention, Nate and I had developed what we thought of as armadillo armour – solid, unbreakable – so those curious or pitying glances bounced right off us.

'Isn't he clumsy, poor lad!' a stranger once remarked as Flynn manoeuvred himself awkwardly onto a climbing frame.

'He has cerebral palsy,' I explained, taking care not to let any annoyance creep into my voice.

'Oh my God, I'm so sorry!' The elderly woman clasped a hand over her mouth.

'No, please don't apologise,' I assured her. 'You weren't to know.' I smiled to mask my irritation at her having made the comment in the first place.

Crucially, Nate and I stopped taking exception to phrases such as 'gross motor function' ('He's our son, for God's sake – not a malfunctioning car!'). We were the devoted parents of a thriving little boy, supported by dedicated professionals and the other parents we met through groups we attended. And, once they knew why Flynn couldn't scale that climbing frame quite as adeptly as other kids of his age, those strangers in the park were unfailingly kind.

Plus, we had Flynn's grandparents. Judy's – ahem – *views* can be somewhat hard to stomach; however, she was happy to babysit, and we accepted her offers gratefully. Until his sudden death from heart failure, we also had quietly-spoken Arthur, my father-in-law, whose shed was filled with tools and half-built things, and was a perpetual source of fascination for Flynn. Then there are my own parents, Cathy and Brendan, who have always doted on Flynn and never once complained about that eight-hour drive from St Ives to visit us. My older sister Marie, whilst rather formidable and living way down in Brighton, has also been attentive and unfailingly generous at birthdays in providing the table tennis, the bike and the Xbox console that we would have struggled to afford.

And so we managed, and Flynn became a teenager who was just as unthinking and irritating as any other. However, he is also – and I realise I'm naturally biased here – the most fantastic young man: determined and proud, having constantly surpassed anyone else's predictions of what he might achieve. And I try to *never* forget that, even when I discover he's doctored an old passport in order to create a fake ID, and stolen whisky miniatures from what we grandly term our 'drinks cabinet' and filled the empty boxes with chalks and Christmas tree baubles because, of course, that way, we'd never know!

Cerebral palsy is just another part of him, like his humour and brilliance at playing guitar, despite his difficulties; like his determination to perfect the microwave cake-cooking method and his whisky-thieving tendencies.

Having arrived at the shop now, I unlock the door and switch on the lights. Most days I'm here on my own; Vicky is overseeing the re-fitting of a second shop in Solworth. I'm doing the rounds, checking that everything is perfectly arranged, when my mobile trills: an unknown number.

'Hello?'

'Just me,' Nate says. 'I'm ringing from the work phone. Sorry, I'm sure you're busy—'

'Look, Nate, I thought I'd explained—'

'Yes,' he says hotly, 'but I was just thinking, how about I drive Flynn over to Abby's – I mean, to *yours* – for your movie-and-pizza thing tomorrow night?'

My back teeth clamp together. 'I'd really just like some time with him. Can't you understand we need—'

'Of course I do,' he says, clearly mustering every ounce of his willpower in order to sound calm. 'I just want to give him a lift, all right? I'm not going to hang around. I won't *get in the way . . .*'

I lower myself onto the chair behind the counter. 'No, I know that. I just—'

'I only want to see you for five minutes, if that's all right?' he cuts in. 'Just *five minutes*. I assume that's not too much to ask?'

'Okay, okay! Of course that's fine—'

'Great,' he announces, verging on manic now. 'I'll look forward to it.'

'Me too,' I mutter, glancing around the empty shop and resorting to fibbing now: 'But sorry, I really have to go, Nate. A customer has just walked in.'

Chapter Eleven

Nate

So, my wife needs extra therapy now, with the woman who put her up to all of this. I'm sorry, but I can't help thinking of Rachel in that way. After all, weren't we fine before she came along? Isn't therapy supposed to make you calmer and happier, rather than stirring things up and driving you to write crazed notes?

Still, at least Sinead has agreed to see me tomorrow, if only briefly. I remind myself of this as I park up and saunter towards the Solworth test centre. Also: it's *good* that Flynn is feeling up to movie-and-pizza nights with his mum. I have no desire for there to be any kind of rift between them. I just wish I was fucking invited, that's all.

Filling my lungs with crisp morning air, I make a point of breezing into the office with a definite spring in my step, like the sodding Easter bunny, in order to transmit the message that, while things might be a little tricky right now, I am coping admirably.

Everyone is here – Liv, Eric, Nadira – chatting, drinking coffee and sorting out paperwork for the day's tests. After a few pleasantries, and being handed a coffee by Eric, I perch on the edge of my desk and clear my throat. 'Look, I don't want to make a massive deal out of this, but I suppose I should tell you that Sinead left me last week.'

Everyone stares, aghast. Liv is first to speak. 'My God, Nate. You mean . . . you've broken up?'

'Well, it sort of looks that way. But we'll see—'

'Why on earth didn't you say something?' Eric exclaims. 'Why didn't you just tell us, or call me—'

'I didn't really know how.' I shrug.

'Oh, Nate, you poor, poor thing . . .' Now Nadira is up out of her seat and hugging me, followed by Liv, resulting in a sort of cuddling *clump*, which I absolutely don't want right now.

'You should have told us last week,' Liv chastises me. 'We're your *friends* . . .'

'Really, I'm okay . . .' I manage to extricate myself and back away to my desk, where I add, hurriedly, 'Please, I don't want a fuss over this. Maybe we'll be able to sort things out. I have no idea. But right now I just want to get on with work, keep busy, and try to focus on that . . .'

'If you're sure you're okay,' Liv offers, exhaling heavily at the awfulness of it all. I can't even look over at Eric, although I can sense him staring at me. Recently, there was talk of us all going away for a weekend on the coast somewhere: two couples plus Flynn. Now our cosy little group has crumbled.

'I really am,' I say firmly, grabbing my paperwork for the first candidate and glancing over towards the internal window, which is only partially obscured by flimsy vertical blinds. 'Ah – she's here now. Better go.'

'Good luck, mate,' says Eric, frowning in concern.

'If there's anything you need,' Liv calls after me as I shoot through the door, perhaps a little too hastily as the girl flinches, startled, at the sight of me bounding towards her.

'Hello!' I beam at her. 'I'm Nate. I'm your examiner today. You're Julianna?'

'Yes, that's right,' she squeaks.

'Could I just see your provisional licence and theory test pass certificate, please?'

She shows me her documents, and we step out into the car park where we go through the preliminaries: the sight test and general vehicle-related questions. By the time we set off in her instructor's car, she seems to have gathered herself together. In fact, Julianna drives extremely well. Will Flynn allow me to teach him to drive? I wonder. Even with his condition, there is no reason why he wouldn't be capable of learning. We might not even need to have a car specially adapted for him, although it's impossible to know without a proper assessment. I shake off the unsettling realisation that this might be the first Flynn-related issue that Sinead and I will deal with as separated parents. Until now, we've always been a tight-knit team.

My God – *Where will we both sit at his wedding?*

I catch my thoughts hurtling off in a ridiculous direction, and try to wrestle them back to the matter in hand. However, now, a particularly depressing realisation is infiltrating my brain: he's just sacked me as his guitar teacher. Why on earth would he want me to teach him to drive?

Concentrate, I tell myself silently. Fortunately, Julianna continues to drive with extreme competence. The test ends, and I tell her she's passed.

'Thank you so much,' she says, grinning. 'Can't wait to

tell Mum and Dad!' And off she skips, already snatching her phone from her bag in order to share the good news with her two-parent family.

My next candidate passes too, and the one after that, which lifts my spirits a little. Despite our reputations, we examiners gain no pleasure in telling someone they haven't passed. However, my last candidate of the day – a chunky red-haired chap named Angus Pew – drives in such an erratic and cavalier fashion, I am forced to use the dual-control brake, which means an automatic fail. Back at the test centre car park, we park up.

I turn to him. 'I'm sorry to tell you, but you didn't pass your test today.'

He gawps at me. 'You're joking, right?'

'No, I'm not joking,' I reply levelly. 'As I said, I'm sorry to tell you—'

'Yeah, I fucking heard you the first time. I'm not deaf.'

I reel back and blink at him. I've been raged at in this kind of scenario plenty of times; one guy tried to grab at my shirt, and another spat at me as we parted company. As examiners, we just have to try to steel ourselves against abuse. 'There's no need to swear at me,' I tell Angus Pew wearily. 'Would you like me to explain why you didn't pass?'

'No, I bloody wouldn't,' he snaps. 'What difference would that make?'

'Well, some candidates find it helpful to know for next time—'

'You know what *you* might find helpful?' he growls, cheeks reddened, a purplish vein bulging from his forehead.

'I'm sorry, I don't quite—'

'*You* might find it helpful to know that I work in a restaurant in Hesslevale . . .'

I frown at him, confused as to why he is telling me this.

'. . . so you'd better watch out,' he concludes with a sneer.

I blink at him, uncomprehending for a moment. 'Are you saying you know where I live?' I ask.

'Yeah. Well, I know you live in Hesslevale. I've seen you out and about. You're kind of hard to miss, being the height you are—'

'And what d'you mean, that I should "watch out"?'

He fixes me with watery grey eyes. 'I happen to work in a restaurant kitchen. That's all I'm saying . . .'

My stomach turns as I study this man, just an ordinary bloke in his early thirties, pale-faced, substantial belly straining against his stripy T-shirt. 'You're not . . . *threatening* me, are you?'

Angus Pew shrugs.

'Are you saying that, if I eat in your restaurant, you might . . . do something to my food?'

'I might. I might not. Who knows?'

I glare at him as we both climb out of the car. 'So, which restaurant d'you work in?'

'Ha! Now, that would be telling, wouldn't it?' He grunts and gives me a frankly menacing stare before loping off, leaving my head swirling with the many ways in which a seemingly innocent lasagne might be contaminated. Is he talking saliva, snot . . . or worse? This is far from ideal if I'm planning to treat Sinead to lots of meals out as, apparently, I make *no effort re us as a couple.*

Perhaps it's just as well that she doesn't feel up to going out to dinner with me just yet.

*

After an uneventful evening – with Flynn being cordial but distant – I greet Tuesday with a little more optimism.

100

This evening, after work, I am seeing Sinead. In those precious five minutes when I drop off our son, I shall not only show my appreciation of her, but prove that I have taken her criticisms on board, and am working through them steadily.

Today, I am working from a different test centre, with another team – in the larger, further-away town of Brokely – and so I'm spared the concerned looks and gentle quizzings from colleagues. At lunchtime, I'm almost grateful for the failure of my iPhone-recovery method. As the rice didn't absorb the bathwater within, a trip to the phone shop for a replacement mobile keeps me occupied. However, it also takes way longer than expected, leaving me no time to peruse the shops and choose a gift for Sinead.

Still, no matter. I'll be able to pick up something for her on the way home. It's not the price tag that's important, but the thoughtfulness; I learnt this from the leopard skirt episode. It cost me a fortune, frankly – more than I'd imagined it possible to spend on a piece of animal-print material the size of a cushion cover – and resulted only in disappointment. 'Nate,' she'd exclaimed, gawping at it, 'did you confuse me with Bet Lynch in 1987?'

Unfortunately, after the final test of the day, Kevin, the Brokely test centre manager, wants to run through a new admin procedure with me, which results in me leaving much later than I'd anticipated.

In fact, as I set off for home at 6.15 p.m., I'm now rather concerned about where I might buy Sinead a present at all. The supermarkets will still be open, but what would I choose for her there? A pair of tights, a bar of soap, a jar of speciality marmalade? None would convey the message that I view her as wonderful and incredibly desirable. Of course . . . flowers would be perfect. *No spontaneity in our lives*, she wrote. Well, I'll prove her wrong on that count! Visualising her delighted face when festooned with blooms, I pull up at the garage just outside Hesslevale and virtually leap from my car.

Luckily, there are plenty of flowers stashed in green plastic tubs outside the shop. Most appear to be carnations and chrysanthemums in zingy colours, which always strike me as particularly cheerful. As opposed to, say, lilies, which bring to mind illness and death, and is clearly not the message I want to convey.

I choose a bunch of yellow chrysanths, decide it looks rather stingy and add red ones, then orange – and then sod it, a whole load of those flecked carnations that look like they've been doodled on with felt tips. The effect of them all together is quite dazzling – like an outrageous sunset. I manhandle the whacking bouquet into the shop, then carry it back out to my car, attracting several bemused glances and one 'Ooh, someone's a lucky lady!' remark from a woman in a pink coat.

Will Sinead think she's lucky? I wonder. At least, will she decide that I'm not quite the lazy, self-centred arse that she had me down for?

I set off for home, glancing back when I stop at a red light to see that the stems are leaking water from their cellophane wrappings all over the back seat of my car. Sinead once remarked to Flynn, rather unnecessarily, I thought, that I am 'anal' about my vehicle – meaning I'm not especially keen on it being scattered with smashed cheese and onion crisps and putrefying apple cores. How they giggled together about the time I was dismayed to discover that a half-litre beaker of Ribena had puddled onto the carpet. I suppose she was right, in that I do prefer my car's interior to be reasonably clean and dry. But now I'm thinking: sodden upholstery is of no concern if my gesture puts a smile on my darling wife's face.

Chapter Twelve

Back home, Flynn is slathering bagels with Philadelphia cheese when I march in with my love offering. 'Who are they for?' he asks, shrinking away as if they might combust in his face.

'For Mum, of course,' I reply, dumping them on the kitchen worktop and wondering how best to present them. As separate bunches in their wrappers? No – that would look cheap, I decide. Better to unify them into one gigantic *shrub*. 'So, how was your day?' I ask him.

'Uh, okay,' he says, clearly far too agog at the blooms to engage in any sort of meaningful exchange.

I pick up a few fallen leaves and look at him. 'You're seeing Mum tonight, aren't you?'

'Erm, yeah.' His cheeks redden.

'It's fine, you know,' I say, overcome by an urge to hug him but aware that it probably wouldn't be welcomed. 'I mean, it's great you're spending time with her,' I add. 'It's important that you still see her, and can talk to her about anything that's bothering—'

'Dad,' he interrupts, turning back to the crumb-strewn bread board, 'can we just leave it?'

'Oh, sure!' I reply in an overly-bright voice. 'I'll just give you a lift over and drop off her flowers, okay?'

He turns to face me and frowns. 'Why did you buy her flowers? It's not her birthday.'

'No, it's not.' I pause. 'I don't need an excuse, do I?'

He squints at them and bites his lip. 'You just never do, that's all.' He's right, of course – but that's all going to change.

As Flynn drifts upstairs to change out of his school clothes, I try to figure out how to make the flowers look extra-special. Clearly, I should present them in a vase, and not as a massive, dripping clump. However, when I search the kitchen for a receptacle that's big enough, nothing comes close. I consider the enormous stainless steel stock pot that Sinead always used when Flynn's friends descended on our house, and she'd dish up bolognaise for the hungry hordes (for some reason, that petered out when they reached their teens. These days the only evidence of food being consumed by his mates is the odd oil-stained pizza box on his bedroom floor). A bouquet in a stock pot would look ridiculous, I decide, and might even trigger a wave of melancholic nostalgia for 'those mass catering days', as she fondly refers to them.

Continuing my search, I step out into our back garden, followed by Scout. All I can find is a watering can, which lacks elegance – plus, shamefully, a small turd lying in what we optimistically term our 'herb-aceous border', and which I bag up, hurriedly, and sling into the wheelie bin.

Rummaging in our shed now, I find an old zinc bucket. This'll have to do, and could possibly even be considered quite stylish in certain circles. I'm sure I've seen tiny silvery containers filled with hydrangeas in florists' windows.

Well, this is just a bigger version, I decide as I carry it indoors, fill it with water and plonk in the blooms.

There. Well, no – not *quite* there. The flowers still need arranging. It dawns on me now why people attend flower arranging classes – which I've always regarded as a bizarre concept – because, clearly, there is an art to this.

'Can we go soon, Dad?' Flynn calls through from the living room while I try, ineffectually, to fluff up the blooms.

'Yeah, in a minute.' I frown at the flowers, wondering what's missing from my outlandish offering because it doesn't look right. Leaves, that's it. A proper bouquet doesn't consist of just flowers; it has spriggy bits too. I glance through our gleaming kitchen window. There's bound to be stuff in the garden I can use.

To avoid being observed by Flynn – who'll probably conclude that I've gone quite mad – I carry the bucket outside so I can fix my 'arrangement' out there, in privacy. A sense of unease starts to build in me as I investigate the garden for the right kind of leaves. Taking flowers to my wife shouldn't feel like such an almighty deal, but, of course, it is. In fact, I'm feeling precisely how I used to just before a performance. Despite playing in several bands – and being a reasonably competent lead and rhythm guitarist – I was always beset with nerves, just as I am now. This feels like a new kind of stage fright; a sense of dread at playing the part of the newly-dumped husband, trying to make everything better with a bouquet.

'Say it with flowers,' the old Interflora ad used to go. So, what am I trying to say here?

I'm sorry. I love, you Sinead. I'll never let you down again.

Having pulled up some large, floppy leaves by the shed, I plunge them into the bucket and assess my offering. *You don't consider my needs*, she scrawled on that list. Well, what she doesn't need is a load of dock leaves, for crying out loud. I yank them out and toss them onto the lawn, then scan the garden for more eye-pleasing specimens. Ferns are growing at the fence which divides our garden from Howard and Katrina's. Ferns are frondy and pretty, I decide, also realising now that our garden requires serious attention; i.e., more than a perfunctory weeding session and mowing of the lawn. It's only late May, yet our borders are already filling with dandelions. Even at the garden's peak in midsummer, they are home to just a meagre selection of unremarkable plants. If I'd spent every Saturday out here in a planting and weeding frenzy, erecting trellises and creating elaborate rockeries like Howard does, would Sinead have left me?

Howard doesn't even have a record collection. He owns about five CDs; all terrible – I've checked them when we've been over there. 'I'm not really into music,' he explained. I moved swiftly away from the atrocities, as if I might be somehow contaminated by standing too close to Shakin' Stevens' Greatest Hits, or anything by Jimmy Nail.

'He's not into music!' I hissed to Sinead later. 'Isn't that like saying, I don't like food, or air?' She muttered something about trying to be less judgemental, and everyone being entitled to their own personal tastes – or did I think a liking for *Crocodile Shoes* warranted a custodial sentence?

Well, yes, in actual fact, I did.

The guilty party is in his kitchen now. I keep glimpsing him bobbing about, being his usual all-round, excellent self – no doubt *listening* to Katrina and absolutely not taking her for granted, ever. Monty is out in their garden, sniffing around. If he were to crouch in readiness for doing a dump, Howard would be out there in a jiffy, poo bag in hand. It's a wonder Monty even shits at all.

Aware of my anxiety building, I tug out a clump of ferns, shake the earth off them and plonk them in the bucket with the flowers. But it still doesn't look right, and now Howard and Katrina's back door is opening. It's Katrina who appears – a tall, powerfully-built woman with a penchant for tight jodhpur-type trousers, despite having no contact with horses, ever. She strides towards me and beams over the fence.

'Hi, Nate.' Her gaze drops to the bucket. 'Aw, are you throwing out those flowers?'

'Erm, no – I'm arranging them,' I explain with a strained smile.

'Wow. With ferns, I see. Very inventive!' Katrina laughs and tosses back her glossy brown mane. 'You're obviously a man of hidden talents.'

Not according to my wife. 'Ha. Well, um, I'd better get on . . .'

Aware of her bemused gaze, I hurry back inside and summon Flynn, as if, yet again, he's been the one delaying our departure.

We set off in my car. 'Are you really giving that to Mum?' Flynn asks, swivelling to frown at the bucket of blooms, which is resting on a protective newspaper layer on the back seat.

'Yes,' I reply. 'I thought I'd surprise her.'

'I think you'll do *that*,' he exclaims.

I glance at him and clear my throat. 'We haven't sat down and talked about the whole Mum thing, have we?'

'No, we haven't,' he replies dully.

He turns to look out of the side window, as if something

108

fascinating is happening in Hesslevale town centre on a rather dismal Tuesday evening. I suppose I should be relieved that he seems reasonably accepting about our new situation. Maybe he assumes his mother and I are having some kind of blip, and everything'll be back to normal pretty soon. In more optimistic moments, I can almost convince myself that that's the case – and she'll be home again before the tofu she left in our fridge exceeds its expiry date.

'D'you *want* to talk to me about anything?' I ask.

'No! No, I don't. It's nothing to do with me.' He shudders visibly.

'Okay, but if you ever feel you need to—'

'It's all right, thanks,' he says quickly.

I'm about to add something else, along the lines that I'm always here for him if ever he needs to talk – but he's made it quite clear that me being 'always here' is not exactly a positive for him. I know it's ridiculous to feel spurned over this, just as it is to envy the forthcoming movie-and-pizza scenario with his mum. And I know it's quite mad of me to try and think of ways to make *our* evenings fun . . . but how about a horror night? Sinead hates scary movies. That's something Flynn could only do with me. We could order in a Deliveroo; we've never done that before. That would be fun, watching our creepy film and waiting for our burgers and fries to arrive! On second thoughts, maybe he regards every evening with me as a horror night. So, how about playing some games together? If I dug out Pass the Pigs, would he find that fun in a nostalgic way? Or would it just remind him of all those Christmases when we were all together, and his beloved maternal grandparents would be visiting from Cornwall, and there'd be a constant flow of drinks and chocolates and laughter?

Oh my God, *Christmas* . . .

I am blinking back actual tears as we turn into Aspen Grove, where Abby lives. Hopefully Flynn won't notice as he's still gazing out of the passenger side window. So this is where my wife is staying now: among the primped gardens with their box-fresh tables and chairs. The lawns are all mown, their edges clipped, barely a blade out of place. You could eat your dinner off these sparkling patios. We have visited Abby before, when she moved in in December – but it didn't strike me then how sterile this estate is. For one thing, it was dark, and the occupied houses had fairy lights and Christmas trees twinkling in their front windows. I told Sinead that I could see the appeal of a brand new house, as opposed to a shambly Victorian terrace, as bits wouldn't keep pinging off it. But of course, that was different. Back then, my wife didn't *live* here.

I pull up outside Abby's yellow-brick semi and look at Flynn. 'Well, here we are!' I announce, as if he is nine years old and I am dropping him off for an exciting sleepover.

'Yeah,' he mutters, clambering out of the car and heading for the door, which has already opened. Sinead is standing there, smiling expectantly, and wearing an extremely pretty blue fitted dress that I haven't seen for ages. Having wiped at my face, I climb out too and shove my hands into my jeans pockets, not knowing what to do with myself.

Now Sinead is hugging Flynn, as if I am not here. 'Hey, darling, so good to see you! I've been looking forward to this all day.'

'Hey, Mum . . .'

I open the back door of my car and lift out the bucket. Loitering a few feet away, I clutch the unwieldy receptacle crammed with flowers and ferns to my chest. At least there's no sign of Abby. That would've been even more awkward, considering that I regard her as my friend too (what'll happen there? Oh, I guess she's made it quite clear where her allegiance lies).

Flynn and his mother pull apart, and she smiles and pats his arm. 'In you go, sweetie. I won't be a minute . . .' She glances at me. *I'll just deal with this bucket-wielding nutter who's lurking here . . .*

Obediently, and without so much as a nod goodbye, he heads into the house.

'Hi,' Sinead says, possibly trying for a smile, although her mouth remains flat.

'Hi,' I say. 'Um, I just thought I'd bring him over . . .'

'Yes, you said you were going to. That was nice of you.' Her gaze drops to my love offering. 'What's this?'

'I, er . . . bought you a present.' I step towards her, lifting it so she can fully appreciate the spectacle of jarring red, orange and yellow flowers and a load of bedraggled foliage.

Her blue eyes look pained as she blinks up at me. 'Wow. They're quite, um . . .'

'I realised I couldn't remember the last time I bought you flowers,' I add hastily. 'I'm sorry, love. I haven't been very good at that kind of thing. It's not that I haven't wanted to do nice things for you. Just that it hasn't crossed my mind. But, you know – now you've made it clear how you feel—'

'Nate, I—'

'I really will try and be a lot more thoughtful and considerate from now on.' I swallow hard and hold out my gift to her, which she takes, wincing, then places carefully on the flagstone.

111

She straightens up and looks at me. 'Nate . . .' She pauses, as if struggling to find the right words. I glance down at her present. Some of the carnations have already started to droop over the sides of the bucket. 'Where did you get these?' she asks.

'From, um, the petrol station,' I mutter.

'Right.' She presses her lips together. 'Thanks, Nate. That was very . . . *thoughtful* of you.'

Did she mean that, or is she being sarcastic? I study her face, trying to read her expression. 'Well, um . . . I'll come back later and pick up Flynn . . .'

'No, don't worry about that. I'm not sure what time that'll be . . .'

'You could call me, though, couldn't you? When he's ready to come home?' *When you've had your pizza and movies and fun . . .*

'It's fine, Nate,' she says firmly. 'I'll bring him home. Bye for now. And . . . thanks again.'

And with that, Sinead carries our dented old bucket crammed with undergrowth into Abby's house, and firmly shuts the door.

Chapter Thirteen

Sinead

'He brought you petrol station chrysanths in a *bucket*?' Rachel exclaims.

'Yes,' I reply. 'It was so bizarre, but, you know – also sort of touching, although not in the way he intended. More like a child's Mother's Day gesture gone terribly wrong.' Rachel nods, but looks rather blank. 'You know how kids present their mums with wonky presents?' I add. 'One year, Flynn brought me breakfast in bed of buttered digestives garnished with slabs of apple—'

'And did you appreciate the gesture?' she asks.

'The apple biscuits? Yes, of course!'

'No, the bucket . . .'

'Oh. Well, yes, I suppose I did, but it also seemed kind of . . . sad, you know? For some reason, he'd also stuffed in some weeds that he'd torn up from God knows where . . .'

Rachel nods gravely. 'His presentation skills could have been better.'

'Yes, I suppose it's not a particular skill of his. I mean, he probably hasn't wrapped a Christmas or birthday present in about a decade . . . what is it with men and this unwillingness to acquaint themselves with scissors and Sellotape, like it's some kind of logistical nightmare that only women can deal with?' I pause. 'So I'm not sure why he tried his hand at flower arranging . . .'

Rachel raises a plucked brow. 'So, did you feel Nate was *mocking* you by bringing you those chrysanths?'

'Mocking me?' I exclaim. 'No, of course not. Why would he do that?'

She looks taken aback. 'Erm, well, you've talked a lot about being overwhelmed by domesticity, and feeling that you've lost your identity as a creative person. You're grieving, in a way . . .'

'Grieving? What d'you mean?'

'Grieving the loss of your old self,' she clarifies. 'For the person you once were – fun, youthful, showing great promise, heralded as a future star with the world laid out before you . . .'

Christ, and seeing her is supposed to make me feel better?

'. . . and understandably, that's caused a deep sense of resentment,' she goes on. 'Perhaps you've interpreted the bucket – and its association with cleaning – as being integral to domestic drudgery . . .'

'No,' I say emphatically, 'I haven't interpreted it as *anything*. Nate's not the kind of person to give me a present with an underlying message. I mean, when he gave me an awful skirt for my birthday – a skin-tight, leopard-print mini – he wasn't thinking, "I'll buy her this to signify that she looks a bit cheap . . ."'

Rachel blinks, clearly confused now.

'He probably just thought it was sexy,' I add.

'Really?'

'Yes, and with the flowers, I'm sure he was just trying to be kind and make things right.'

I run my tongue around my dry mouth, wondering now whether I did the right thing, in keeping tonight's appointment after seeing Rachel on Monday too. However, I needed someone to talk to after that awkward evening with Flynn. The whole day, I'd been desperate to see my boy. However, it had felt so forced and contrived, sitting there in Abby's living room, eating pizza together. Abby was working at the pub, and I'd found myself almost wishing she was there with us, diffusing the tension. Flynn was quiet and gloomy, responding to most of my questions with monosyllables and shrugs.

He doesn't want to be here, I decided – a realisation that made me feel as if I'd been kicked.

'So,' Rachel continues, 'it's now a week since you left Nate, is that right?'

'Yes.' God, a week. It's been terrible, frankly: keeping up a chirpy facade in the shop, and trying not to drone on too much to Abby, who's been lovely – but I know she has her own life too.

'Shall we go back to the list you wrote?' Rachel suggests. 'We haven't really talked about that in much detail.'

I nod. 'Yes, okay.'

'Did you find it . . . cathartic, to put it all down on paper?'

'Erm, I'm not sure.'

'Well, how *did* you feel?'

'Pretty angry, I suppose. As I told you, I left Nate straight afterwards—'

'And do you feel that was the right thing to do?'

'I don't know. I mean, yes – when I saw it all written down, I knew I couldn't stand it anymore. But I thought

115

I'd feel better by now, in that at least I'd made a decision.' I push back my dishevelled hair that's at least two months overdue a cut. I look a fright these days. Even Abby has started giving me worrying looks.

'What about the *good* points you'd put on your list?' Rachel asks.

I stare at her. 'The good points?'

'Yes,' she says briskly. 'Remember we talked about you writing down all the negative *and* positive aspects of your marriage?'

I twist my fingers together, feeling like my teenage self, who'd just been told by a friend that there was *another* exam question on the reverse side of the paper – one I hadn't noticed, which meant an automatic fail. 'Yes, I do remember that now,' I murmur.

Rachel shuffles on her chair. 'But you just focused on the negatives.'

'Yes. They, erm, kind of ran away with me . . .'

'You didn't put down any good points at all?'

'Um, no, I didn't.'

'Ah.' She nods. 'Well, okay, that's how you were feeling that night. You were upset and angry – and that's *fine* . . .'

I glance at the school-style wall clock behind her. Somehow, it seems to beam the time into Rachel's brain via the back of her head as, without ever turning to look at it, she always knows precisely when our hour is up. Right on cue, she says, 'So, that's the end of our session today, Sinead. Would you like to meet next Thursday? Or something sooner, perhaps?'

I hesitate. 'Can we leave it for a little while? I think I need time to mull over a few things.'

'Of course, yes,' she says in a clipped tone. 'Just call me whenever you'd like another appointment.'

'I will, thank you.' I pay and thank her again, sensing a certain coolness emanating from her as I leave, as if I have somehow disappointed her, either by ballsing up the list exercise, or ducking out of our regular sessions.

Out in the street, I pass the restaurant of a faceless hotel, in which a cluster of besuited men are all gathered around the salad bar. Flynn was obsessed with salad bars as a little boy: being allowed to heap his plate with potato salad and sweetcorn and sprinkle bacon bits all over the top. Why is *everything* making me nostalgic these days? Next thing, I'll be welling up when I spot a can of Ambrosia Creamed Rice in the supermarket – another childhood favourite of Flynn's.

My phone rings, and I pull it from my bag, expecting it to be Nate; however, it's Michelle, my old college friend. 'Hey,' I exclaim, 'are you back already?' For the past six months, she has been on an artist's residency in New York. To my shame, I've been terrible about keeping in touch. Chatty texts have remained largely unanswered, Facebook rarely checked.

'No, not until next week. You've been awfully quiet, hon. I've been worried about you. Everything okay?'

I hesitate. Whilst I'd rather not break the news about leaving Nate right now, I can't pretend everything's okay either. I haven't even told Vicky, my boss, yet. My own *parents* don't even know. They'd jump into Dad's knackered old pick-up truck and descend to fuss over me, and that's really not what I need. They'd also tell Marie, my sister, who has always been of the opinion that, as a high-ranking nurse, she knows absolutely everything, whilst I am merely an arty, ditsy jewellery person, barely capable of locating a matching pair of shoes.

'Not so good, actually,' I start. 'I've . . . well, I've left

117

Nate. I've moved out and left Flynn with him. Things just weren't good, so I'm staying at Abby's—'

'Oh, my God. What happened?'

By the time I've climbed into my car, I have spilled it all out: about fuelling myself with lady petrol, writing that list, Nate coming over with the bucket of flowers – and the worst part, feeling as if I've walked out on Flynn too (which, of course, I have; never mind my clumsy attempt to make things right with a crappy movie and a pizza). 'Sorry to splurge all this when you're away,' I add, sitting in the driver's seat now.

'Don't be crazy. I mean, I knew you were unhappy. I just didn't realise quite how bad things were. Why didn't you say? You could have called or messaged me—'

'I know, but it just happened. It wasn't really planned. Anyway, I didn't want to heap all of that on you.'

'Well, I need to see you. I'm back a week today, so how about the Friday?'

'Won't you be jet-lagged?'

'I'll be *fine*. I'll have to be anyway. There's a bit of a gathering with the old gang and we'll need you there, okay?'

'A gathering?' I almost laugh at her suggestion.

'Look, I know what you're thinking, but it won't be a huge night, I promise. Just a bite to eat in Fletcher's for old times' sake . . .'

Ah, Fletcher's: purveyors of murky bean dips and fierce Argentinian reds, and our beloved haunt as students. 'Who's "we"?' I ask cautiously.

'Just George, Aisha and Brett.'

'Brett?' I repeat. 'You mean Brett O'Hara?'

'Yeah! C'mon, it might be just what you need.'

No, I think: *if I needed anything, it would be to see*

you on my own. But then, Michelle was always like this: the organiser and fixer, grabbing at any excuse for a party. She'd never have let her own life slide, the way I have. 'You do remember how lovely they are,' she adds.

'Yes, of course I do . . .'

An image swirls into my mind, of an evening – no, many evenings, all rolled into one – with all of us sitting around Michelle's scruffy oak table in her basement flat close to our college in Leeds. Cheap wine flowed, someone was usually playing guitar, *everyone* was smoking copiously and Brett would be holding court. We were all platonic friends, really, although Michelle and George had a fling that fizzled out after one term, and Brett and I had one of those marathon snogs at a party once, never to be discussed, and certainly never repeated. Everyone fancied Brett, as I did, although never in any serious sort of way; he was too flighty, too in demand – I couldn't have coped with the competition. In contrast, my college boyfriends were more the quiet, unassuming types. But those nights – with the five of us gathered around Michelle's table – were the highlight for me really. Barely out of our teens, we still had that unshakeable belief that the world was ours for the taking. Since then, Michelle's career has flown; she's had numerous exhibitions and prestigious commissions. I've heard through the grapevine that everyone else is doing pretty well too.

'Aisha got in touch to say she'd run into the boys at an exhibition a couple of weeks ago,' Michelle continues now. '*Please* come. Everyone wants to see you. We don't have to talk about Nate, if you don't want to. When's the last time you saw everyone? Was it George and Petra's wedding?'

'It must be,' I say, 'and that was, what – ten years ago?

119

Aisha was there too, wasn't she? But Brett . . . well, I can't remember the last time I saw him.'

Actually, I do remember. It was a couple of years after Flynn was born, and I was Christmas shopping by myself in Leeds, where everyone – including Michelle – still lives. Brett spotted me in WH Smith and came bounding over, and we caught up on each other's news. While I'd pretty much put my jewellery business on the back-burner, his career as a graphic designer was flourishing. 'You'll get back into it, though, won't you?' he asked.

'Maybe one day,' I replied.

'But you must! Promise me you will?'

I'd laughed, and promised, and we'd hugged and gone our separate ways.

'Please don't mention this to anyone,' I tell Michelle now, 'but I've been seeing this woman, a therapist . . .'

'Oh, there's no shame in that,' she says. 'Virtually everyone in New York sees someone. Seriously, to *not* have a therapist here – at least, amongst the people I've met – would seem as weird as not having a dentist—'

'But this is Yorkshire, not New York,' I remind her.

'Well, if she seems to "get" you, then I think it's a great idea. So, what would she say about a night out with your old friends?'

I smile. 'She'd probably say go—'

'Then you've got to come!'

Now I'm laughing at her forthrightness; my old friend who was always the life and soul. 'Yes, but I'm not sure she's such a great therapist, actually.'

'Well, *I'm* saying it, then,' Michelle insists, and I know she's smiling. 'We'll see you at Fletcher's next Friday at eight – and *no* backing out.'

Chapter Fourteen

Nate

Some testing situations I've had to deal with since Sinead left me:

My colleagues tiptoeing around me and being ever so concerned, as if I have come to work covered in a mysterious rash.

Liv offering to drop me off a casserole (politely declined due to invalid/bedpan vibes). Nadira even bringing me in a *cake*.

A brief, rather awkward phone conversation with my high-achieving brother Joe, head honcho at a pharmaceutical company who talks as if a war's going on: 'Hi, I gather from Mum that all's not too well on the home front?' 'Yes, that's about it, I suppose.' 'Ah well. Chin up, take care of yourself, won't you? Let me know if you need anything? Bye!'

Eric asking repeatedly if I'd like to go for a drink.

Ditto Paolo. 'You shouldn't shut yourself away,' he warned when I told him about Sinead's lukewarm response to the flowers. I wasn't shutting myself away, I insisted. I was going to work and coming home, picking up groceries, cooking dinner, doing housework, walking Scout, setting mousetraps and disposing of the occasional carcass, much to Flynn's fascination and disgust. One morning, the worktop was splattered with blood. Thank God Sinead wasn't here to see that. This is how bleak things have become: that I'm scrabbling for reasons as to why it's a *good* thing that my wife has left me.

On top of all that, I've been trying to figure out which of my faults I should attend to next – and wondering if there's any point, actually. After all, I have already had an altercation with Mum, scrubbed the house like a maniac, mowed the lawn and begun to deal with our apparent infestation. As Sinead wasn't here to witness any of that, it's hardly going to help my case. I've considered emailing her photos of the traps, strategically positioned and baited with bacon ('Darling, you were right all along. There wasn't just the one!'). But would that mark me as unhinged?

Sinead isn't even coming round at lunchtimes to let Scout out anymore. 'I'll walk him during the day,' Katrina offered, kindly, after I'd explained that Sinead had moved out. 'Please let us know if there's anything else we can do, Nate.' Katrina doesn't have a paid job – she seems to fill her time with charity lunches and suchlike – and insisted she's out with *Mounty* anyway. I just hope he doesn't sexually harass Scout.

The rest of the week passed in a bit of a blur. On Friday afternoon, I explained to Liv that I wouldn't be coming to her fiftieth birthday barbecue on Saturday night; I simply wasn't feeling very sociable. I'd taken in a bottle of champagne and a birthday card for her and was eager to beetle off home.

'But it's going to be *great*,' she said, looking crestfallen. 'My sister's doing this thing where you drill a hole in a watermelon and pour in a bottle of vodka. Then you carve it up into chunks of boozy fruit.'

'Sounds delicious!' I said, trying to sound impressed.

'Chet's making those paneer kebabs you loved last time,' Nadira chipped in.

'And I'm doing that marinated lamb,' Eric added, bringing to mind the last do at Liv's when Sinead looked so gorgeous in a little red dress, and we all drank sangria and watched the sun go down over the fields.

No, I insisted – I'd be no fun. I didn't want to spoil the gathering.

And now, on this rather grim Friday evening, I am installed on the sofa at home, trying to ward off self-pity by reading a thriller, set in 1960s Berlin. I was racing through it before 'It' happened. Now it could be the boiler instruction booklet, for all it grips my attention. Flynn is out at a gig, which is fine – I don't expect him to stay home just to keep me company – so I channel-hop for a while. Sinead and I have never been huge telly watchers, preferring to hang out, chat, read and listen to music. At least I'd *assumed* she enjoyed those sort of evenings, before I learnt her true feelings about my record collection.

I turn off the TV, toss the remote onto the coffee table with such force that it skids off and lands on the floor, and glare at the rows of albums. Neatly stored on apparently terrible shelves, they represent a lifetime's love of music. Okay – not my *entire* life. I'd like to think I have a few more years left in me yet. However, intense record buying really belongs to one's youth, when music means pretty much everything. These albums of mine inspired and brought joy; they were the soundtrack to the best and worst times. It's no exaggeration to say that they represented a sort of guidebook for life.

Could Springsteen help me now?

I select the first album I ever bought, at age thirteen. Although perhaps not a favourite of die-hard fans, *Born in the USA* is Springsteen's biggest commercial success. I stretch out on the sofa with Scout on my lap, and listen to the whole of side one, then get up and flip it over to side two. Perhaps it's ridiculous, at forty-three, to expect a lyric to jump out and inspire me. In fact, the only thought in my head is why on earth Sinead found it so offensive.

As I've disposed of her original list – actually it fell to bits – I go upstairs and open the document on my laptop where I typed it all out. I print off a copy and study it. *Your bloody record collection,* she wrote. I fold it neatly and slip it into the side of my pants drawer.

When I bring my laptop downstairs, side two is still playing. As it's a record I seldom listen to these days, I'd have expected a rush of nostalgia on hearing it. But not tonight. Springsteen – in fact, *all* of my musical heroes – have served only to irritate my wife and son ('old dead guys!') and therefore no longer have any place in my life.

So – sod it – they can damn well go.

Settled at the kitchen table now, I do a quick Google search on my laptop: 'Records wanted', 'vinyl for sale', all the permutations. There are plenty of people in Leeds, Bradford and Huddersfield, offering to buy entire collections – then I spot something closer to home:

STAN'S RECORDS
95 Bingham Road, Solworth, West Yorkshire
We buy all vinyl. Albums, 12" and 7" singles.
Excellent prices paid.
Home visits and free valuations arranged.

There's a mobile number. I hesitate to call because it's so late. No, not because it's late; it's only 9.25 p.m, so that's just an excuse. I wander through the living room, my gaze scanning row upon row of records I've collected over the years.

I just want to persuade Sinead to come home. Clearly, that's going to be no mean feat, which means there's no time to waste. The record finishes. I replace it in its sleeve, filed back under 'S'.

'Let's play a joke on Dad,' Sinead once giggled to Flynn, deliberately loud enough for me to overhear. 'Let's change Dad's filing system so all the bands starting with "The" – The Beatles, The Stones, The Who and all that – go under "T".' They actually started to do it. I pretended to 'catch' them in cahoots, and laughed along as the two of them collapsed, clutching each other, on the living room floor. Our little gang. I thought it'd be the three of us forever.

I wasn't that bad, was I? We had fun as a family . . . didn't we?

Inhaling deeply, I tap out Stan's number on my mobile. A voicemail message kicks in, and I clear my throat in readiness.

'Hi,' I say, 'I'm looking to sell a record collection of, uh, probably something like a thousand albums. I really have no idea how many there are. They're mainly sixties, seventies, eighties – all in pretty good nick. Call me if you're interested, okay? My name's Nate.'

Satisfied that I won't hear anything until tomorrow, I turn on the TV again. It's all terrible stuff: bickering families, a dreary quiz show, the graphic filming of intestinal operations.

My phone rings and I dive for it. 'Hi, is that Nate?' asks a male voice I don't recognise.

125

'Yes?'

'It's Stan. Stan from Stan's Records . . .'

'Ah, right, yes . . .' Christ – he's on the ball.

'You just called?'

'Um, yeah—'

'So, I'm in Solworth – you probably realised that. Could you bring your collection over to my shop sometime?'

'There's a record shop in Solworth?' This piques my interest – but then, my vinyl-buying days are over.

'Ah, well, yeah – we're a bit tucked away and opening hours are pretty sketchy . . .'

'Sorry,' I cut in, 'but it really is a huge collection. I was hoping you could take a look at it at my place, if that's okay. I'm in Hesslevale . . .'

'Yeah, sure – but I'm heading over to France tomorrow with a mate. We'll be away for two or three weeks, doing some gigs, buying up records.' He pauses. 'You might want to call someone else, if you're looking to get rid of them in a hurry. House clearance, is it?'

'No, no – it's my own collection . . .'

'Ah, right. Family pressure to get rid of them?' He chuckles, then, without waiting for a response, adds, 'I'll give you a call when I'm back, all right? And if you're still selling, I'll be right over.'

'Great.' I clear my dry throat.

'It's quality vinyl, isn't it?' Stan asks. 'I'm not being funny, mate, but I'm only looking for saleable stuff.'

'Oh, yeah, it's top quality,' I reply in a perky tone, as if I'm looking to sell a ratty old sideboard that I never liked much anyway.

*

On Saturday – marking my second weekend as a newly single man – Sinead calls, asking if it's okay to 'pop over' in an hour or so. At first, this feels like excellent news. But it soon transpires that she's not coming specifically to see me, but merely to pick up more of her stuff. Stuff that seemed to be disappearing in small quantities when she was still dropping in on Scout at lunchtimes, and now, it appears, is vital to her very existence.

'What d'you want to take?' I ask, pacing around the kitchen, phone clamped to my ear.

'Just, you know – my things.'

'What things?'

'Er, clothes and stuff,' she says lightly. 'Books, toiletries, shoes, some records . . .'

'Records?' I bark.

She pauses. 'Well, yes, a few of them *are* mine, you know. Half a dozen or so . . .'

Christ, I'd forgotten about those disco compilations she used to love dancing around to with Michelle and the rest of her college mates, whenever they came over for their occasional girlie nights. Those evenings seemed to fall off the radar, for some reason; maybe Sinead didn't have the energy or inclination anymore. 'Yeah, of course,' I murmur. 'I'll get them together for you.'

'Thanks. Um . . . it *is* okay for me to come over, isn't it? I was planning to wait until you're out one evening but . . . you know . . .'

No, I never socialise these days. I just watch shit telly, set mousetraps and try to read. 'It's fine,' I say firmly, finishing the call and realising that at least I'm wearing decent jeans and a newish T-shirt – and our son is out yet again.

*

And that really is a good thing, as I wouldn't have wanted him here right now as Sinead potters away in our bedroom, bundling the rest of her clothes into enormous plastic sacks.

'Remember your dressing gown,' I remark as I observe her from the doorway.

'Yes, thank you, Nate,' she mutters, investigating drawers now and pulling out all those pretty lacy slips and fancy knickers she used to pack whenever we had a weekend away in the early days.

In the early days. How long is it since I took her somewhere special, and we spent all night in our hotel room caressing and—

My attention is caught by a glimpse of pastel pink lace, poking out of one of the carrier bags. It's a camisole, if I remember rightly – if that's the proper term. The one she wore that time we went to Paris for the first time together, *Oh, God* . . .

'I think your spare slippers are under the bed,' I add.

'Hmm.'

'And remember that corduroy jacket you hung in my side of the wardrobe, 'cause you didn't have space—'

Sinead turns to me and winces. 'D'you mind not standing there watching me doing this?'

'I'm only trying to help . . .' I stop myself. My mother said exactly that last week. Christ.

'It's just a bit off-putting,' she adds.

'Oh. Yes, of course. Sorry.' I stomp downstairs so she can get on with removing her every possession from our property.

Our property. What will happen to this, our jointly-owned home? I can't even think about that right now. Anyway, Flynn has marched in, greeting me with a perfunctory 'Hey' in the hallway.

'Mum's here,' I explain. 'She's, um, just collecting some of her stuff.'

'Oh – right . . .' He virtually shoves me aside in order to head upstairs to greet her, and they fall into a clearly audible conversation.

At least, it's audible from where I'm lurking, halfway upstairs, ear cocked:

'Hey, darling. I wasn't sure if I'd see you today . . .'

'Yeah, just been out.'

'Rehearsing?'

'Just going through some songs at Max's . . .'

'Going well, is it?'

'Kind of, but my hand's been a bit stiff lately, this bit here . . .'

Has it? He hasn't mentioned this to me!

'Oh, really?' she says. 'Let me see, love . . .' Mumble-mumble . . . 'Is it that bit there?'

'Yeah. It's kind of annoying . . .'

'I'm sure it is. Maybe you should see Dr Kadow? You might need that cream again—' There's more muttering while I stand here, lunatic eavesdropping Dad, who's clearly so low in the family pecking order that he's not even party to a discussion on our son's condition.

I know I'm being ridiculous, and that this is about Flynn, not me – Flynn who, apparently, has been suffering from stiffness in his hands and is merely telling his mum because she's the one he's always tended to go to with such matters. Why *is* that anyway? Have I been unapproachable, or too preoccupied with work, never truly here for him? Maybe he just prefers to confide in her, rather than in me. Perhaps he just *loves her more*. Aware that I am now regarding our parenting as a ridiculous competition – one which I have clearly lost – I head into

129

the living room and try to focus on gathering up her records instead.

Chic, Sister Sledge, The Isley Brothers, a couple of disco compilations. Good-time records. My heart seems to twist as I slip them into a carrier bag.

As Sinead and Flynn appear downstairs, laden with bags, I realise I have cocked up yet again. 'I'd have helped you if you'd said,' I mutter, hating the petulance that's lacing my voice.

'Oh, we managed fine, thanks,' she says coolly, dropping a bulging carrier bag at her feet.

I glance at Flynn – or rather, specially at Flynn's hands. He shuffles uncomfortably, clearly uneasy at being with his mother and me, together. As he scoots off to the back garden, already murmuring into his phone, Sinead and I start to carry her things out to her car and load up the boot. In they go, all those bags, one of them containing the pink lacy camisole that she looked so beautiful in, I could hardly believe my good fortune to be in a Parisian hotel room with her. In an open box, I glimpse her red and white spotty dressing gown and pot of face powder, her cleanser and various other mysterious creams. There's her manicure kit, a hairbrush and a bottle of body lotion that matches her posh shower gel (incidentally, the gel is all used up; in some feeble act of rebellion, I've been using it liberally every day). There are the remaining bits and pieces from when she was still making jewellery, heaped into wicker baskets and now stacked neatly in the boot.

She hurries back inside, presumably to say bye to Flynn, then she's out again and we're muttering awkward good-byes on the pavement, and she's off.

*

I make dinner at five o'clock, which feels oddly early, but I can't think what else to do. It's a rather speedy affair – another stir-fry, this time with mushrooms. Now I remember that Flynn hates mushrooms. As I watch him pick them out, I raise the subject of his stiff hand – 'I just overheard you saying to Mum' – but it's *fine*, he says, matter apparently closed. How am I supposed to support him if he won't tell me what's going on?

We eat in silence for a few moments.

'Dad?' He looks up from his bowl.

'Uh-huh?'

'I think there's someone at the door?'

At first, I assume he's resorting to that tactic he used to employ when he was little, on the rare occasions when he and I were having dinner alone. *Dad, did you hear that? Something's happening outside!* I'd hurry to the window and when I came back, some offending item – usually a dastardly vegetable – would have disappeared from his plate. I once found a cauliflower floret dumped in a pot plant.

But no – someone really is knocking. My heart seems to stop. She's back! It's all been a terrible mistake. She arrived at Abby's and stared at all those boxes and bags in the boot of her car, and thought: *no, I can't do this* . . .

I drop my fork in my bowl and march through the hallway and fling open the front door.

Eric is standing there, a hesitant smile on his face. 'Okay, look – I *know* what you're going to say.'

I stare at him. Why is he here?

'What I'm going to say about what?' I ask, genuinely baffled.

He grimaces. 'Well, Sarah and I had a talk, and then we

spoke to Liv and Nadira. None of us are happy about you hiding yourself away, and it's only a barbecue—'

'Oh, I can't go to Liv's barbecue,' I say firmly. 'I told you, I'm just not up to socialising right now. I mean, it's kind of you to stop by and everything but . . .' I break off and register Eric and Sarah's blue Mazda parked across the street. Sarah catches my eye from the driver's seat and beams encouragingly. I glance back into the house; the house which has, since Sinead's departure today, seemed even more bleak with all the odd spaces where her things used to be. Her jars and potions, her dressing gown and jewellery: all gone.

'C'mon,' Eric offers. 'It's always a laugh at her place and you could do with a few beers and a bit of fun.'

I study his face for a moment and see a friend who's been thoughtful enough to drop by on some sort of rescue mission. He thinks he's doing the right thing when, in fact, what I'm really more inclined to do is flop on the sofa and neck a bottle of wine.

'Okay,' I murmur. 'I s'pose I could just show my face. But I won't be hanging around for long, all right? I know you'll want to stay late, but I can just get a cab home . . .'

'Yeah, sure! Just a bit of chat, couple of drinks. Nothing too taxing.' He nods encouragingly.

I inhale deeply. Flynn has plans for tonight, not that he needs me hanging around and bothering him. 'Give me a few minutes to get myself together, all right?' I say, raising a smile.

'Great. You go and get ready. Don't worry about booze – we've got plenty in the car. But maybe give your hair a comb—'

'My hair?' I go to touch it and suspect it's sticking up

all over the place. I must've looked a sight for Sinead and didn't realise.

'Yeah. I know you're having a shit time, but it *is* a party. Got to make an effort for your public, right?' Eric is grinning now, poking fun. 'Also,' he adds, dropping his gaze a little, 'you might want to put your T-shirt on the right way round.'

Chapter Fifteen

So, ten days after I learned that my marriage is over, I am on my way to a barbecue where I'm likely to be harangued into eating some kind of vodka-watermelon slush puppy.

A birthday party populated by a disproportionally large percentage of driving examiners, which, apparently, Eric is looking forward to tremendously, judging by the way he and his wife Sarah are chatting about it merrily in the car. 'That last one was brilliant, wasn't it?' he remarks, glancing back at me.

'Hilarious,' agrees Sarah, who's driving. Clearly, they have planned to *jolly* me out of my malaise.

From the back seat, I murmur in agreement and watch the neat red-brick terraces of Hesslevale's outer reaches give way to softly rolling hills.

'At least, *Eric* was hilarious,' Sarah adds with a snigger.

'You know what that means, don't you, Nate?' Eric catches my eye in the rear-view mirror.

I force a stiff smile. 'Yeah.'

'It means he was slaughtered,' she adds. 'So tipsy he fell into that cactus, remember?' They both laugh loudly, thankfully oblivious to the fact that their banter – the easy, teasing communication of a couple who are still very much in love – is serving only to plummet me further into a cesspit of gloom.

It's not that they have chosen to ignore the glaring fact that Sinead has left me. We got all that out of the way when I emerged from my house – T-shirt corrected, hair combed into some semblance of order – and was greeted by hugs and gushing sympathy by Sarah, whom I know is terribly fond of both of us. I disentangled myself and thanked her for her concern, asking if we could leave it there, just for today. It was the only way I could think of to get through the evening; i.e., to pretend it hasn't happened.

'Think there'll be karaoke again?' Eric muses.

If there is, I may have to commit hara-kiri with a barbecue fork.

'Hope so,' Sarah enthuses, for she is the karaoke type – and I don't mean that in a snidey way. She has a rich and confident voice, and on several occasions I have been happy to sit back with my beer and enjoy her hearty rendition of *Suspicious Minds*.

We can't go on togethuuurrrrr . . .

But not today, thank you very much.

'See that box next to you, Nate?' Eric remarks.

I glance at the transparent plastic container of raw meat, oozing blood, which is sitting beside me on the back seat. My stomach shifts uneasily. 'Your marinated lamb?'

'Yeah. Garlic, oregano, mint, lemon juice. Best left for twenty-four hours, if you've got the time. Tenderises it, then you get the smokiness from the barbecue coals . . .' Eric smacks his lips.

'Sounds delicious,' I remark.

'It's his signature dish now,' adds Sarah. 'He's started growing mint especially for it. What a ponce!'

'It grows itself really,' he chuckles. 'Runs bloody rampant . . .'

I blink at the passing fields, willing my friends to stop overcompensating and be a little less cheery. But then, they are cheery people; it's me who's the miserable old sod now. I start thinking of other friends of ours – people Sinead and I have grown close to through Flynn's school and Scouts and various CP groups – and how I'm going to break it to everyone that we're no longer together. As for Eric and Sarah – well, I'll miss those evenings at theirs, over on the other side of Hesslevale, the pair of them always so relaxed and convivial, our glasses constantly refilled.

Of course, I remind myself, they might still invite me . . . all by myself. I'm sure they'd love that, me sitting there, all sour-faced on their sofa, and everyone being careful not to mention Sinead. Plus, there's no reason why I can't invite them over for fantastically fun evenings at *my* house. Dismal stir-fries aside, I like to think I'm more than competent in the kitchen. However, whenever I'm cooking for friends there's always a whiff of stress in the air, a slick of perspiration on my brow, and one of the side dishes is usually left in the oven to be discovered, a charred heap, several days later ('What *was* this?' Sinead would snigger before tipping it into the bin). On those sociable evenings at our place – and I can hardly bear to think of them as being in the past tense – her role was to be the fun one, handing out dishes of nuts and being sparkling company while I sweated and yelped in the kitchen and ran my burnt finger under the cold tap.

'Um, I hope you don't mind me asking,' Sarah says now, 'but is Flynn okay? I mean, how d'you think he's taking things?'

'He seems okay so far,' I reply, picturing him virtually manhandling me out of the door, hissing, *Of course you're going. Eric's here for you, and I told you I've got people coming over*. He can be terribly forceful when he wants to be.

'I know it'll be hard for him, but you're a brilliant dad, Nate,' she offers. 'You'll make sure it all works out.'

My eyeballs seem to prickle. 'I don't know about that, but it's kind of you to say so.'

She catches my gaze in the rear-view mirror. 'I'm sorry. I know you don't want to talk about this now.'

'I'd rather not, if that's okay,' I say quickly, at which she apologises profusely, then steers the conversation to her and Eric's own boys, Johnny and Ryan, both of whom are flourishing at some kind of sports college. I try to listen and contribute to the conversation, feeling like a hostage in their family saloon. 'Can we stop off so I can buy some booze?' I ask, rather belatedly, as Liv's village comes into view.

'Oh, don't worry about that,' Eric says. 'I told you – we've got plenty with us . . .'

'But I'd feel better if I took something. There's a shop here, isn't there? I'm sure they'll have wine . . .'

'No need,' Eric insists.

I sigh heavily and sit back, aware of the subtle tilts of Eric and Sarah's heads as they exchange a silent but clearly understandable message: *D'you really think he's okay?* However, jollity is restored as we turn off the main road and into the village, which consists mainly of huddled stone cottages and the aforementioned shop, which I see

137

now has closed down, its window whitewashed – so no chance of dashing in for emergency wine anyway.

We turn into the newer cul-de-sac and park close to the end house, which Liv shares with her husband Steve and their two daughters. I check my watch as we all climb out of the car: 6.10 p.m. I'll stay for an hour, I decide as we all file into the garden. I reckon I'll just about be able to hold out that long, then I'll sneak off home.

Liv appears through the clusters of guests in a white dress emblazoned with red poppies. 'Hey, good to see you,' she exclaims, hugging each of us in turn and accepting Eric and Sarah's crate of lamb and clinking bags of bottles gratefully. 'Wow, you are a star, Eric,' she gasps. Perhaps, amidst all the enthusing over his marinade, she won't notice that I've come empty-handed. She turns to me. 'You okay, love? I'm so glad you've come . . .'

'Um, I'm glad too,' I say half-heartedly.

'I know it's not easy . . .' She squeezes my arm.

'It's fine, honestly. It's great!'

Liv's husband Steve – a rugby-playing bear of a bloke – offers us drinks, and soon Liv is stationed back at the barbie (Steve is never allowed within a five-metre radius of the thing). Sipping beer from a bottle, I hover on the fringes of a group of examiners, all of whom I know from working across various test centres in our area.

Although dark clouds are gathering, everyone seems in a jovial mood already. Nadira and her husband Chet have arrived. A terribly good-looking couple, they are so tactile with each other that I am seized by an urge to vault Liv's fence and run across the neighbouring fields, all the way home. Of course, I can't expect everyone else to stop expressing affection just because my wife no longer wants to be with me.

'So, I asked this guy to please take the next right,' says Martin, a newly-qualified examiner with a dense brown beard, 'and he turns to me and goes, "Nah, mate, that's not the quickest way back."' He laughs and bites into his hot dog. 'So I say, "I'm actually giving you a direction. Could you take the next right, please?" But the man's shaking his head, saying, "Look, I know it like the back of my hand around here. Lived here man and boy," until I'm practically driven to shouting, "You do understand that this is your test, don't you? We're not just out on a casual *drive* . . ."'

Now Nadira is acting out the time when a candidate had a sudden dramatic nosebleed that splashed all over her shirt.

Petra, an older lady with a reputation for being rather fierce, tells us, 'I kept saying, "The lights have changed to green now. You can move on . . ." And then I looked at him properly and realised he'd *died*.'

Everyone laughs in that horrified way; it's our ability to find humour in the awfulness that keeps us going sometimes. I know we're not miners or surgeons and that, from an outsider's point of view, we do little more than sit in the passenger seat, being utter bastards. But we are just doing a job, albeit a much-derided one, rather like tax inspectors or parking attendants – and it's not always an easy one (take Angus Pew, threatening to contaminate my food in his restaurant). We are offered cash bribes and even sexual favours; colleagues of mine have been promised blow jobs and even entire nights of passion in exchange for that elusive pass certificate. Although that's never happened to me, I have had a woman trying to thrust a giant Toblerone at me.

Of course, gifts of any sort are always politely – but *firmly* – turned down.

139

More stories come, but I am finding it impossible to pay proper attention to all the banter around me. I can't bring myself to eat anything, either, despite Liv's teenage daughter Molly touring the garden with trays piled high with succulent burgers and hot dogs.

'Try some of this then,' Molly says, now brandishing a platter of the famous watermelon which, as it turns out, isn't a slush puppy sort of affair at all, but just chunks of seemingly innocent fruit.

'That does look good,' I say, taking a piece, in the hope that it'll quell the bitter taste that seems to have developed in my mouth. Bitter, because Sinead should be here at my side.

Now Liv's sister, who's wearing a kind of kaftan over tight pink trousers, is making a shouty announcement through a microphone that the karaoke is about to begin. The gaggle of children all whoop with delight.

'Me first!' yells Ava, Liv and Steve's youngest, a late baby who arrived when they were well into their forties, and who's around six or seven, I think – Sinead would remember her exact age, her favourite colour and probably her birthday, if pushed.

A backing track begins. I munch on the watermelon slice as Ava and her friends blare out an enthusiastic rendition of Dolly Parton's *Joleen*.

Karaoke proves to be a huge success, no doubt helped along by the fact that wine and beer are in full flow now. As no one else seems interested in the watermelon, I tuck into another slice from the tray which has been dumped, conveniently, within arm's reach. Liv and Steve's garden is filling up with more friends and neighbours, and as dusk falls some of the guests start dancing on the patio. I exchange pleasantries, and make a pretence of joining in with the odd bit of chat, but really I'm feeling very far away from the actual proceedings as I nibble on more vodka-infused fruit.

It's extremely moreish, and not due to the alcohol content – at least, I don't *think* it's that – but because my mouth is terribly dry, and watermelon is quenching. Sinead might have left me, but at least I've had my sodding five a day. More like ten, probably. I should be the poster guy for some government heath campaign. Also, munching away gives me something to occupy myself with while everyone else chats and laughs and takes their turn on the karaoke. Because what else would I do otherwise? I can't think of any amusing anecdotes to contribute, apart from finding a note from my wife, listing the nineteen reasons (naturally, I've counted them) why she doesn't love me anymore.

And I can't imagine *that'd* get many laughs.

'Nate, c'mon – give us a song!' Steve is in my face now, cheeks flushed, beaming encouragingly.

'Oh, I'm not really a karaoke kind of guy,' I protest with an awkward laugh.

'But all those bands you were in . . .'

'Yeah, but as the guitarist, not the singer . . .'

'Aw, go on,' Nadira exclaims, grabbing my arm. 'Let's do a duet!'

'No, I can't, really. You know I have a terrible voice . . .' I check my watch, astounded that it's just gone 9 p.m. Somehow, three hours have slipped by. I'm drunk, I realise. Slowly and steadily I've ingested enough vodka watermelon to partially anaesthetise myself from the horror of the past ten days. Nadira pleads some more, then sashays off to blast out *Lost in Music* with Chet. I look around the garden, at the glowing glass lanterns and silvery fairy lights that seem to have appeared suddenly, turning a garden in an ordinary cul-de-sac into a magical grotto. Sensing myself wobbling, I grip a wooden bird table for support.

What a lovely garden this is, I decide. Liv and Steve's home is a modern semi with nothing to distinguish it from the other houses in the road, but what they've done with the space is remarkable. While their neighbours' gardens seem to consist of neatly-clipped rectangular lawns, Liv and Steve have carved theirs up into intimate spaces with cleverly-placed hedges and shrubs. Narrow brick paths weave in and out, leading you from one nook to the next. Several wrought-iron benches, ancient stone birdbaths and many other ornamental delights are hidden at the far end of the garden, away from the revellers.

I know this because I seem to have blundered away from the main party where Liv is now belting out *Come Fly With Me*, a Sinatra classic and a must at this kind of event. Will anyone dare to murder a Springsteen number, I wonder? If Sinead were here, she might have urged me to, virtually shoving me onto the stage. But she's not here, she's at Abby's, perhaps re-watching *The Sopranos*, or maybe shagging some new lover somewhere, looking sensational in her pink camisole – and, anyway, I'm bloody *fine*, because I am not alone either. I have the watermelon tray with me, which I am now cradling to my chest, like a long-lost friend.

Down here, away from the off-key karaoke and those meaty barbecue smells, I feel calmer. I am right at the bottom of the garden now, at the fence that divides it from the rolling farmland beyond, and I seem to have found a little house.

It's a Wendy house, constructed from rather grubby

primary-coloured plastic sections. But right now, as rain begins to fall, it seems as inviting as a boutique hotel. I look down at the watermelon tray. How embarrassing, sneaking off with the whole lot. And I gave Flynn a hard time for nicking those whisky miniatures from our cupboard! But never mind. No one will know as, from what I can make out, everyone seems to be heading indoors. While the karaoke machine is protected by an awning, clearly no one wants to stand outside in the rain, and soon the garden is deserted.

Wiping my wet face with my jacket sleeve, I realise that now would be the perfect opportunity to call a taxi and sneak off home without any fuss. I pat my jeans pocket; thankfully, my phone is still there. Would it seem rude to leave without saying goodbye? Would anyone actually notice? As the rain falls more heavily, I push open the Wendy house door and crouch down to enter it, grateful for a few moments' respite while I decide what to do.

Due to my height, I have to stoop considerably as I take in my new surroundings. This was probably Molly's house before it was Ava's. It certainly feels as if it's been here for a very long time. Long grass has grown around its base, and rain patters insistently on the mottled roof. There are just two items of furniture in here: a child-sized table and chair, both with stubby, cylindrical legs. Squinting in the gloom – weak light is filtering in through the tiny window and open door – I lower myself gingerly onto the chair, which wobbles under my weight. For sustenance, I bite into another slice of watermelon. What tastes like neat spirit floods my mouth. I'm wondering now about the effectiveness of tipping in an entire bottle of vodka through a hole, in terms of even distribution of booze. Surely certain areas absorb more than others?

I pull my phone out of my pocket, with the vague intention of scrolling for a taxi company, and notice a text from Flynn: *Okay if I go stay at Max's tonight?*

Replying takes a certain degree of tussling with auto-correct. *Yes no pob*, I finally manage to reply after multiple stabbings, hoping that sounds normal. And now, hunched on the teeny baby-chair, and without planning what I'm going to say, I call Sinead.

'Nate?' She answers immediately, and sounds alarmed.

'Hey, hello there, love!' I slur.

There's a beat's silence. 'What's happening? Is everything okay?'

'Yeah! Just thought I'd call you. I'm at Liv's barbecue . . .' I have adopted my best sober voice, the one I used as a teenager when I'd been out with my mates and would be confronted by my flinty-eyed mother on my return home.

'Oh.' Sinead pauses. 'So you decided to go, then?'

'Yeah, I'm here!' I reply cheerily. 'I'm here and it's *great*. It's so fun . . .'

She clears her throat. 'So, who's there?'

'Everyone!'

'Erm, well, that's good . . .' Is it? *Why* is it good? 'You sound sort of echoey,' she adds.

'I'm just inside,' I explain, gripping the plastic table for support.

'Oh. Right. Well, it's good that you felt up to it,' she adds, as if I am no longer her relatively sane husband, aged forty-three, but a fragile elderly relative who has just been released from a psychiatric unit.

'It's great,' I babble on. 'It's a really great party . . .'

She sighs audibly. 'So, you're enjoying yourself, are you?'

I glance around the interior of the Wendy house, with

144

its mouldering plastic walls and beleaguered grass carpet. The tray on the table is littered with watermelon rinds, and yet more are scattered around my feet. I must have scoffed a load more without realising.

'It's brilliant,' I reply, rubbing at my scratchy eyes now.

'So, what's happening?'

'Oh, there's karaoke—'

'Karaoke?'

'Yeah, it's great!' I touch my face, which appears to be wet. As I'm sheltered in here, I don't think it's rain.

'But you hate karaoke,' Sinead reminds me.

'Not anymore . . .'

'Nate . . .' She hesitates. 'Just how drunk are you?'

'Not at all,' I fib. 'Not one bit!'

We fall into silence, and I register a small, dark thing slithering up one of the walls of the house. Actually, it's not so small: it's possibly the largest, fattest slug I have ever seen, glistening and obese. It's more like a seal, I decide. If I wasn't so pissed I'd take a picture of it to show Flynn.

'Let's talk some other time,' Sinead says gently, 'when you're sober, okay? And I'm glad you're out, having a good time.' With that, she rings off.

For several minutes I sit there, a giant on the baby-chair, staring at my phone as if Sinead might burst out of it, or at least text me to say she still loves me. And then I go to check my watch – and it's not there.

My father's watch is gone from my wrist. I kneel down on the ground and fumble about, but it's so dark I can hardly see anything. I try to turn my mobile into a torch, the way Flynn does with his without thinking about it, but I can't remember how to do it. Is everything different with this new replacement phone? At one point I must press

145

the wrong thing because my own face appears on the screen, sweaty and stressed, and I appear to have taken a terrible selfie. And then I seem to be muttering to myself *through* my phone. Is this what they call Facetime?

Telling myself not to panic, I sit on the ground, breathing slowly and deeply and trying to figure out where the watch might be. It must be in the garden somewhere . . . but where on earth would I look? It feels like I've been wandering all over, for hours.

Overcome by exhaustion, I curl up on my side on the lumpy ground and close my eyes, with the intention of resting until I can summon the energy to hunt for my watch, and then call a taxi home. But that doesn't happen. Instead, I find myself drifting away to a happier place where there is no karaoke, no *Joleen*, and I haven't turned up booze-less (and wife-less) at a party.

Rather than sharing a Wendy house with a slug, I am now at the seaside – Scarborough or Whitby, it doesn't really matter where – and Sinead and I are sitting on a checked blanket in the late evening sunshine. My beautiful wife is leaning on my shoulder, and Flynn is just a little boy, making a giant sandcastle. He loved making sand-castles, and sometimes they'd be so elaborate, with turrets and moats and driftwood drawbridges, that passers-by would stop to compliment him on his work.

On the day in my mind, we've bought him one of those plastic windmills that spin in the wind, and he's stuck it carefully on top of his castle. I remember this moment like it happened yesterday. It's the day one of Flynn's therapists at the hospital had told us she was amazed by the improvement in the strength and coordination of his arms. She even went to find a couple of students so they could meet him and see how brilliantly he was doing. She gave him a jelly lolly shaped like a cat and said he was a hero. To celebrate, we drove straight to the coast.

And now, just like any other ordinary kid, he is digging away in the sand with his green plastic spade, and I don't think I have ever felt happier in my whole life.

Chapter Sixteen

'Christ, boy! Get *off* me . . .'

It's Scout who's woken me. No, it can't be Scout, because I'm not in bed. A quick scan of my surroundings confirms that this isn't even our house. It appears to be a shed of some sort – have I been taken hostage? – and, more pressingly, I seem to have some kind of *beast* slobbering all over me.

'Wolfie? Wolfie!' a woman's voice cuts through the night air.

I try to back away from the over-affectionate animal. Now I can see it has greyish fur and a gaping, panting mouth, from which huge canine teeth gleam.

'Wolfie! C'mon, boy!' the woman's voice comes again.

'Er, I think he's in here,' I call out, remembering now where I am: in a tiny plastic house at the bottom of Liv's garden. The dog turns – it is definitely a dog – and shoots out through the door.

*

'There you are,' the woman exclaims. 'Were you hiding in that little house, silly boy?' The footsteps outside grow closer. *Please just go away,* I will this unknown female, but now a human face has appeared at the child-sized door. 'Oh, hello!' the woman exclaims.

'Hello,' I reply, scrambling up to a kneeling position.

Her eyes widen in surprise. 'My God, you're not *living* in here, are you?'

'No, of course not!' I make some semblance of dusting myself down, then stoop to ease myself out of the house. 'I was just, uh . . . sheltering from the rain . . .'

She looks me up and down as I straighten up. Even in the darkness, she looks faintly familiar, although I don't remember seeing her at the barbecue. 'Well, it's not unheard of . . .' She grins. 'You know how people find someone living in their potting shed, or under their caravan, and they'd never even realised they were there?'

'Yes, haha,' I say stiffly. 'But no, I don't live in there. The facilities are a bit basic, to be honest . . .'

The woman laughs. Short and slim, she is wearing skinny jeans, muddied black boots and a huge moss green and unfortunately hoodless jacket. Her drenched hair is plastered to her head. 'Supposed to be at Liv and Steve's party, are you?'

'Yep, that's right.' I glance down at the grass-stained knees of my jeans, and glimpse further smearings on the arms of my jacket.

'Were you playing hide-and-seek with the kids?'

'No.' I laugh involuntarily. 'As I said, I was just—'

'. . . Sheltering?'

I nod, aware of her studying my face with amusement. I rub at it with the flat of my hand in case it's splattered

149

with mud. Miraculously, the sleep I had – and I have no concept of how long I was lying there – seems to have at least partially sobered me up. Less happily, a hangover is already setting in.

'I *know* you,' she adds, stepping closer.

I peer at her in the moonlight. 'You look familiar too . . .'

She chuckles. 'Don't you remember me?'

I shake my head. 'I'm sorry, but I can't place you. I've had quite a bit to drink, and I've just woken up—'

'Well, *you're* not someone I'll ever forget in a hurry. Imprinted on my brain, you are, like some terrible tattoo . . .'

I step back from her. 'I'm sorry . . .?'

'You don't look so scary now, though!' She emits a loud, barky laugh that ricochets across the garden. 'But I'd never have imagined, with a job like yours, you'd be the type of guy to end up smashed out of your box in a Wendy house . . .'

Now it's starting to make sense. I blink at her, trying to bring her into sharp focus. 'You're . . . Tanzie, aren't you?'

'Yeah, that's right. And you're Nate . . .' I nod and take in the sight of her. Her hair is chin-length and purplish, with a tiny fringe like several of Sinead's art school mates used to have when they were about twenty-two. Only, I know for certain that Tanzie is around forty, and that she failed her eleventh driving test.

'I'm so sorry for all those tears last time,' she says, as we start to make our way through the garden.

'Oh, please don't worry,' I assure her. 'People react in all sorts of ways. It's quite normal really.'

She looks at me and smiles as she clips on Wolfie's lead. It's still raining steadily and the night has turned cold and bleak. 'But you know I'm not usually like that. Honestly – I take most things in my stride. I knew there was a good chance I'd fail. My boyfriend says I'm a crap driver . . .'

'I'm sure you're not,' I say, keen to escape now and call a taxi. 'Virtually everyone has the capacity to pass with decent tuition.'

'Yeah, well, I made a complete arse of myself that day and I'm sorry. It must be so embarrassing when people do that.'

'I'm kind of used to it,' I murmur, brushing flecks of grass from the right thigh of my jeans.

She shrugs and nods towards the house. 'You going back in, then? Gary said we were invited 'cause he re-floored their kitchen. I haven't met them myself. But we had a bit of a situation tonight and I wasn't really in the frame of mind to meet new people . . .' Tanzie drops her gaze to her rather forlorn-looking soggy dog.

'Gary?' I ask.

'My boyfriend,' she clarifies. 'Or maybe' – she shudders slightly – 'I should say *partner*.'

'Right. So, er . . . what kind of situation did you have?' I know it's none of my business, but I'm a little concerned about her now.

'Don't want to get into that,' she says impatiently. 'I'm only out because this monster got through the fence and took himself off for a little adventure.'

I manage a weary smile and glance towards Liv's back door. Music is audible – *We Are Family* by Sister Sledge, one of Sinead's beloved girls' night in tracks – accompanied by the cheers of a well-oiled houseful all having a wonderful time. I very much doubt if my presence is being missed.

151

'You know,' I start, 'I've had a bit of a night of it too. I've also managed to lose my watch, so I'm just going to have a good hunt for it in the garden—'

'In the rain?' Tanzie cuts in. 'In the *dark*?'

'Well, er, I need to really. It's important for me to find it.'

'I'll help you then,' she says firmly.

'Oh, no, please don't do that. It's a horrible night. I can manage fine by myself, and then I'll call a taxi home . . .'

'Sorry,' she says firmly, shaking her head at my apparent ineptitude, 'but this time, *I'm* the one who's in charge.'

So that's what we do, Tanzie, Wolfie and I. We comb the various lawns, rummage in the shrubbery and investigate clusters of abandoned glasses and plates stacked on every horizontal surface.

'You were right,' I concede finally. 'It's too dark and miserable out here to be doing this.'

'I'm happy to keep looking,' Tanzie says blithely. 'Is it special to you, this watch?'

'Well, um, it was my dad's,' I tell her. 'It was left to me when he died.'

She turns to me, aghast. 'We must find it then!'

'Thanks, but it feels as if we're just going over the same ground now. I'll ask Liv to keep a look-out when she's clearing up the garden, and if there's no joy, then I'll come back and have another look . . .' I pause and push back my sodden hair. 'I'm really grateful for your help. It's so kind of you.'

'I'm just sorry we couldn't find it,' she says with a sigh, like a child who's failed at a treasure hunt.

'Well, we tried. I think I'll just call a cab now, and wait at the front of the house for it.' I smile tightly.

'But you'll get soaked,' Tanzie retorts. 'Go inside and

152

make your call from there. I'd better head back home myself . . .'

I hesitate, imagining the scenario if I slope into Liv's house and join the throng with my muddied clothes and possibly bloodshot eyes. I seem to remember phoning Sinead at some point this evening, and crying. What was our conversation about again? I can barely recall it and can only hope I didn't beg her to come back to me. Will I ever be capable of behaving normally again?

Tanzie is peering at me, looking solemn now, perhaps picking up on my reticence. 'I s'pose you feel a bit of a prat, don't you? Collapsing pissed in the Wendy house . . .'

I laugh awkwardly. 'I didn't collapse pissed!'

She chuckles and tugs on her dog's lead. 'Okay, *I* believe you. Tell you what, then – you can come back with me and call your taxi from our place. Gary's a pain in the arse – he's had a fair few beers himself tonight – but don't be scared, he won't bite . . .'

I blink at her, keen to avoid visiting the house of a woman I don't even know, at least not personally – not to mention encountering this Gary person, with whom she has had some kind of 'situation'. Christ knows, I have enough of a situation of my own to deal with right now. However, somehow I am unable to access the words to explain why I'd rather wait for my taxi in the street, becoming even wetter. And so I find myself falling into step with Tanzie and her bedraggled dog, in the rain. We leave Liv's pristine cul-de-sac, and make our way along a nondescript country lane, where the only buildings appear to be tumbledown barns and outhouses.

'We only moved here in January,' she tells me. 'We were right in the middle of Hesslevale before, just behind the library, you know?' I nod, sensing a chill settling into my bones. 'I loved it there,' Tanzie continues, 'being so near to school and work and being able to get a nice coffee and feel like there was life going on around us. But it turned out our place was riddled with asbestos.' She snorts. 'Nice to see guys in full-cover body suits storming into the flat you'd rented, oblivious, for three years . . .'

'So, you had to move?' I ask, deciding not to mention that I live in Hesslevale too. No need to divulge any personal information.

'Yeah. Had to find somewhere in a real hurry, and this place turned up, pretty cheap.' She pauses. 'We're just down here . . .' We turn into an unmade single track road, heavily pitted with rain-filled potholes and bordered by unruly hedges. There are no streetlights here. Tanzie pulls a torch from an enormous jacket pocket, which emits a feeble yellow glow.

Feeling distinctly out of my depth now, I start to plan my excuse as to why I can't actually go to her house, not when she might actually be mad, and not planning to merely offer me shelter but wreak revenge for her eleven failed driving tests in the form of an axe through the back of my skull.

'Here we are!' she announces cheerfully as a ramshackle cottage comes into view. My heart seems to sink as it confirms my worst fears. Even in the dark, I can see that its roof is sagging and clumped with moss, its peeling walls possibly last whitewashed around forty years ago. It looks like the kind of place from which one leaves dismembered, wrapped in black polythene, then flung into a ditch or possibly devoured by her dog. There probably is no 'Gary'. So this is how my evening ends: being subjected to all kinds of humiliations and pain, simply

154

due to being a committed employee of the Driver and Vehicle Standards Agency. This wouldn't have happened if I'd opted for accountancy, like my dad.

I glance at Tanzie, who is marching along at quite a pace now, with Wolfie trotting alongside her. An ageing yellow van – actually more rust than yellow – is parked next to the house. I squint and read the writing on its side: 'The Lino King'. I turn to Tanzie. 'Whose is that?'

'Gary's,' she says with a dry laugh. 'He has a flooring business – only, lino's not the only thing he lays.'

'*Sorry?*' I turn and stare at her.

Tanzie grunts in derision and stomps towards it. I frown, confused now. Did she mean 'lay' as in other women – i.e., implying philandering tendencies – or merely in a flooring context? i.e., *Lino's not the only thing he lays. He is equally happy to install vinyl flooring, tiles, carpet, slate – even cork, if anyone still has that . . .*

I glance back at Tanzie, then at the van. There's a badly-painted lion next to the lettering, with a luxuriant mane and a frankly terrifying human face. Or maybe the lion actually looks quite friendly, and it's just my hangover setting in, triggering paranoia.

Giving the van one last, fretful glance, I follow Tanzie into the cottage, mustering all the courage I possess for meeting this Gary person, and my certain doom.

Chapter Seventeen

The cramped and dingy living room is dominated by a TV blaring out *Ramsay's Kitchen Nightmares*, and the multi-tattooed presence of the Lino King himself.

'Hey!' He swings round from the screen and regards me with surprise.

'Gary, this is Nate,' Tanzie explains. She pulls off her rain-drenched jacket and jams it over a radiator.

'Hey, Nate.' He is solidly built with cropped dark hair, handsome in that beefy, action-movie-hero sort of way, and dressed in a tight black T-shirt and grubby-looking jeans.

'Hi, Gary,' I say, adopting a perky tone, as if I am friend whom he's been expecting, rather than a stranger whose hangover is definitely taking hold.

As unobtrusively as I can manage, I check the time on my phone: 11.27 p.m. Definitely time to return to the relative sanctuary of home.

'Nate's a friend of Liv and Steve's,' Tanzie offers.

'The driving test woman?' he asks in a slow drawl.

Oh, God, I will Tanzie, *please don't tell him I'm a*

driving test person too – in fact, the very person who 'failed' you on several of your own tests. I can't imagine my insistence that I'm just 'a passive observer' would hold much truck here.

'That's right,' she says, unclipping her dog's lead. 'We, uh, got chatting when I was out looking for Wolfie and I said he could call a taxi home from here.'

Gary frowns. 'Use our house phone, you mean?'

'No, no, on his mobile,' she clarifies. 'It was just, um, a bit rowdy at Liv and Steve's for making a call, and it's still pouring down . . .'

He nods, apparently satisfied with this bizarre explanation as to why I have interrupted his evening. It occurs to me that, if this had been Sinead and I, then *I'd* have been the one out dog-hunting in the rain. 'I did their kitchen floor,' Gary tells me. 'What did you think of it?'

I toy with the idea of enthusing over the excellent standard of work. However, right now I doubt if I could pull it off. 'It was a garden party,' I explain. 'I didn't actually go into the house—'

'A *garden party*?' he crows, adopting an aristocratic tone.

'Well, a barbecue,' I say quickly.

'You said we were invited, Gary,' Tanzie remarks with a frown.

Choosing to ignore this, he drops his gaze to the front of my shirt. 'Were you in a fight?'

I glance down, registering for the first time that it's not only muddy but also liberally splashed with pinkish liquid. 'Oh, that's just watermelon juice—'

'*Watermelon juice!*' he crows, as if I'd said asses' milk, and I wonder now if everything I say will be deemed amusing enough for him to repeat.

I catch Tanzie glancing at him in irritation, and wonder again what kind of 'situation' they had earlier tonight.

'Well, I won't take up any more of your evening,' I say. 'I'll just call my taxi now.' I start to scroll for the local cab company on my phone.

'You need to warm up,' Tanzie retorts. 'Come through to the kitchen and have a cuppa with me. *Then* you can call a cab . . .'

'Uh, well, just a quick one,' I say, relieved to at least leave the room Gary's in.

In the even dingier kitchen she tells me to sit at the table. 'Give me your jacket,' she commands.

'Oh, no, it's fine . . .'

'For goodness' sake, *give* it to me,' she says, exasperation lacing her voice. 'C'mon – the heating's on. It'll dry off a bit.' Obediently, I take it off and hand it to her. She pushes up a row of bras on the radiator and stuffs it beside them. The demise of my marriage seems to have triggered a state of utter passiveness in me, to the point that I will do anything anyone – even a near-stranger with a comically tiny fringe – tells me to do.

Over the blare of Gordon Ramsay in the living room, Tanzie hands me a mug of tea and fills me in on her life. 'It's driving me mad, living out here,' she announces. 'Forty years old and I'm living in a dump like this. The only good thing is, the girl from the farm down the lane comes over to walk Wolfie when we're at work. But, God, I miss the buzz of Hesslevale . . .'

I smile at that; whilst my home town is sizeable enough to have its own secondary school and several primaries, it's hardly a metropolis. 'Too sleepy for you out here, is it?' I suggest.

'Yeah, there's that – and transport's a nightmare. I work

158

in Hesslevale and the buses don't coincide with my shifts. I seem to spend half my life waiting in the bloody bus shelter.' She takes the seat opposite and eyes me levelly across the table. '*That's* why I was so desperate to pass my driving test.'

'Yes, of course.' I sip my scalding tea.

'So, whereabouts d'you live, Nate?'

'Er, in Hesslevale, actually.'

Tanzie blinks at me in surprise. 'Really? In the posh bit, I suppose?'

I smile briefly. 'Nope – we're probably in the *least* posh bit . . .' I glance briefly around the kitchen. There is barely more headroom in here than there was in the Wendy house. Chipped gloss-painted shelves are crammed with piled-up crockery, and a low-watt bulb with a yellowing shade dangles over the table. 'So, what's your job?' I ask, merely to show polite interest.

'I'm a waitress, for my sins. You know Burger Bill's at the bottom of the high street?'

'Yes, I do,' I reply, although it's not somewhere Sinead and I have ever visited. The sign in the window boasts MASSIVE FLAVOURS – which everyone knows just means bucketloads of salt. Still, I *am* hungry now, I realise. Ravenous, in fact, having only ingested fruit that's approximately ninety-eight per cent water (okay, booze) since that lacklustre stir-fry with Flynn. I couldn't face any of the barbecued offerings at Liv's.

As if reading my mind, Tanzie fetches me a Penguin biscuit, which I accept gratefully. I devour it in two bites, then glance at my mobile on the table, wondering how soon I can make my escape without seeming rude. Tanzie gets up to prod at my jacket, announcing that 'it's drying out already'; she is a tiny thing really, barely five feet tall. Her level of concern is quite touching.

'Like another biscuit?' she asks, plonking a dented tin in front of me.

'Yes please. You're being very kind. Thank you.'

'Aw, it's no problem. Got a sweet tooth, have you?'

'I suppose so, yes . . .'

'We do great desserts at Bill's,' she goes on. 'Tell you what – if you come in when I'm there I'll slip you a knickerbocker glory on the house.'

'Oh, that's very sweet of you.' Naturally, I have no intention of taking her up on this.

'You will drop in, won't you? Bring your wife?'

Ah, she must have registered my wedding ring. 'Erm, the thing is, my wife's not really a burger kind of person . . .'

She pulls a crestfallen face. 'It's probably not your date night kind of place, then . . .'

'Probably not,' I agree. *Because nowhere is anymore.* I clear my throat, aware of a creeping sense that I really shouldn't be here, and that right now I would very much like to be safely installed in my own home. As Flynn is staying over at Max's tonight, I won't even have to put on a pretence of being normal. I'll be able to slob around, a fine example of a newly-single middle-aged male with my muddied knees and juice-splattered T-shirt, probably reeking of vodka. However, I am also slightly concerned about the 'situation' Tanzie mentioned earlier. Surely Gary isn't violent to her?

'So, is it just the two of you here?' I venture.

'Nope, my youngest is still at home,' she explains. 'My other two are long grown up. Robbie works offshore as a commercial diver. He's an underwater welder up in Scotland, works on the oil rigs . . .'

'Really?' I exclaim. 'But surely he can't be—'

160

'I was a young mum,' Tanzie cuts in with a smile. 'Had him at sixteen, and he's twenty-four now, so he's properly qualified and everything. I'm very proud of him.'

I study this birdlike woman who's raised a child to manhood, yet seems incapable of fully concentrating behind the wheel of a car. 'I'm sure you are,' I murmur. 'I imagine it's terrifying too, though . . .'

'*Life's* terrifying, isn't it?' she says blithely. 'You just have to take things as they come and deal with it. And then there's Ashley, she's twenty-two, lives down south with her boyfriend. Just had a baby of her own . . .'

'So you're a grandmother?' I exclaim.

She nods. 'Yeah. Just the one so far. A beauty, but quite enough to be going on with . . .' She beams. 'And then there's Kayla, she's sixteen, still at school – in theory. Goes to Hesslevale High. D'you have any kids?'

'Yes, just the one. He's sixteen . . .'

'Which school?'

'Um . . . he's at Hesslevale too. His name's Flynn. Flynn Turner.' It seems wrong, somehow, to share details about my family with a candidate – but then I am sitting in her kitchen, and she'd be bound to ask anyway.

'What's he into, then?'

'Erm, the usual stuff – gaming, bit of reading, hanging out with his mates. And he plays guitar – that's his main thing . . .' She nods, clearly genuinely interested. I hesitate, knowing it'll seem rude if I seem eager to leave, but aware that the conversation will probably work its way round to my wife. 'I'll just order my cab, if you don't mind,' I add, making the call.

Hello, begins the recorded message, *you've reached Hesslevale Cars. All our operators are busy at the moment . . .*

161

I sip my tea and wait with my phone still clamped to my ear, trying to adopt a casual expression so it doesn't look as if I am desperate to get out of here. Tanzie smiles, and I find myself wondering whether she'll book another driving test, or just give up; it sounds awful, but I hope she knocks it on the head. It's extremely rare, but some people just aren't cut out for driving. She seems terribly well-meaning – although she puts on a tough front – and after last time, with all the crying, I'm not sure if she should put herself through that again.

The cab company's message rolls on and on over terrible tinny music. Tanzie checks my jacket again, taking it off the radiator and shaking it out, as if to try to accelerate the drying. I watch as something seems to catch her attention, and her expression changes. I follow her gaze to a small piece of folded paper, lying on her kitchen floor.

My printed-out copy of Sinead's list has fallen out of my pocket.

As I jump up to retrieve it, Tanzie bobs down and grabs it from the floor. I stare at her, phone still gripped to my ear.

Hello, you've reached Hesslevale Cars . . .

'They're busy,' I tell her as I finish the call abruptly.

She nods, still holding the folded-up list. 'Well, it is Saturday night.'

'Yeah, I guess so.'

A smile plays on her lips. 'I'd drive you home myself, but, you know—'

'It'd be highly illegal,' I say distractedly, sitting back down. 'Erm, that thing you picked up. I think it belongs to me—'

'Oh, does it?' She peers at it as if she has only just remembered she has it in her hand. Gordon Ramsay is still

162

shouting in the living room; something about this being 'no way to store fish!' I realise I am still clutching the Penguin wrapper as Tanzie unfolds the note carefully. What the hell is she doing? I seem to be incapable of asking her to hand it to me.

She is frowning thoughtfully at the list. For some reason, it must seem perfectly fine to her to examine someone else's personal paperwork – something that's fallen out of a pocket, and could be *anything*. 'Er, Tanzie?' I say. 'That bit of paper there . . . it's actually mine.'

'Yeah,' she mutters with a dismissive wave of her hand. I watch her, astounded by her audacity as she starts to read it.

Perhaps that's why I just let her do it: because I'm too stunned to stop her. *Go ahead, then! You've given me tea and two Penguins, which you seem to think gives you the right to read my private stuff . . .*

I don't know if she's a terribly slow reader, or if the passage of time has warped somehow, but it feels like forever as I sit there, knowing I could jump up and snatch it from her grasp – but what would be the point? She'll have read enough to get the gist. She might as well be fully aware of my every shortcoming; in fact, perhaps Gary would like to read it too, when his programme finishes? From the living room comes his rumbly laughter and the pop of a can being opened. Clearly, Saturday night is in full swing around here.

Tanzie looks up, her gaze seeming to penetrate my frontal lobe. 'What actually *is* this, Nate?'

'Er, could I just have it please?'

She hands it to me and sits back down on the chair opposite. 'Sorry,' she mutters. 'I really shouldn't have read it. I don't know what got into me.'

163

'It's all right.' I jam it into my jeans pocket.

'It's from your wife, right?'

I nod. 'As you'll have gathered, she's not terribly impressed with me at the moment.'

'Yeah, I can see that,' she murmurs.

'In fact, she left me ten days ago. I found the list one morning, and she'd already gone. So we're separated.' I glance down at my phone, wondering if an operator at Hesslevale Cars has become available yet.

She exhales loudly. 'God, you poor thing. And she took Flynn with her?'

'No, no – he's still with me . . .'

'The cow!' she exclaims.

'It's not like that,' I say quickly, because right now it feels imperative to explain that Sinead is not the baddie here; there *is* no baddie. Or, if there is, it must be me, with my poo-shirking tendencies and deep love of Springsteen which, clearly, I should have grown out of by now. 'It's been . . . tough,' I add. 'Tough for Sinead, I mean. I suppose most of it – looking after Flynn, the house, all the day-to-day stuff – fell to her . . .'

'She sounds so resentful,' Tanzie remarks.

'Yes, she does.' I pause. She has already branded Sinead a 'cow' for leaving Flynn with me. I dread to think what she'd call her if she knew about his condition.

'Couldn't she have told you, though? Given you the chance to work things out?'

'I wish she had,' I say with a shrug.

She shoots a quick look towards the open kitchen door. 'Me and my ex – the kids' dad, I mean – should've talked more and tried to fix things. We were idiots really. We had the first two kids so young, then Kayla came along as a little surprise and that kind of finished us off. I was stuck at home again – isolated and probably depressed – and I guess I blamed Neil for that.' She pauses and shrugs. 'Maybe we should've . . . I don't know, *seen someone*. A relationship person, I mean. Everyone goes for counselling these days, don't they?'

'I suppose so,' I reply, wondering if Sinead felt isolated too. I suppose the possibility has never occurred to me.

'Anyway,' she adds, 'Neil's with someone else now, down in London – two more kids – and I met Gary. So here I am, stuck out in the wilds by myself for a lot of the time . . .'

'But you said your youngest – Kayla – still lives with you?'

'In theory, yeah, but she spends most of her time at her best friend's Paige's house. It's all, "The Rileys this, the Rileys that", with their shower that squirts you from all angles and a tap that boiling water comes out of . . .' She snorts derisively.

'Are teenagers really excited by boiling water taps?'

'Seems like it.' She laughs. 'Anyway, never mind us. It's *you* we're talking about—'

'Looks that way,' I say with a faint smile.

'All that stuff she put,' she murmurs. 'Can I see it again? The list, I mean?'

Hell, why not? I retrieve it from my pocket and hand it back to her.

Her face softens as she re-reads it. 'What's this about your bloody record collection?'

I shrug. 'I have no idea. Maybe she's just run out of tolerance where Bruce Springsteen's concerned . . .'

'Springsteen?' She pulls a face, as if a foul smell has infiltrated the kitchen. 'That American patriot crap by a guy in double denim?'

For a moment, everything seems to stop as I stare at her across the table with its myriad of scuffs and stains. Something else is happening too. Perhaps it's the restorative properties of the tea, or the Penguin biscuits, or her disparaging comment about Bruce that causes the final residue of my drunkenness-stroke-hangover to disappear instantly. It's as if I have sprung back, and fully regained my faculties. Although I'm sure a police officer would believe otherwise, I feel as if I would be perfectly capable of conducting a driving test right now. 'Patriot crap?' I repeat. 'No – that's *not* what he's about.'

Tanzie's eyes widen. For the first time, I register how intensely green they are, the effect perhaps heightened by the strange purplish hue of her hair. 'What *is* he about then?' she asks, resting her pointy chin on her hands.

'Well, I assume you mean *Born in the USA* . . .'

'Yeah, of course . . .'

'It's not a patriotic song,' I say firmly. 'In fact, it's quite the opposite. Have you ever listened to the lyrics properly?'

She shrugs and shakes her head. 'Can't say I have. Like I said, he's not my cup of tea.'

'Well, it's about a guy coming back from Vietnam with all the promises of, "Oh, America will look after you because you're a hero. You've been off to fight and now you'll be given a good job and be properly taken care of."' I study Tanzie's rapt expression. 'Only, it doesn't happen that way,' I continue, 'and all the promises count for nothing because he's just flung on the slagheap like he doesn't matter at all. It's the very *opposite* of the American dream. It's ironic, don't you see?' She nods mutely. Even Gordon Ramsay seems to have piped down. 'It's about someone who's given their all, only to be tossed aside like a piece of crap . . .'

166

'Like you!' Tanzie interjects, at which I laugh, mirthlessly, astounded at her bluntness.

'Well, I haven't fought in Vietnam,' I point out. 'The only fight I've had in recent years was with a candidate who tried to grab at my shirt, and all I did was restrain him.'

'I don't mean that,' she retorts. 'I mean, you've given your all too, haven't you? To your family, I mean?'

'I don't know about that,' I bluster.

'Oh, come on, Nate. I can tell what kind of guy you are. You've got a good heart. I know that for a fact . . .'

'Do you?' I ask, confused now. What *is* she on about?

'Yes, I do. I mean, the way you've brought up your boy and dealt with all that stuff. He has a disability, right?'

I stare at her across the table, prickling with defensiveness now. What has her daughter been saying about him? 'Well, yes – he has mild cerebral palsy,' I murmur.

'Yeah, I know,' she carries on in her matter-of-fact way. 'Kayla's mentioned him. But anyway, never mind that. With you—'

'What on earth does this have to do with—'

'The way you just spoke,' she cuts in, 'with that forcefulness, like you cared *so much*. And I assumed you were just this shy, retiring, buttoned-up kind of guy!'

'Really?' I ask, dumfounded.

'Yeah. And all you were talking about was some clapped-out middle-aged bloke in a bandana . . .'

'He's not just a middle-aged bloke in a bandana! What's all this focus on his clothes?'

'Technically a bandana's an *accessory*,' she says with a grin.

'But no one cares what he wears,' I retort. 'He's a musician, not a fashion model—' I break off as Gary saunters in. He throws Tanzie an irritated look as he helps himself to a can of lager from the fridge. Perhaps he reckons she should be waitressing here too, replenishing his supplies? Tanzie glares at him, relaxing again only when he disappears back to the living room.

'So, what's going to happen with you and your wife now?' she asks.

I shuffle on the wooden chair. 'Well, er, I've come up with a sort of plan, actually.'

'What kind of plan?' She leans forward with interest.

'Um, what I thought was, if I could work through Sinead's list, point by point, then maybe she'd decide our marriage was worth another chance after all.' I pause, wondering why on earth I am telling her this. But then, she is sort of forcing it out of me – and at this point, I am beyond caring what anyone thinks of my situation. Maybe I should just take out an ad announcing our split in the *Hesslevale Gazette*? 'But, actually,' I add, 'I don't think it's working.'

'Why not?' she asks.

'Well, it seems to me like her mind's made up.'

Tanzie frowns at me. 'Are you sure?'

I drain the last of my tea. 'Looks like it. I mean, we've talked since, and she's spelt it all out – and I took her some flowers the other day but that didn't seem to go down very well at all.'

'Really? I *love* flowers . . .'

'Hmm, well, she didn't seem too impressed.'

Tanzie flutters a hand as if trying to waft away my negativity. 'So, apart from that, what have you actually done off the list?'

I pause, *really* keen to order my cab now. The last thing I need is to delve into all of this. Plus, I have Scout to let out when I get home, and these damp, dirty clothes to deal with.

'Erm, I'm just starting out really,' I mutter.

'Right, so which of these have you put right?' She jabs at the crumpled sheet of paper on the table.

Oh, to hell with it. I might as well give her all the information she needs, then I can call my taxi and leave. 'Okay, so you see where it says I leave too much to her?' Tanzie glances down and nods. 'Well, I've done loads in the house. It's probably the cleanest it's ever been . . .'

Her eyes narrow. 'You think your wife will come back just because you've run the hoover about?'

'No, not *just* because of that,' I reply irritably.

She throws me a stern look. Now, I reckon, she is perfectly capable of standing up to the Lino King through there. 'So, what else have you done since she left you?'

Christ, she's really wasted as a burger bar waitress. She'd make a first-class interrogator. 'I've, er, mown the lawn . . .'

'Big deal!'

'Not just that,' I say quickly. 'See where she put "Your mother"?'

'Uh-huh . . .'

I swallow hard, feeling as if I am being interviewed for a job, and failing badly. 'I made it clear to Mum that it wasn't on, her bad-mouthing Sinead . . .' I tail off, registering a distinct lack of approval. 'And I've called a guy who's coming round with a view to buying my record collection. . . .'

'Your Bruce Springsteens?' she gasps. Ah, now I can see she's impressed. Hang on. Why do I care what this woman thinks of me?

'They're only records,' I say blithely. 'If they're bothering

169

Sinead that much, they can go.' I shrug, to demonstrate that it's of little consequence really. 'Oh, and I've mentioned the flowers . . .'

Tanzie raises a brow. 'What kind were they?'

'Carnations and things – I forget what the others are called – from the garage . . .'

'From the *garage*?' she gasps.

'Yes, I was late back from work—'

'Did you grab her a bottle of anti-freeze while you were at it?' she crows, sliding the list back to me.

'I thought the flowers were enough,' I mutter, deciding not to add that I 'arranged' them in a bucket.

'So, that's it, is it?' she says curtly. 'That's basically all you're planning to do to win her back?'

'No, of course not,' I protest. 'I'm going to do *lots* more . . .' I pause and glance at my bare wrist, then check the time on my phone: 12.20 a.m.

'Can I just say something?' she remarks.

'Go ahead.'

'Well, I just think you're going about this all wrong.'

I look at her, knowing I should try the taxi company again right now. But I am also desperate, and if she can offer a crumb of advice, then I'm prepared to sit here for a few minutes more. 'What d'you mean?' I ask.

She pushes back her still-damp hair. 'If you really want her back, I think you should forget about the crappy flowers and the hoovering and concentrate on the important stuff. *If* you don't mind me saying . . .'

'Like what?'

'Well, reading that list, as a woman . . . I think I know *exactly* what she's getting at.'

'Do you?' I ask. *Tell me then,* I will her. *Tell me what the hell to do because I really could do with some help.*

170

'Yeah. I mean, just try to understand what she's actually trying to tell you here. It's not really about shelves or records or mousetraps, is it?'

'Isn't it? I have no idea. My mate Paolo reckons—'

She shakes her head impatiently. 'Never mind what a *bloke* says. This list – well, it's about feeling neglected, un-cared-for and probably depressed. I mean, she's had years of this, hasn't she? Years of looking after the family and feeling put-upon . . .'

'D'you really think so?'

'Of course she has. She's done the lion's share of looking after a disabled child . . .'

'Tanzie, d'you mind not referring to him as—'

'And maybe she's lost herself along the way. Lost her identity, I mean, and any sense of how to be happy. Have you ever asked her if she's depressed?'

'Er, not really. She did see the doctor a while ago . . .'

'And what happened then?'

'She got some pills,' I reply, 'but I think she stopped taking them.'

'You *think*?' she exclaims, with an eye roll.

I nod, aware of a gnawing sense of shame now. But then, how can Tanzie possibly know anything about my marriage, when she hasn't even met my wife?

'What you need to do is show her you care about her *properly*,' she continues, 'as a woman, an individual, and not just Flynn's mum. Never mind setting the mousetraps and shouting at your mother—'

'I didn't *shout* . . .'

'You know how you talked about Bruce Springsteen just then? How revved up you were?'

I nod wordlessly.

'Approach it like that. Show her you're passionate about

171

putting things right – and I don't mean by squirting a bit of Mr Sheen about the place . . .'

'We don't use Mr Sheen,' I mutter.

'I mean, show her that you love and respect her.' She wrinkles her nose. 'I can't believe you belittled her job . . .'

'Honestly, I don't think I have!'

'Well, she thinks you have. What does she do anyway?'

'She works in a gift shop called, uh, Tawny Owl or something.'

'Tawny Owl?'

'Or Snowy Owl . . .'

'Nate, what kind of owl is it? You don't even know!'

No wonder she left you, she means.

I scrunch up the Penguin wrapper. 'I've just forgotten. God, that sounds awful, doesn't it?'

'It does, actually,' she retorts, 'but it's not too late to show her how much you want things to change.' She leans back and smooths down her damp hair. 'Self-pity is terribly unattractive,' she adds. 'So, when you've calmed down and stopped drowning your sorrows and collapsing in Wendy houses—'

'I *didn't* collapse,' I protest.

'Then you can get yourself some gumption, a *backbone,* and start to be the kind of husband and father she wants you to be. Do all *that,* and I promise you everything'll work out.'

I blink at Tanzie, momentarily lost for words. I have never met anyone quite like her. I had no idea she could be so forthright, so presumptuous – so damn bossy actually – when she sat there sobbing in her driving instructor's car. 'D'you reckon that'll work, then?' I ask finally.

She nods. 'Yeah, of course it will. But next time you buy her a present, don't stop off at the petrol station, will you?'

'No, I definitely won't,' I say, quite bewildered now as I pick up my phone and finally manage to speak to an actual human being at Hesslevale Cars.

Fifteen minutes later, I am wearing my almost-dry jacket, having thanked Tanzie profusely and called out a cheery goodbye to Gary, who didn't even turn around from the TV.

Installed in the back of a pine-scented minicab, I look out at the wet, black night, feeling somehow lighter as we speed along the country lanes.

Maybe that's why my wife has been seeing a therapist: because she simply needed to offload. Well, I understand that a little more now. While I still have no idea what the future holds, a new sense of purpose has settled over me; it's time to look forward, to be positive and strong for Sinead, for Flynn – for *all* of us.

By sheer fluke tonight I found someone of my own to offload to. And as Sinead once told me after a Rachel session, it's good to talk.

Chapter Eighteen

Tanzie

Burger Bill's is unusually busy this Sunday afternoon. There have been rumblings about the place closing, which would be a real pain. I mean, I moan about the buses, and sometimes having to arrive in Hesslevale two hours before my shift starts. But being jobless would be worse. It's just getting terribly competitive around here with so many restaurants all jostling for attention in the middle of town.

Dressed in the particularly unattractive uniform of tangerine tunic and my own shapeless black trousers, I deliver burgers, ribs and chicken wings – plus fries, *copious* fries – to the party of eight who are all drinking beers and wine and shouting over each other at the circular table by the window.

'Could I have pickles? Did I *ask* for pickles when we ordered, love?'

'Yes, you did. There are pickles on your burger . . .'

'And we wanted extra mustard on the side?'

'Yep, I'll bring that right now . . .'

'Is there barbecue sauce on this?'

'Yes—'

'Are you sure?' A paunchy thirty-something male with a silly, greasy little ponytail whips the top off his bun and examines the burger, as if it might jump up and snap at his face. 'Okay, darling, there *is* sauce – but you've been a bit mean with it, naughty girl. That's just a *dribble* . . .'

I fix on my bland, nothing-ruffles-me face. I'm as adept at putting it on as I am my lipstick. 'I'll bring you some more,' I tell him. 'It's not a problem.'

'Well, yeah. I'd like a lot more than that!'

I can bring you the giant plastic tub it comes in, if you like – and tip it over your fat, smug head. Would that be enough sauce for you?

'She doesn't assemble the burgers,' remarks a blonde girl in a tight pink top. 'She just brings them to the table.'

'And she does it very charmingly too,' ponytail man says with a patronising smile.

I smile back – tersely – managing to resist telling them that I'm not just a 'she', in fact I do have a name, it's why I wear a badge saying TANZIE. But heck, who cares what they call me? As I collect a dish of extra sauce from the kitchen, I find myself thinking instead about Nate – as I have numerous times over the past two weeks, since I virtually frogmarched him back to my place. Should I have left him alone, all wet, muddy and disorientated in Liv and Steve's garden? I know I went a bit over the top, lecturing him on how he might win his wife back. As if it's any of my damn business! In fact, I've looked out for him, pretty much every time I've been in Hesslevale – just for the chance to say, 'Sorry, I really didn't mean to go on at you that night. I felt sorry for you, and I just wanted to help you really.' But there's been no sign of him around town. Maybe he's glanced into Bill's and spotted me in

175

my terrible uniform. After sobbing when I failed my last driving test, and then banging on at him about his wife's list, he probably has me down as a nutjob.

Anyway, I'm one to talk about how *anyone* should get their life together. Six shifts a week, I'm doing at the moment, putting up with the attitude that any woman who works in a place like Bill's is fair game when it comes to the comments. The near-constant stream of 'darlings' and 'babe'; the assumption that I enjoy any kind of male attention. 'Cheer up, honey,' some creep drawled last week. 'Is it your menopause or something? Are you *drying up*?'

Unfortunately my boss, Stefanos – known as Stef – was there at the time, so I just gritted my teeth and fell into my joking-with-the-punters tone: 'Not quite yet. But don't worry – I'm a ticking time bomb. I'll let you know when it all kicks off.' It might not be arse gropes and boob stares like the younger waitresses have to put up with, but it's bad enough.

Until three years ago, I had a great job. I was PA for the Managing Director of Brogan Mitchell Pies, a company that started small, selling savoury pies around the Pennine towns of Yorkshire, and grew quickly, expanding to supply all the main supermarkets; it was phenomenal. I'd been there from the start, when it was just Brogan himself – who I knew from secondary school – and four women in the nearby factory, on a small industrial estate towards the northern edge of Hesslevale.

When the factory could no longer cope with demand, Brogan bought a bigger place, closer to Solworth, although our offices remained where we had always been. But there were teething problems with the new factory. The pastry was wrong, the meat substandard, and customers complained. Brogan realised he would have to make regular checks to ensure that the new, twenty-strong workforce were doing things properly.

The stress was taking its toll. One morning, following a late-night mash-up for his birthday, Brogan was stopped in his car by police and breathalysed. Still over the limit from the night before, he was fined and given a two-year ban. Now he needed a PA who could drive him back and forth from office to factory every day.

'I'd like that to be you, Tanzie,' he said. I'd had a few driving lessons, and vowed to knuckle down and pass my test as quickly as possible. He said he could get by with taxis in the meantime, if I could book a test right away and pass either that one, or the one after that – two chances. Talk about pressure! But Brogan had given me a real opportunity in hiring me, and I knew I was lucky to have that job.

I'd grown up in Solworth and left school without any qualifications. By the time my friends were heading off to college and uni, I was already a mum. While they were all excited about choosing throws and cushions for their student halls, I was living at my parents' place with my boyfriend Neil and our baby boy, and battling with nappies and night feeds and all that. When my friends talked about modules and lectures and freshers' week, it could have been a foreign language. All I managed throughout my twenties was the odd supermarket job, fitted in around the kids.

I failed that first driving test, probably due to nerves more than anything else – and by the time the next one rolled around I'd worked myself into such a state that it was inevitable I'd screw up. I tried to impress on the examiner how important it was for me to pass – just to be pleasant and make conversation. That was Nate. I can't believe I was terrified of a guy who gets tanked at a barbecue and ends up crawling into a little plastic house, like an inebriated teenager! 'I'm sure it *is* important,' he'd said, with not a flicker of empathy. *Are you an actual human being?* I'd thought irritably, *or don't you have any emotions at all?*

And now, as I sit in Burger Bill's back yard on my afternoon break, I turn over the whole Nate/Sinead scenario in my head. That crazy list, and her walking out with no warning: I know I gave Nate a telling-off for being a crappy husband, but still, it seems pretty drastic. Leaving her kid as well! I know Flynn's not a baby – but still. When Neil and I split, it never occurred to me to not have the children stay with me. I know I'm being sexist. Plenty of men walk out on their kids without so much as a backward glance – and no one vilifies *them*.

But can Nate really be so terrible as a husband and dad? He seems thoughtful and kind; qualities I'd have sneered at once, but which seem to grow in importance, the older you get. Handsome, too, with those intense dark eyes behind wire-rimmed specs and that slightly wonky smile. I only noticed that when he was round at my place that night. I suppose, when you're about to sit a driving test, the last thing on your mind is whether or not the examiner is fanciable. But yeah – he definitely is. He has that long-legged, gangly thing going on too, which is appealing. You could do a lot worse, Sinead, I decide. Yep, now I'm trying to beam my opinions through the airwaves to a woman I've never met, like *I* know the first thing about relationships.

Something-owl, that's the shop his wife works in. I pull out my phone from my pocket and try googling a few owl species, then type in the more obvious 'owl-gift-shop-Hesslevale'. Up it pops: Little Owl. Funny that Nate knows

178

literally *thousands* of rules of the road – yet can't even remember the name of it. I go to the shop's website and click on 'Meet our team'. There's a woman with a brunette pixie cut and a slash of red lipstick: 'Hi, I'm Vicky,' the caption reads. 'It was always my dream to open a shop of beautiful gift ideas and call it Little Owl!'

And then there's a blonde woman with a kind, sweet face, a pinkish complexion and bright blue eyes. 'I'm Sinead, and I work in Little Owl, helping you to choose that perfect gift for someone special. I look forward to meeting you very soon!'

She looks like the kind of woman who'd take care to pack a nutritionally balanced lunchbox for her kid. I'd have thought she was the *last* person to scrawl a demented note and walk out on her son.

I slip my phone back in my pocket, stuff my half-eaten burger into the bin, and finish my carton of weak coffee. Then I head back into the restaurant for another four hours of serving the great British public.

The volume around the rowdy table has cranked up several notches. Carmina, the other waitress who's on today, gives me a knowing look as the ponytailed man snaps his fingers and shouts, 'When you've got a *minute*, please?'

'He's just asked if I have a boyfriend,' she mutters. 'I told him it was none of his business. He said he was only trying to be friendly—'

'Aw, you've probably hurt his feelings,' I remark, and we both snigger.

'He must be at least forty . . .'

'God,' I exclaim. 'Almost dead!'

'Sod him,' Carmina says with a smirk. 'I don't care. This is my last shift—'

179

'Has that come round so soon?' I exclaim, with a prickle of envy.

'Yeah!' She's beaming now. At eighteen years old, Carmina has only been working here in order to amass the funds for her trip to Thailand, before she heads off to university in the autumn. It's just been a stopgap to her. It's not her *life*.

'Could we order some desserts, please?' That's the pink-top woman from the circular table.

I zoom over with a smile. As Stef always says, 'It costs nothing to be nice.' The astronomical cost of driving lessons and tests, and the fact that Gary never seems to bring home anything like I'd expect him to earn, means I'm always grateful for tips. Luckily, Stef lets us keep our tips, rather than shoving them into the till like they do in some places.

After Driving Test Fuck-up Number Two, this was the only job I could find in a hurry. At least it was local, I thought. I could walk here from our flat. And it would only be temporary. I'd lost my job at Brogan Mitchell, soon to be replaced by a girl called Lilli, with an 'i', who looked barely old enough to cross a road by herself, let alone drive a car. I met her when I bumped into the whole gang on a night out. They were all gathered around a big table in the Lamb and Flag. I'd just popped in with my friend Maggie and, of course, my former workmates spotted me and beckoned us over.

Lilli had the kind of skin that's so smooth and even, you'd wonder if she actually has pores. 'You must stay in touch, Tanz,' Brogan said, squirming uncomfortably. 'I'll always look out for you, you know.' Yeah – sure he would.

Of course I didn't keep in touch. What would we have

talked about: the brilliance of Lilli's driving? Recent developments in the savoury pie industry? Still, a yearning to drive had its hooks in me. In the past three years, since I've been serving burgers, I went on to sit eight more driving tests.

Then last month I failed for the eleventh time.

Normally I don't fall to pieces. I just try to brush it off and focus on the next time. But that day I was sobbing like a little kid, and snot was pouring out of my nose. Poor Nate just sat there, waiting for me to finish.

I wasn't crying because I'd been under pressure to pass for work. There was no job at stake. No, that time, it was about something that mattered much more – and I flunked it, just as Gary said I would.

That's the end of your test. I am sorry, but you haven't passed. Would you like me to explain why?

No-bloody-thank-you, I wouldn't. It was Mum who once told me that only a raving idiot keeps going back for more helpings of the same old crap.

So I'm done with driving. That's the easy part. The other stuff – the *major fault* in my life – is going to be a whole lot harder to fix.

Chapter Nineteen

Kayla, my youngest, is allergic to her phone. At least she is when it's me trying to speak to her. What's the point of paying for her mobile if she refuses to communicate with me? At least half the week she stays over at her best friend's place. She even keeps her best dressing gown there. 'Oh, I'm leaving it at Paige's now!' she told me, when I asked where it had gone. Sounds trivial, I know, but it didn't half feel like a kick in the teeth.

'Paige's is just handier for school, Mum,' she keeps telling me – and, yes, there is that, although she is eligible for the free school bus. 'And I love their place,' she added. 'It's so calm and relaxed there.' Hmm, *that* was harder to take. Not that I begrudge Kayla having friends, because life's been tough for her, after her dad and I split up. This was five years ago. Her older sister had just left home, so it wasn't the best time – not that there ever is one.

I finished at Bill's at six today and had a quick glass of wine in the diner with Carmina to celebrate her freedom and forthcoming trip. And now, instead of hanging about for the next bus, I've decided to drop in at Paige's and at least check in with Kayla and remind her that she does in fact have a mum.

The evening has turned cool and breezy by the time I reach Paige's estate, not that that's what they call Aspen Grove. No, it's a *development* in yellowish brick, with all kinds of pillars and columns decorating the houses, and those ultra-bright bedding plants in the front gardens that never look quite real. I've been here before but I've only met Paige's parents briefly. Both solicitors, they seem to be either at work, or bounding out for a run with plastic water bottles strapped to their chests in special elasticated holders, as if they are about to cross a desert.

Paige's house is the biggest and fanciest here. It's been quite a climb up a long, steep hill. I take a moment to steady my breath and rap on the front door, then wait patiently for someone to answer.

'Oh, hi, Tanzie!' It's Paige who opens the door. She's a stunning girl with long, golden hair, huge blue eyes and braces across her seemingly perfect top teeth.

'Hi, Paige. Hope you don't mind me dropping by. Is Kayla still here?'

Paige blinks at me as if I might be about to storm in and try to kidnap her. 'Yeah.' She turns away. 'Kayla? It's your mum!'

I swallow and wait, trying to ignore a tight ball of indignation that's growing inside me now. *I'm her mother, for God's sake. Aren't you going to invite me in?*

Paige is standing there, waiting, arms folded across her pristine white top. Perhaps she's worried I'll contaminate her shiny home with the greasy whiff from Burger Bill's if she asks me to step inside. Actually, she'd have a point there. I know it clings to my clothes, my hair – even my skin, probably. Sometimes I'm conscious of the person sitting next to me on the bus trying to edge away, as if the fatty smell might transfer from my sleeve onto theirs, and seep through the material to their arm.

Now Paige has wandered back into the wide, polished-floored hallway, leaving me stranded on the doorstep as if I'm a delivery person waiting for a signature for a parcel.

Ah – *finally* here comes my daughter, face chalky-pale, shoulder-length dark hair all tangly and loose. 'Mum! Hey.' She smiles resignedly.

'Hi, love. I had a while to wait for my bus, and you haven't been answering your phone—'

Kayla winces. 'Forgot to charge it. Sorry . . .'

I decide not to challenge her feeble excuse. 'That's okay. You've been here since Friday night, though, and I'm missing you . . .' I realise, with horror, that a wobble has crept into my voice.

'Have you?' She beams her beautiful wide smile. 'I s'pose I am pretty wonderful really.'

We both chuckle. 'So, what've you been up to, then?'

'Just watching films, chatting, hanging out. Nothing much . . .'

'Are you coming home tonight?' I ask, aware of a note of hope in my voice.

Kayla shrugs. 'Er, I don't think so, Mum. It's just, with school tomorrow, it's so much easier to go from here—'

'And you've got everything you need, have you? Enough clean clothes and stuff?'

'Yeah, yeah. I'm fine. Paige's mum's been washing stuff for me.'

I clear my throat. 'Why don't you just come back with me, love? We can watch something together and have a catch-up. You could get the bus to school in the morning—'

'I'd rather stay here, Mum.' She drops her gaze. I could *demand* that she comes home with me now – but what would be the point, and who could blame her for enjoying being here, being 'treated like one of the family' (ouch!) as she once put it?

'Give me a hug, then,' I say suddenly, overcome by an urge to hold her.

Kayla laughs awkwardly, then we fold our arms around each other. It doesn't matter that I am standing here on the doorstep, virtually have to *beg* for time with my daughter, because it's so good to feel her close.

We pull apart. 'I'd better get off, then,' I say.

'Okay, Mum.' Concern flickers in her greenish eyes. 'Love you.'

Love-you: all the girls say it that way, sing-song, like a doorbell jingle, and I suppose it's kind of lost its meaning.

All the same, I hold the words close as we say goodbye.

*

No wonder she prefers it here, I decide as I head down the hill. Of course, I know it's not solely due to Paige living so close to school. It's Gary too – not that he's actually been horrible to her. I mean, he hasn't shouted at her or been violent or anything. He's just an unpleasant presence, radiating his bad moods and plonked there, inert on the sofa like a bloody great silverback gorilla. Actually, a gorilla would be preferable. It wouldn't have the telly blaring, or litter the floor with its cans.

A gorilla wouldn't tell me I'm thick and useless and should never have even bothered to take all those driving tests.

As I near the bottom of the estate, where the newest

houses are empty and still up for sale, a slim, blonde woman appears and starts striding up the hill towards me. At first, I barely register her. I am too busy thinking about Kayla's pink fluffy dressing gown dangling from a hook on the door in Paige's bedroom, and telling myself that only a mad idiot would feel jealous. Then I glance at the woman again. Her long hair is loose and a bit dishevelled. She is wearing a cotton dress, patterned all over with little blue flowers, and a flimsy navy blue jacket on top, plus flat Mary Janes, the kind of style some women (like her) manage to look cute in. I'd just look like a middle-aged woman stomping about in a child's shoes.

I slide my gaze over towards her as we pass each other. Now I realise I know her face. I saw it earlier today, during my break at work: the blonde woman on the Little Owl website. Sinead, Nate's wife.

She catches my eye and smiles briefly, as if she's just on her way home to her nice, normal house, and her lovely husband.

I stop and watch her trotting up the hill, all jaunty, like she doesn't have a care in the world. You'd never guess she was capable of writing a note like that – about all her resentments about mice and records and his mother . . . What else was on it? Oh yes – his crappy attempts at DIY. At least he had a go, I think bitterly, heading out of the estate now and along the lane, past the single-storey building that used to be Brogan Mitchell's pie factory.

You'd think, being a tradesman, Gary would be willing to do the odd job around our cottage – but no. The shelf that fell down in our bedroom is propped up against the wall, my books stacked in untidy piles all around it.

'Your fault,' he said, 'for putting too many books on it.'

'But it's a bookshelf!' I'd argued.

He'd rolled his eyes. 'I've just done a full day's work, Tanz. Maybe you should spend less money on books, and less time reading?'

I was about to remind him that the books I devour – biographies of people with interesting lives, doing things that matter – are from charity shops and generally only cost a couple of quid. But we'd been there before, many times. Gary doesn't see the point of reading anything.

I was also tempted to ask what had happened to the charming man who'd seemed so generous and attentive when we first started going out. He'd come to carpet Brogan Mitchell's offices when we had our refit, and flirted and charmed me with loads of calls after the job had finished, until I finally agreed to go for a drink with him. I wasn't bothered about having a boyfriend, but why not just go, the girls in the office kept saying? *He's handsome and sexy,* they reckoned. *If you don't, one of us will!*

He'd seemed lovely at first: never married, no kids, bit of a free spirit and lots of fun. Bloody good-looking, too, in that slightly rough-around-the-edges sort of way, like the waltzer guys my friends and I all fancied when the fair came to town. I could hardly believe he was attracted to me. Seriously, I was almost embarrassed to put up Facebook pictures of the two of us, imagining people thinking, 'How did she manage to nab *him*?' It's not great, being the less attractive partner. But then, it wasn't his looks that hooked me really, but his generosity and mad sense of humour (surely anyone who'd come up with 'The Lino King' for his business name had to be a decent guy?).

In our early days together, he drove us all over Yorkshire on weekends in his yellow van: to the seaside, on shopping trips to Leeds, even to the theatre a couple of times, to see shows. Kayla came along with us sometimes, when she wasn't staying over at a friend's. Even she seemed to like him at first. He was the kind of man who, when he took you out, insisted on buying a programme and ice creams in the interval, and then maybe going somewhere afterwards. We had so much fun. Neil and I had never done any of that. Not that I blamed him – we were young and broke, with a family – but it was a new and lovely experience to have all that.

There were signs, though, a year or so in, after we'd moved into the flat just off Hesslevale high street. I wanted to believe that Gary worked hard, grafting long hours; that I was just being paranoid. I told myself I was worrying unnecessarily when someone started calling our landline and, whenever I answered, there'd just be silence, punctuated by the odd, sharp breath, and then they'd hang up.

'Who d'you think it is?' I asked him one evening in bed.

'Just some nutter,' Gary replied.

I told myself I was being overly suspicious when I overheard two of Gary's friends chuckling together at a wedding we'd been invited to: 'See Gary's still up to his old tricks?'

'Yes, haha – the John Lewis of carpet laying.'

'John Lewis?'

'Never knowingly under-shagged.'

Just stupid drunk men gossiping, I told myself.

I also convinced myself I was being ridiculous when a salmon-coloured bra turned up in our laundry basket two weeks ago. With its huge rigid cups, it certainly wasn't mine – or Kayla's. So how the hell had it got there?

'Nothing to do with me,' Gary countered, when I dangled it in front of him.

'Are you sure? Please, whatever it is – just be honest with me.' I stood there, shaking with fury and humiliation.

188

'Maybe one of your friends left it,' he suggested, although none of them would wear a horror like that, and anyway, they never stayed over. They hardly ever visited either. I'd go to Maggie's or Andrea's or Toni's instead, or we'd meet at the pub. I knew they didn't like Gary.

So how the hell had the salmon bra come into our flat?

I had to get out of the house, and set off with Wolfie. As I marched along the dark, narrow lane, I convinced myself there must be some innocent reason for it being there. Stupidly, I let Wolfie off his lead by the modern cul-de-sac, and he spotted a rabbit and legged it. Gary had pointed out Liv and Steve's house to me when he'd been doing some work for them. Wolfie shot in through their gate, and I crept into the garden to look for him. That's when I found Nate.

When I lay it all out, about the bra and Gary's reaction to it . . . well, I must seem like the world's biggest mug – but I wanted to believe that everything was okay.

A bit like Nate, I decide, as I perch on the narrow bench in the bus shelter. He must have known something was wrong. You can't be married to someone who's that unhappy and resentful and not have a clue.

A head-in-the-sand approach – *that's* what he must have adopted, just like I did, even before the appearance of that mysterious bra.

On the day I sat my last driving test, I woke up to a clear, bright morning. Gary had already left, without even wishing me luck: he'd had to set off early for a big job in Bradford. I didn't think anything of it.

My driving instructor, Jason, came to pick me up. As usual, I was using his car to do my test. 'Just pretend it's a normal day,' he said cheerfully. 'Tell yourself you can drive perfectly well, and it's only forty minutes of your life. Remember you can have plenty of minors and still pass. No one expects you to be perfect.'

Jason is my third driving instructor. The first one started to become 'unavailable' when I failed the fourth time, and the second one said I might benefit from 'a fresh approach' (i.e., not *his* approach). Jason is a nicely-mannered young man, probably only a couple of years older than my eldest. He was chatting away as he drove, about a documentary on wolves in Alaska he'd watched the night before. I was only half-listening as we came into the outskirts of Solworth. To be honest, I was too busy trying to convince myself that that *wasn't* Gary's van I'd just glimpsed, parked in a side street of terraced houses. We'd passed too quickly for me to see whether it had a lion painted on the side. But it was the right shade of yellow, and all scuffed and rusting like Gary's, and you don't see many vans like that.

We arrived at the test centre fifteen minutes early, and I excused myself and went to use the loo. I didn't care that anyone might hear me through the flimsy cubicle partition as I made the call on my mobile. I had to speak to Gary. I couldn't possibly focus on emergency stops and reversing round corners without knowing the truth.

'Tanz?' he barked, sounding distracted. 'What's up?'

'Um, I wanted to let you know I'm at the test centre now, just about to do my test.'

'Oh, right. Good luck with that, then.'

'Thanks,' I said. 'It's just, you forgot to say that this morning, so I thought I'd call you now to give you the chance.'

He grunted. He really thought I was just winding him

up. 'Ha, yeah. Sorry about that. But, you know, I'm not sure you're really cut out for driving . . .'

'Thanks!'

'Oh, c'mon, Tanz. Concentration's not really your thing, is it? You're just so easily distracted—' *Well, stuff you!* 'Anyway, I've said sorry,' he went on. 'It was just so early when I left. I didn't want to be late for this job—'

'The job in Bradford?' I cut in.

'Yeah,' he replied, calm as anything.

My hand was shaking but I managed to steady my breathing so he wouldn't realise anything was wrong. 'And that's where you are now, is it? At the job?'

'Yeah, that's right. Look, I'd better go, got a ton of stuff to get started on here . . .'

I cleared my throat. 'Carpet, is it?'

'Er, some of it, yeah . . .'

'Shagpile?'

'Uh? What are you on about?'

Someone had come into the loos. I could hear them shuffling about, then having a pee in the next cubicle. 'Gary,' I said carefully, 'I'm sure I saw your van on the way here. You're in Solworth right now, aren't you?'

'What *are* you on about?' he snapped.

'Your van! I'm sure I saw it parked down a side street. So, what were you doing—'

'Jesus Christ.' He sniggered as if I was a raving idiot. 'You're just stressed, that's all. I don't know why you keep putting yourself through this. Catch you later – and good luck . . . *again.* Just try and hold it together this time, okay?'

I will, I told myself as I left the loo and sat next to Jason in the waiting room. *I'll hold it together all right.*

191

I'll pass and that'll bloody show you. What I'd actually like to do is drive over your foot.

So, yes, Nate – it really mattered that time, more than the others. But you'll never know quite how much.

The bus pulls up at the stop. I step on and say hi to the driver, who I know by sight. As I take a seat, I spot a few other regular passengers who use this service to trundle back and forth from Hesslevale, to the various villages scattered around to the south. There's the elderly lady who talks to herself, and the man with black-framed specs who always has tons of carrier bags clustered around his feet. The young mum is there, her baby asleep in her arms in a blanket of marshmallow pink.

Soft rain starts to hit the windows as I scroll for Kayla on my phone and text her a heart, not caring if she thinks I've gone soppy. I press send, then glance out at the gently sloping hills, and try to figure out what I'm going to do with the rest of my life.

Chapter Twenty

Sinead

'Morning, can I help you with anything?'

'Just browsing, thanks.' It's Monday morning, and my first customer is impeccably groomed, her navy blazer from somewhere like Jaeger or Hobbs, the upper end of the high street that still feels too posh and grown-up for me, even if I could afford to shop there. She is perusing the photo frames I arranged along a wall, strewn with the tissue-paper flowers I made, strung on fine thread. While I might not make intricate silver jewellery these days, there must still be a kernel of creativity lurking somewhere inside me. However, right now I am unpacking fairy lights whilst mentally compiling another list, this time entitled:

Reasons Why I am Not a Monster.

Because only a monster leaves her child, doesn't she? Never mind Abby insisting repeatedly over the past month that it's *not* Flynn I've left, I'm still not always there for my son, and these days he doesn't seem terribly keen to spend time with me.

Of course we've hung out together plenty of times. I've cooked for him at Abby's – his favourite lasagnes and cottage pies, hefty wintry meals even though we are well into June. I've suggested going to the movies ('Nothing I really want to see, Mum'), and managed to tempt/bribe him to come on shopping trips to Solworth for new clothes and Xbox games, attempting to assuage my guilt by lavishing money on him (which I can barely afford as I'll need to scrape together a deposit and rent for a place of my own at some point; I can't even think about talking to Nate about dividing up our finances just yet). On one such outing, I bought myself a cherry-red jacket, which Flynn blinked at, startled, as I carried it to the till, muttering, 'You *sure* about that, Mum? It's very . . . bright!'

I *want* to feel bright, I decided as I jabbed my debit card into the machine, although I suspected it would take more than an outlandish jacket to make that happen.

So, yes, we've been doing stuff together, yet each time I've suspected that Flynn was eager to escape back home to Nate or, better still, be with his friends. If I were a proper mum – a *good* one – I'd have stayed with his dad and kept our family intact.

Meanwhile – somewhat shamefully – I have been 'getting out there' again, as my friends put it, by which they mean socialising, going out after dark and not just on hasty dashes to the supermarket for wine.

'You can't just sit in every night and brood,' Abby said one evening, not unkindly. So we've had a few nights out – just dinner and drinks locally – and, although I'd been on the verge of cancelling, I dolled myself up to meet up with my old art college gang last week. I took the train to Leeds, and the moment I spotted Michelle, Aisha and George, waving from a corner table in our beloved old bar, I knew I'd done the right thing. A few minutes later, Brett shot in amidst a flurry of apologies.

194

'Wow, Sinead – look at you!' he exclaimed. 'You look amazing. Younger, even, than last time I saw you. Is time going in *reverse*?'

'I don't think so,' I laughed, but maybe he was right, and I did look a little more like my pre-motherhood self. He'd still looked so cool and handsome, that time I'd run into him in WH Smith's – as he did that night at Fletcher's. But that time, I'd been wearing some dumpy mum outfit, and was still being woken by Flynn most nights.

As we fell into easy conversation, I felt glad that I'd made an effort, and that Abby had virtually pushed me out of the door. Michelle told us about her stint in New York – complete with brief love affair – and Brett had us in stitches by divulging that his latest relationship came to an end because he couldn't pronounce 'quinoa'.

'Oh, come on,' I insisted, laughing. 'That *can't* be the real reason.'

'No, it really was.' He grinned, and just for a moment I remembered how it had felt to kiss him, all those years ago; a party kiss between friends that had caused fireworks to explode in my head, and was never referred to again. 'Hannah reckoned I kept saying it wrong just to wind her up,' he added. 'But it was probably the final straw in her long list of my failings.' Hmmm. And then it was my turn to explain that I'd left Nate. Although everyone was sympathetic, they didn't dwell on it; it wasn't a night for tears or an analysis of what had gone wrong. Aisha filled us all in on her life as an art teacher, and her tentative forays into online dating since her divorce. *No one's life is neat and tidy,* I reflected as we bickered good-naturedly over the wording of Aisha's dating profile. Even George had his fair share of romantic disasters before finding love with the extremely gorgeous Petra.

As for Brett, my college crush, there had been a couple of long-term relationships, as far as I gathered, plus a smattering of short-lived flings. I'd already known he has a son, Corey, who's ten years old and lives with his ex, an arrangement which no one seemed to find appalling that night.

So, couples – *parents* – break up, yet everything can work out okay. This seemed mildly reassuring. Then came the question I'd had semi-dreaded. 'You are back to doing your jewellery, aren't you?' Brett asked.

I cleared my throat, remembering his declaration by the confectionery shelves in WH Smith: *You're the rising star! I saw that big feature about you. Aisha sent it to me. Promise you won't take too much time out?*

'I'm afraid I kind of let things slide,' I admitted.

'Well,' Brett said briskly, 'you can always pick things up again. You can't let your talent go to waste.' I insisted that it had been too long, and I was out of touch – but he wouldn't hear of it. By then several wines down, I glanced around the table, wondering why I'd let it go, just as I'd let these friendships drift. Well, not anymore, I decided, as we hugged and said our goodbyes; while my business might have been history, I very much needed these friends back in my life.

Brett insisted on walking me to the station because he was 'going that way'. Was he really? I wondered. 'Please keep in touch,' he said as we exchanged numbers. Of course I will, I told him. He hugged me again and kissed me lightly on the cheek. I think I must have smiled the whole train journey home.

It doesn't really matter that he hasn't texted or called; in fact it's probably for the best. I serve my customer – she buys an elegant white china vase – and check my phone as she leaves. There's a text from Mum, who's been bombarding me with messages since I finally told her I'd left Nate. I'm keeping her at bay from visiting – just. Even she has been a little judgemental: *'Don't you think Flynn should really be with you?'*

My phone buzzes with a call; it's Nate. At least he's stopped bombarding me now. 'Hi,' I say. 'I'm actually at work . . .'

'Yes, I know – I am too. I'll be quick . . .'

'Is everything okay?' A young couple have wandered in, and I greet them with a bright smile.

'Yes. I mean – well, you know how things are, so no, not really. I was just wondering if we could meet up sometime? Have a drink, or even dinner . . . I mean, I know you said you weren't ready. But that was weeks ago now, and I thought maybe now you'd—'

'I can't really discuss this now,' I murmur.

'There's nothing *to* discuss. Can't we just arrange a night?'

'Nate, I have customers here.'

'And God forbid you upset your customers!'

I open my mouth, lost for words for a moment. *Please don't do this,* I will him silently. *Please just accept what I've done and try to get on with your life, like I am, even though it's bloody terrible.*

'Can I just ask you something?' he says.

'Uh-huh,' I say non-committally.

'D'you think I've let you down?'

'Nate, please . . .' A wave of nausea hits me. I don't know if it's the smell of Little Owl, all the scented candles, oil diffusers and chakra-balancing hot-water-bottle covers, but there's something about this place that is almost stifling these days.

197

'Couldn't you have given me a chance, instead of springing this on me?' he barks. 'If you'd told me how you felt, then maybe I could have tried harder and fixed things. Why didn't you at least say something?'

Feeling quite sick now, I hold the phone away from my ear for a moment.

'. . . could have communicated,' he rants on, which is rich, seeing as I tried to communicate how unhappy I was, countless times. I even showed him my packet of anti-depressants, for God's sake, as if that would ram the point home.

Do they have any side effects? he'd asked.

Well, yes, Dr Monroe said they can affect your libido a bit.

Oh, he'd said, smirking. *I hope it's in the right way!*

Now, though, he's not joking. He is raving on, not even listening when I try to interject, and all the while my customers are drifting around the shop, and I should be assisting them, trying to make a sale.

'I really have to go now,' I cut in, finishing the call abruptly when they bring a bronze-framed mirror to the counter. As I tissue-wrap it, I am aware of blinking back tears.

'Are you okay?' the woman asks, clearly concerned.

'Yes, I'm fine, thank you.' I force a tight smile. 'Kids,' I add with a small laugh, as if that explains everything. But better for her to think I've had an obstinate teenager on the phone than a distraught husband.

Guilt gnaws away at me all afternoon. It doesn't help that the shop is deathly quiet for the rest of the day; sometimes I wish my work was more hectic, like Nate's is, although God knows he moaned about it often enough.

'D'you think I should have just put up with everything as

198

it was, and stayed with Nate?' I ask Abby later over dinner in front of the TV.

'Why are you saying this?' Abby places her fork in her pasta bowl. 'Has he phoned you again?'

I nod. 'He's so upset, Abs. It's unbearable . . .'

'Of course he is,' she says gently. 'The fact is, he wants to still be together. Have you ever thought that you might just need a break? That you might get back together, I mean, as long as things could be different?'

I shake my head. 'I can't imagine Nate changing for anyone.'

Abby looks at me. 'D'you think you really meant everything you put on that list? I'm sorry, I might sound a bit dense here, but I never quite understood what it was about.'

'Well, you know Rachel suggested I wrote it,' I remind her. 'She said it would help to clarify my thoughts.'

'Right. Like a sort of diary?' She adjusts her sleek blonde ponytail.

'Yeah. Only she meant for me to list the good *and* the bad things, so I could get a clearer picture – and I forgot to write down any of the good.'

'You know what I think?' she offers gently. 'I think you just need more time, away from everything for a little while. You can stay here as long as you like, you know.'

'But it's been a month already . . .'

'That's fine,' she insists. 'Just think of that spare room as yours.' She smiles and squeezes my hand. 'I just want to take care of you for a bit. Maybe *that's* the thing, d'you think? This is no one's fault. But you just haven't been taken care of for a very long time.'

'Yes, maybe you're right.' I wipe at my eyes. 'Abs,' I add, 'I don't know what I'd do without you.'

'Hey.' She pushes a strand of hair from my face. 'Remember I've known Nate for twenty-odd years, and I do realise what he's like. I know he's not the best communicator, and he doesn't always remember to show appreciation, or that he cares—'

'Tell me about it,' I say dryly.

'But, you know he does love you, don't you?'

'Yes, I know.' Something seems to twist inside me.

Her mobile rings on the coffee table, and I see her hesitate to answer it.

'Take it,' I say. 'I'm fine – honestly . . .' I jump up and go through to the kitchen to wash our supper things. Abby appears a few moments later.

'Hon, I'm sorry – Phoebe's had to go home. She's not feeling well. I don't like to think of Brian manning the bar by himself, so I really should go in . . .'

'Off you go,' I tell her. 'I'll be fine here. I'll probably just have an early night.'

She ums and ahs some more, and now it's my turn to insist she goes, which leaves me alone, replaying today's conversation with Nate.

Couldn't you have given me a chance, instead of springing this on me?

Given him a chance! What did he think I was trying to do when I suggested we went for couples counselling?

'What do we need that for?' he'd exclaimed as we stood face to face in our kitchen. 'We're fine, aren't we?'

'I don't feel fine,' I'd retorted. 'I feel completely over-burdened, to be honest, like we're not a proper couple anymore. It's as if we happen to live in the same house. Come on, Nate. You must feel it too . . .'

'I don't feel *anything*—'

'Well, that much is true!' I'd exclaimed.

200

He fell into a sulk then, his default setting when things don't go his way. 'There's no way I'm lying on a stranger's couch, telling them my innermost feelings,' he huffed.

'Because you don't have any,' I shot back, at which he tossed the oven gloves across the kitchen – probably the most violent gesture he's ever made.

'And therapists don't have couches,' I added. 'That's only in films.'

'Therapy,' he repeated witheringly. 'Isn't it all about raking over your childhood, crying because you weren't allowed – I don't know – a trampoline at seven years old?'

Fury bubbled up in me then. 'Why can't you take this seriously? Why can't we talk about something that matters for once?'

Nate glared at me. 'We can – of course we can. I just don't think there's any point in actually *paying* someone—'

'Of course there's a point, if you care about us. Is that what you're saying? That you don't care enough to try to make things better?'

We both flinched at the sound of the front door opening. Flynn was home. 'If you think you need therapy,' Nate mumbled, 'then why don't you just see someone by yourself?'

When I remember all that, resentment starts to build in me again – and I know I was right to leave him. And now, having tried, unsuccessfully, to settle in front of the TV, I pour a glass of wine and fiddle with my phone, replying to a text from Michelle, checking on how I'm doing.

I'm lucky, I decide, to have friends who care; but I can't stay at Abby's forever. When I have a place of my own, I'll ask Flynn if he wants to live with me. That would be better; the two of us together, close enough to Nate so he can see him whenever he wants – although, of course, it's quite likely that he'll choose to stay with his dad.

It's just gone nine, and I'm finishing my second glass of wine when my phone rings. Nate again, I imagine, grabbing it from the coffee table and vowing to be firmer this time: *Don't phone me at work unless it's an actual emergency!* But it's not Nate's name on the screen. It's Brett.

'Hi!' I say in surprise, aware that I shouldn't be so pleased to hear from him.

'Hey,' he says brightly. 'Hope it's okay to call?'

'Of course it is, yes. It's lovely to hear from you.'

'So good to catch up, wasn't it? That was such a fun night.'

'It was,' I say truthfully, figuring now that of course he's calling to organise another gathering; a party or some kind of event.

'So, how are things going?'

'Getting there, I think,' I fib.

'That's good to hear. So, um, I was just wondering if you fancied a drink sometime?'

Just us? I want to ask – but of course that's what he means. 'That would be lovely,' I say.

'Great. Well, look – I'm sorry I haven't called until now. I wasn't sure, you know, if it'd be okay with all the stuff that's been happening.' He pauses. 'But it really was lovely to see you again. Are you free any nights this week?'

'Um, I think so,' I say, feigning uncertainty.

'Well, look, I have a client in Hesslevale. I'm working on rebranding for a pie company and I thought maybe, if we could get together after my meeting, we could have dinner or something?'

202

So not just a drink, but dinner. 'That sounds great,' I say, as if all of this is perfectly normal. I shrug off a wave of guilt. 'So, when's your meeting?'

'I wanted to check with you first. How about Thursday? Are you free then?'

I find myself smiling as I wander through to Abby's kitchen and top up my glass. 'Thursday's good for me,' I say. 'Shall we chat nearer the time and sort out a time and place?'

'Yes, let's do that,' Brett says. We finish the call, and as I climb into Abby's spare bed, I reassure myself that of course it's okay to meet him. It's just dinner, after all. A catch-up with an old friend; that's definitely all it's going to be. But still, for the first time since I wrote that damned list, I feel a sense of lightness settling over me as I drift off to sleep.

Chapter Twenty-One

Nate

Although I'm grateful for their concern, it's also something of a relief that Liv, Eric and Nadira have calmed down about my newly single state. I am no longer the subject of fretful glances or copious invitations to go round to dinner. Naturally, they were all taken aback when I snuck off from Liv's barbecue without saying goodbye. However, nearly three weeks on – and over a month since Sinead left me – my only real regret about that night is the fact that my watch still hasn't been found.

'Would you, erm . . . mind checking inside the Wendy house?' I asked, last time I brought it up.

'The Wendy house?' Liv spluttered. 'How on earth would it have got in there?'

I shrugged. 'I, er, just thought it might be worth a look . . .'

'What were you doing in the Wendy house?' She'd stared at me.

I considered explaining that I'd been sheltering from the rain – because, of course, that would have seemed normal when there was a perfectly serviceable, proper

204

house just a few metres away, *where everyone else went*. 'I just, er, sat in it for a few minutes,' I muttered. 'I sort of needed to be by myself.'

'Ava did mention that she found a load of watermelon skins in there,' Liv added.

'Probably taken in by foxes,' I remarked, suddenly the nature expert.

'Then they must have taken the tray in there too,' she said with a smile.

A little light teasing, I could cope with. In fact, for the first time in my life, I'm thankful for the non-stop nature of my working days. If it wasn't for Flynn, I'd volunteer to work Saturdays too – not that our weekends together amount to much really. Whilst they still stretch on interminably, at least the hours fly by at the test centres. I only manage a hasty phone exchange with Stan – of Stan's Records – who's back from his travels and suggests coming over to view my collection tonight.

'That okay for you?' he asks.

'Yes, sure,' I say, reminding myself why I'm doing this. *Your bloody record collection*, she wrote.

Back home on this rain-lashed Tuesday evening, I make fish fingers, oven chips and baked beans for the two of us – foods Sinead would never contemplate eating – and try, unsuccessfully, to engage Flynn in some chat about school, his teachers, his subjects. I know he excels at maths, music and history, whereas English he's not so hot on . . . at least, I *think* that's still the case. Tonight, though, my conversation openers come out sounding so clunky, I am almost relieved when he dumps his cutlery on his empty plate, then proceeds to make himself one of his beloved microwave cakes: ingredients chucked into a mug, stirred, then nuked for three minutes.

Leaving a flurry of flour and cocoa powder in his wake, he carries his concoction through to the living room.

'D'you have much homework tonight?' I ask, hovering in the doorway.

'Nah.' He's spooning the gloopy mess into his mouth with gusto, as if I hadn't made him any dinner at all.

'You don't seem to have much at the moment, do you?'

He merely shrugs and focuses on the contents of his mug.

Has homework stopped then? I want to ask. *Or are you still being given the normal amount but just never bothering to do it?* It doesn't feel like the right moment to prod him about this – but then, when *is* the right time? I don't want 'pays no attention to Flynn's education' to be added to my list of shortcomings.

'I meant to tell you,' I add, 'someone's coming round tonight to look at my records.'

'To *look* at them?' He frowns.

'I mean, to buy them, possibly. I'm hoping he'll take the lot.'

Flynn throws me a confused look. Admittedly, I was hoping for a more shocked response.

We look at each other for a moment, and I wait for him to cry out, *No, Dad, please! You can't possibly do that!*

'Why?' he asks, spooning in more cake.

I shrug. 'I just thought we could use the space.'

Flynn glances around at row upon row of neatly-aligned albums, then turns back to me. 'Have we got money trouble or something?'

'No,' I exclaim. 'Well, no more than usual. No – I just thought, do I really need to hang onto hundreds of records we hardly ever play? I mean, as you said, they're not *your* thing at all, so really, I just—' I stop babbling at the sound of a sharp rap on the door, and go to answer it.

Stan and I greet each other briskly. He is possibly aged around sixty, although it's tricky to tell. Short and thin and with an unseasonal tan, he has a fifties-style quiff, a triumph of styling and liberal usage of product, considering his dramatically receded hairline.

'Thanks for coming . . .' I form a tight smile and shake his hand.

'No problem. Thanks for calling me.' He follows me into the living room.

'This is my son Flynn,' I add.

'Hi, mate.' Stan beams at him. 'So, is it you who's persuaded your old man to part with his collection?'

'Er, not exactly,' Flynn says with an awkward laugh as he gathers himself up from the sofa. I catch him assessing Stan's black shirt, its collar embellished with white embroidery, as he zooms out of the room.

'Okay then,' Stan says, swaggering towards my records, his skinny legs tightly encased in drainpipe jeans. 'This is the lot, is it?'

'Yep, that's it,' I reply.

His wide smile creases his weathered face. 'It comes to a lot of people, this. You know when it's the right time, don't you?'

No, actually, I am only doing this to please my wife. 'I guess so,' I murmur, silently urging him to wrap up this transaction as swiftly as possible. It's like the last time I had to have a tooth pulled out. 'There's no saving this beauty, I'm afraid,' my dentist said. Then, rather than just yanking it out, he proceeded to chat away, gathering his implements together – rather sadistically, I felt – whilst trying to engage me in bloke-chat about golf, and the best way to go about treating a rotting fence, as if I'd share his interests, simply as a fellow male.

Stan is clearly in no hurry to leave. Records are pulled from the shelves, examined and discussed, then slotted neatly back into place. An hour – then two – drift by. Music booms down from Flynn's bedroom. I'd expected Stan to flick through my collection, but now he's accepted my rather half-hearted offer of a mug of tea, and then he spots my Fender which happened to be propped up in the corner of the living room, and we get to talking about guitars and records and bands we love. It turns out that Stan is a drummer. Although we have never played together, we know numerous people in common.

'I knew your face was familiar,' he says. 'Still playing these days?'

'No, that's all in the past for me,' I reply.

Stan nods. 'Other stuff gets in the way, doesn't it?'

'It certainly does,' I say, affecting a shrug to show that I don't care really.

Now Stan has arranged himself cross-legged on the floor, despite the sofa and armchairs being available. He pulls out a small, ratty notebook from a jeans pocket, plus a stubby pencil. 'Give me a minute to figure this out . . .'

The minute stretches to five, then ten, fifteen, and finally, he shows me the figure he's written down. 'I think that's fair, do you?'

'Yep, sounds good to me,' I say briskly, not really caring about the money at all. '. . . So, um . . . d'you want to take them tonight?'

'Might as well. I find it's best to deal with something like this right away.' He gives me a wry look, as if he knows what I'm thinking. 'Strike while the iron's hot, kinda thing.'

I blink at him. 'Are you worried I might change my mind?'

'It does happen.' Stan chuckles. 'Sentimental value and all that.'

I raise a smile. I can't bring myself to dislike the man; he's been perfectly decent company and, after all, I called *him*.

'Shall we pack them up now, then?' I suggest. 'D'you have boxes and stuff?'

'Yeah, plenty out in the van.'

And so the two of us pack up my entire collection into plastic crates. I'm relieved that Stan hasn't suggested I ask Flynn to help, as he'd struggle to lift hefty boxes of vinyl and, anyway, he's still holed up in his bedroom. Stan and I march back and forth from our living room to his battered old unmarked white van.

It's around half-ten, and I'm passing Stan a crate of back-breaking weight, when Howard and Katrina's front door opens.

'Hi there!' Howard says, bounding out with Monty straining on his lead.

'Hey, Howard,' I say with a tense smile.

'What's happening here, then?' His gaze lands upon the crate in my arms.

'Erm, this is Stan,' I explain. 'He's just bought my record collection.'

'Whoa, good work, Nate!' Howard beams. 'I've always said to Kristina – all those records, gathering dust and taking up so much room. How can Sinead even—' He catches himself and flushes. 'I mean, er, each to their own, of course. But who plays vinyl in this day and age?'

'Plenty of people,' Stan retorts. 'It's back, mate – big time, especially with the youngsters . . .'

'What, the old gramophone?' Howard chortles.

'Flynn has a turntable,' I remark dryly.

'Ah, yeah – but that'll be all new stuff. Not *old* stuff, clogging up your life . . .' Like he'd know anything about new *or* old stuff, with his collection of precisely four atrocities. 'Anyway, onwards and upwards, eh, Nate?' Howard barks. 'Nothing like a good old declutter to clear the head, haha!' Mercifully, Monty pulls hard on his lead, virtually dragging my neighbour down the street.

'Hmmmph,' Stan mutters as he reaches into a jacket pocket and pulls out a chequebook. 'I'm old-school,' he adds. 'Cheque okay with you?'

'Yes, of course.' He scribbles it, and I take it from him, feeling as if I have just sold one of my children.

'You know what?' he adds, tweaking his quiff. 'Most of the houses I go to, it's just a disinterested relative selling off a collection that they couldn't give a stuff about. So it's been great to meet someone like you, with music in your blood. You should come and meet the guys I play with. It's nothing serious – just a bunch of mates getting a few songs together, and we could do with some fresh input. D'you fancy that?'

'Erm, I'm not sure at the moment . . .' I picture a living room populated by several sixty-somethings, all wearing embroidered-collared shirts.

'Ah, well, the offer's there,' Stan says with a shrug, climbing into his van. He waves from the driver's side window, and off he goes, taking with him every album I have ever owned. The sight of his scrappy vehicle disappearing around the corner reminds me of standing here, in this very spot, watching Sinead drive away. Although I'm not married to Stan, obviously, I'm still hit by a wave of desolation as I step back inside.

Time to move on, I tell myself silently. *Time to grow up once and for all.*

In the living room now, I stare at the empty shelves. They look awful without my alphabetised albums – tatty and scuffed, and conspicuously bare. What shall I put on them instead? Pot plants? Cacti? Should I go to – I don't know – John Lewis for some vases and other decorative stuff? I'm not sure I'd have a clue what to choose. Sinead was always the one who had strong opinions on home furnishings and how things should look.

No, I decide: the shelves were built for records, and now I don't have any, they simply have to go. I fetch my rarely-used toolbox from the shed and, as quietly as possible so as not to alert Flynn, I disassemble them piece by piece. If only my wife could see me now, working quickly and efficiently, with a screwdriver! It turns out that taking them to bits is a lot simpler than building the darn things. Once the whole structure's in bits, I carry the sections out to the garden and prop them against the shed. Perhaps they'll be adopted as a shelter for wild-life? As far as Sinead is concerned, they'd be a darn sight more useful that way.

Back inside, as if to underline how truly together I am now, I put on a wash, mop the kitchen floor and, for some reason, find myself wondering whether Tanzie Miles had long to wait for her bus home tonight.

Chapter Twenty-Two

Sinead

Brett hurries into the pub, wet from the rain and looking around for me. I jump up from my corner seat and wave.

'Sorry I'm late,' he says, and kisses my cheek.

'It's fine. I've only been here five minutes,' I say truthfully.

'Well, this is nice.' Brett looks around the pub's small, cosy lounge, in which virtually every inch of wallspace is covered with framed sepia photographs of Hesslevale in days gone by.

'It's the pub that time forgot,' I say, smiling.

'It's lovely. I'm so glad places like this still exist. So, what are you having?' he asks.

'I'm fine just now, thanks.' I indicate the glass of wine I've already started to steady my nerves.

Brett nods, and as he orders a beer from the elderly lady at the bar, I decide that the Dog and Duck was a perfect choice for this wet Thursday night. Somewhat forgotten these days, it's tucked away down by the river, well away from the town centre where – I must admit, the possibility crossed my mind – there'd be zero chance of us running into Nate on a night out with Paolo or Eric.

Not that I have anything to hide, I remind myself as Brett heads back to our table. Of course I am allowed to go out and meet friends. 'So, how did your meeting go?' I ask him.

'The usual kind of scenario,' he replies. 'They had their own ideas, and I had mine, so it involved loads of discussion and compromise, but hopefully everyone'll be happy with the end result.' He grins and shrugs, and I decide he's ageing terribly well: there are a few lines around his clear blue eyes, and his short dark hair is greying just a touch, but his youthful sparkle's still there. The wide, warm smile, not to mention his trim body – he's wearing a smart navy blue shirt and black jeans – all add up to one pretty attractive package.

'I'm sure they will,' I say. 'What is it you're doing for them?'

'Well, they're a savoury pie company,' he explains.

'Brogan Mitchell? Everyone knows them around here—'

'That's the one. So they're looking for a new logo, packaging design – it'll be rolled out onto all of their vehicles and products, that kind of thing.' He says it so casually, as if it's nothing much at all.

'I've checked out your website,' I tell him, deciding not to mention that I've pored over his Facebook page too. 'You're a brilliant designer, Brett. Your work's sort of retro, which I love – but fresh and modern too.'

He smiles. 'Thank you, I'm glad you think so – but anyway, enough about that. What about you?' His gaze meets mine, and he adds, 'I assume your jewellery business is hardly top of your concerns right now . . .'

'No, it's not,' I say quickly.

Brett nods. 'I wasn't just trying to flatter you, that time we ran into each other in Smith's. D'you remember that day?'

'Yes, of course,' I say, a tad too eagerly. I resist the urge to tell him I remember precisely what he said: *You shouldn't let your talent go to waste.* 'But honestly,' I add, 'I'm living with a friend right now, so first I need to sort out somewhere of my own to live, and of course, there's the whole business with Nate, and trying to smooth things over with Flynn as best I can.'

He sips his beer. 'We don't have to talk about any of that, if you'd rather not.'

'No, it's all right, really. What I mean is, it's not a taboo subject.'

'Okay,' he says gently, 'so what actually happened?'

It strikes me as strange, as I skim over events of the past few years, that it all starts to tumble out far more easily than when I'm sitting in Rachel's sparse therapy room. However, I remember now that Brett was always one of those 'easy to talk to' people – in that he genuinely listens, interjecting only now and then. I remember from college when he'd often end up with a drunk girl trying to latch onto him, babbling about her rotten boyfriend or how her lecturer didn't 'get' what she was trying to do with her art. He was always kind to them – save the occasional surreptitious eye roll – and I lost count of the times he, sometimes aided by George, went off on missions to find a tipsy girl's friends and make sure she was taken safely home.

With just one glass of wine downed, I find myself telling Brett how Nate and I slipped into that state that so many long-term couples find themselves in: merely existing together. With a lack of thought and tenderness, virtually

214

zero meaningful communication, sex about three times a year – I actually tell Brett this, I can hardly believe it – you're left with a marriage that's little more than a legal arrangement.

'I can imagine how that must've felt,' he says.

'You haven't been married, though, or with anyone for that long.' I catch myself. 'Sorry – that sounded terribly judgemental. I didn't mean—'

'Don't worry,' Brett cuts in. 'You're right. Vanessa and I managed four years, but of course, we have Corey. We still get along . . .'

'Then there was the quinoa girl,' I remind him with a smile.

He chuckles. 'Hannah. Six months.' His eyes glint playfully. 'I'm making them seem like jail sentences, but actually, you know, they were good relationships at the time.'

I consider this. Will I ever be able to look back at my marriage and consider it 'good'?

'So, with you,' he continues, 'there was no one single thing that made you leave?'

'You mean, did he have an affair or something?' I shake my head. 'No, Nate would never have done that. In fact, the final straw was something terribly trivial . . .' I pause, realising how trite this is going to sound. 'We have mice, you see. And I'd been on at him to set the traps, and he just wouldn't.' I smile wryly. 'I know it sounds ridiculous that I couldn't bring myself to set a few stupid traps . . .'

'Sounds reasonable to me. It's the way they might snap down on your fingers when you're edging them into position, right?'

'Yes,' I say, relieved that he seems to understand, rather

than viewing me as merely feeble. 'So, it was sort of that – although of course, that wasn't the real reason.'

'I didn't imagine you'd have walked out on your marriage because of a few mice,' he says with a smile. Now we fall into talking about Flynn, and Brett's son Corey, who shares a love of guitar playing. 'Flynn can play guitar?' he says in surprise.

'Yes.' I nod. 'Nate taught him. He helped him work around the limitations with his hand mobility and came up with different ways for playing tricky chords.'

'Wow.' He blows out air. 'That's impressive.'

'Yeah, Flynn's very dedicated,' I say, wondering now if he was referring to Nate.

We have another round of drinks – Brett travelled by train today – and then a third. I tell him about my depression, medication and therapy (gratifyingly, he doesn't grab his jacket and leave), then the conversation lightens as we catch up on gossip about various characters from our student days. By the time I go to the ladies', I realise a whole two hours have flown by, during which we haven't even touched upon the subject of where we might go for dinner. More crucially, I haven't felt sad, or remorseful, since he walked into the pub. I'm just aware of wishing we could slow down time, and eke out the evening, as I make our way back to our table.

We finish our drinks, and decide on a quick supper at the bistro at the far end of town; another rather forgotten haunt, which is half-empty and feels pleasingly old-fashioned with its candles in bottles dribbled with wax. We both order fish, and share sides of green beans with balsamic, a ceramic pot of dauphinoise potatoes, and yet more wine. And only now, in the flickering candlelight, with jazz playing softly, do I start to wonder what this night is really all about.

'We should do this again,' Brett says, setting down his cutlery onto his empty plate.

'I'd love to,' I say. 'Honestly, apart from our reunion night, it's pretty much the only time I've actually felt a little bit more like my old self.' I pause. 'Since it happened, you know.'

'Well, I'm glad to hear that.' Brett looks at me across the table, and something stirs in me, just as it did all those years ago, at that party, when we found ourselves kissing in a darkened hallway. His arms slid around me that night, and one thought rang loud and clear in my head – *I am kissing Brett O'Hara!* – as I leaned back into the thick layer of coats and jackets hanging on hooks behind me.

The waitress clears our table. As Brett has to catch the last train back to Leeds, we decline dessert and coffee. There's a small, good-natured verbal tussle as I insist on splitting the bill, and then I'm pulling on my new red jacket over the simple navy blue dress I chose so carefully tonight. My hair, which I scooped up into some approximation of a casual updo, has partly come undone, but I don't care about that now.

It doesn't occur to me that anyone could spot us together as we start to walk through the back streets towards the railway station – because we are not doing anything wrong. Nor am I taken aback when we stop outside the station entrance, and Brett says, rather hesitantly, 'I have to tell you, Sinead, you look absolutely lovely tonight.'

I smile, sensing my cheeks flushing. 'Thank you. You look good too. I've really enjoyed myself, you know. It was just what I needed.'

'Me too, after a whole afternoon of pie-talk.'

I laugh, and we pause for a moment, both of us feeling

217

a spark between us; I know he senses it too, because he touches the side of my face, and then my heart seems to stop as he kisses me – not on the cheek this time, like an old college friend might, but softly on the lips.

It's not like that long-ago kiss at the party, which we realised afterwards had carried on for the entire duration of the hostess's compilation CD. No, this one lasts perhaps a second or two. But I can still feel it, gentle as a feather on my lips, as we say our goodbyes, and he hurries away to catch his last train home. He turns and waves, then disappears from sight.

For a few moments I just stand there in the deserted street, thinking: *I have just kissed Brett O'Hara.* In the days that followed the student party, when it became clear that we would just carry on as friends – that he certainly wasn't looking for a serious girlfriend – I could barely look him in the eye. I just nurtured my secret crush, and even distanced myself for a while, in my heroic attempt to show that I held no romantic yearnings for him whatsoever.

However, tonight I am neither embarrassed nor ashamed as I start to walk home. And when guilt niggles at me – guilt at how Nate and Flynn would react, if they knew – I steel myself and firmly push it away.

Chapter Twenty-Three

Nate

Despite Sinead's insistence that she's still 'not ready' for an evening out with me, the last few days have passed in a not entirely disastrous fashion, in terms of working my way through The List. The records and shitty shelves have gone, and I've woken up on several mornings to be greeted by yet more mouse carcasses (*carci*?). More significantly, Flynn and I seem to have fallen into a new routine of him getting up for school with only minimal nagging (clearly, he is respecting my boundaries, whatever they might be!). Just as well Sinead doesn't know that he is enjoying his new-style breakfast (Oreos, juice), despite my suggestions for healthier options.

Mum has also called several times, and I hope I've handled her kindly but firmly. 'I'm worried about you, Nate.' 'I'm okay, Mum. Really.' 'You say that – but I know you. You bottle things up. Can I come over, cook something for you?' 'Mum – I can cook perfectly well, thank you!' And I really am fine – well, fine-*ish* – whiling away the evenings trying to read the same chapter of that Berlin book over and over. And tonight, on this wet Thursday,

I even allowed myself to be hauled out for a few beers by Paolo, as Flynn was heading over to Max's yet again.

Like last time, we chose the Wheatsheaf over the Lamb and Flag (due to the Abby issue: I'm hopeful that I *will* be able to see her again, and visit her pub, once the dust has settled. I'm just not quite sure how long dust takes to settle in this kind of scenario). Anyway, the Wheat, as it's known, was pleasantly buzzing by 8 p.m., and Paolo was buoyant company, full of amusing stories about rewiring a house and discovering a dead crow in an attic, and some lady trying to plant a kiss on his lips when he had only come around to fit a new centre light. This happens to Paolo. Women gravitate towards him – not that he would ever take advantage of any such situation, so devoted is he to the beautiful Bea.

In return, I hope I amused him by telling him about a candidate of mine who reeked of booze – after a heavy session the night before – and another who, when told she'd failed, asked, 'Could we just erase all that and start the test over again?' Like there are second chances in life.

As for my second chance with Sinead, we touched on it only briefly. Paolo was baffled, but amused, when I told him about my Tanzie encounter at Liv's barbecue. 'I'd never fraternise with a candidate normally,' I added.

'I wouldn't call it fraternising,' he said with a grin. 'Sounds more like you were taken hostage.'

'Actually,' I remarked, 'she was pretty helpful about how I might persuade Sinead to come back home.'

'In what way?' he exclaimed.

I started to explain that it was all about showing I cared about her as an individual with needs and dreams of her own. 'Although I'm not quite sure how I'm going to prove that I'm a better person now, if she won't even agree to spend any proper time with me.'

'She won't see you at all?' he asked, frowning.

'Oh, just briefly, whenever I've dropped Flynn over at Abby's.' That's how I always refer to that smart, modern house; I can't bear to say 'her place'.

'Can't you just buy her something really thoughtful, that she'll love?'

I shook my head. 'This isn't about giving her material things.'

'Oh, come on,' he urged me, 'how about buying her something special, like, um . . . lingerie?'

'Lingerie,' I spluttered, 'when we've split up? It hardly seems like the right kind of present, timing-wise.'

Paolo chuckled. 'I don't mean tacky stuff. I mean something frighteningly expensive that she'd never buy herself. What d'you call those silky things for the top half . . .?'

Unfortunately, this brought to mind the scrap of gauzy pink fabric I'd spotted poking out of the box when Sinead was bagging up her possessions. 'Not sure,' I said. 'I've never been good on the names of women's underwear. I mean, it could never be my specialist subject—'

'Just as well it never comes up in the pub quiz,' he said with a smile. 'God, I used to study that stuff as a teenager. Pored over all these mail-order books that used to come into the house. Studied it like I was preparing for an exam.'

'Pervert,' I sniggered, draining my glass.

'Oh, c'mon,' he guffawed. 'Don't tell me you didn't have a quick wank over the underwear section in your mum's Grattan catalogue.'

I spluttered. 'I don't think she ever got the Grattan's catalogue.'

'Well, it didn't have to be Grattan. It could've been Littlewoods or—'

'I think she got the Next directory,' I added.

'There you go, then. Bet you had a good pore over that . . .'

'I was more interested in the storage solutions section,' I retorted.

Paolo rolled his eyes, and we laughed. 'Bet you were. But I guess people are into all kinds of weird shit. My cousin had a thing about Esther Rantzen and her big teeth.' This caused me to choke on a mouthful of beer which, while hardly decorous, cheered me up no end and reassured me, as we said goodnight and I started to make my way home, that perhaps the world as I knew it hadn't ended.

Thank God for friends, I reflected, suspecting that drunken sentimentality might have been taking hold. Although I'd only had three pints, they had certainly rushed to my head – perhaps because I hadn't bothered with a proper dinner, just scoffed some sad-loner Jacob's crackers and cheese. Just as well I'd booked a day off tomorrow – if only due to Liv nagging that I really must start taking some of the copious leave I had stacked up, and she really wouldn't have me just working and working without ever taking a break.

Chips, I decided: that was what was needed now. A lovely bag of steaming, salty chips – only, when I passed the most popular chippie, on the high street, they were just closing for the night. There's another one, which I thought may be open later, tucked away down by the railway station, so that's where I headed, feeling quite buoyant for a man who'd recently been dumped by his wife.

The chippie was open, and I started on my bag of steaming fries as soon as I stepped back outside. I was just thinking that nothing tastes better than hot fried potato when you're a bit pissed when I happened to spot a couple strolling along a few metres ahead of me. The man, I barely registered. But the woman . . . well, this was happening to me now and again: my heart sort of clenching whenever I spotted someone who looked a little like Sinead.

I'd seen phantom Sineads striding around Solworth while I'd been conducting tests, and yet more when I was out walking Scout. And here was another one, stopping now in front of the railway station's entrance.

I stood dead still and posted a chip into my mouth, suddenly not hungry at all. My God, she looked like my wife from the back. It was the hair colour, the shape of her shoulders and neck, and the way she carried herself. But the woman's hair was styled in a way that Sinead never does hers, and she was wearing a swingy red jacket that, whilst eye-catching and stylish, wouldn't be my wife's kind of thing at all. And anyway, she was with her man.

The couple turned to each other and kissed. Something about the sight of two people being so tender and affectionate caused my whole body to ache. One of them was obviously going to catch a train. For that moment, they looked as if it was actually quite painful for them to part.

I knew I shouldn't be standing there, staring like some kind of lunatic. So I turned quickly, dumped my barely-touched bag of chips into the nearest litter bin, and bent my head against the rain as I hurried home.

Chapter Twenty-Four

I spend my Friday off gardening, fiddling about on guitar and listening to music on Spotify on my laptop (I have to say, it lacks the depth and quality of vinyl; on the plus side, as it requires no physical storage, it cannot be deemed an eyesore). While it's all pleasant enough, as the afternoon drifts on, I find myself looking forward to Flynn coming home from school. I've decided to suggest a pizza and movie night of our own tonight, as long as he doesn't have other plans.

However, when he appears, it transpires that he *is* intending to watch a film tonight – but not with me. Sinead is taking him to the cinema in Bradford. A proper city night out! Well, good for them. After a perfunctory résumé of his day, he rushes off. Apparently, she is parked in our street; they need to leave immediately as they're eating out before the film. Pizza, probably. What's wrong with the gigantic Marks & Spencer pepperoni – plus extra treats – that I went out specially for this afternoon?

Well, sod *that*, I decide, after he's gone, hurt that Sinead couldn't even bear to come to the house and say hello.

And now, having been unable to tempt Flynn with my ciabatta doughballs with garlic butter dip, I hardly feel like tucking into them either. In fact, why shouldn't I go out for dinner too, by myself? That'll show them! So, where to choose for my own night out? Of course, there's still Angus Pew's food contamination issue, which gnaws away at the worry centre of my brain from time to time. None of the pubs are terribly appealing; I'd probably be spotted by someone I know – a situation I'd rather avoid.

Look – there's Nate Turner, having dinner all by himself on a Friday night. Have you heard that his wife left him?

I know where to go. The fact that it's somewhere Sinead and I would never frequent serves only to heighten its appeal, as I won't be plagued by unwelcome thoughts, such as, 'What would she order?' Or, 'Oh, look – sea bass. My wife's favourite fish!' No, I decide, sensing my appetite building now, Sinead definitely *wouldn't* be thrilled by my restaurant of choice tonight.

Only four of the dozen or so tables in Burger Bill's are occupied when I arrive just after 9 p.m. 'A *thousand* permutations?' I exclaim, looking up at Tanzie in her tangerine shirt, which I have to say clashes startlingly with the purplish hue of her hair.

'That's right,' she says with a broad smile.

'But . . . how can that even be possible?'

She jabs at the enormous laminated menu I'm holding. 'Well, with your patties you've got the option of beef, chicken, salmon or veggie. Then there are eleven cheese options, thirty-two toppings and twenty-one sauces . . .' She pauses for breath. 'Are you any good at maths?'

'Not bad, but I'll take your word for it . . .' I focus back at the shiny menu, the white type on a black background proving a devil to read. The thumping music and orange walls, not to mention the squiggly graphics of dancing gherkins on the menu, suggest that the place is aimed at a somewhat younger demographic. However, Tanzie's cheery manner is making me glad I decided to come here after all. 'I'm not used to this much choice,' I add.

'The point is that customers can build their own meal,' she says patiently.

I look back at the menu, conscious that Tanzie has other tables to attend to – but now, with the knowledge that the patty/topping/sauce permutations are virtually infinite, I am trapped in indecision.

'D'you like beef?' she suggests.

Oh God, beef. As Sinead will only eat creatures from the sea, and not land, we never have it at home. 'I do, yes. I *love* beef.'

'Well, that's what I always go for,' she says brightly. 'The dirty beef burger with crispy salad, pickles, Monterey Jack cheese, piri piri sauce . . .'

'What exactly is a dirty burger?'

'It just means messy and juicy with big flavours,' she explains.

'Tons of salt, yes.' My stomach growls in anticipation. 'And piri piri sauce . . . what's that?'

She laughs. 'Where have you *been*, Nate? It's just hot sauce, with chillies in. You sound just like my dad. He's so suspicious and weird about food . . .'

'Hey, I'm not weird . . .'

'He won't even eat pasta, for goodness' sake,' she cuts in. 'I mean, pasta! I forget it's not actually British, don't you?'

'Absolutely . . .'

'God help the lady who tried to serve it up to him in

his care home: "I hope you're not expecting me to eat this foreign muck!"' She honks with laughter. 'You're okay with fries, I take it?'

'Yes, of course,' I say. She chuckles, and I realise that, while I have shared an alarming amount of detail about my private life with her – under duress, I might add – I know very little about hers, bar the basic details. It's not that I particularly *want* to know more about her. However, she is bright and engaging and seems terribly kind, if a little overwhelming, and I can't quite get my head around why she has landed herself with a slob like Gary.

'Anything else?' she asks.

'Just a Coke please.' I glance furtively towards the door to the kitchen. 'Can I ask you something?'

'Go ahead.'

'Um . . . d'you know all the chefs who work here?'

'Yeah, of course I do. There's usually two at a time. It's Ted and Richard tonight . . .'

I lower my voice to a whisper. 'There isn't an Angus Pew working here?'

'Never heard of him,' she replies, frowning. 'Why d'you ask?'

'Just someone I'm hoping to avoid,' I say quickly.

Now Tanzie is studying me intently, and I realise my mistake in bringing this up. 'C'mon,' she urges, 'you can't start to tell me and then not.' Across the restaurant, a woman raises a hand to attract Tanzie's attention.

'It's nothing,' I mutter, scanning the room. 'Just a guy who failed his test with me. Said he's a chef at some restaurant in Hesslevale – he wouldn't tell me which one – and if he sees me eating there . . .' I tail off with a shudder.

'You mean, he'll do something to your food?' Her green eyes widen.

'He threatened to, yeah.'

'What, like, spit on it or something?'

'I've no idea, he didn't specify . . .'

'Or put snot on it?'

'I don't know! Can we leave it now, please?'

'God,' she says, grimacing. 'Well, don't worry – you're safe here.' With a pat of my arm, off she goes, leaving me to study my surroundings with feigned interest, as if I have arrived from some distant planet where there are no burger joints; then, stuck for how to occupy myself, I turn my attention to my phone and prod at it, finally settling on the list function.

My plan is to make notes about the points on Sinead's list which I might try to tackle next. I inhale deeply and run through it in my head. Obviously, I know it off by heart; *this* could be my specialist subject. But I can't think of anything to note down. My brain is drained, my energies consumed by the anticipation of a vast platter of fast food.

'You look miles away there,' Tanzie remarks as she brings my burger, which is surprisingly delicious: a veritable feast of sizzling red meat, cheese, fat and salt, all jammed together with wooden sticks and involving a mere cursory nod towards greenery. It's like being in a service station caff with one of the bands again – only everything is bigger and juicer than I can ever remember. The chips, heaped generously in a silvery receptacle (I knew zinc buckets were trendy!) are equally pleasing. In case I'm not quite sending myself off to the coronary ward, I sprinkle extra salt all over everything. *See what you think about that, Sinead!*

228

'How was that?' Tanzie asks when I've devoured the lot.

'Really good, thank you,' I enthuse.

'You sound amazed.' She laughs. By now, the other remaining customers are getting ready to leave; minutes later, it's just me and Tanzie. Looking rather tired now, she plonks herself down on the chair opposite.

'So, is that your shift over for the night?' I ask.

She grimaces. 'Pretty much. Just got to wipe the tables and cash up . . .'

'How will you get home?' Somehow, I can't imagine Gary rousing himself to come and fetch her.

'Last bus,' she replies. 'Twenty past eleven.'

I frown at her. 'It's only just gone ten now. That's an awfully long wait. Will you hang about in here?'

'No, Ted'll want to lock up before then. I'll just wait at the bus stop,' she says matter-of-factly.

I glance at the rain-streaked window, then back at Tanzie. 'For, what, over an hour? In this weather?'

She laughs, in the way that Flynn does, when I'm being patronising for perhaps suggesting that he might deign to wear proper, watertight shoes, and not flimsy canvas articles, in three-inch snow. 'I *am* a grown-up, and this is Hesslevale, remember. There's no crime here . . .'

'The Happy Fryer's window was smashed last weekend!'

'. . . and there is actually a bus shelter.' She gives me a bemused look. 'Not that *you* ever have to lower yourself to using public transport . . .'

'Of course I do,' I retort.

'When did you last take the bus, then?'

'Erm . . .' I roll up my paper napkin into a skinny sausage and frown. 'It must be when we took Flynn to the safari park . . .'

'That's not a public transport bus,' Tanzie retorts.

'Of course it is. It's for lots of people – the general public . . .'

'The general public don't pay twenty quid to be driven round a safari park . . .'

I laugh in disbelief. I know she's winding me up, but now it feels imperative to win this debate. 'They do, actually,' I retort. 'And there's a choice, you know – you can either drive around in your own car . . .'

'*If* you can drive,' she chips in.

'Yes, of course – or you can take the bus—'

'Which is painted in zebra stripes.'

'And your point is . . .?'

Tanzie chuckles. 'Normal buses aren't zebra-striped. Anyway, look – here I am, babbling away when you're sitting there, waiting for your bill.' She springs up and makes for the counter.

'I'm not in any rush,' I call after her, because, actually, I am enjoying her company. It's far preferable to sitting at home alone.

She returns with my bill, then attends to the tables with her squirty disinfectant and cloth.

'Erm, I could give you a lift home, if you like,' I call over. 'It's awful weather and I really don't like the idea of you standing out there by yourself.'

She puts down the plastic bottle. 'Thanks, but it's fine. I do it all the time.'

'Well, I'd be happy to. I'd just have to let Flynn know, in case he comes home when I'm out—'

'Are you allowed to do that?'

'You mean, give you a lift? I don't see why not—'

She beams at me. 'I mean as a *driving examiner.* Are you allowed to give a lift to someone when you've done loads of their tests?'

I pause. 'Yes, of course I am.'

She hands me the card machine to settle up my bill, and I slide a generous tip rather self-consciously under my glass.

'I really do think you could've passed last time,' I add as I tap in my PIN number. 'You nearly nailed it. If you hadn't been so distracted—'

'I'm not looking for an assessment of my driving right now,' she says with a snort, 'but, actually, I will take your offer of a lift home, kind sir. So, where's your chariot?'

Chapter Twenty-Five

The drive to Tanzie's only takes twenty minutes, and she uses the time efficiently in order to grill me about my progress with The List. 'So, your records have gone?' she asks.

'Yep, all sold . . .'

'Even the Bruce Springsteens?'

'Even the Bruce Springsteens!'

She stares in wonder from the passenger seat. 'Well, she can't say you're not committed.'

'Maybe I *should* be committed,' I mutter, which she seems not to hear.

'So, what's next?'

'That's the tricky part,' I reply as we speed along the dark country road. 'I mean, it's easy to pick up Scout's poos and tackle the laundry and all that . . .'

'Why didn't you do it all before then?' she asks with a sly grin, and I frown, wondering whether or not she is teasing.

'I would have if she'd asked.'

She exhales through her nose. 'Women don't always *want* to have to ask. I mean, why should we?'

I glance at her. She seems to be harbouring a grudge against men in general; understandable, I guess, considering the specimen she's living with. *Lino's not the only thing he lays*, she reckons. Maybe her ex, Neil, was of that type too. I am keen to show her that I am not of that camp – not because I care what she thinks of me, but simply because it's not true.

'Nate?' she prompts me. 'Why should a woman have to ask her husband to do stuff?'

'Because it's useful to communicate?' I suggest.

She blinks at me, exasperated. 'Yes, but asking implies that it's the woman who's meant to be in charge, and he's just helping.'

'I've always been willing to help,' I insist, which seems to rile her even further. Perhaps it's not just Sinead I'm capable of irritating to the point of combustion – but the whole of womankind.

'You're still thinking of it as *helping*,' she says slowly, as if I am eight, 'when really it should be an equal partnership.'

'Oh. Yes, I see what you mean.' I focus on the road ahead, deciding right now that I won't be going in for a cuppa this time, even if she tries to lure me with a Penguin biscuit.

'So,' she adds in a calmer tone, 'how about the stuff on her list about you being a better, more thoughtful husband? The deeper stuff, I mean?'

'Ah, yes . . .' I run through them silently, relieved that she's stopped haranguing me for a moment or two. *You don't consider my needs,* is the one that springs to mind. 'I guess she thinks I took it for granted that she gave up her jewellery business to look after Flynn,' I murmur, more to myself than to Tanzie.

'She had a jewellery business?'

'Yeah, a pretty successful one too. She was in all the glossy magazines – *Elle, Marie Claire* . . .' I glance at Tanzie, who looks nonplussed. I'm guessing that she isn't a glossy magazine kind of person.

'Couldn't she get that up and running again?' she suggests.

'I suppose so, but—'

'Why couldn't she, with your support?'

'It's not as simple as that,' I say, feeling a little agitated myself now. 'I mean, she has a job—'

'Yeah, in a gift shop . . .'

'And she needs an income, especially as we're not together anymore . . .' I tail off, remembering that, if I can't put things right, then sometime pretty soon we'll be sorting out our finances and dividing everything up. The very thought fills me with dread, because then, it'll be final. There'll be no list to work from – no project. It'll be solicitors and divorce and the rest of my life spent without her . . . 'Anyway,' I add, 'enough about me. How have things been with you lately?'

'All right, I s'pose.' She throws me a guarded look. She has a certain expression, I realise, that she adopts when she is less sure of herself; a determined face, chin jutting out, as if she is trying to project an air of defiance.

We fall into silence, and I wonder what Flynn made of my hasty text: *Went out to dinner, giving someone a lift home, back v soon.*

'It's just . . . I hope you don't mind me bringing it up,' I add.

'Bringing what up?' she asks.

'Well, that night I was round at yours, you mentioned . . .' I pause. 'Um, you said there'd been a bit of a situation at home, that's all. And that worried me a bit.'

'Oh, that,' she mutters. 'Yeah, that was nothing . . .'

'Really?'

She nods mutely. 'Oh, all right. You want to know what happened that night?'

'Only if you feel comfortable telling me . . .'

'Okay, well – ever since then I've been sort of wishing Gary was trans.'

I throw her an incredulous look. 'You mean, you wish he liked wearing women's clothes?'

'Yeah. Well, underwear, specifically. In fact, a gigantic pink bra, even *more* specifically—'

'I'm sorry, you've kind of lost me now . . .'

'I found this bra,' she says emphatically, 'in our laundry basket that night, just before I stormed out with Wolfie and found *you*. We'd had a row about it. That was the situation I was talking about . . .'

'I see,' I murmur, turning off the wipers now the rain has finally subsided.

'Hideous thing, it was,' she continues. 'Definitely not mine . . .'

I inhale deeply, wondering what to do with this piece of information. I've never had a woman confide in me like this before. 'So, you think the bra might be Gary's?' I venture, giving her a quick look.

'No,' she retorts, as if I'm an idiot. 'I was only joking. But it belongs to *someone*, obviously.' She shrugs. 'He denies getting up to anything, but I know he's lying through his teeth.'

'Are you sure?' I ask.

Tanzie nods. 'Remember my last driving test?'

'Yes, of course.' *It's embedded in my brain . . .*

'Well, that day, on the way to the test centre, I spotted Gary's van parked where it shouldn't have been. He said

235

he was over in Bradford doing a job, but I spotted it in a side street on the edge of Solworth . . .'

'Right. That does sound odd . . .'

'That's why I was so distracted,' she adds.

'No, honestly, you drove pretty well that day!'

'Hmm,' she murmurs. 'Anyway, I phoned him just before I did my test. He was still adamant that he was in Bradford laying someone's floor . . .'

'Right. Could you have made a mistake, though? I mean, might it have been another van?'

'I don't think so,' she says, frowning.

We fall into silence for a few moments. 'And with the bra, well . . . are you sure there's no other explanation? I mean, could a visitor – a friend of yours – have left it at your place?'

Tanzie snorts. 'No one ever stays over. We don't have the space, and anyway, my friends can't stand Gary . . .'

I focus on the road ahead, trying to figure out other ways in which a rogue bra might have deposited itself in a random laundry basket. 'Could a bird have flown in through an open window with it?'

'Yeah – that's probably it,' she says, laughing bitterly now. 'I see birds flying around with bras dangling from their beaks all the time.'

I chuckle as I turn down her narrow unlit lane. 'Well, stranger things have happened. Or, you know how things get stuck to your shoe sometimes?'

She smirks as I park next to the rusting yellow van. It strikes me, not for the first time, that Gary could get off his lazy arse and pick up his wife after a lengthy shift.

'I bet that's it,' she exclaims. 'I'm living in the middle of nowhere, where's there's underwear strewn all over the place – and it got tangled up in my heel.' She laughs dryly. 'What are the chances of that?'

I smile at her, then glance out at the cottage that's silhouetted against the haze from the moon. 'Well, I'm sorry things aren't great between you and Gary. I do know how that feels . . .' I hesitate. 'I mean, sort of. But it's been nice talking to you tonight. You've cheered me up, so thank you for that . . .'

Tanzie musters a grin. '*And* you enjoyed your dirty burger.'

'Yes, I really did!'

Her smile settles. She is unconventionally pretty, I decide, with those striking green eyes and the oddly-tinted hair. I find myself wondering what colour it is really, probably because no other woman I know would choose that kind of shade. 'Nice talking to you too,' she says. 'Sorry about going on a bit. About the bra, I mean. I do tell my friends this kind of stuff, but sometimes I get the feeling they've heard enough, you know? About me and Gary, I mean. I s'pose there's only so many times they can tell me to leave him, and for me not to do anything about it . . .'

'I guess so,' I say, feeling rather out of my depth now.

'Maybe I should write a list of his faults?' she asks with a wry smile, then seems to catch herself. 'Sorry, Nate. I know it's not funny . . .'

'It's fine,' I say, truthfully. 'And, please, if you're ever stuck for getting home – I mean, if you miss a bus, or are going to have to wait ages, you can just call me, okay? If I'm home, it's not a problem . . .'

'That's *so* sweet of you,' she exclaims, 'but if I was really stuck, I'd just get a taxi—'

'I'm just saying, if you need me, it's fine.' She looks at

237

me as if she's about to protest some more, then agrees to take my number and taps it into her contacts.

'Okay,' she says breezily. 'I mean, I probably won't ever call, but—' She breaks off, then – startlingly – she throws her arms around my neck and hugs me.

I reel back, sensing myself blushing. 'Well, enjoy the rest of your evening,' I bluster, keen to escape now, back to Flynn – if he's home by now – and Scout, and my quiet, undramatic house.

'I'll try to,' she says. 'And thanks again. You're a good person, Nate . . .' She flashes another grin as she climbs out of my car. 'Considering you failed me all those times . . .'

I smile weakly. 'Will you book another test, d'you think?'

'Oh, I very much doubt it. Unless . . . would you be allowed to examine me?'

I laugh awkwardly at her choice of phrase.

'Swing me a favour?' she adds with a wink. 'Be a bit more lenient now we know each other—'

'You must know I couldn't do that!' I say, aghast.

'I'm *joking*,' she says, laughing.

'Anyway,' I add, 'technically, we're supposed to declare it if a candidate is a friend—'

She crooks a brow. 'Are we friends now, then?'

I look up at her. So brazen and opinionated: she really is something else. But I have to admit, the prospect of bumping into her from time to time doesn't exactly appal me during this particularly testing stage of my life. 'If we go by the guidelines set out by the Driver and Vehicle Standards Agency,' I reply, 'then yes, I guess we are.'

Chapter Twenty-Six

Sinead

A week has passed since my evening with Brett, and we've just met up again. It was just a quick coffee this time, after another of his meetings at Brogan Mitchell Pies. I felt more nervy this time, not due to being with Brett; we chatted easily, and my heartbeat seemed to quicken when our hands brushed under the table. However, it was just gone six – town was still busy – and we were installed in a coffee shop right on the high street. Several people I know vaguely popped in for takeaways and said a quick hello. We hugged briefly just before we parted outside the cafe – Brett was driving home this time – and I found myself panicking in case anyone (well, Nate, really) might happen to spot us and leap to the conclusion that this strikingly handsome man is the real reason I walked out.

'It's great to be in touch again,' Brett added with a warm smile.

'It really is,' I agreed, unable to stop myself from scanning the vicinity for any familiar faces. Then off he went, and with my head bowed, I speed-walked towards Abby's, sort of relieved that she'd be on duty at the Lamb and Flag until much later. Although she knew I was meeting Brett, and wasn't remotely judgemental, I was looking forward to a little time alone.

Brett and I have been texting and chatting most days – but where is this going, if anywhere at all? Of course, it would be way too soon for me to be dating – which we are definitely not. Flynn would be horrified, justifiably; anyway, I'm not remotely in the frame of mind to get involved with anyone right now. We're just mates hanging out, and in some ways it's precisely the *right* time to rekindle a friendship with someone from the past. There's something about being with a person who knew the younger you – before mortgages, pension plans and all that – that reminds you that you were young once, and full of life, the kind of girl who'd concoct a cauldron of rocket-fuel punch for a spur-of-the-moment party.

Never for one minute have I regretted or resented anything I've had to deal with regarding Flynn. However, spur-of-the-moment *anything* hasn't featured in my life for a very long time.

I let myself into Abby's house. As I take off my jacket, my phone trills from inside my bag at my feet. I grab at it; Nate again. 'Hi,' I say, hoping he doesn't detect the note of alarm in my voice. Did he spot me and Brett after all?

'Hi, love,' he says, sounding hesitant. 'Look, I, um . . .' He clears his throat. 'I just wanted to catch you for a quick chat. Is it a good time?'

'Er, yes, it's fine. I'm just in.' I wander through to the kitchen and fill the kettle.

'Well, look – I just wanted to say, I'm so sorry about

240

how I've been with you lately. Going off on one, I mean, when you were in the shop that time—'

'That's all right,' I say quickly, wondering why he's bringing that up now. We have talked several times since, about matters concerning Flynn: businesslike calls, conducted as swiftly as possible.

'I know I can be a real idiot,' he adds.

'Honestly, it's okay,' I murmur, still a little surprised by his apology.

'I really would like to see you,' Nate adds. 'I promise I won't get on at you or give you a hard time. I'd just like to . . . talk, in a more relaxed way. Would that be okay?'

I hesitate, trying to picture us out together in a restaurant or bar. Should I tell him I've seen Brett for dinner and a coffee? I can't imagine it would go down terribly well – but I'll mention it when I see him, in case Brett and I are spotted out and about, and Nate gets to hear of it. After all, I have nothing to hide.

'Yes, we can do that,' I say cautiously. 'I mean, go out somewhere, if you'd like to.'

'Like to?' Nate exclaims. 'Of course I would! Shall we have dinner then? Somewhere a bit special?'

'Oh, I don't really know if—'

'Is tomorrow night any good for you?' he asks eagerly.

Oh, God, that soon? 'Saturday would be better,' I say. *An extra day to build myself up for it.*

'Great! That's fantastic. I'll book somewhere then.' He pauses. 'I'm so pleased you've said yes. I know this is really hard for you, as much as it is for me. But I'll make sure we have a lovely evening, okay?' His voice cracks. I know he's upset again, and that I am the cause, and I can't help hating myself for it.

'Okay,' I murmur.

Our conversation falters, and I hear his intake of breath. 'Oh, darling,' he says, 'I know I shouldn't say this, but I'm *so* happy I'm going to be seeing you.'

*

Never mind a cup of tea right now. Instead, I am driven outside by a fierce desire for wine. There's no corner shop near Abby's; just the supermarket at the bottom of the hill. Here, I wander the aisles, choosing wine, then toothpaste, shampoo and shower gel so it doesn't look as if I am *just* buying wine – as if anyone would care what's in my basket. Without thinking, I toss in a box of tampons too, as I never seem to have any handy when I come on. It occurs to me then: when did I last have a period? It feels like quite a while ago – but then, perhaps all the upset has disrupted my cycle. Can sadness and guilt actually do that?

I stand there for a moment, trying to pinpoint precisely when it was – but nothing comes. However, I do remember the last occasion when Nate and I ended up making love, a few days before I left him . . .

A sense of dread creeps over me. *Surely* I can't be pregnant. I'm too old for that. Never mind the fact that we're not together and it would be an absolute disaster. I'm probably having an early menopause, I decide. It's my body's way of punishing me for walking out on my son.

Even so, I should find out for certain, just to put my mind at rest. Glancing furtively around, as if I am about to steal a bottle of conditioner, I drop a pregnancy test into my basket. Then, solely for concealment purposes, I place a packet of facial wipes on top.

242

Half an hour later I am standing alone in Abby's bathroom, holding the plastic stick and staring at two pink lines in the window, thinking, it can't be.

It *really* can't. We have done it precisely twice in something like six months, the last time being one of those angry shags – when you've bickered and then it turns into a brief flurry of, if not passion, pretty intense feelings swirling around. Then, afterwards, you go to sleep back to back.

I glance down. I'm still clutching the white stick, wondering if I'm seeing things or interpreting it incorrectly. But it's quite simple really. Either there is a second pink line, or there isn't. And there is most definitely a line.

Dread washes over me when I realise how happy Nate'll be, with smiles and hugs and tears, probably – and then devastated all over again.

Once upon a time, we wanted another child so much. This almost seems unfair – like winning the lottery the first time you buy a ticket, when your friends have had syndicates for decades – but then, it doesn't *feel* like a win. Far from it.

Abby and her ex tried for most of their married life, spending thousands on treatments along the way. And here I am, seemingly pregnant and recently separated, too old for a baby and not remotely wanting another child now. Before all this mess happened, I thought I was a pretty decent person. I never realised I am capable of causing so much hurt. But I know in my heart, as I wrap the stick in loo roll and drop it into the bin, that I simply cannot have another baby with Nate.

Chapter Twenty-Seven

Nate

Since I managed to persuade Sinead to come to dinner with me, I've felt slightly more optimistic about our future, to the point where I'm thinking: okay, perhaps it's just a break she wants. Understandably, I realise now, she was sick to the back teeth of me being so shabby and neglectful. I've changed, though. Really, I have.

'You're making pretty good progress,' Tanzie agrees as she skims through my printed-out copy of The List, which is now annotated with my various pencilled notes.

'Thanks,' I say as she hands it back to me. 'It really helped, talking it through with you.'

'Glad to be of service,' she says with a wide smile. 'It's good to see you're taking it seriously. I'm sure she'll appreciate it, Nate.'

'Well, I hope so.' I sip my coffee, wishing she'd sit down with me for a moment – but of course, she's working. It just seemed natural to pop in and see her for a catch-up, and it feels sort of right, having a new place to go to since my world turned upside down.

A tall, well-built man with slicked-back dark hair

– her boss, I'm guessing – glances over from the counter area.

'I suppose I hadn't really understood what the real problem was,' I add.

Tanzie nods. 'You'd been focusing on the minor things . . .'

I nod. 'When it wasn't really about those at all.'

As she leaves my table to attend to a newly-arrived group, I skim through the list again.

You don't listen to me.

You take me for granted.

You don't consider my needs . . .

The above three, I feel, can be rolled into one. While they're a little abstract, I hope Sinead will realise when I see her tomorrow night that I am trying to do my best as a husband and dad, after years of her feeling overburdened.

On the Flynn side of things, I took another day's leave today to accompany him to an appointment (not that I am expecting gales of applause for taking my son to hospital!). A new kind of muscle relaxant is to be administered in the hope of easing the stiffness in his hand. At first, I could sense resentment radiating from him as I sat beside him in the consultancy room; but we got along better as the day progressed, and we stopped off to buy him some trainers, plus guitar strings, on the way home. It shames me now to realise how often Sinead has taken time off work due to Flynn's numerous appointments, and it rarely occurred to me that perhaps I should do so more often.

No effort made re us as a couple . . .

This one, I am especially pleased about. I have booked a table for two at Elliot's on the edge of town, and I know she's going to love it.

245

You leave too much to me.

Tricky to address, seeing as we are not together at present, but if I can coax her back to the house after Elliot's, then I hope she'll be impressed by how smooth-running and gleaming everything is. I'm not expecting her to stay the night or anything; just that we might be able to prolong our evening for as long as possible.

You belittle my job and show no interest in it.

Topic number one, for our night out: does she regret giving up her jewellery business? How can I support her to get things started again, if that's what she wants? I am considering writing an agenda to consult secretly when she nips to the loo.

No spontaneity in our lives.

Perhaps an agenda might highlight my lack of impulsiveness. However, I hope to plan something spontaneous for her forthcoming birthday (can 'planning' and 'spontaneous' go together? I guess I can bend the rules).

Your bloody record collection.

Now in Stan's possession.

Your terrible attempts at DIY.

Now propped up in the garden and providing shelter for a hedgehog, as far as I can gather.

. . . and your blank refusal to get the professionals in.

As there's been nothing I've needed a tradesman for, I have yet to be able to demonstrate my willingness to fork out enormous amounts of cash to have various jobs done. Perhaps I can think of something that needs attending to? Should we have an unnecessary new patio laid?

Handing me a wodge of tenners to buy my own Christmas present . . .

Mindful of this – and of the ill-chosen leopard skirt – I shall take extra care over selecting her birthday gift.

Perhaps I could ask Tanzie to help me choose something? I look around to ask, but she is heading towards a table brandishing a tray laden with drinks.

Woolly boundaries re Flynn . . .

Whilst he's ditched me – without warning – as his personal guitar tutor, we do at least seem to be rubbing along okay. Although I should probably address the Oreos-for-breakast issue, none of his teeth appear to have crumbled – yet. Anyway, now doesn't seem to be the right time to suddenly come over all stern Victorian father, if that's what she means.

Mouse issue (traps!!!).

Carcass tally to date: eleven. Okay, so there wasn't just the one . . .

You treat me like an idiot (i.e., always texting to remind me not to leave things on trains).

Our evening at Elliot's will hopefully allow me to show her that this is not the case.

Don't make me feel special.

Ditto . . .

On and on it goes. I'd like to consult Tanzie for more Sinead-pleasing suggestions, but now the diner is filling up with teenagers wandering in after school, and she's far too busy, darting in and out of the kitchen with trays of food. Anyway, I should really go home and cook something nutritious for Flynn.

I pay for my coffee and thank her for listening yet again. 'I meant to say,' I add, beaming, 'I've booked a table for Elliot's for tomorrow night.'

She blinks at me and her face falls. 'Aw, Nate – you should've said. I'm working this Saturday!'

'Uh, no, I actually mean for Sinead and me,' I bluster, sensing myself reddening. My God: has she got the wrong

247

idea about us? I mean, I'm married (technically), and she lives with someone, and I'd never . . . I mean, I hadn't even *thought* . . .

'Of course,' Tanzie murmurs, looking down at her flat boots. 'I hope you have a fun night.'

I rub at my suddenly clammy forehead. 'I'm sorry, Tanzie. Really, I am. I didn't mean—'

Her face breaks into a grin. 'I'm joking,' she exclaims, laughing now. 'God, Nate. Why d'you take everything so seriously? That's brilliant. It's meant to be lovely. Kayla's been – her friend Paige's parents took her for a family celebration—'

'Well, I thought she'd like it,' I say, still sweating a little.

'Of course she will. *Now* you're getting it, aren't you?'

'I hope so,' I say, realising as I leave that I didn't ask if she found out who owned that pink bra. Although I don't want her to think of me as an unthinking arsehole either, perhaps the middle of her shift in the diner was neither the time nor the place to bring it up.

Still, it's puzzling me as I stride home. If Gary is sleeping around, then why on earth does she put up with it? She's bright and attractive, and she strikes me as being no pushover. After all, she's brought up three children – on her own for much of it, as far as I can gather. It's quite baffling. Perhaps, quite simply, she still loves him.

Back home, I check the final points on Sinead's list. There's the one about her therapist: *Keep referring to Rachel as 'your shrink' (i.e., making a joke of it and so belittling the issue).*

From now on, the word 'shrink' will be banished from my vocabulary and nothing she mentions will be belittled, ever again. I'll even go to couples counselling with her if she suggests it again. The very thought makes my back teeth clench together, but it'd be worth it, if she thinks it would help.

Constant untidiness . . .

Well, she can't accuse me of that anymore. At the first opportunity I shall show her round our house in the manner of an eager estate agent.

YOUR MOTHER!

Hmm, well, Mum seems to have gone quiet again. Sulking, probably, that I haven't taken her up on offers to come round and cook for me, as I'm incapable of operating a gas hob (I'm sure all will be fine – when she next needs a dog-sitting favour).

Refusal to pick up Scout's poos in garden!!!

These days, anyone could inspect our lawn with a magnifying glass, and they'd never guess we owned an animal of any kind.

So I'm getting there. While there's still work to be done, I feel sure that tomorrow, Sinead will realise I am trying, at least. And that I'm prepared to do anything to win her back.

*

And so Saturday comes, the thought of our date (an actual *date*!) keeping me going all day to the point where I'm not even riled by the elderly bloke who bangs the backs of my legs with his shopping trolley as I wait in the supermarket checkout queue.

When I run into Eric and Sarah in the high street, my change of demeanour must be apparent. 'You're looking a bit cheerier,' Eric remarks. 'Good day off yesterday?'

'Not bad,' I remark, then, as if I'd asked my crush to the school disco, I add, 'Sinead and I are going out for dinner tonight. I asked her, and she said yes!'

'That's fantastic,' Sarah says, squeezing my arm. 'Oh, Nate. Maybe she's having a change of heart? I do hope so.'

'Who knows?' I say, but of course, that's what I'm hoping for too. There's a flurry of 'good lucks!' as we part, and I march home, swinging my carrier bags of groceries, allowing myself to enjoy a wave of optimism for once.

Back home, Flynn has Max and Luke round. Impressively – although Sinead would probably beg to differ – they seize the sack of oven chips I've brought home and cook them, along with an impressive quantity of sausages. It may be less than six weeks since Sinead left me, but I'm finding it hard to believe that we ever had tofu and kale nestling in our fridge.

With almost three hours to go – it's just gone five, and I booked our table for eight – I take Scout on a long, meandering walk, more to kill time than anything else, and return to a riot of messy plates dotted about the kitchen. Over the sound of the boys' guitars upstairs, I clear up, then shave – a double-shave, actually, just in case . . . though, I can't imagine there'll be any kissing tonight. But Sinead always preferred me clean-shaven to stubbly ('Sandpaper face,' she'd remark, not entirely affectionately), so why not be ready, just in case? This is followed by possibly the longest shower of my life, interrupted only because Flynn bangs on the door, saying Luke is desperate for the loo. All that remains is to transform myself into an impressive vision of manhood (at least, as much as I can possibly muster).

'You're going out?' Flynn asks, appraising my appearance as he opens his bedroom door.

I glance down, as if surprised to see that I am in fact wearing a favourite shirt (a subtle burgundy check), my newest jeans, and have even attacked my shoes with a duster. 'Just meeting up with Mum,' I say casually.

'Oh.' This seems to surprise him and, with his friends being here, I don't want to go into any explanation. I'm sure he doesn't want to either.

'We're just grabbing a bite to eat,' I add, as if all of this is quite normal and recent events had never happened.

'That's nice,' he says warily. Behind him, I glimpse Luke and Max lounging, guitars strewn about.

'I'm sure it will be.' I beam into the room like an awkward teacher on his first day with a new class. 'So, everything okay here?'

Luke nods. 'Yeah.'

'Okay. Well, have fun, lads.' Did that sound patronising? Is 'fun' a word they associate with the kind of birthday parties where there'd be jelly and cake? 'Bye, then,' I add quickly.

'Bye, Dad,' Flynn says, and closes his bedroom door.

I head outside to the waiting taxi. Better not drive tonight, I decided earlier; I'll certainly need a drink, though not so much that I start ranting and raving, begging her to come home. It feels like a first date now, such is my state of anxious anticipation. As the taxi pulls off, I'm spiralling back to my actual first date with Sinead, after we'd met and exchanged numbers at the All Saints gig. *Really enjoyed meeting you,* I'd said, when I'd mustered the courage to call her. *Wondered if you'd like to go for a drink sometime?* Funny how certain conversations imprint themselves on your brain. *Please-say-yes-please-say-yes.* Numerous times, I'd picked up the phone in my shared house – having waited until all my housemates were out – and started to tap out the digits. But I kept losing my nerve. Women have no idea what it's like for blokes, having to do this stuff, poised for rejection. What would a beautiful girl like Sinead want with a geek like me?

Yes, she'd said, that would be lovely. No, she wasn't free the following night (dammit, why had I sounded so keen?). Or the next night, come to that. It was clear that her social life was far more interesting than mine. In five days' time, she could see me – but it was worth the wait. There she'd been, sitting in the pub, close to her flat in Leeds: my train from Hesslevale had been delayed, so I was late. As this was in the days before social media, the only picture of her I'd been able to access was the one that had imprinted itself on my brain. When I walked towards her, I realised that image hadn't done her justice. As her delicate face broke into the sunniest smile, she was even more lovely than I'd remembered.

I glance out of the taxi window now as we stop at red lights in town. Across the street, Burger Bill's looks busy tonight. I glimpse a young waitress with blonde pigtails, then a flash of purplish hair: Tanzie. It's raining lightly now. So much rain this summer – more than I can ever remember. I hope she doesn't have to hang about for ages at the bus stop tonight. I study the garish orange sign, depicting a cartoon burglar in stripy T-shirt and mask, biting into a burger of enormous proportions. Then the taxi moves off, and it's not Tanzie who's occupying my thoughts, but my wife once more.

'I'll pick you up in a cab,' I'd suggested, when I called Sinead to tell her I'd booked the table.

'No thanks,' she said firmly. 'I'll be fine making my own way there.'

It occurred to me that perhaps she was trying to minimise the amount of time she would have to spend in

252

my company – or perhaps she wanted to keep her options open, in case she had a sudden urge to make a quick getaway? But now I decide I was just being paranoid. She agreed to come, didn't she? Which suggests that she wants to see me. Maybe she just wants to make it clear how terribly unhappy she's been. Oh, I realise now that I should have known all along, as the signs were there: the listlessness, the muttered complaints, the pills she was taking for a few months around the start of the year. Maybe someone had removed my brain and replaced it with pillow stuffing. But I truly had no idea of how bad things had become.

We're almost at the restaurant now, and the rain is falling more heavily. The cab driver puts on the radio – and Bruce Springsteen fills the car.

I sit back and smile, deciding it's a good omen. My God, how I've missed her just being there at home, and lying beside me at night. It'll be all I can do not to take her in my arms and kiss her passionately on her beautiful mouth.

I close my eyes for a moment and allow the lyrics to flood into my head. They are intensely moving and are doing a sterling job of blowing away my anxieties. In terms of passion and energy, no one else touches Springsteen, as far as I am concerned. 'American patriot crap by some guy in double denim,' according to renowned rock critic Tanzie Miles. But what does *she* know?

The driver pulls up outside Elliot's. I pay him and virtually bound into the restaurant.

'Hi, d'you have a reservation?' asks the immaculate young woman who greets me.

'Yes, it's Turner. Table for two . . .'

I glance around as she checks the screen at a small counter area. The restaurant is around two-thirds full, beautifully lit with elegant sixties-style table lamps, and bold, splashy abstracts adorn the walls. For a moment, I feel like that ill-formed musician of twenty-four years who was set on impressing his new girlfriend. I took Sinead to a French restaurant once, and was appalled to discover that the menu was actually in French – in Hesslevale! What was happening to the place? I racked my brain for any remnants of schoolboy French, but all I could remember was, *Ou est la pharmacie*? Luckily, Sinead knew enough to find her way around the menu, and made me laugh by ramping up her French accent as we ordered.

'Here you are. Could you come with me, please?' the woman says now.

'Great, thank you.' I inhale deeply and follow her to a table at the back of the restaurant.

'Is this okay for you?' She smiles pleasantly.

Okay? It's bloody perfect! 'It's lovely, thanks,' I say, trying to sound as if I come to places like this all the time. It *is* perfect, too. If I'd walked in and been allowed to choose any table, this would be it, tucked away in a corner by a window consisting of tiny panes, overlooking a shrub-filled garden.

'Can I get you something to drink to start with?' she asks.

'Yes please.' I pick up the wine menu and stare at it. Should I order a bottle for both of us? *You treat me like an idiot* . . . No, better let her choose the wine. 'Just a glass of house white for now, please,' I say, hoping that doesn't make me sound like a halfwit.

'Sure.' The woman beams and disappears, leaving me to gaze at the entrance in anticipation of the arrival of my wife.

An older couple drifts in, smiling and sparkly, the

woman's red dress encrusted with tiny beads. Once upon a time I might have thought her outfit a bit too ritzy for a restaurant in Hesslevale – albeit a posh one – but now I can see that she's dressed for an occasion, perhaps an anniversary. Sixteen years, Sinead and I have been married. I should have made an effort on our last anniversary – but what's the correct material to mark it with? It's easy with the biggies – silver, golden – but with the others it's stuff like paper and tin. I mean, what do you give someone for a tin anniversary? A trowel for the garden? Quite rightly, Sinead would have clonked me over the head with it.

Now, as I sit here, my gaze locked upon the restaurant's entrance, I remember Paolo making a big thing of his and Bea's 'wood' anniversary. In the pub one night, he told me how he'd had a personalised plaque made, depicting the beachside cabin they'd stayed in on honeymoon, carved from a piece of oak. At the time, I'd thought that was touching – if a bit over the top. But perhaps that's the level of thought and imagination that's required in order to show one's devotion? If it is, then so be it – I'll have a poem embroidered onto a tablecloth for our 'linen' anniversary if that's what it takes (or have I missed the boat with 'linen'?).

I'm still mulling over presents; specifically Sinead's birthday now, which is coming up in two weeks' time. Then my tumbling thoughts halt abruptly as here she is, a vision in a pale blue dress under a neat black jacket.

My heart quickens as I jump up from my seat. She is greeted at the entrance by a bearded young man who takes her jacket. She smiles broadly, thanking him. Now she's glancing around the room, her eyes meeting mine as she makes her way towards me. She is wearing pinkish lipstick, and her hair in a style I've never seen before, or at least – shamefully – perhaps not registered; could that be Abby's influence? It suggests, disconcertingly, that things are moving on without my involvement but admittedly, it suits her very much. It's all piled up, slightly haphazardly, apart from springy curls which have escaped – maybe that's deliberate? – to bounce around her finely-boned cheeks.

She arrives at our table and I give her a brief hug. 'Hello, love,' I say.

'Hello Nate.' There's a smile, so small it's barely perceptible – but it's there.

'You look wonderful,' I add.

'Oh, thank you,' she says as she sits down. We look at each other, and although neither of us seems to know what to say next, it feels anything but awkward to me.

I'm on Fire, Bruce Springsteen belted out in the taxi. And now I – a lanky, speccy driving examiner from Huddersfield – am on fire too.

Chapter Twenty-Eight

As she's driven here, she won't be having any wine. While this is mildly disappointing, it is of course her choice.

'I just thought it'd be easier,' she explains, turning to ask the waitress for a sparkling water.

'Right. So, are you on a health kick?' Ouch. I regret asking this immediately. Like saying 'your shrink', it's probably one of those dated phrases that'll mark me out as being stuck in some Neanderthal time warp.

'I just didn't feel like drinking tonight,' she says lightly.

'Easing off on the lady petrol, then?'

Sinead's eyes widen. God, what possessed me to say *that*? I meant it as a joke but it came out sounding as if I have her down as a borderline alcoholic.

'Sorry,' I mutter. 'I'm talking rubbish. Take no notice of me.'

'It's all right.' Her tone softens, and a hint of a smile plays on her lips.

'I'm a bit all over the place,' I add as we grab at the menus.

'Me too,' Sinead says, glancing around the restaurant.

'This is really lovely, though. Thanks for booking it. It's a real treat.'

'Oh, that's okay.' I look at her across the table. Could this be it? I wonder. Can I possibly begin to hope that, after tonight, she might consider coming back to me? 'I love that dress,' I add.

'It's ancient,' she says.

'Still fits you perfectly, though.' In fact, I am bluffing as I don't remember seeing it before. What have I been doing these past few years? Blundering around with a sack over my head? 'Anyway, thanks for agreeing to come,' I add. 'I just thought, after everything that's happened, it'd be nice for us to have some time—'

'It's okay,' she says quickly. 'You don't have to explain. It's good to see you too.'

My heart swells at that. So it's good to see me! At least, she is clearly not finding my presence completely abhorrent. I smile and look back at my menu, although it could be a list of the brackets and screws stocked by B&Q for all I am able to focus on it. I adjust my specs, my eyes lighting upon something termed 'fanned rump of lamb', which sounds tempting. However, considering Sinead's pescatarian tendencies, perhaps it would be unseemly to chomp away at an infant sheep in front of her (I've never quite understood why fish are different. I mean, they have hearts and faces, just as lambs do – although not legs. Is that what gets her? That, basic shape-wise at least, they're not so different to dogs, and it would seem like a small step away from eating Scout?). Catching my thoughts racing, I try to calm them. Anyway, now is not the time to question her dietary choices.

She chooses wild salmon, and I dither over copying her – which might seem rather lame, seeing as it's not what

258

I'd go for normally – but eventually opt for tuna steak. We order, and with her encouragement I ask for a second glass of wine, as my first one seems to have been quaffed extremely quickly by an invisible, extremely thirsty thief.

'Just because I'm not drinking doesn't mean that you shouldn't,' she points out.

'Okay.'

'Just relax,' she adds. 'We don't have to be on best behaviour with each other, do we?'

'Oh, I thought you might prefer it to me being my usual disgusting, obnoxious self—'

'Nate, I've *never* thought—'

'I'm joking,' I say quickly, wondering at what point I will stop saying the wrong thing, and be able to act normally. 'So, um . . .'

'So, how have you been?' she asks.

I clear my throat. '*You* know. You can imagine how things are, I'm sure.'

Sinead nods. 'I'm sorry, Nate. I wish we could have met up before now but I just haven't felt able to.' She pauses. 'D'you understand that?'

'Yes, of course,' I murmur, on best behaviour still.

'How d'you think Flynn seems at the moment?'

I consider this, as I'm not entirely sure of the answer myself. 'I think he's okay. The lads are round tonight. Oh, and I took him for an appointment yesterday, about that stiffness in his hand . . .'

'I was going to do that,' she says, frowning.

'Well, it was all fine,' I say quickly. 'You know what he's like – he's convinced he doesn't need either of us with him anymore—'

'So it was yesterday? I'd have taken the time off!'

'You didn't need to. I dealt with it.'

259

Her face settles into a frown. I'd actually thought she'd be pleased that I'd taken him and not bothered her. 'Did you see Dr Kadow?' she asks.

'Yeah, he was great. There's a bit of inflammation, he said, so Flynn has some cream—'

'Nate, I'm happy to do those appointments with Flynn,' she asserts. Now I'm not sure whether she's annoyed because she thinks I am incapable of sitting and conversing with a doctor, or just that I hadn't mentioned the appointment. It was just an oversight, that was all, and I have been trying to avoid bothering her with too many calls.

'I know you are,' I say now, grateful to the waitress for bringing my second, gratifyingly large glass of wine.

'Will you let me know when the next appointment is?' Sinead asks as I take a big sip.

'Of course, yes.' Duly chastised, I eye my glass, deciding I mustn't swig it as quickly as the first one.

We lapse into an awkward silence. *You leave too much to me,* she wrote in her angry scrawl. I'd assumed she meant not only domestic tasks, but matters concerning Flynn's school and medical stuff too. But have I got this wrong? Is Dr Kadow supposed to be her department, in the division of responsibilities?

'In other news,' I say, affecting a jovial tone, 'Flynn seems to have sacked me as his guitar teacher.'

She shuffles on her seat. 'So he told you, then.'

I blink at her. 'Yes. So, did you know he was going to do that?'

'Um, he just mentioned it in passing.' She pulls a pained face. 'He said he just wanted to do his own thing musically, that was all.'

I allow this information to settle for a moment. So it had been discussed, and Sinead hadn't thought to pick up the phone and let me know. 'Oh, it's fine,' I say breezily, turning to thank the waitress as Sinead's salmon, and my tuna-I-now-wish-was-lamb arrive.

'He just said he prefers to pick up new stuff from tutorials on YouTube,' Sinead explains.

'So he'd rather learn from strangers than from me?' I exclaim.

'Nate, it's not like that,' she murmurs, glancing around distractedly.

'. . . I mean,' I go on, 'is YouTube really awash with guitar tutors who are used to working with kids with CP?'

'I don't think that's the point—'

'And I *do* know him pretty well,' I charge on, 'and what he's capable of, how to work with his limitations. We started when he was eight, d'you remember?'

'Yes, of course I remember.'

'And people said, don't be disappointed if it's too difficult for him . . .'

'Nate,' she cuts in, more firmly now. 'Please – this wasn't meant as a criticism of you. It's nothing to do with you, actually – it's to do with him being sixteen. He'll come round eventually when he's a bit older and past this phase . . .'

'Yeah, when he's fifty and I'm about to croak it,' I mutter.

'Nate!' she exclaims.

'I'm joking . . .'

She looks at me and tips her head to one side, and for a moment I wonder if that's a gesture she's picked up from her therapist. 'I can tell you've taken it to heart,' she adds gently, 'but look at everything he's learned from you up to this point.'

'Like what?' I ask, genuinely unable to think of a single

thing right now, and wondering if it was such a great idea to invite her here so soon, with everything still so raw and hurtful.

'Oh, come on,' she says, starting to tuck into her fish. 'What about riding a bike, when so many people said he might never be able to do it?'

'Well, yeah,' I remark, prodding at my virtually raw tuna.

'And all those other things we take for granted now, like him tying his shoelaces and learning to swim and managing cutlery properly—'

'*He* learnt those things,' I say blithely. 'You know how determined he's always been, how he'd never give up on anything, once he had an idea in his head. It didn't come from me.'

'Nate, that's not true! You've always had more patience with that kind of thing than I have.'

'Oh, I don't think—'

'You *do*, honestly,' she says, her voice rising. 'Why can't you just take a compliment?' She stops and sips her water. 'You're so good at taking a seemingly straightforward task and breaking it down into simple, easily-understandable steps . . .'

'Really?' I ask, conscious of a tiny kernel of pride growing inside me.

'Yes!' she exclaims. 'That's probably why you're such a good guitar teacher.'

'Well, Flynn doesn't seem to think so, does he?' She chooses to ignore this remark.

'. . . *And* you were a brilliant driving instructor,' she goes on. 'So patient and unflappable. Everyone said so. I was always being accosted by people coming up to me in town, saying, "Your Nate is so great!"'

Your Nate. My insides seem to clench.

'So please,' she continues, more calmly now, 'allow yourself to take some credit for everything you've done to help Flynn over the years.'

I consider this, wondering how to respond, so unaccustomed am I to such a compliment. However, there's no need to say anything as Sinead has excused herself – 'Just been feeling a bit queasy' – and makes for the loo.

Queasy? I hope her fish is okay. I peer at it, but it looks perfectly fine, and I'm not about to lean over and sniff it in a place like this. Instead, I take a moment to allow her words to sink in. Perhaps, due to focusing on her list so much, I'd forgotten I'm actually good at anything. After all, being left a document detailing your faults doesn't exactly fire up your self-esteem.

It sounded pretty heartfelt, though, what Sinead said just now. I mean, some compliments seem to just trip off the tongue: 'You're so funny/handsome/sexy', etc, not that I've ever been bestowed with any of those. Being told you're 'good at breaking down tasks' isn't quite as thrilling as someone saying, 'Your penis is incredible. I didn't know they made them so big!' But at least she seemed to really mean it.

Yet, if I'm so great at all that, then why did she leave me? I guess my general usefulness wasn't enough to make her stick around. As for my flaws, well, there were enough to fill a lined sheet of A4; perhaps, when she weighed it all up, they simply outnumbered my good points. She reappears, and I quickly push those dark thoughts away as she sits back down.

'So, how are things at the shop?' I ask. *You belittle my job and show no interest in it.*

263

'Okay,' she says, 'although I've been thinking, maybe I've been there long enough.'

'Are you going to look for something else?'

She twiddles the strand of hair that's hanging so prettily at the left side of her face. 'Actually, I'm thinking I might get a small jewellery studio together again.'

'Really? Is there room for that at Abby's?'

'Erm, I'm not planning to be there forever, you know.'

'No, of course not,' I say quickly. 'I, er . . . guess you'll soon be looking around for your own place?'

Our eyes meet again and I'm seized by an urge to hold her. 'Let's not talk about that tonight,' she murmurs.

I muster a faint smile and we eat in silence for a few moments. 'We should have a list of all the stuff we're not allowed to talk about,' I add.

'Yeah,' she says, smiling too. 'That might help. So, tell me, what've you been doing?'

I ponder this as we finish our main courses, deciding not to mention my rather bizarre new friend, who's been counselling me on how to repair my marriage. 'I've been thinking about that list you left me,' I say carefully.

'Please, Nate, can we leave that too? I was upset, it all just poured out . . .'

I lean forward. 'No, listen. It's been quite helpful actually, and with some of the things – well, all of them probably – you were quite right.'

'Like what?' she asks with a frown as our plates are whisked away.

'Like, "Your bloody record collection".'

'Oh, that.' She looks down and shakes her head.

'It was obviously bothering you,' I venture, trying not to sound at all embittered, 'so I've sold it.'

264

She stares at me as if I have just torn off my clothes. 'You've sold it? You mean, all your records?'

'Yes!' I say with a note of triumph.

I look at my wife, who seems horrified. 'No – please tell me you're kidding. I didn't mean *that* . . .'

I shrug and go to sip more wine, and realise my second glass is empty. 'Well, it's done and dusted now, and it's okay. The shelves they were on have gone too.'

'What d'you mean, they've gone?'

'It's fine,' I say. 'You were probably right. I mean, some of the records I'd had since I was fifteen, and they were hardly ever played. So I just decided . . .' I tail off, realising I'm winging it here, making up what she wants to hear. 'I decided there was no point on clinging onto tired old stuff just for sentimental reasons.' Hang on. *Tired old stuff?*

'Well, I think that's a terrible shame,' Sinead murmurs. 'I mean, music was always a huge part of your life. D'you think you'll ever be in a band again?'

'Oh, I can't imagine it really,' I mutter, baffled now. If she didn't mind my record collection, then why did it appear on her list?

'But why not?' she asks. 'You work hard. You deserve some fun—'

I laugh involuntarily. This is somewhat hard to take seriously, considering she is the very reason that life has been distinctly *un*-fun lately. 'Weirdly enough,' I remark, 'the guy who bought my records asked if I'd like to jam with him and his mates sometime.'

'You should! It'd be good for you,' Sinead asserts, as if I am a socially inept teenager, mooting the possibility of mingling with other human beings. 'Don't you miss playing?' she goes on. 'That whole side of your life used

265

to be so vital to you. I loved that – that you were passionate about something. It was *everything* to you—'

'I don't really think about it anymore,' I murmur.

Our waitress glides over and we study the dessert menus, although I have no interest in anything on it. It was challenging enough for me to plough through that main course.

'Just a chamomile tea for me,' Sinead says. 'Oh, and I'll have a sorbet too, please.'

'No coffee?' I ask.

'I'm a bit off it at the moment,' she says. Now, this is odd. No booze, fine – clearly, she'd sensibly decided to keep a clear head tonight. But to forgo what I'd imagine would be an excellent coffee? She's always downed tons of the stuff – something like a pint first thing in the morning, and always after dinner on the rare occasions we ate out.

Her tea arrives in a glass with a silvery handle, her sorbet in a tiny porcelain cup. To keep her company, I chose a dark chocolate tart, which I am now chipping away at with a lack of enthusiasm. And now, as she sips her pale tea – I'd love to order more wine, but know I shouldn't – I am aware of the unspoken issue that's been smouldering away at the back of my brain all night.

I place my fork on my plate. 'D'you mind if I ask you a question?'

She looks at me and flushes, and right then I know there's something. Something else that wasn't on the list, and perhaps wasn't even about me, after all. She hasn't even touched her sorbet yet. 'Of course you can,' she says. 'What is it?'

'I, er . . . just can't help wondering if there's something else, that's all. Something you haven't told me, I mean

266

– about us, and our marriage. Can I just ask . . .' I break off and look at her. Now her cheeks are even pinker and she's fiddling with her tea glass, and prodding at her hair.

I swallow hard. She's already answered my question for me; *she's been seeing someone else.* I've tried to dismiss the possibility, not because Sinead isn't beautiful, clever and desirable – Christ, any sane man would want her – but due to the fact that I couldn't bear the thought of her being with some other man.

'Are you . . . in love with someone else?' I ask, as levelly as I can manage.

She meets my gaze, and all at once the flush drains from her cheeks until they are chalky-pale. 'No, of course I'm not. It's hardly been any time at all, Nate. It's the *last* thing I'm looking for . . .'

'Come on, I can tell there's something going on,' I say, more sharply than I intended. 'Please tell me. I just need to know. Who is it?'

She clears her throat and looks away, as if the view of the lantern-lit garden has caught her interest for the first time.

I am aware of our waitress glancing over as she strides past, perhaps registering that we are a couple who are having a *bit of a situation.* But I don't care. All the possibilities are whirring through my mind: the various dads Sinead's known, through her social life as a mum, making friends with everyone – far more than I ever did. Should I have gone to more playgroups and parent meet-ups, more days out to the zoo, or the coast, with hordes of other mums and dads? What the hell was I doing when all that was going on?

Could it be one of those bouncy, infinitely capable dads who seemed to be able to juggle numerous children whilst reading a picture book and flipping pancakes in the pan? I'm sure plenty of them must have fancied my wife. She always seemed so vivacious – never weighed down by the parenting thing at all, at least not until the last year or so, when she appeared a little less sparkly. Or maybe it really is some charmer who wandered into the gift shop, just as I imagined, asking for pomegranate candles . . .

This is it, then, I decide, looking around the restaurant, where everyone else seems to be having a lovely time. Our break-up wasn't about me failing to set mousetraps or leaving the odd dog turd lying in the grass. And now, I feel as if I am floating – a bit pissed, probably, after two huge glasses of wine – as she folds her fingers together and tells me what's really been going on.

Chapter Twenty-Nine

'Okay, look, I *have* been out with someone, but it was just for a drink,' she says. 'Well, drink and a quick dinner,' she adds, 'and then coffee one other time. But it really doesn't mean anything at all.'

'Oh,' is all I can say. I glance down at my tart, sitting there on its small white plate. It now looks too perfect, like it was moulded out of brown plastic. So, while I've been selling my records and dragging our shelves into the garden, she's been sleeping with someone else.

'Nate, honestly,' she insists. 'He's just a friend—'

'Who is it?' I blurt out, my eyes fixed on hers.

Sinead clamps her lips together and pauses, as if weighing up the likelihood of whether I'll make a scene. 'D'you remember me talking about Brett O'Hara from college?'

'Vaguely,' I say huffily, although yes, I do – in shimmering detail, now she's mentioned him. The one everyone fancied, she said: the 'college hottie'. The one she'd kissed once, and it had been mortifying, because they were mates. The one who's clearly intimately acquainted with her sensational body right now. Just a friend? It's clear from her face that there's no 'just' about it at all.

'I wasn't even sure about telling you,' she adds with a dismissive shrug.

'I'm sure you weren't,' I mutter.

'Not because I was being secretive. I just didn't want to upset you, okay? And I'm only mentioning it now in case you've heard some gossip. I didn't want you jumping to conclusions . . .'

'Of course I'm jumping to conclusions!'

'Could you please try and hear what I'm saying?' she snaps. *You don't listen to me . . .*

She frowns and drains the last of her pee-coloured tea. Her sorbet still remains untouched. 'I'll tell you exactly what happened, all right?' she says firmly. 'Michelle came back from New York. I met up with her and some others – George, Aisha . . . remember them?'

I nod curtly. I don't give a shit about George or Aisha.

'. . . And Brett happened to come along too' – just happened to, because he was passing? – 'and it was lovely to see him,' she goes on. 'After all the upset and stress, and how I've been feeling lately, it was so good to relax and have fun and remember the old times . . .'

Before I came along, she means. Before I wrecked all her fun.

'. . . And then, um, I met Brett again another night,' she continues.

'Just the two of you that time, for dinner?'

Sinead nods. 'He was in Hesslevale for a meeting.'

'Right. That was handy . . .'

'We're just *friends*, Nate,' she stresses again. 'We were talking about my jewellery business and how I could get started again. I was really fired up—'

270

Bet she was. I, however, am not quite so on fire now. 'And then you had coffee another time?'

'Nate, could you please stop grilling me?' she hisses, which seems a little unfair. 'Yes,' she adds. 'He had another meeting . . .'

'So many meetings!' I remark bitterly, at which the red dress lady throws me a startled look.

'Please don't be like this,' Sinead mutters.

I look down at my empty glass, wishing it would miraculously fill itself with alcohol. 'I just need to know if you were seeing him when you were still with me.'

'Of course I wasn't! Christ, Nate, if you carry on like this, I'm leaving—'

'No, don't do that,' I say quickly. 'So, are you seeing him again?'

'Erm . . . probably. Okay – yes, I will. Honestly, it's *nothing*.' She looks at me across the table and reaches for my hand, her eyes glinting with tears now. 'I'm so sorry, Nate. I've been so awful to you, but you do realise . . . I didn't leave you because of someone else, don't you? You have to believe that.'

I nod mutely, realising my own eyes are misting now.

'It wasn't about all those things on the list either.'

I stare at her, baffled now. 'What was it then?'

Sinead sighs and rubs at her eyes. As if only just remembering it's sitting there, she has a spoonful of lemon sorbet.

'D'you remember when we used to take Flynn to the beach,' she starts, 'and he was mad about making elaborate sandcastles just so he could watch the waves come in and wash them away?'

'Yeah,' I mutter, wondering what this has to do with anything.

'So, d'you remember how he used to like watching

271

each wave dissolve a bit more of the castle, until finally, a last one would crash over it, and the whole thing would be gone?'

I nod, utterly lost now. 'What does that have to do with us now?'

'Well, it wasn't one thing that made me anxious and depressed and have to see the doctor and then get therapy. It was wave after wave, year upon year, dissolving me bit by bit until, well—' Sinead breaks off, her voice cracking. Now, it's as if the entire restaurant, and all the people in it, have faded to nothing. 'Don't you see, Nate? It was as if *I'd* been washed away, dissolved onto the beach. There's was literally nothing left of me.'

For a moment, I can't think of a single thing to say. I want to tell her I'm sorry, that I wish I'd known and done more, wish she'd tried to tell me all of this before it was too late – then my attention is caught by a man who's appeared, briefly, at the circular window in the door that leads to the kitchen. Pale face. Short red hair, messily gelled.

You'd better watch out when you're eating out locally, that's all I can say.

When I glance over again, he's still there at the window: Angus Pew, my deranged candidate. I look down at my tart, wondering if it's been contaminated – but never mind that, my wife has just eaten a wild salmon steak, with braised greens, and said she felt queasy earlier, plus a spoonful of sorbet.

She stops and gives me a curious look. 'Are you okay, Nate?'

'Er, yeah.' I glance back at the door to the kitchen. Another flash of red hair, and a glimpse of a pasty arm. I'd imagined him working in a more downmarket place, not somewhere like this. But then, chefs can probably turn their hand to anything, from flipping burgers at Bill's to— There he is again! A rumbly laugh emits from the kitchen as Sinead lifts another spoonful of sorbet towards her mouth. 'Don't eat that!' I bark at her.

She flinches and drops the spoon. 'What?'

'Don't eat any more of it, okay?'

'What's wrong—' Our waitress, who was swanning past, turns to us in alarm.

'D'you feel all right?' I exclaim. 'You said you felt a bit sick earlier . . .'

'Not sick exactly,' Sinead says, still looking bewildered. 'Just kind of nauseous. I've had it quite a lot lately. You see, I wanted to tell—'

'It's bloody him!' I exclaim, catching yet another glimpse of his round, smug face as I leap up and shove back my chair.

'Nate, what the hell?' Sinead is staring up at me, aghast, but I'm no longer registering my wife as I storm towards the kitchen, shove open the swing door and march in.

The kitchen is all silvery units and things steaming and hissing on a gigantic hob.

'Hey, mate!' An older man whirls around from tending an enormous pot.

'Is Angus Pew here?' I shout.

A younger chef, his collarbones jutting above a baggy T-shirt, strides towards me. 'What's going on?'

'I'm looking for someone,' I bellow, glancing wildly around. 'A ginger-haired guy. Angus Pew, sat his driving test, threatened to do something to my food if he saw me in his—'

'Jesus Christ,' the older man says, wiping his hands on a cloth. 'What are you accusing us of here?'

273

'I don't know. Spitting on my wife's wild salmon? I have no idea—'

'Fuck's sake!' the younger one exclaims.

'Get out of here,' thunders the older man. 'Just get the hell out or I'm calling the police . . .'

I step back. 'Where is he? I need the names of everyone who's working here!'

'Nate, what the hell are you doing?' Sinead is standing behind me now, grabbing at my arm, pulling at the shirt I chose so carefully and ironed to perfection. 'What's got into you?' she cries. 'Have you gone completely mad?'

'It's not me who's mad,' I snap. 'It's him, wherever he is. It's – it's *assault*, that's what it is. Poisoning someone . . .'

'Who's poisoned?' Sinead gasps, and at that moment a back door opens, and in steps the ginger-haired man who, I can see now, isn't Angus Pew after all. He is pale-skinned and red-haired, just like my candidate – but a good few inches taller. I have never seen this young man before in my life.

I stare at him, aware of the three chefs' eyes upon me. The older man is tapping out something on his mobile. 'I'm so sorry,' I mutter, stepping back towards the door now. 'I thought he was somebody else . . .'

'Get this nutter out of here,' the younger man snaps.

'It's fine, it was a mistake. I'm going now . . .' I turn and hurry out of the kitchen, aware of everyone in the restaurant staring at me. The lady in the red dress is gawping with her fork halfway to her mouth.

Sinead follows me, then barges past, storming towards our table – the one we were so lucky to get tonight. She grabs her bag from beside her chair and swings round to where our waitress is hovering, looking distinctly alarmed. 'Could I have my jacket, please?' Sinead asks her.

'Yes, of course.' The waitress scurries away.

Sinead turns back to me. 'Have you lost your mind, Nate?'

'No! I just thought . . .'

'What an end to our evening,' she exclaims, eyes brimming with tears now. 'I thought it might be possible for us to have a nice time. I thought, maybe, when I told you . . .' I watch as a tear slides down her face. She wipes at her cheek as the waitress approaches with her jacket.

'Please, darling,' I start, trying to reach for her hand, 'I'm sorry. You see, there was this guy, this candidate, and when he failed his test he threatened . . .' I stop. There's no point. Sinead has already turned, gripping her jacket in one hand, and is marching briskly towards the exit. As I stand there, helpless, it strikes me that she's leaving again, and here I am just watching her go. And as she disappears, I sit back down, looking first at Sinead's barely-touched dessert, then around for the waitress so I can ask for the bill.

A couple of other diners catch my eye, and I realise the place has fallen oddly quiet. It takes a few minutes for conversations to resume. I sit there and wait, trying to act like I'm fine. But all I can think is, it's a cold, wet night out there, and Sinead hasn't put on her jacket.

Chapter Thirty

Tanzie

I'm sorry, but when Nate tells me about the Angus-Pew-mistaken-identity thing I can't stop laughing. I know it's terrible, and that he'd piled all his hopes on that posh dinner at Elliot's – but storming into the kitchen just because he saw a flash of red hair? 'Oh, God, Nate,' I say, dabbing at my eyes with a Burger Bill's paper napkin. 'I'd never had you down as having a violent temper.'

'I wasn't being violent,' he insists. 'I was just, you know, *concerned* . . .'

I perch on the chair beside him and realise some of my mascara has transferred onto the napkin. Nate brought Flynn into the diner today after school – a drizzly, grey-skied Thursday – and what a handsome boy he is. You can tell he has *something* by the way he moves and holds himself, but he was sweet and cheerful (I mean, why wouldn't he be? All I knew before I met him was from what Kayla had said; that you'd 'hardly know really', and that he's an 'amazing guitarist').

In fact, he reminded me of my eldest, Robbie, when he was that age. *Such a nice boy,* everyone said. I know that sounds bland, but he really was. We had a couple of difficult years when his dad had left, and Robbie was staying out all night, dabbling with pills and God knows what. Most people think, 'How quaint!' when they come to Hesslevale. They see the renovated mills, the pretty river and canal with all the houseboats, and have no idea there's a drug thing going on here. But of course there is. It goes on everywhere. Maybe it's because I'm a small woman and not a big, strong man like his father – but I couldn't control Robbie at all. If I asked what he'd taken he'd just laugh in my face. But then, by the time he was nineteen he'd got into college, and became obsessed with diving, getting all the qualifications – and now he's offshore, earning a fortune.

So Flynn reminded me a little of Robbie, when he was a slightly awkward sixteen-year-old too.

Nate introduced us: 'This is Tanzie. I did her driving test.' (Test-singular.)

'Hiya,' Flynn said, and that was that. Of course, Nate wasn't about to add, 'And since then, she's seen me mashed out of my brains staggering out of a Wendy house and been advising me on how to win back your mother. In fact, we are *friends* now, according to the guidelines set out by the Driving Standards Agency,' or whatever they're called. Anyway, there was barely time to say much more, as Flynn scoffed his burger like a half-starved thing – 'That was great!' he enthused as I took his plate away – and then he was off, bolting out the door to meet friends and, naturally, leaving his dad to pay the bill.

Nate is looking at me now, as he stirs his coffee. 'You think I'm crazy, don't you, wrecking the evening like that?'

'Well, you obviously have some anger lurking in you somewhere,' I remark.

277

He smirks. 'I did throw an oven glove once.'

'Whoah. Steady on,' I say, chuckling, then quickly scan the restaurant to check that no one needs attending to. The place has quietened down now. We have the after-school flurry (most of them just want chips), but we'll be busy again in an hour or so. 'So, how's Flynn doing?' I ask. 'I mean, how's he handling living with his crazed, oven-glove-throwing dad?'

'We seem to be managing okay,' Nate replies, then adds, 'I mean, I'm tolerated. That's why I brought him here – just to try to have some proper time with him.' He smiles. 'And he sat down for, what, about fifteen minutes . . .' He breaks off. 'Is your daughter like that?'

'Kayla?'

'Yes, Kayla,' he says quickly, as if trying to show that he remembered her name, although I wouldn't have expected him to.

'Oh, yeah,' I say. 'I told you about her fascination with her best friend Paige's place . . .'

'With the fancy all-angles shower?'

So he was listening after all. 'That's the one. Yeah, I'd just love her to be at home more, you know? Did your parents ever say to you, "You treat this place like a hotel?"'

'Not really,' he says, looking a bit bashful. 'I wasn't one of those teenagers who was out all the time. I mean, I had friends of course, but I was also with Dad a lot, making things, building stuff . . .'

'What kind of stuff?'

'Oh, anything really. Dad was into making model steam engines, proper miniature machines with pistons and valves and – oh, God, that sounds so geeky . . .'

'It doesn't,' I say. In fact it does a little, but I always liked a man who had the patience to make things from scratch. Gary managed to persuade me he was like that; funny how a man can go from building you a double bed, and I don't mean flat-pack – he literally impressed the pants off me – to refusing to fix some fallen-down bookshelves.

'We spent hours together,' Nate adds. 'We were kind of inseparable.'

I nod, touched that he's telling me this. He doesn't strike me as a man who shares any personal information easily. 'I don't suppose Liv ever found his watch?'

'Nope.' He shakes his head. 'She said she's looked everywhere, but no luck.'

'Aw, that's a real shame.'

We fall into silence for a moment. If Stef was in, I wouldn't be sitting here with Nate – but he's not, so I am.

'Flynn's a lovely boy,' I add, in the hope of lifting his mood. 'You must be very proud of him.'

'Oh, I am of course. But, you know – he's just like any other teenager in many ways.'

I smile. 'Yeah, it's not an easy phase, is it? I wish Kayla *would* treat our place like a hotel. You know, use the facilities, throw a few towels about, lie around in a fluffy dressing gown—'

'. . . Raid the minibar,' he chips in.

'Exactly. Maybe I should have one installed in her bedroom. At least that way, I'd see her occasionally.'

Nate smiles kindly. He has a lovely smile; wide and open, unguarded. You don't notice that when he's sitting there in the car with his examiner's face on: calm, professional, emotionless.

'Don't you wish there was an instruction book to tell you how to be a parent to teenagers?' I ask.

'God, yes,' he says eagerly. 'I'd certainly buy it.'

''Cause sometimes,' I add, 'I really think I'm losing it, Nate. Seriously. It's like I'm not her mum anymore. Like she's *disowned* me. Can I tell you something that'll probably sound mad?'

He frowns and takes off his specs. I haven't seen him without them before. His eyes are chocolaty brown, with crows' lines and slight shadows beneath – tired dad eyes – and radiate kindness. 'If you like,' he says hesitantly.

I laugh dryly. 'I feel like I can talk to you, you know? Isn't that weird? I mean, I hardly know you really.'

'Well,' he says with a smile, 'maybe you've just figured out, who on earth is he going to tell?' He twists his fingers together. He's still wearing his wedding ring, of course. It's a medium-width plain gold band – the kind you'd expect.

I twiddle with the vinegar bottle on the table. 'I'm only with Gary because of Kayla.'

'Really?' His eyes widen.

'Yeah.' I nod. 'You see, when me and Neil split up, even though it wasn't all my fault – it wasn't anyone's fault really – I felt like a big failure. I saw my own mum sticking with Dad until he had to move to a care home – even though he'd been a shit to her really. Drinking, squandering their money, getting off with other women, that kind of stuff. Mum was tough, though. I think she thought it was kind of heroic to put up with all of that.'

Nate is looking at me, really listening, I can tell. Sometimes it feels as if no one really does. 'And when me and Neil broke up,' I continue, 'she thought I'd given up too easily. I mean, compared to Dad, Neil was a saint! He never hurt me or cheated on me, which made him perfect in her eyes. And then I met Gary, and even when things started to go wrong, I wanted to show Kayla that I could make a relationship work, that her hopeless mother wasn't going to be a failure all over again.'

I pause for breath. Nate looks at me, as if a little stunned by my outpouring. 'You're not a failure,' he says carefully. 'Far from it, from what I can tell.'

'Huh.' I shrug. 'That's very sweet of you.'

He frowns. 'But is that the right thing to do, d'you think? Sticking with him, I mean?'

'Stand by your man and all that?' I snort. 'I really don't know anymore.' I scan the room and realise I *really* shouldn't just be sitting here, even though there are only two other customers, drinking coffee, and they haven't asked for their bill yet. 'Thanks for letting me babble on,' I add.

'Oh, you're welcome. And you haven't been babbling at all. This has been really nice.'

I smile and get up from the chair. 'Want me to slip you a knickerbocker glory?' I wink theatrically and drop my voice to a whisper. '*On the house?*'

'Tempting, but I'm all done, thank you.'

'Not even a banana split with squirty cream?'

'Some other time, maybe.' He gives me a bemused look. 'But, um, just before you go . . . can I ask you something?'

'We don't give out our secret hot sauce recipe, Nate.'

He chuckles awkwardly. Now it's him who's twisting the vinegar bottle round and round.

'Actually,' I add, 'it comes out of a three-litre plastic carton, like engine oil.'

We look at each other, and he smirks. 'Erm, it's not that,' he murmurs. 'You might think it's out of order, actually . . .'

'No, I won't,' I say, sensing myself reddening now, 'unless

281

you're about to say something really pervy, and I really don't think you're the type . . .' Oh God, what made me say that? Of course he's not. He's an upstanding man – a guardian of the highways, or however driving examiners see themselves. Even so, there was a flicker of something then, and with a jolt, the possibility occurs to me . . . Does Nate want to ask me out? Maybe I shouldn't have told him all that stuff about Gary. I know Nate's single now – sort of – but I'm definitely not, and even if Gary's shagging half of Yorkshire I'd never go with anyone behind his back. But still, the thought of . . . well, someone like Nate, liking *me* . . .

I look down at him. 'C'mon, Nate. Just spit it out. What d'you want to ask me?'

He chuckles, and now he's blushing too. He puts his glasses back on and rakes back his light brown hair. 'Okay – please do say if this is something you'd rather not do . . .'

'Of course I will . . .'

'Well, um, I was wondering, if you had the time and wouldn't find it a completely awful experience . . .' He beams hopefully.

I realise I am holding my breath.

'. . . It's Sinead's birthday a week on Saturday,' he adds. 'I don't suppose you'd help me to choose a present for her?'

Chapter Thirty-One

Sinead

It's Abby who suggested I did another test. Abby who went through round after round of IVF, with all the hope and crashing disappointment, and would have given anything to be a mum.

'And that was positive too?' Rachel asks now.

'Yes.'

'How do you feel about this pregnancy?'

'Pretty awful,' I admit.

'And why is that, Sinead?' As usual, her expression remains entirely passive. Sometimes I wonder if she is a robot, plugged into the wall. In fact, even though I decided to restart my weekly sessions, I'm starting to wonder if she is the right person for me. Hesslevale is awash with therapists of every description – you could have someone interpret the veins on your eyeballs whilst wafting smouldering rosemary in your face if that's what you wanted. It seems crazy now that I chose her because of her kind answerphone voice.

'There are so many reasons,' I tell her.

'Maybe you could talk about some of them?'

'Okay,' I start, 'there's the fact that we're separated, obviously. We did want another child after Flynn – very much – but that was so long ago, and after I miscarried, we decided . . .' I hesitate, picturing the two of us back then. Nate was still playing with bands and driving all over the UK. Month after month, we'd be on tenterhooks until my period arrived. He bought us enormous mobile phones – so I could alert him with the good or bad news, wherever he happened to be. 'After a year or so of that, we decided to try and forget about it,' I continue. 'I mean, we never used contraception – but we didn't conceive again either.'

Rachel smooths back her liquorice-black bob. 'I see. So, if we could go back to the reasons why this isn't a good situation for you now . . .'

What *is* she talking about? I am almost forty-four! Nate and I are heading for a divorce! 'Even if we were still together, I'm too old, and I haven't been looking after myself properly. I know I've been drinking more than I should . . .'

'Is this anything to do with Flynn?' she asks, which stops me short.

'You mean, how he'd react to having a little brother or sister?' I glance at the clock, willing our time to be up. 'I'm sure he'd be shocked initially,' I venture.

'I mean, are you worried that the same thing might happen that happened to Flynn?'

Ah, she's referring to cerebral palsy. I prickle with annoyance. 'We'd be no more at risk than anyone else. Our consultants have always been very clear on that point—'

'Oh, I didn't know.' Her cheeks flush.

'Anyway, it's nothing to do with that,' I continue. 'What I mean is, I'd want to go into a pregnancy in a positive frame of mind, really *wanting* the baby and doing things properly. It's just the way I am.'

It's true; after we had Flynn – who was a delightful surprise – I researched, researched, researched, in the hope of giving us the best chance of having another child. Even recently, just out of interest, I read up on what a pregnant woman should and shouldn't eat these days. Talk about information overload! I remembered that shellfish and unpasteurised cheese should be avoided – but now I learnt that fish which may contain high levels of mercury can be risky too.

Curled up on Abby's spare bed, I skimmed the list: swordfish, shark, king mackerel. It seems crazy that I was even reading that stuff, because even then I'd decided I wouldn't be continuing with the pregnancy. Maybe it was just as well. While I was confident I'd never had the latter two, I *had* had swordfish, that night with Michelle, Brett and the others at Fletcher's. I might as well have guzzled the contents of a thermometer, I decided.

'Sinead,' Rachel says now, 'remember that thousands of women go about their daily lives, eating and drinking whatever they like, until they find out they're pregnant. And, in most cases, everything is fine.'

Really? And how would *she* know? 'Yes, but I'm sure virtually every one of those women worries themselves sick too.'

'Hmm. So, how far into the pregnancy are you?'

'About seven weeks,' I say flatly. 'It was quite easy to pinpoint when I conceived, actually, seeing as it's not exactly a regular occurrence—'

'And do you have any thoughts of what you might do?'

285

Any thoughts? Is she mad? I've been thinking of nothing else. 'I don't think I can go through with it,' I murmur.

Rachel's greyish-blue eyes meet mine. 'And what does Nate think about that?'

'He doesn't know yet.'

'You haven't told him?' A flicker of surprise crosses her face. Surely, in her line of work, she's heard more alarming things than this?

'I was going to tell him on Saturday night,' I say quickly. 'He'd booked a lovely restaurant, and I thought we could talk it over, and I could explain my reasons, and he'd – well, I knew he'd want the baby, very much. But I also hoped he might come round to understand that it wasn't a very good idea for us.'

'But you *didn't* tell him?' Rachel ventures.

'Well, er – no. There was a bit of a scene . . .' Her expression has settled back into its normal placid facade. 'He thought someone in the kitchen had tried to poison us,' I add.

'Really?' Rachel exclaims.

I nod. 'He seems very paranoid.' *Of course he is,* I remind myself. *You left him a list of his personality flaws, so what the hell do you expect?*

'There's a lot to think about, isn't there?' she remarks.

'Yes, there is.' *And you're not helping.* 'It was a terrible night,' I add. 'He also asked me if I've been seeing someone else and, well, I have been out with an old friend a couple of times . . .'

'I see . . .' Her eyebrows shoot up. *And with you being pregnant?* is what her tone implies.

'Yes,' I say quickly. 'I mean, I just thought it was best to be honest, when Nate asked me outright. Brett's an old college friend, that's all. It felt so good to be with someone who listened, and cared – at least, about me being more than a wife and a mother . . .' Her expression has set. Does she think I'm awful?

I glance around the room as silence settles around us. There are just two chairs, a small low table between us, bearing a jumbo box of Kleenex, and a bookshelf housing various enlightening tomes: *Be Your Own Guiding Light. Rediscovering Closeness After Infidelity. Taming the Butterfly Within.* I can sense Rachel tuning into the wall clock behind her, reading it through the back of her head. You don't get any free extras with therapy. It's not like having a friendly hairdresser who says, 'Pop in for a free fringe trim in between times, just to keep things in shape.'

'Okay,' she says levelly, 'so we can talk about that more next time. But I'm afraid we've come to the end of our session today . . .'

Well, thank Christ for that. It feels like it's been rumbling on for *weeks*. I pay up, never as grateful to get out of that room. But what now? I reflect as I leave the building. I'm pregnant with Nate's child. The single time we've had sex since Christmas, we somehow managed to conceive. Despite all the odds being against us, it happened. I'm still certain that going ahead with it would be a terrible idea, but now a rogue thought snags at me: *what if . . .?* After all, people have done crazier things. And numerous women have gone through a pregnancy – and raised a child – alone . . .

Stepping out into the street now, I pull my phone from my pocket; I always have it on silent when I'm with Rachel. There's a missed call from Brett. I blink at his name, wondering whether to call back or at least text him. I hesitate, then plunge it back into my pocket and decide there are more pressing issues for me to consider right now.

Chapter Thirty-Two

Nate

On perhaps the most bizarre Saturday afternoon of my entire life, I am out shopping with Tanzie, in York, for my wife's birthday present. I chose York as I was keen to find something special and different, and had an idea that the shops here are more of the quirky type. More than in Hesslevale, anyway – which has decent gift shops of its own. But as Sinead works in one of them, she's probably pretty au fait with the stock in all of the others. Bradford and Leeds are fine, for practical shopping – but I wanted this to be a fun day for Tanzie too. She told me she'd never been to York before, when we figured out the details for our day.

'You've never been to York?' I gasped.

'No,' she said, a tad defensively. 'Why is that so weird to you?'

Because it's an incredibly well-known historic city, I thought, and it happens to be within easy reach of the town where you work, and used to live; I mean, trains and buses go there. It's hardly Bangkok. 'It's not weird,' I replied. 'Just surprising.' Now, though, I'm glad it's the first time she's been here because I have never known anyone to be so openly thrilled by everything around her.

'My God, it's all so *old*,' she exclaims as we start to meander through the cobbled streets.

'Well, yes – it's a Roman town. It was founded something like two thousand years ago . . .'

'And it's still standing,' she marvels.

'I think there's still the odd original structure,' I say with a smile. 'Most of what you see is medieval, although they did find a whole Viking settlement beneath what's ground level now, with the remains of houses, fireplaces, even toilets—'

She stops suddenly, and I swing around to see what's grabbed her attention. 'Look at *that*,' she exclaims. 'Oh, I love it . . .' I follow her gaze towards the window of New Look. 'That dress,' she adds, beaming at me. 'Isn't it gorgeous?'

I arrange my face into what I hope is an expression of appreciation at the skimpy silver frock. 'It's very striking,' I agree.

'I'm trying not to spend any money,' she adds, 'but, God, I'm in love with it. D'you think it'd suit me?'

'I'm sure it would,' I say, silently urging her to move along. I have never been one of those men who's comfortable hanging around women's changing rooms and commenting helpfully. 'They're fine,' I told Sinead one time when she pulled back the curtain, expecting my considered opinion on the fifth pair of jeans she'd tried on that day.

'Fine?' she shot back. 'Well, thanks for that – I was actually going to buy these!'

'Well, you should. They look great.' But too late: she'd

already flounced back into the changing room, to reappear a few minutes later with the announcement that 'I think I've done enough shopping, actually.'

Tanzie gazes at the dress some more, then shakes her head emphatically. 'Sorry, Nate. I hardly ever come shopping so I'm a bit of a kid in a sweet shop. But we're not here for me. We're here for you – I mean, for Sinead. C'mon, let's get a coffee and we can form a plan.'

We wander some more, with Tanzie oohing and ahhing at the numerous tea shops – 'So many to choose from!' – finally settling on one that's so chintzy, it's a little like finding oneself in an elderly auntie's front room.

'So, what I was thinking,' she says, stirring her coffee, 'is that she works in a gift shop so she won't want any of that bog-standard gift-shop kind of stuff.'

'Right,' I say. 'That's probably a good point.' In fact, after the debacle at Elliot's, I am aware that I must get this just right. Luckily, Sinead and I are on speaking terms again – albeit in the form of brief, terse phone conversations – for which I am grateful.

'Have *you* thought of anything?' Tanzie asks.

I take a bite of my extremely delicious Eccles cake. 'Actually, I was thinking of something to wear. That's partly why I asked you along. I thought maybe – as a woman – you could steer me in the right direction—' I break off, realising how inept I must sound; plus, Sinead's style is nothing like Tanzie's. As she sips her coffee thoughtfully, I fill her in on the leopard skirt debacle and how I have never been terribly successful in choosing clothes for my wife.

'Yeah,' Tanzie says. 'Her style's quite quirky, isn't it? Cute, a bit arty . . .'

I peer at her across my fluted-edged cup. 'Oh, have you met her? Did you pop into her shop?'

'Um, not exactly,' she says, shuffling uncomfortably. 'I just googled it. Little Owl, I mean – there's a picture of her on the website . . .'

'Really?' Admittedly, I have never taken a look myself. Christ, I really have shown no interest in her job.

'Yeah. That sounds a bit weird and stalkery, doesn't it? I'm sorry.' She snaps off a bit of shortbread biscuit and pops it into her mouth.

'No, not at all . . .'

'And then I went to see Kayla one time,' she continues, regaining her usual breezy tone, 'at her friend Paige's. Remember I told you about—'

'The boiling-water-tap house? Yes.'

'Well, I saw Sinead there too. I mean, I spotted her in the street.'

'Right,' I say, taking this in. 'So, er, whereabouts does Paige live?' I ask, trying to sound casual, and not that I'm trying to squirrel out information on my wife's movements.

'In that new estate behind the old pie factory,' Tanzie replies. 'Aspen Grove, I think it is.'

'Oh! That's where Abby lives. What I mean is, that's where Sinead's living too, at the moment . . .' I decide to steer our conversation back to the matter in hand. 'So, anyway, d'you think something to wear is a good idea?'

'Sure – if it's the right kind of thing. If it's something pretty that says, "I love you, you gorgeous, adorable woman", and not, say, a brown jumper.'

'What would a brown jumper say?' I ask with a smile.

'"I find you unsexy and dull".'

'And I don't want *that* . . .' I pause. 'My friend Paolo suggested I should buy her some lingerie . . .'

291

'Oh, I'm not sure about that.' Tanzie shakes her head emphatically.

'Why not?'

'Well, that would be saying, "I see you as a sexual being". I mean, I'm sure you do, but, timing-wise it's not quite the right message—' She breaks off and pushes back her tinted hair, which today has assumed the darker hue of an aubergine. 'You don't want frumpy, and you don't want full-on sexy either.'

I nod. 'Complicated, isn't it?'

'Yeah . . .' She chews at her lip. 'Hang on, what's that shop called again?'

'Which one? Could you narrow it down for me a bit?'

She munches thoughtfully on the remains of her short-bread and washes it down with her coffee. 'Oh – you know. Cotton prints, fifties-style, kinda virginal-looking . . .' Now she's lost me completely. 'My friend Maggie had an apron from there. You must know it, Nate. *Everything* has flowers on . . .'

'Erm, Topshop?'

'You don't get aprons in Topshop!' she sniggers. I extract my phone from my pocket, intending to identify it by googling – but then, what would I google? Tanzie glances around the cafe in which, coincidentally, every surface seems to bear a jangly floral design. Then her gaze seems to light upon something. 'Excuse me!' she barks, at which a woman turns around from her table. 'See your bag? Where's it from, if you don't mind me asking?'

The woman glances round at the satchel dangling from her chair. 'Er, Cath Kidston,' she replies.

'Cath Kidston!' Tanzie repeats triumphantly, as if she's just nailed a crucial question at the pub quiz. 'That's it.

292

Thanks.' She turns back to me. 'They call it modern vintage . . .'

'Isn't that a contradiction in terms?' I ask as a teenage waitress places our bill on a doily-lined plate on our table.

'Yeah – but it's just the thing. It's kind of twee, but a certain kind of woman can pull it off.' She grins, and after a brief, heated argument about who'll pay our bill – 'Tanzie, of course I can buy you a coffee and a biscuit!' – we leave the cafe.

As it turns out, Cath Kidston is just a couple of streets away. I realise pretty quickly that, while it certainly has that retro look that Sinead tends to go for, many of the items are decidedly domestic. And if I've learnt one lesson recently, it's that my wife will no more appreciate a peg bag or set of tea towels than those garage fore-court flowers presented in a bucket she already owned anyway.

Tanzie moves on to the clothing section. She herself is wearing skinny jeans, a thin sweater that has some kind of sparkle to it, and a dark blue jacket which might be real leather or possibly fake, with numerous zips and pockets. A voluminous purple suede bag is slung over her shoulder.

We flick through rails of jumpers together, like some bizarre couple.

'How about this?' Now she is holding up dress after dress against herself, emblazoned with rabbits and teddies, some wearing spectacles. One is entirely patterned in guinea pigs.

'That's not a frock,' I retort. 'It's an *infestation*.'

She splutters and replaces it on the rail. 'Sorry, Nate. I don't think I'm being very helpful.'

I inhale deeply and look around. 'You are, but I think I need to get out of here.'

We find ourselves in a bookshop next. To my shame, I'm surprised to see Tanzie veering enthusiastically towards the biographies section. Here, she flicks through one after another, at one point shunning my offer of help and clambering onto a stool in order to reach a top shelf.

'You like reading?' I ask as she jumps back down.

'God, yeah. I'm always buying books . . .'

'Can I get you one, as a thank you for helping me out today?'

'No,' she exclaims, stuffing the book back onto the shelf, in the incorrect section, as it happens. It triggers a slight frisson of unease in me, as used to happen when anyone replaced one of my albums in the wrong place (not a problem I'll have to live with anymore!). 'They're so expensive here,' she adds. 'A tenner, some of them.' She shakes her head emphatically. 'I get mine from charity shops.'

We move on to more shops, where we peruse jewellery, handbags and fancy toiletries, the kind of things I'd imagine some women would be excited by, but perhaps not my wife. Hungry now, I moot the possibility of taking Tanzie for a late lunch. Again, she protests – 'Can't we just have a sandwich on a bench?' – but the afternoon is turning cooler, and I manage to persuade her to stop off at a tapas restaurant tucked down a cobbled lane. The menu seems to baffle her.

'A lot of people go for our set lunchtime selection,' explains the helpful waiter, so that's what we do.

Tanzie seems to love it, her only criticism being that 'the dishes are tiny, aren't they? It wasn't like this when I went to Spain.'

'You've been to Spain?' I ask, trying to mask my surprise.

'Yeah,' she says, tucking into the patatas bravas. 'Me and Neil took the kids. Our last holiday together. Bit of a disaster, really . . .'

'Weren't you getting on well then?'

'It wasn't that,' she retorts. 'Silly bugger was too macho for sunscreen. Said he'd never needed it in his life.' She sniggers. 'Yeah – but that's because he'd never been out of Yorkshire before. So he burnt from head to foot, had to be seen by the Spanish doctor . . .'

I smile at that. She makes it sound as if there was only one in the entire country.

'So, where are we with the birthday present?' she asks now, after a swig of Coke.

'I'm a bit stuck, to be honest.'

'Yeah. Sorry we haven't found anything.'

'Oh, don't be sorry,' I say. 'I'm having a really lovely day. It's fun.' I catch myself and laugh. 'I've never said that about shopping before . . .'

Tanzie laughs too. 'There's a first time for everything. So, anyway . . .' She leans forward. 'Tell me about your job, Mr-Examiner-Man. What's it really like?'

I shrug and wonder how to explain it. 'I suppose it's just as you'd imagine, really.'

'What's the worst thing, though? I mean, which part of the job d'you hate?'

I consider this, deciding not to go into the threats I've received, or the odd violent outburst. 'Well, occasionally you get a candidate with awful BO.' I pause and look at her. 'I know that sounds mean. It's just, when you're trapped in a car for forty minutes . . .'

'Why can't people just wear deodorant?' she muses.

295

'No idea. Maybe they do, but they're so nervous their sweat breaks right through it.'

'Yeah.' She nods. 'I don't blame you, you know.'

'For minding about people with BO?'

'No,' she exclaims, 'for failing me all those times.'

'Oh,' I murmur, experiencing a surge of guilt; the only time it's happened regarding a candidate in all of my ten years in the job.

Tapas devoured, she rests her fork in a terracotta bowl. 'You were just doing your job,' she adds.

'Well, that's what I try to do, to the best of my abilities . . .' I pause, keen to move on from the subject. 'Are you all finished? Shall we go?'

'Sure,' she says with a smile. 'Looks like it's brightening up out there . . .'

And so it has as we step back outside. The sky has turned a pale, clear blue, and the half-timbered shops are bathed in sunlight. Wondering aloud where to go next, we find ourselves drifting into not another shop, but the Castle Museum. Here, Tanzie is enthralled by reconstructions of Victorian shops, and gazes around in awe like a child visiting a museum for the very first time. Then it's onwards to the Minster, where the splendour of the stained glass windows renders her speechless for a few moments.

'I'm not a churchgoer – are you, Nate?' she asks in a reverential whisper.

'No, not at all,' I whisper back.

'But honestly, if there was one like this near me I'd be tempted to just go and sit and think about things, you know? I mean, life and stuff . . .'

'I probably would too,' I murmur, knowing exactly what she means.

'That's a pretty over-the-top church!' she adds as we step back outside. I smile, genuinely enjoying Tanzie's un-jaded attitude. 'I'm having such a fun day, Nate,' she adds.

'Me too,' I say truthfully. 'And I really appreciate you coming with me.' Now I'm wondering how I might put my other plan into action – because I have decided to buy another gift, apart from Sinead's. Tanzie has been such fun and engaging company, at a time when I could barely remember laughing at anything, and I want to show my appreciation. 'D'you mind if I nip off for a few minutes by myself?' I ask.

She looks taken aback briefly, then smiles again. 'No, of course not.' Having lost our bearings now in the twisty streets, we have ended up outside the bookshop again. 'I'll wait for you in there,' she says. 'You'll know where to find me.'

We part company, and I head for the shop I have in mind, which suddenly seems far more daunting than it did from outside. In fact, the silver dress she had admired in the window of New Look is nowhere to be seen in the actual store, despite my thorough search.

Sinead always said I'm a 'typical male' in that I'll do almost anything to avoid asking for help – which I suppose is true. The trouble is, in here it's virtually impossible to distinguish the staff from the customers. Finally, spotting a girl folding knitwear on a table, I venture over. 'Excuse me,' I say, feeling terribly old and out of place, 'there's a silver dress in the window. I wondered where I might find it?'

She gawps at me as if I have asked whereabouts in the store I might locate fish. 'What's it like?'

The one that looks like it's made out of Bacofoil. 'Erm,

297

it's shiny and silvery, without sleeves, I think . . .' She blinks at me and wanders away. Confused as to whether I'm supposed to follow her, I trail after the girl, in the manner of a dad coming to collect his teenage daughter from a party – smiling apologetically whenever any of these children make brief eye contact, and thanking her profusely when she finally jabs at several silver dresses dangling from a rail.

Now, what size might Tanzie be? I flick through the selection, wondering whether she might be annoyed at me buying it for her – but then, I want to treat her. Is she a size twelve, maybe? Or a ten? Wary of causing offence in the manner of Sinead's leopard skirt, I examine dress after dress, deciding eventually to go 'by eye' (she is *tiny*) and, to play doubly safe, requesting a gift receipt at the till.

Back in the bookshop I find her engrossed in the memoirs of some TV star I have never heard of. 'Oh, here you are!' She grins, jumps up and shoves it back on the shelf. 'So, where to next?'

'I'm not sure.' I beam at her, clutching the New Look carrier bag. 'Actually, I don't know if I can face any more shops today.'

She peers down at the bag. 'So, you've got the present, then?'

'Um, this is for you actually . . .' I hand it to her.

'For me?' she exclaims. 'What for?'

'Just to say thank you,' I reply, sensing myself reddening now. 'If it doesn't fit, or you don't like it, there's a receipt in the bag . . .'

She pulls it out and holds it up. 'Bloody hell, Nate! You bought this for me?'

'Yes, but as I said, if you don't like—'

'I *love* it,' she exclaims, throwing her arms around me and kissing me noisily on the cheek. 'Thank you. You really are a sweetheart. Now, look – I hope you don't mind about this. I haven't bought you anything, but I do have a surprise for you too . . .'

'What sort of surprise?'

She grimaces. 'I'm not sure how you're going to take this. Maybe I should've mentioned it before. It's just, with us being here in York anyway, and it mattering so much to Andrea . . .' She folds the silver dress carefully and places it back in its bag.

'Who's Andrea?' I ask. While I've enjoyed Tanzie's company today, I hadn't factored in meeting up with any of her friends.

'My best mate,' she says, as if it should be obvious. 'It's her first night here, you see. The ones she's done in Solworth and Bradford have been brilliant – but this is all new territory to her. She's not sure how it'll go. So I'd said we'd pop in, just to show a bit of support . . .'

'Is it a cafe or something?' I ask, frowning.

'Oh, no – nothing like that. It's a club night. Eighties. Just a one-off for now but if it goes well it could be regular—'

'Tanzie, I can't go to a *club*,' I exclaim.

Her face seems to fall. 'Why not?'

'Because . . . I am not the clubbing type.'

'Neither am I,' she announces, which I suspect is a fib. 'But this isn't your normal kind of club.'

'No, it's eighties. You said.' We are leaving the bookshop now, stepping back out into the cobbled lane.

She looks at me. 'It'll be fine. Honestly – we don't have to stay late. I know you're driving. We can just show our faces, say hello, have a bit of a dance . . .'

299

'I'm really not up for that,' I blurt out, as if she's suggested a trip to a naturist beach.

Tanzie rolls her eyes at me. 'Okay – you go home then. I'll go to the club on my own.'

I glance at her. Although she's suggested this entirely un-grumpily, I can sense how much she wants company. 'But then, how would you get home?' I ask.

Tanzie shrugs. 'I could catch the last train. Honestly, it's not a problem.'

'But then, what about getting home from Hesslevale station?'

'Oh, I'll just get a taxi.' She shrugs. 'Sorry, Nate. I thought you might be up for it, but I won't try to bully you into something you don't want to do . . .'

I study my shoes for a moment. 'It's just, you know – eighties music . . .'

'Yeah.' She chuckles. 'Although, isn't Springsteen eighties too?'

'I can't imagine he'll be top of the playlist,' I say with a smile.

'No, maybe not. It'll be a laugh, though. I'll need to find somewhere to change—'

'But you look fine as you are,' I say truthfully.

'Yeah – but it's a theme night.'

I stare at her. Along with 'there'll be karaoke', 'theme night' is one of those phrases to strike terror into my heart. 'You mean, you're changing into an eighties outfit?'

'Well, yeah,' she says, as if that's obvious too. She pats her shoulder bag.

'So, you planned this for tonight? I mean, when I picked you up this morning you knew you'd be going to this club?'

She winces and smiles. 'Yeah. I didn't want to freak you out. I thought, if I just dropped it in at the end of the day . . .'

The end of the day. She's right; the shops are closing, the crowds are thinning and I still have no gift for my wife's birthday. I look at Tanzie, knowing with absolute certainty that I have no desire to venture into an eighties night – but nor am I happy about leaving her here after she's been such charming company all afternoon.

I inhale deeply. 'So, we'd just pop in, would we? And not stay long?'

'Of course!' Her face brightens. 'Doors open at eight. We can hang about somewhere, get a coffee, and go as soon as it opens. Don't worry. I'll look after you. You don't even have to dance.'

I chuckle. 'You really don't want to see me on a dance floor . . .'

Laughing now, she links her arm in mine, a gesture that would startle me normally but actually feels entirely natural – and even rather comforting.

'Just one drink, okay?' I add.

'Just the one, I promise.' She affects a serious face.

'And then we're off home.'

Tanzie nods. 'Like I said, we're just showing our faces. Andrea'll be so pleased to meet you and you'll *love* it, I know. There's a band on and everything. Maybe I should just get changed at the club . . .'

I look down at my navy blue shirt, black jacket and dark jeans. 'I'm just going like this, obviously. I mean, I'm not planning on being part of any *theme* . . .'

Tanzie nods. 'You look fine. Don't worry. You can just be the boring one out of Kajagoogoo—'

I frown, trying to conjure up an image from a long-ago episode of *Top of the Pops*. 'Was there a boring one in Kajagoogoo?'

Tanzie's face breaks into a grin. 'Well, there is now.'

Chapter Thirty-Three

The club is sandwiched between a Chinese takeaway and a dry-cleaner's, and goes by the unprepossessing name of Rumours. When we arrive, the place is virtually deserted. But never mind. We are only staying for one drink.

'So you've come!' gushes Tanzie's friend Andrea, a statuesque redhead wearing what looks like a leotard, and fishnet tights, plus a tutu of fluorescent pink netting.

Tanzie chuckles. 'Yeah. Managed to persuade him!' She turns to me and smiles. 'Andrea, this is Nate. Be gentle with him. He's of a slightly nervous disposition . . .'

Andrea feigns concern. 'Aw, not your kind of thing, is it, Nate?'

'Well, not until now,' I reply with a faint laugh, not wishing to seem like a killjoy.

'I'm off to get changed,' Tanzie announces, darting away to the ladies'.

Andrea grins at me. 'You'll love it, Nate. Next time, you'll be turning up in costume. Tall, handsome man like you, I can see you as . . .' She looks me up and down. 'Tony Hadley, maybe? From Spandau Ballet?'

303

'Really?' I muse, as if considering it as an actual possibility.

'Oh, yeah. You're very dashing for an examiner guy . . .' She laughs. 'So, what're you drinking? It's on the house . . .'

'Oh, that's very kind. Just a Coke, please.'

'Not a cocktail?' She feigns disappointment. 'Not a Long Island iced tea? You've probably forgotten how good they taste . . .'

'Thanks, but I'm driving,' I say quickly, at which she strides off to the bar.

Alone now, I take in my surroundings. If clubs aren't my natural habitat at the best of times, a near-empty one seems particularly dismal, and I'm not convinced that the atmosphere will improve as the place fills up. The walls are painted black, liberally scuffed, and a mirrorball dangles forlornly over the dance floor. As for Long Island iced teas, I do in fact recall the craze, but no one ordered them for their 'taste'. They downed the vicious blend of tequila, vodka, gin and Christ knows what else in order to achieve inebriation with minimal messing about. I would no more order one at forty-three years old than tip exploding candy into my mouth.

Over by the bar, Boy George is flirting with Clare Grogan (or perhaps she's half of Strawberry Switchblade? There's certainly an abundance of polka dots going on) over what I vaguely recognise as an A-ha track. There's a portly Michael Jackson in a suit and trilby – plus one glove, nice touch – and now I spot the arrival of Adam Ant, accompanied by several others in what I assume is just your general eighties attire. I even glimpse a couple of the kids from Fame. There are bubble perms, ra-ra skirts – even fluorescent knitted legwarmers. While I

304

can appreciate that the fifties, sixties and even seventies had their allure, style-wise, the eighties doesn't do it for me. A woman strolls past in those high-waisted jeans all the girls used to wear, plus a white shirt and a fluffy permed wig (early Kylie?). Perhaps guessing each clubber's identity will keep me occupied for the half hour or so before we can get the hell out of here.

And now, from out of the ladies', Tanzie appears like a vision in a swishy – and worryingly flammable-looking – blonde wig, plus some sort of shiny red bodysuit and a short skirt, also red, worn over the top. I reel back as she bounds towards me.

She smiles and tweaks her wig. 'Sorry I couldn't wear the dress you bought me. I kinda had it all planned out, you see.' She juts out a hip, and in one swift movement rips the skirt entirely off her body.

'Have you torn it?' I exclaim.

'No! Don't you remember that bit?' She is now standing before me in just the skin-tight bodysuit, and it's a little unnerving.

'That bit of what?' I ask.

'Their *Eurovision* performance.' She chuckles and shakes her head at me, as if everyone knows that. 'I adapted the skirt myself,' she adds, 'with Velcro.'

I nod, trying to look suitably impressed. 'That was very resourceful of you.'

She smiles broadly and refixes her attire. 'It's a crucial part, the skirt-ripping . . .'

'I have to say,' I remark, 'I don't remember Agnetha doing that.'

'Agnetha?' She gawps at me. 'Who d'you think I am, Nate?'

'Er, aren't you Agnetha from Abba?'

'Abba were seventies,' she guffaws. 'God, Nate. I thought you were a music fan, with all those records you have – I mean *had* . . .'

'Yes, but not—'

'I'm Cheryl out of Bucks Fizz,' she announces, turning to accept her cocktail from Andrea. 'He thought I was Agnetha!'

I fix on a benign smile as the two women chortle over my idiocy.

'So . . . it's definitely just one drink?' I murmur to Tanzie as Andrea shimmies away.

'Yeah-yeah,' she says quickly, nodding along to the music now: a Duran Duran track, if I remember rightly. Naturally, the DJ – a balding chap with an immense stomach – will be favouring chart hits tonight. Human League are next, followed by Tears for Fears and – I almost feel a slight connection here – Kajagoogoo. The dance floor, which has been filling steadily, now features a whole gaggle of Limahls.

'Isn't it amazing,' Tanzie marvels, 'that we thought the mullet was a pretty hot haircut at the time?'

I laugh. 'I suppose we did. It didn't reach my part of the world though.'

'Oh, there were a few of them dotted around Solworth . . .'

'Is that where you grew up?' To my shame, I haven't asked her about her childhood.

'Yeah. But my first boyfriend was more your Robert Smith type.'

'So you liked The Cure?' I ask, interest piqued, and wonder what we'd have made of each other if our paths had ever crossed. Through my later teens and early twenties, I often went to gigs in Solworth. There's only a handful of decent pubs, so I'd imagine we've have been in the same vicinity.

'Loved them,' Tanzie enthuses. 'Did you?'

'Oh, yes, I was quite a fan . . .' Perhaps by some kind of telepathy, *Friday I'm in Love* fills the room.

We both smile, and she grabs my hand and pulls me towards the dance floor. 'Did you have the spiky hair, the smudgy red lipstick?'

'I didn't quite go that far,' I say, laughing and shaking her off.

'My boyfriend did. Malcolm, his name was. Oh, come on, Nate – just this one . . .'

I shake my head grimly, and Tanzie skitters away, merging with what is now quite a lively crowd. Startlingly, she proceeds to throw herself around, still clutching her glass and swigging from it occasionally.

I stand back and watch, knowing precisely how Sinead would react if she were here now. She'd probably have a bit of a dance, and we'd remark how busy the club was so early in the night. 'Because everyone has to get home for their babysitters,' she'd laugh. But she'd enjoy it only in an *ironic* way, and she wouldn't be swigging a Long Island iced tea or wearing a cheap wig and a detachable skirt.

From the dance floor, Tanzie gesticulates for me to join her. I grin and pull my phone from my pocket, indicating that I must make a call. It's not just a dance-floor-avoidance tactic. I called Flynn earlier, but he didn't pick up. Now, at a quarter to nine, I am aware that I should make contact, in the rare event that he might have started to wonder where I am.

I step into the dingy foyer and scroll for his number.

'Hey, Dad,' he says. 'Where are you?'

307

'Still out in York. I've tried to call you a couple of times. Everything okay? You at home?'

'Yeah. I'm fine. Did you find a present for Mum?'

'Er, not yet,' I reply.

He pauses, and I can sense him tuning into the Bucks Fizz track that's playing. I remember it now: *Making Your Mind Up.* I can even recall the ripping-off-skirts part of their routine; Christ, how does that sort of thing embed itself in your brain?

'Where are *you*?' Flynn asks. 'What's that awful music?'

'Bucks Fizz.'

'Are you . . . drunk, Dad?'

'No! Of course I'm not. But I'm, er, at a club . . .'

'A what?'

I sip my Coke. 'Um, d'you remember I said Tanzie was going to help me find a present for—'

'You're shopping for Mum's birthday in a *club*?'

'Er, not exactly. Tanzie wanted to come . . . you do remember Tanzie from Burger Bill's?'

'Uh, yeah?' I can sense his bewilderment radiating across the forty-odd miles from our house.

'Well, it's her friend's event,' I prattle on. 'I'll be home very soon.'

'Oh, don't rush, Dad,' he says, his voice laced with amusement now.

'No, seriously – I'm leaving in a minute. So, are you okay?'

'Yeah – you've already asked that . . .'

I step back as a woman swishes into the club wearing a black dress of cobwebby lace and a cascading dark wig. Kate Bush, I decide. Clever. 'Just don't do anything daft,' I say over the thumping intro to Ultravox's *Vienna*.

'Don't worry, Dad. I'm just sticking knives into the

toaster – stuff like that. See you later. And have fun at the club!'

He ends our call with a snort, and by the time I've rejoined the throng in the main room, a band are setting up on the stage. I'm aware of a twinge of nostalgia as I watch them chatting and joking, the camaraderie of a bunch of musicians of a certain age. Realising the drummer looks familiar, I try to figure out where I've seen that well-worn face.

Now he's peering over at me, this man in jeans and a black shirt with an embroidered collar. With his clearly dyed hair combed into some semblance of a quiff, he doesn't quite fit in with the other, shaven-headed men – and nor does he seem to match the eighties vibe. It dawns on me, as the record ends, that it's Stan, purveyor of second-hand vinyl.

I fetch myself another Coke, and a second cocktail for Tanzie, which she accepts with enthusiasm as the band starts to play. While eighties cover bands aren't my sort of thing, this one is remarkably tight and energetic. We listen, and Tanzie flits off to dance again, seemingly accepting now that I won't be persuaded to join her. They play track after track, and the atmosphere is one of sheer enjoyment. There's nothing like live music to grab you, as far as I'm concerned. Instead of itching to leave, I'm now quite happy to enjoy the performance – not for the song choices particularly, but their proficiency as musicians.

Tanzie returns to my side.

'See the drummer?' I shout over the music. 'He's the one who made off with my records.'

'Made off with them?' Tanzie says, laughing. 'I thought there was money involved. I assumed it was *consensual* . . .'

I chuckle at her turn of phrase, and she darts off to fetch us more drinks. As she returns, the singer – a tall, narrow man with angular cheekbones and sideburns – announces they'll be back after a break.

'Hey – I thought it was you.' Now Stan has appeared in front of us.

'Hi Stan,' I say brightly. 'Great band you have there.'

'Cheers, buddy.' His gaze flicks to Tanzie. 'So, I'm guessing you're the one who finally put your foot down about all those records of his!'

'Oh, Tanzie's not my wife,' I say quickly.

'Ah, right.' He waggles a brow.

'She's just a friend,' I add, at which Stan smirks, clearly of the opinion that a man and a woman couldn't possibly socialise platonically. 'So, d'you fancy doing a number with us, Nate?' he asks.

'Maybe sometime,' I say vaguely, having no intention of ever doing so.

'No, I mean right now, or at least after our break. C'mon, I was telling the guys about you. They all remember you from way back when . . .' *From way back when.* Like one of those old, dead guys. Like Chuck-fucking-Berry. 'This kind of stuff,' Stan continues, slapping an arm around my shoulders, 'you could play with your eyes shut. It doesn't have to be cheesy, though. How about we do a Cure track? Bit of variety for the punters?'

'Thanks for asking me, but I really don't think so,' I say firmly.

'Aw, just the one number. Why not?'

Because . . . Hell, what could I say? That I haven't performed in over a decade, and no longer have the nerve? Or that my own son won't even deign to play music with me and, right now, the thought of performing in public

310

– even to a middle-aged crowd in mullet wigs – is bringing me out in a light sweat? Yet, as I glance around at the other band members, all of whom look as if they've thoroughly enjoyed themselves so far, I'm also aware of wanting to be part of something again. It's that urge to belong, to be part of a collective endeavour: the very opposite of being a driving examiner, when it's just you and some bloke who wants to daub snot on your food.

I thought my urge to play with a band had left me years ago. Yet now here it is, rearing its head – at an eighties night, of all places.

'You can play Norm's Gibson,' Stan continues, indicating a tall, skinny man sipping a pint at the bar. 'I've already okayed it with him. He's talking about leaving. Work commitments mean he can't put in the rehearsal time. So we're keeping our eyes open for someone new . . .'

'But I work full-time,' I say quickly.

'Yeah – we all do. I mean, between manning the shop and running about all over the place, picking up collections like yours – they're selling fast, by the way . . .' Stan tails off, as if he's lost his thread. 'Anyway,' he adds quickly, 'why not join us for one song? Come over and meet the guys. We'll figure out what we can play. It'll be like falling off a log to an old pro like you . . .' He beams an encouraging smile, and saunters back to join his bandmates.

Tanzie grins at me, green eyes wide and sort of sparkling. 'So, are you going to do it?'

I take a sip of my Coke. 'Old pro, he said. Made me sound about eighty-seven.'

'Stop dodging the issue,' she chastises me.

I laugh, realising our one drink has stretched to three. Weirdly, though – even though I am unable to anaesthetise

311

myself with booze against the strains of *Club Tropicana* – I am not averse to staying a *little* longer.

Tanzie tosses back her blonde wig. 'You really should do it, Nate. Go on, let yourself go a bit. Live a little . . .'

I smile at her, still not entirely sure how a seemingly straightforward shopping trip has ended up like this. The DJ puts on Bowie's *Let's Dance*, a track I'm particularly fond of. People are dancing, arms waving, and a sense of exuberance fills the club as I am transported back to my own younger self, overcome with excitement on playing this record for the first time.

'So, will you do it?' Tanzie urges. 'Go on, please!'

I look at her, jiggling enthusiastically on the spot, clutching a tall glass of brown liquid with a wedge of lime jammed over the rim. 'Okay,' I say. 'I'll do it.'

'Brilliant! Oh my God, I'm in the company of a rock star . . .'

'Hardly,' I splutter, but sensing my spirits soaring all the same. And that's how I end up accepting the loan of Norm's rather battered Gibson, and find myself in a hastily muttered discussion with the band. My heart quickens as I step up onto the stage.

We don't play a Cure track, as originally suggested in order to lure me – but Haircut 100's *Fantastic Day*. If my former bandmates could see me now. But then, it has been a fantastic day, in the weirdest sort of way. I have been to a cathedral – or an 'over-the-top church' – and examined dresses covered in guinea pigs. I have chatted and laughed and agreed that tapas come in rather small dishes, and – crucially – almost forgotten the terrible events of the past few weeks.

Christ, I've almost felt *young* again.

The song rings out in all its jangly glory, and I find

myself smiling inanely despite not really knowing the track, but, heck, it's hardly difficult. And when I look out across the dance floor, all I see are delighted faces; Michael Jackson flinging himself around with abandon, Clare Grogan jumping and Kate Bush punching the air. Then it's over, and I almost wish I could stay up there for another song . . . but Norm has reappeared to reclaim his guitar.

'That was excellent, mate,' he says, slapping my back.

'Ha, well, I did my best.' I glance over at Stan, who gives me thumbs up from behind his drum kit, and step back down off the stage.

'You were *great*,' Tanzie says, squeezing my arm. 'See, you were all nervous, but once you were up there it all came back.' She gives me a warm, wide smile. 'It was like riding a bike, wasn't it? Or driving a car, even . . .'

I laugh, and we finish our drinks.

Although I can't stomach another Coke, I can tell that Tanzie is enjoying her cocktails. 'Like another?' I suggest.

'Yes please, if you're sure?'

'It's fine,' I say. 'I'll just nip to the loo first, okay?' She nods, and I head off to find the dismal gents' at the end of a graffitied corridor. I'd assumed I'd done my time in venues with lurid scribblings on the walls, but heck, this place isn't so bad. Like in most divey clubs, once it fills with people and music you stop paying attention to the decor.

As I head back to the main room, my phone rings in my jeans back pocket. It'll be Flynn, I decide, grabbing at it. Christ, I hope everything really is okay at home. Was the knives/toaster thing really a joke?

'Nate?' It's not Flynn, but my wife.

'Sinead! Hi, love. Is everything all right?'

A man of around my age, in faded jeans, a denim waistcoat and a bandana (Bruce Springsteen?) saunters past me.

'I'm not sure,' she replies hesitantly. 'I, um, really don't know how to say this . . .'

I lean against the scuffed wall, sensing my rush of elation ebbing away rapidly. So my earlier hunch was right: my wife is in love with someone else. Maybe it's Brett O'Hara – or perhaps it's some other guy I've never heard of. Was she telling the truth when she said she hadn't been seeing someone when we were still together?

'What is it?' I murmur, looking down at the sticky floor.

'I, er . . . look, Nate, I wanted to tell you face to face, at Elliot's, but it all ended so badly that night . . .'

'Why are you crying? *Please* just tell me.' I glance to my left. Tanzie is standing there in her shiny red ensemble, wig askew.

'You okay, Nate?' she asks, frowning.

'Yes, I'm fine,' I say distractedly, and turn away.

'Who was that?' Sinead asks.

'Oh, just someone. So, what's wrong?'

I glance around and see Tanzie's face. Gone is the exuberance of a woman who loves to dance, fuelled by cocktails. Her green eyes meet mine, and there's a flicker of, well, I don't know what – disappointment, perhaps. She turns and makes for the ladies' loos.

'I'm not sure if it *is* wrong,' Sinead blurts out, 'or what it is. But I'm . . . I'm pregnant, Nate. That time, a few days before I left – can you believe it actually happened?'

I stand there for a moment, gripping my phone, oblivious now to whatever track is booming out in the main room.

314

At first, I wonder if I have heard her correctly, as it takes a moment or two for me to make sense of her words.

'Nate?' she prompts me. 'Did you hear—'

'We're going to have a baby,' is all I can say as tears stream down my face.

'Yes,' Sinead says, and she's crying too. 'Yes, Nate – we are.'

Chapter Thirty-Four

July turns hotter, and Sinead and I have started seeing each other again since her big announcement a week ago. I mean seeing as in simply *seeing*, meeting up for chats and coffee. Actually, she seems to prefer chamomile tea now, having ditched caffeine as she did during her other pregnancies. So, we are friends again – sort of.

'Let's just see what happens,' she says, when I go over to Abby's with a cake on her birthday on a blisteringly hot Saturday. It was all I could think of by way of a present, and I didn't even bake it myself. Instead, I asked The Homemade Cake Company in Hesslevale to rustle up a carrot cake, Sinead's favourite. No decoration or message on top: just richly swirled with creamy icing.

Luckily, she seems pleased as she cuts slices for me, Flynn and herself in Abby's kitchen. The insistent rain of June has made way for warm, balmy days. On this sundrenched afternoon, Abby is working at the pub. I haven't seen her since Sinead moved in with her. I guess it's kind of awkward.

I haven't seen anything of Tanzie either, since the night

at Rumours last week. Of course I was delighted with the news – wouldn't this bring Sinead and I back together? – and I told her so. Tanzie had hugged me again ('See, I *told* you everything would work out!') but refused my offer of a lift home; she was having too good a time at the club. 'I can stay at Andrea's sister's tonight,' she'd said. 'She lives in York. I'm not working tomorrow so no need to rush back.' I'd driven home aware of not being wholly in control of my faculties, despite having stuck to Coke all night. *She's pregnant,* was all I kept thinking. *It's some kind of miracle. This time, I'll make sure I'm the very best husband and father I can possibly be.*

And now Sinead, whilst perhaps not being quite as thrilled as when we conceived all those years ago, seems quietly happy about the prospect of us having another baby together.

We've also been speaking every day on the phone, mainly to talk about Flynn, about how he might be planning to fill the forthcoming summer holidays, as well as how she is feeling (pretty tired, and sick now and then – the heady scent at Little Owl tends to trigger a wave of nausea in her). Naturally, I have asked her about Brett, and she's insisted she hasn't met up with him again. However, there is no talk of Sinead moving back in with us.

'How d'you feel about the baby, really?' I ask Flynn, as the two of us walk home from Abby's later that afternoon, having left Sinead settling down for a nap.

'*God,* Dad,' he retorts. 'It's fine. 'Course it is.'

'You really mean that?'

He flashes me a quick look. 'Okay, it *is* a bit weird . . . but it's all right.'

Hmm. *Weird-but-all-right.* I guess, coming from a sixteen-year-old, this counts for wild enthusiasm.

'I mean,' he adds, 'are you and Mum going to get back together, or what?'

'I wish I could answer that,' I murmur. 'But honestly – I have no idea.'

'So, what'll happen when the baby's born?'

'I don't know about that either at the moment.'

'Have you *asked* her to move back?' I glance at my son who looks like an adult; he's adult-sized, certainly, with his light brown fringe perpetually flicking into his dark eyes, and a hint of beard growth smattering his angular chin.

'Of course I have,' I reply.

'What did she say?'

'She wants to see how things go.'

'And what does—'

'Look, Flynn,' I cut in, picking up on his exasperation as we make our way through town, 'I really can't predict how things'll turn out. I'm sorry, but this is the best I can do at the moment.'

He huffs and grunts, accelerating his walking speed now, as if trying to minimise the chance of being spotted in public with me. I'd assumed we'd left that phase behind – the horror at walking at my side. But then, at just gone five, the town is still busy, and of course it would be mortifying for him to be spotted by anyone. I'd only suggested walking over to Abby's so we could pick up Sinead's birthday cake en route. Plus, in the event that our visit was awkward, I'd thought Flynn and I could talk things over on the way back. However now, as he's clearly unwilling to talk, the trek home seems interminable.

I had also thought we might stop off for a burger at

Bill's, but now it seems like less than a brilliant idea. I'm not sure what I'd say to Tanzie, if she's even in there today. I haven't seen her since our York day a week ago. Although she was perfectly lovely about it, the news of Sinead's pregnancy kind of altered the mood somewhat. Suddenly, I felt foolish, being in a tawdry club surrounded by people in fluorescent netting and wigs. So I don't glance into Bill's as we pass. I just hope she'll get around to sorting out the Gary stuff. It still baffles me why such a sparky and, I have to say, quite brilliant woman stays with a halfwit who's blatantly putting it about.

Back home now, I let us into our house. The rest of Saturday evening seems to stretch like never-ending elastic, especially after Flynn has headed out to a gathering at his friend Luke's. I know it's normal, for a teenager to find friends' homes more appealing than their own – just like Kayla does, virtually moving in with that other family by the sounds of it. Anyway, I don't expect Flynn to stay home to keep me company. At least he has good friends, and an active social life, and Sinead and I are getting along.

'Life's not so bad, is it?' I ask Scout, as he jumps up onto the sofa with me. He just blinks at me, and stretches out on my lap as I try not to think about Sinead and Abby enjoying her birthday evening together, and how it should be me who's with her right now.

*

Still, my newly single life fills itself, somehow. I have a quick drink with Paolo on Sunday lunchtime, who reckons the baby will bring us back together: 'Definitely,' he states firmly in the Wheatsheaf's sun-dappled beer garden.

'Babies make *everything* all right.' He chuckles. 'Who'd have thought it, eh?'

'Who'd have thought what?' I ask, genuinely perplexed.

'That you still had it in you . . .'

'I'm only forty-three,' I remind him, laughing now – but, yes, I am quite amazed too. All those months and years of trying, then it's happened now. I like to believe it's fate.

'She'll soon be back home with you,' Paolo adds.

I shake my head. 'I really don't know. I mean, God, I hope so. But these days, you know . . .' I pause, enjoying the warmth of the sun on my face. 'Well, I don't want to take anything for granted anymore. But it's . . . well, I suppose I'm just willing to wait and see. I mean, what else can I do?'

We part company and I head home, meandering through town on this warm afternoon, having declined Paolo's well-meaning invitation to a family dinner. Things *are* looking better, I try to reassure myself. Obviously, I'd prefer to know that she still loves me – or is at least prepared to give me another chance. However, even if Sinead doesn't want us to get back together, at least she *does* want the baby . . . so perhaps there is hope for us after all.

Later that afternoon, I clean the kitchen and then try again to immerse myself in that wretched Berlin book. When that fails to grip me, I walk Scout for miles along the towpath beside the canal. One benefit of being left by one's wife is that you end up with a very fit dog.

That evening, following a flurry of persistent calls and texts on her part, I have Mum over for a bite to eat. Once I've made it clear that my marriage isn't up for discussion, we actually manage not to snap at each other. However, I decide not to break the news of the pregnancy to her, and asked Flynn not to either – at least, not just yet. Plenty of time for that further down the line when I have a clearer idea of how things will pan out with me and Sinead.

'Well, you seem to be coping quite well,' Mum says, arching a brow as I make her an after-dinner coffee. Like she expected rubbish to be cascading out of the kitchen bin all over the floor.

When she's gone, I manage to resist the temptation to tap on Flynn's bedroom door and ask if he fancies a jam on guitar with me, just for fun, like we used to. Not a lesson – *definitely* not a lesson. I even get so far as to hovering, needily, at his closed bedroom door. Fortunately for both of us, his mobile rings, and I take this as a cue to retreat back downstairs and leave the poor boy alone.

So, yes, life is continuing in a rather curious way. However, while I am still conscious of odd spaces all around the house where Sinead's things used to be, I *am* managing, as Mum so rightly observed. And next morning, when I show up at the Solway test centre to start the working week, it seems my fortunes have taken a turn for the better.

Sitting there, on my desk, is my father's watch.

I look over at Liv, who is grinning at me. 'You found it?' I pick it up and examine it, at once soothed by its weightiness in my hand.

She comes over and perches on the edge of my desk. 'I'd like to take credit, but it was actually a neighbour of mine. Well, not a neighbour exactly – they live way down the lane in a little old cottage. Her bloke floored our kitchen. Bit of a creep, to be honest. The kind of guy who stares at your boobs and thinks you don't notice . . .' Her green eyes glint with amusement. 'I hadn't realised he lives with Tanzie Miles, the one who's failed, what, nine tests—'

'Eleven,' I correct her.

'Poor woman!'

'Yeah – on both counts . . .' Baffled now, I turn the watch over to check for damage – but it seems perfect. 'But how did *she* manage to find it?'

'She was out walking her dog and we got chatting in the street,' Liv explains. 'She asked if she could have a quick look around in the garden for it. Apparently, she knew all about you losing it at my barbecue . . .' Clearly, Liv is struggling not to grill me about this. 'She wasn't *at* my party, though. They were invited, but didn't turn up—'

'Er, no, we just sort of ran into each other,' I say quickly, grabbing a wad of paperwork from my desk in order to convey my keenness to get on. Eric strolls in, shortly followed by Nadira, and there's a brief exchange of greetings. I'm keen to wrap up this conversation without everyone being involved.

'Apparently, you're friends?' Liv ventures, regarding me with rapt interest.

'Erm, sort of,' I bluster, sensing my face glowing.

'Who's friends?' Eric asks.

'No one,' I say quickly. Thankfully, he and Nadira fall into a conversation of their own.

Liv smirks. 'Anyway, it wasn't so much a *quick* look,' she adds. 'She was out there for ages. I offered to help, even though I'd already had a good search. She said no, she'd be systematic and it'd be easier to do it on her own. She seemed pretty determined . . .'

'Amazing,' I say, fixing the watch onto my wrist now.

Liv nods. 'She found it stuffed in the privet hedge. Well, in a nest, really—'

'In a *nest*?' I exclaim.

'Yeah.' She laughs. 'But it hadn't been put there by a bird. Guess who'd been amusing herself by making a nest for magpies, when my party was going on?'

'Ava?' I know Liv's youngest is an inventive child.

'That's right.' She shakes her head in mock exasperation. 'And she'd found your watch, lying in the long grass by the Wendy house. Instead of bringing it into the house, like any sensible child would, she put it in her nest for the birds . . .'

'Thank you so much. Honestly, I thought I'd never see it again—'

'I can't believe it still works,' she adds, 'after all the rain we've had!'

I smile. 'It's good quality, I guess . . .'

'Oh, so your watch turned up?' Eric remarks, glancing over. 'That's brilliant!'

'Yeah.' I fix on a broad smile as the sound of chatter filters through from the waiting room; looks like my first candidate has arrived.

Liv gives me another bemused grin as Eric fills the kettle. 'I think Tanzie's the one you really need to thank,' she adds with a smirk. 'Don't you?'

However, Tanzie isn't at Bill's when I drop by on my way home. 'She had to leave in a hurry,' explains a younger waitress, carrying a tray laden with ice cream desserts.

'Oh, wasn't she feeling well?' I ask.

'No, it was something to do with school,' the girl says briskly, sending the clear message that she doesn't have time to chat.

'Right. Well, thanks,' I say, stepping outside and deciding to text her instead. However, when I pull my phone from my pocket, I discover it's out of charge; in the excitement of being reunited with Dad's watch, I hadn't thought to check it. Still, I can charge it at home and send a message then. As I climb into my car, I picture Tanzie, combing Liv's garden, astounded that she took the trouble to do that for me. I'm also wondering if she's found an occasion to wear the silver dress yet.

Apparently, you're friends, Liv said, arching an eyebrow. Well, yes, we are. We might have stumbled across each other in bizarre circumstances, but I value her being in my life now – and not just because of the watch. I'm formulating a thank-you message in my mind as I pull up outside our house and step into the hallway.

'Nate?' My wife's voice rings through from the living room.

'Sinead?' I am surprised – but delighted – that she's here, until she strides through towards me and I see her stricken face.

'I've been trying to call you!' she blurts out.

I blink at her. 'What's wrong? Is everything okay?'

'No, it's not,' she declares. 'It's really *not* okay, Nate. Christ. Why was your phone off?'

'It was out of charge. I'm sorry. Come here, tell me what's wrong . . .' I go to embrace her, but she shrugs me off.

'I'm fine. It's nothing to do with the baby. At least, not the one in here . . .' She jabs at her still-flat stomach. 'Come through.' I follow her into the living room where Flynn is curled up on the sofa, earphones stuffed in, glued to his laptop.

'Hey, Flynn, everything okay?'

'Um . . . not really.' He resolutely refuses to look up. It's as if he is trying to block out the world.

'What's the matter?' I ask, but he merely looks at Sinead.

324

She looms over him, hands plonked on her narrow hips. 'Honey, *please* take those earphones out. We need to talk about this now that Dad's home.' She bobs down and squashes onto the sofa beside him.

'What's going on?' I ask, lowering myself on the armchair opposite as Flynn pulls out the earphones and tosses them to his other side.

'I was called into school this afternoon,' Sinead remarks tersely.

'What for?' *Tanzie had to go in too.* I try to shake off a creeping sense of unease that these events might be connected.

Sinead's eyes are watering, and she wipes at them impatiently with the back of her hand. 'Mrs Wrightson called me. Said there'd been an unfortunate incident – some graffiti sprayed on the back wall, the one overlooking the playing field . . .'

That feeling of unease is growing stronger now. 'What kind of graffiti?'

Sinead glances at our son. His lips are pursed, his dark eyes lowered. 'I'm sorry to have to say it again, darling,' she murmurs, at which he shrugs. She looks at me. 'It said, "Flynn Turner is a spastic".'

'What? That's disgusting!' It feels like a punch to my gut. *Spastic:* a word we detest, obviously, and one I'd assumed – optimistically, I suppose – had almost faded into obsolescence. Those taunts on the bus that Flynn endured seemed so long ago – but that single word propels us right back.

'Yeah, I know,' Sinead murmurs. 'Charming, huh?'

I exhale. 'Flynn?' He raises his gaze to meet my eyes. 'Are you okay, son?'

'Yeah, s'pose so,' he drawls, clearly trying to shrug it off.

325

'I'm really sorry this has happened to you. Do they have any idea who did it?'

He shakes his head. 'Doesn't matter.'

'It does matter, Flynn,' I say firmly. 'My God – they have to make it clear that this is completely unacceptable. What on earth possessed someone to do that? It's so *hateful*—'

'Nate, listen,' Sinead cuts in. 'They said a girl called Kayla Miles had a can of red spray paint in her bag.'

'Kayla Miles?' I gasp. 'Are you sure?'

Sinead frowns at me. 'D'you *know* this girl?'

'No,' I say quickly. 'No – I've never met her. But I do know her mother.' I look at Flynn, who has now gathered up his earphones and is tipping them from one hand to the other. 'Remember Tanzie, the waitress in Burger Bill's?'

'Yeah?' Flynn says with a nod.

'Well, I'm pretty sure this Kayla is her daughter . . .'

'Is that the Tanzie who's failed her driving test about a zillion times?' Sinead's blue-eyed gaze is fixed on me.

'Yes, it is,' I reply, feeling quite heady with anger now.

Flynn scrambles up and makes for the door. 'Look, I've had enough of this today. I don't want to make a massive thing about it, okay?'

'But it *is* a massive thing!' Sinead exclaims.

'Yeah, well – it's happened and it's all going to get cleaned off the wall by tomorrow. They can get special stuff.'

As if that makes it okay, I reflect bleakly as he stomps upstairs. The words will be gone, but everyone will have seen them and discussed them endlessly. They'll linger in people's minds, long after the 'special stuff' has been used to scour them away.

I look at Sinead who is regarding me oddly, perhaps

326

still angry that she couldn't reach me by phone – or because I am somehow acquainted with this girl's mother.

'So, Tanzie Miles works in the Burger place?' she remarks.

'Yes, that's right.' I watch Sinead as she takes this in. Although there's no visible bump yet, she has that 'thing' about her already; a certain glow to her, the suggestion that there is another life inside. It still feels like nothing short of miraculous.

'D'you know her quite well, then?' she asks.

'Our paths have just crossed,' I reply, aware that I am understating things somewhat. However, now doesn't feel like the right time to go into the vodka watermelon scenario, or the fact that Tanzie has scrutinised my wife's extremely personal list and advised me on how to proceed. I can't even contemplate telling her about our shopping day in York, convulsing with laughter over the guinea pig dress, or our foray to an eighties night.

Sinead rests her chin on her clasped hands. 'I didn't know you even liked burgers these days.'

I clear my throat. 'We just got chatting the night of Liv's barbecue, and I've popped into the restaurant a couple of times. She's a nice person. She's just been friendly—'

'You want to hang out with someone whose daughter—'

'No, of course I don't,' I say firmly. 'But do we know this for sure? That it really was Kayla, I mean?'

'I think the evidence was pretty damning, Nate!' she snaps.

'Okay, okay. I'm not saying it *wasn't* her. I just think we have to be certain—'

'Are you sure?' she barks, eyes flashing. 'Because it sounds as if you're pretty tight with her mum!'

My heart pounds as we glare at each other across

327

the living room. It feels terribly sparse now, following the removal of my records and the shelves that housed them.

'That's ridiculous,' I say, keen to curtail this exchange. Flynn will be able to hear everything – his parents rowing is the last thing he needs – and it's not getting us anywhere. I worry, too, that it can't be good for the baby, Sinead being so het up. 'I'll go into school myself,' I add, 'and ask for a meeting with Mrs, Mrs uh—'

'Mrs Wrightson.'

I clear my throat. 'Yes. She's the year head, right?'

'The *deputy* head.'

'Okay.' Bloody hell – it feels like I'm the one on trial here.

'I don't think that'll help,' Sinead adds, her tone softening.

'Well, it might.'

She purses her lips. 'I *knew* that Tanzie woman had a thing about you. That's why she keeps failing on purpose, just for an excuse to see you over and over again—' Her eyes well up.

Christ, I thought we were talking about the trouble at school? 'Don't be crazy,' I murmur. 'No one would do that. Anyway, she hasn't always had me. When someone applies for a test there's no guarantee who they'll get as their examiner. *You* know that . . .'

'Okay, okay. I'm sorry. I'm just upset, that's all . . .'

'So am I. Christ, Sinead, don't you think I care?'

Tears are rolling down her cheeks now. I step towards her, wrap my arms around her and pull her close. I expect her to edge away, to announce that she's going upstairs to try to talk to Flynn, or that she'd better get back to Abby's. But she doesn't. Instead, she presses herself even closer: so close I can feel her heart beating. There's the patter of Scout's approaching feet on the floorboards. Without looking down, I can sense him standing there, waiting to be included in the hug.

Sinead pulls away from me and scoops him up into her arms. Immediately, he settles into her embrace, as if she has never been away. She looks up at me. 'Nate, I'm so sorry – about everything.'

'Darling, it's okay.' Something seems to have caught in my throat.

'I think I made a mistake,' she adds.

My heart seems to stop. Does that mean she wants to come home?

'Look, I know I've been a bit rubbish,' I say quickly, 'and you were right, to bring up all that stuff – about how crap I've been, how unsupportive—'

'Hey,' she says gently, setting Scout back down on the floor, then winding her arms around me. 'Please, none of it matters now. I just need to be here with you and Flynn and Scout. Is it okay if I come back home?'

Chapter Thirty-Five

Tanzie

She didn't do it. I know my daughter, and she's far from perfect – but she'd never even think of doing such a terrible thing. Spraying *anything* on a wall, I mean, let alone something as vile as that. Kayla doesn't like to stand out or be noticed. She's a quiet girl, and works hard enough to scrape through her exams. Her dad knows that too – not that she sees him that much.

It annoyed me, as Kayla and I sat in Mrs Wrightson's miserable little office, that Neil wasn't there to support her. Silly, I know, as I hadn't even texted him about it. I knew there was no point. I mean, what could he do, down in London? Anyway, he's fully occupied with his new family now, his two little boys. *I'd* stand up for her, though, I decided as soon as I got that call. Stef was good about letting me dash off like that. It just felt wrong – the spray can poking out of Kayla's schoolbag, in full view of everyone in the changing room. If she *was* guilty, she'd have done a better job of hiding it. Even Mrs Wrightson couldn't argue with that.

'Well, I'm sorry,' she said, looking at me levelly across

her cluttered desk, 'but we still have to follow procedure. It's a serious incident—'

'I know it is, but Kayla's saying it wasn't her,' I shot back, willing my voice to stay strong and not wobble.

Mrs Wrightson nodded. She was wearing a grey dress and particularly unattractive earrings shaped like bow ties. 'Kayla?' She looked at my daughter, who was sitting all hunched beside me. 'Are you sure you don't know anything about that can of paint?'

'No, I don't.' She rubbed at her pink eyes and looked down at her lap.

'Kayla's told you that already,' I retorted. 'She'd never seen it before in her life.'

'Yes, I realise that, Mrs Miles.' Mrs Wrightson pulled a tight smile and looked back at Kayla. 'So, what d'you think happened today?'

Kayla sniffed. I had to grip the sides of the plastic chair to stop myself from hugging her, as I knew she'd hate that, being cuddled in a teacher's office.

'Somebody must've put it there,' she murmured.

'Why would anyone do that?' the teacher asked in a superior voice.

'How the hell should she know?' I snapped, lurching forward.

'Please, there's no need to get upset . . .'

'I think there is, actually,' I fumed. 'So, the gym teacher saw the paint, and that was that. Kayla was labelled a vandal, someone who'd insult a boy with—'

'Please, let's try and discuss this calmly.'

'That's what I came here to do,' I blasted out, sensing Kayla folding into herself, trying to shrink away to nothing. Oh, God, I'd gone in there wanting to be firm and logical,

331

and now I was on the verge of slamming my hand on the desk and fighting back tears.

'I know you're upset,' Mrs Wrightson offered, 'but I don't think shouting is going to help—'

'Can we just leave now, please?' I snapped. 'I think Kayla's been through enough today.' Before Mrs Wrightson had even given us permission, I stood up and Kayla followed.

The teacher fiddled with a flashy sapphire ring on her middle finger. 'Yes, of course. And thank you for coming in, Mrs Miles.'

As we left her office, I couldn't shake off my annoyance at not having stood up for Kayla more forcefully. They'd jumped to conclusions, that's what got me. A girl like Paige would never have been blamed without someone checking things out.

I was aware of the odd glance from other kids as we made our way down the corridor, past the framed artwork on the beige walls, and a mosaic of people standing hand in hand, with the slogan 'Every Colour is Beautiful'. Maybe I was just being paranoid. After all, it's a big school – over a thousand kids – and they couldn't *all* have known about Kayla being accused of that terrible thing. Maybe we were getting those looks because I hadn't had time to change out of my Burger Bill's tangerine shirt and my ugly black trousers. I was aware of that familiar, fatty burger smell wafting off me as we stepped out into the cool air.

'Of course I didn't do it,' Kayla says now, on the bus we've waited forty minutes to catch.

'I believe you,' I say. When I try to take hold of her hand, she pulls hers away. At least she hasn't insisted on going to Paige's tonight.

'So, who d'you think might've put that can in your bag?'

'Don't know,' she mutters.

I turn to look at her face. Her cheeks are still pink, irritated by her tears. Her hair is half coming down from its topknot and hanging around her face, looking a bit greasy. Her ears look sore too. She had her first piercings at fourteen, nagged me until I crumbled, eventually coming to the conclusion: is this really worth fighting over? *Pick your battles,* I thought. I took her to Claire's Accessories in Solworth and wandered around the shop, pretending to be fascinated by pouches of something called 'unicorn glitter' while my little girl had her lobes punctured with a gun.

Then came the nagging for a second piercing, which I said a definite no to. I'm not a fan of loads of studs and hoops, all the way up the ears. So she got Paige to do it – Perfect Paige with the big house, the professional parents with their running gadgets and half-marathon boastings on Facebook. One evening, when they were out, Paige found a needle and jabbed it through Kayla's ear. Of course it went pus-y, oozing yellow goo; Kayla needed an antibiotic for the infection.

'It can happen to anyone,' she said defensively, when we came back from the doctor's. 'Paige knew what she was doing.'

'Of course she did,' I retorted. 'If you had a bad tooth, and she offered to pull it out with some rusty old pliers, would you have let her do that too?'

We sit there in silence now, the bus chugging out of Hesslevale and into the country, where it passes through three villages before our stop. 'Okay,' I say eventually, 'so can you at least think of someone who might've wanted to get you into trouble?'

333

Kayla shakes her head.

'Or someone who has it in for Flynn, for some reason?'

'No one does,' she mumbles. 'Everyone likes Flynn.' She wipes a sweatshirt sleeve across her face. 'No one's ever going to believe me, Mum,' she adds.

'Yes, they are,' I say. 'The truth'll come out, and then someone will have to apologise to you. I'll see to that.'

We fall into silence, and she leans into me and closes her eyes. I slide an arm around her as the bus rumbles through narrow country lanes. Despite our horrible day, it feels so good, having my girl close like this. Sometimes I miss her so much, it causes an actual ache. Nate seemed to understand that – how hard it is to feel you're being pushed away by your own kid. What must he be thinking now? I wonder. He'll be furious, naturally – and like everyone else, he'll probably assume Kayla did it. After all, he doesn't know her. I wish he'd met her. Then he'd know she'd never do such a horrible thing.

Of course, he hasn't been in touch about his dad's watch either. I wouldn't expect him to now. I just wanted to do a nice thing for him after our day in York, when he bought me that dress. I feel for my phone in my pocket, itching to call, or at least text him. I picture him standing there, looking ridiculously out of place at Andrea's eighties night, and remember how I just wanted to see him smile and have fun. And that first time we met properly – I mean, not just in a driving test situation – when he was pissed and splattered in pink watermelon juice. I just wanted to hug him then too. My fingers fold around my phone, even though I know I'm the last person he'll want to hear from now.

Back home, Kayla heads straight to her room, while I round up all the mugs and smeary glasses that have been left dotted around the living room. Is this the kind of thing Sinead was so angry about? I can't believe Nate's like Gary, who, incidentally, is still out at work, no call or text to say when he's coming home.

That's a good thing, I decide, as I head out to walk Wolfie down the lane. I don't want to see him right now, and have to explain what happened at school today. I know exactly how it'd play out: another reason why I am a disaster as a mother, a woman, a human being. Well, sod him. I don't care what he thinks anymore. I felt out of control in Mrs Wrightson's shabby office, with her in a position of superiority and me feeling like nothing. I'm sick of feeling like nothing. I won't allow it to happen anymore.

Heading back to the house now, I pause at the farm gate and tap out a text to Nate: *So sorry about what happened at school today. It's disgusting. Please believe me that Kayla had nothing to do with it. I hope Flynn is okay. Feel free to call me anytime, T xx.*

And then, much later, when no reply comes and Gary still hasn't returned home, I climb into bed, making a firm decision to change my life.

Chapter Thirty-Six

Nate

Hesslevale is in full bloom. It's midsummer now, and the island on the town centre roundabout has been cultivated, with vegetables and flowers growing abundantly. Anyone is allowed to take them. It's part of the community gardening project, which Sinead has thrown herself into since she came back to us. Howard from next door – who spearheads the venture – is delighted that she's become involved.

'It's doing me good,' she says, coming in one evening smelling of sunshine with a basket filled with broccoli and nasturtiums – which, apparently, you can eat (flowers in your salad is very Hesslevale). She is still working in the shop, and keeping busy; too busy, I worry sometimes, considering her 'condition' (I know that sounds terribly Victorian).

However, when Sinead has her scan, and we see the curled-up little smudge nestling there – everything apparently fine – we feel reassured enough to start thinking about names. Sophie, Nina, Clara? Leo, Noah, James? I suggest Arthur, after my dad.

'Hmmm. Not sure about that,' Sinead says.

'Or "Arty"?' I add as a joke. 'Arty Turner . . .'

'Arty Farty,' she says, giggling.

'Or how about my dad's middle name?' I suggest.

'What was that again?'

'Charles. Charlie . . .'

'I like Charlie,' she says. 'It's cute but fine for a grown-up too.' She pauses, seeming distracted now as she chops vegetables at the kitchen worktop. 'Can you remember if Flynn's still funny about mushrooms?'

'Yep, no change there,' I reply, surprised that she's asked. Sinead's always had Flynn's dietary likes and dislikes firmly imprinted on her brain.

'I wonder when your likes and dislikes become sort of fixed?' she muses. 'I mean, when your taste buds basically stop changing? Or d'you think there's still the potential to like something you've always hated, even at our ripe old age?'

I smile and wind my arms around her waist. She's wearing her hair up in a messy topknot, and as she resumes chopping, I can't resist kissing the back of her slender neck. 'I think he'll regard mushrooms as the devil's work for the rest of his life.'

'He can have a jar sauce then,' she adds.

'Or I could make something just for him.'

She exhales, sets the knife down on the chopping board and turns to face me. Something is bothering her now, and I assume it's not mushrooms. 'I don't think we should get into making two separate meals, do you?' she asks.

'No, I guess you're right.' I am conscious of being careful to agree with her as much as humanly possible.

She pushes a frond of fair hair from her eyes. 'Nate,'

she says carefully, 'd'you think we should have an amniocentesis?'

I frown and take hold of her hand. I know it's been worrying her, whether or not to have the test, to find out whether our baby has a significant risk of chromosome abnormalities. We're also aware that the test carries a slight risk of causing miscarriage. 'Look, darling,' I say, 'every time we talk about this, we come to the same conclusion, don't we?'

Sinead nods. 'Yes, I know.'

'I mean, if there *was* something . . .' I pause. We both detest the word 'abnormal'. 'Whatever it showed up,' I go on, 'what would we do anyway?'

'We'd carry on with the pregnancy,' she says firmly. 'It's just . . . you do realise I'm ancient, in baby-making terms?'

I enfold her in a hug. 'Hey, come on. Look at all we've been through together. I think we can handle anything life throws at us now, don't you?'

She presses her face into my chest, and when she pulls away she musters a smile. 'Yes, I suppose we can.' She glances down at my watch and touches its face. 'I think it's sweet, how attached you are to that.'

'I lost it, you know,' I say, taking over now in the making of dinner as, looking exhausted, Sinead sits at the kitchen table, where she flips open her laptop. More research, probably. Despite my reassurances that everything will be okay, we are both aware that sixteen years have passed since our son was born. She was just twenty-seven then.

'What did you lose?' she asks vaguely.

'My watch. I lost it at Liv's barbecue . . .' I teeter on the edge of telling her that Tanzie found it. Now we're back together, it feels important not to have any secrets

– however insignificant. One day, I might even work up to telling her about eighties night.

She peers at the screen. 'It says here I shouldn't be eating sprouts.'

'But you don't like sprouts,' I remind her. 'Neither does Flynn, or Mum, for that matter. Remember, we decided not to bother with them last Christmas—'

'Not those kind of sprouts.' She turns around and frowns, as if I am a pupil who's failed to pay proper attention in class. 'I mean sprouted *seeds*, like alfalfa and all that . . .'

'Oh, right,' I say, although I'm not entirely sure what alfalfa seeds look like.

'They're impossible to wash clean,' she adds, focusing back on the screen while I make two sauces – mushroomy for us, tomato and basil for Flynn.

Conversation is rather stilted later at dinner. Was it always like this, I wonder, as Flynn shovels in his pasta as if stoking an engine? Perhaps I'm just being sensitive.

Sinead's back, I remind myself, when she's headed upstairs for a bath and Flynn has wandered off to play guitar in his room, and I am loading the dishwasher. That's all that really matters.

It's when I'm wiping down the worktops that I spot the sheet of paper lying there, beside the fruit bowl.

It's a list, written in her handwriting. For a moment, it feels like my heart has stopped. I pick it up and read:

Swan's feather
Wave crest
Summer cloud
Dandelion clock

I stand there, staring at it, wondering if it's some kind of code, referring to . . . what exactly? I turn at the sound of footsteps on the stairs. Sinead appears, smiling, wrapped up in her dressing gown.

'What's this?' I ask lightly, still clutching the sheet of paper.

'Oh, that's just a list I made.'

'Yes, I see that . . .'

She frowns, then her eyes flicker with knowing and she gasps. 'You didn't think it was something . . . awful, did you?'

'No, no, I just wondered . . .' I place it back on the worktop and squeeze out the dishcloth.

'It's just paint colours, Nate. For the spare room. I mean, for the *baby's* room . . .'

'Oh, yes, of course!'

She stretches up and kisses my cheek. 'We are going to get all that junk out of there, aren't we? And redecorate?'

'Yes, absolutely. I was thinking about that.' I look at my wife, all pink and fragrant from her bath, and take her in my arms.

'It's just, I'm worried it won't be ready for when the baby comes.'

'Hey,' I say gently, 'there's plenty of time—'

'I'd just feel better, if it was all done . . .' She breaks off, and I remember this from the other two pregnancies: the fixating on paint colours, curtains, a lampshade and cot, and how she wouldn't settle until everything was perfect. The baby we lost at ten weeks had had a nursery ready and waiting. I didn't remind her that Flynn had slept in a cot at our bedside for the first year.

'The nesting thing's kicking in, isn't it?' I ask, touching her cheek.

Sinead nods. 'You know what I'm like. Please bear with me.'

'I know,' I say. 'I do remember from the other times. Just leave it to me, okay? I'll clear out the room and we'll have it all ready in no time.'

'Thanks, darling.' She grins now, and seems to relax. 'I just want everything to feel right.'

So I start that evening, even though it does seem a little crazy, with something like six months to go, to be dragging Sinead's old filing cabinet from the spare room and parking it in the corner of our bedroom (there really is nowhere else to put it). It feels a little like arriving at the airport three hours before take-off, as we did on those holidays when Flynn was little: better to hang out in Starbucks for what felt like a week than risk missing our flight.

But then, if it's important to her, it's important to me. I haul out all the boxes of books, old toys and God knows what else we've been hanging onto, and carry them up to the loft. I find a gnarly old tennis ball that belonged to Larry, our lurcher, and Flynn's matted old panda that endured many washing-machine cycles over the years.

Finally, the room is bare, its hint-of-apple walls distinctly grubby, the grey-blue carpet fuzzed with dust. A male voice drifts upstairs from the TV; Sinead and Flynn are watching a documentary about Scientologists. They're fascinated by that kind of stuff. I'm aware of them discussing it, enjoying watching it together. Perhaps everything really will be okay, after all?

All finished for the night, I stand in the doorway and assess the room that will soon be ready for our baby. There were three of us living here when we first moved

341

in, so delighted to own a real house, with a garden – a proper family home. Then, briefly, there were two. Soon there'll be four, I muse, wondering now what those paint colours actually look like – not that I care really. I'd agree to have this room papered with gold leaf if that's what Sinead wanted – because right now, I feel like the luckiest man in the world.

*

Three days later, I'm still trying to remind myself of that when Sinead calls me at work to say she's having strange cramps, and by the time I've rushed home, she is bleeding.

'It'll be okay, darling,' I say, even though – remembering the last time this happened – I know there's a very strong chance that it won't be.

At Solworth hospital I hold her hand tightly as she has another scan. This time, something *is* wrong.

'I'm very sorry,' the young blonde woman says, 'but there's no heartbeat.'

And so our baby has died, and all I can do is hold Sinead as she cries in the hospital bed, and tell her it's no one's fault, that miscarriages happen all the time.

'We'll be okay, my darling,' I soothe her. 'We can try again.' I catch a flash of horror on her pale, drawn face. 'Or we can just be together,' I add, wiping away my own tears now. 'That's all we need, isn't it? To be together. You, me and Flynn.'

Chapter Thirty-Seven

Tanzie

In the end, it's not the uncaring attitude that does it, or even the shagging around. Like Sinead with her list, sometimes it's the little things that tip you over the edge. Only with me, it's not about shoddy DIY or dog poo left in the garden. It's *driving*.

'Gary,' I start, one wet Thursday evening as soon as Kayla has gone to bed, 'I want to sit one more test.'

'No way,' he retorts. 'We're done with all that. You've had a try – God, you've tried. But enough's enough.'

I stare at him, plonked there on the sofa, beer can in hand, family bag of sweet chilli crisps torn open on his lap. 'You can't say that. I want to give it one last try.'

'But you've spent hundreds – thousands – already,' he thunders. 'It's just not going to happen. You need to accept that—'

'I don't need to accept anything,' I insist. 'What I need is to be able to drive. I'm forty years old, Gary. I need that freedom, especially with us living way out here. I'm sick of spending my life waiting for buses. Anyway, if I pass the test and can afford to run a small car, maybe I could leave Bill's and find another job—'

'*What* other job?' He looks at me as if I am stark raving mad.

'I mean a job like I had at Brogan Mitchell that was varied and interesting and not just about carrying food.'

Gary's pale eyes narrow, then he seems to lose interest as he flicks on the TV. He sits there, a hand clamped around the remote control as if it's his penis, but plastic, with buttons all over it. Only, he keeps the remote to himself – no one else is allowed to touch it – whereas with his penis he likes to share it around.

My gaze flicks from the football on TV to the passive face of my boyfriend. I have barely spoken to him since the day he found out about the spray painting at school (he was convinced Kayla was lying), apart from to tell him that the person who planted that can in her bag was a boy called Thomas Darling. Despite the angelic name, he'd taken it badly when Kayla said she didn't want to go out with him – and then he was caught in the act by a caretaker, spraying more obscenities on that same wall. Only this time, Kayla was the subject, and the word 'slag' was involved.

The little shit. He's been suspended now, and Mrs Wrightson called to say that Flynn's mum and dad had been told exactly what had happened. She even apologised, which was big of her. But Nate hasn't been in touch and, despite Kayla's name being cleared, she was relieved when school broke up for summer. She's spending less time at Paige's, and enjoying earning some cash, doing the odd shift in the kitchen at Burger Bill's. I think Stef took pity on us after all the upset.

It's much later, and Gary and I are in bed, when I

raise the driving issue again. 'So, I'm serious about sitting another test,' I say.

He turns and peers at me. His stubble is patchy, and I can smell beer mixed with sour breath. These days, he doesn't always bother to clean his teeth. Perhaps, being a flooring guy, he's hoping they'll go fuzzy like tiny carpet tiles. *That* would be on-brand. How did I once find him irresistible? I suppose he was quite a looker when I met him. Perhaps he still is, but I just can't see it. 'Are you still going on about learning to drive?' he asks gruffly.

'Yes, and I'm going ahead with it. I have enough money saved up. I really want to do this.'

He blows out air. 'Sometimes, you've just got to face facts, Tanz . . .'

'What facts?'

He exhales through his nostrils. 'That your time's passed, you're too long in the tooth—'

'You make me sound like a greyhound that's about to be put down!' I snap.

'Look, I'm tired, okay? Can we just leave this?'

Music is playing in Kayla's room now. She wouldn't normally put it on so late, and I plead silently for Gary not to shout through to tell her to turn it off. Of course, she's trying to blot out our voices. I'm sorry for bickering when she's in earshot, but sometimes you just can't help yourself.

I edge away from him to ensure that our bodies don't touch, even accidentally. He emits a snore, but I suspect he's faking.

Arsehole, I mouth at him. *You duped me. You did everything you could to convince me you were a lovely guy – a catch, for someone like me.*

The snoring grows louder. Shit – he really is asleep. The

bloody cheek. With a surge of anger, I poke him in the side.

'Uh?' he blusters, eyes blinking open.

'Gary,' I say levelly, 'I need to talk to you. I want to talk *now*.'

'Fuck's sake, Tanz. What is it with you tonight?'

'I just want you to tell me the truth.'

He frowns. 'The truth about what?'

'*You* know.'

He mutters under his breath, then sits up, rearranging his half of the duvet irritably as if he's the one being wronged. That time Nate came round, and I read his wife's list, I joked that there was never just one mouse. Well, I'm wondering now if there's never just one woman either. Get away with it once, so why not try it again? Why not have a whole *colony*?

'Tanz, I really need some sleep,' Gary says, affecting a yawn.

I look at him in the dim glow of my bedside lamp, willing myself to remain calm and not shout, or do anything that'd upset Kayla. 'I know you've been seeing someone else,' I say levelly.

'Huh? What're you talking about?'

'That time I took my last driving test, when I saw your van parked in Solworth.'

He smooths a hand over his shaved head, perhaps weighing up whether to lie. 'Oh, *that* . . .'

I glance up at the mottled ceiling, inhaling the damp smell that Gary's told me I've been imagining, but I know it's there. 'You said I'd made a mistake,' I continue. 'But I know it was yours. So, whose house was it?' I sense my heartbeat accelerating, as if I've just downed a strong coffee. I'm hedging my bets as I didn't glimpse the logo

346

or lion's body with his face. But it was the right kind of van, in the precise shade of yellow. He must think I'm a bloody fool.

'Just someone,' Gary mutters.

The thing is, I realise now, I don't care enough to feel angry or betrayed, because I don't want him.

'It was nothing,' Gary adds. 'Anyway, it's all over now.'

With those few words, my entire body seems to deflate, but not in a bad way: it's almost as if all the tension has gone out of it. He's right: it *is* over. Shit, why didn't I realise this months, or even years ago? We lie there in silence for a few minutes. It's so quiet out here in the countryside – creepily quiet. I like hearing sounds of life around me, even at night. I spoke to Stef at work today. He can come over as stern but he's kind, really. I knew he had a flat to let – two bedrooms, perfect for Kayla and me – just round the corner from her school. Although he didn't say it in so many words, I got the feeling he'll let us stay there, until we get settled, for minimum rent.

'Was that pink bra hers?' I ask now.

'Uh, that was just someone who wouldn't leave me alone,' Gary says.

'Oh, poor you,' I say, sensing rage building in me, finally. 'So, what happened? Did she come round when I was at work?'

'Yeah, just showed up out of the blue. Bit of a nutter, to be honest.'

I ease out of bed and stand there, glaring down at him in his silky pyjamas with his chest hair sprouting out. I can't be close to him anymore. I can't ever again.

'Is the pink bra woman the Solworth woman, or are they different?'

He sighs and rubs at his face. 'It's been a bit of a messy time, Tanz.'

I nod, making a conscious attempt to breathe slowly and deeply, in the hope that that'll stop me attacking him with the lamp.

'So . . . did she *forget* her bra, or what? I mean, it was pretty large, Gary – a 38D. And you know I'm not built that way, but even I'd notice if I left someone's house with no bra on . . .'

He purses his lips. 'I think she must've left it there on purpose.'

I choke back a mirthless laugh. 'What, so I'd find it?'

'Fuck knows,' he says with a shrug.

I glance around the dismal room, wondering what happened to me, how I lost my spirit, and why I've carried on as if everything is normal when, deep down, I've known for years.

'Anyway,' he adds, sounding indignant now, 'what about you, that night you went to that eighties club?'

'What about it?' I shoot back.

'Well, you were coming home, and then you weren't. Funny how you went shopping with that driving guy, just to help him out. Then I didn't see you again till the next day . . .'

'I told you, I stayed at Andrea's sister's . . .'

'Yeah?' He sniggers witheringly. 'Got a hotel with that speccy tosser, more like!'

I open my mouth to speak, about to protest that I didn't, and he can check with Andrea if he likes, and that maybe, if he'd really believed that, he'd have grilled me about it when I got home and not now, six weeks later. I glare at him, then I can't look anymore, because he's just not worth it. I stomp away, and grab a sleeping bag from the cupboard in the hallway and drape it over myself on the sofa in the living room. I don't even have the energy to climb into it properly.

I must sleep a little, because when I open my eyes, greyish morning light is filtering in through the window. The call to Stef is quick, done and dusted in five minutes as I stand at the back door while Wolfie potters about, doing his business outside.

When I check on Gary in our bedroom, he's still sound asleep. So is Kayla, when I peep into hers. But it doesn't take much to wake her, and whisper that we're leaving now – a taxi is on its way. For a moment, I'd thought about calling Nate. Didn't he say he'd help me out with a lift, whenever I needed one? But then, he didn't mean at the crack of dawn and, anyway, that was before the awful school stuff, when I thought we were friends. It seems crazy to miss him, considering we'd only seen each other a handful of times, but I do.

I don't blame him, of course. Anyway, he'll be back with Sinead now, which is just as it should be, with their new baby on the way.

As Kayla pulls on jeans and a sweatshirt, I lurk in her doorway as if on guard. 'Where are we going?' she asks, stuffing make-up and a few T-shirts into a bag.

'To Stef's flat.'

'We're staying with Stef?' she exclaims.

'No, not *with* him – he has an empty flat in Hesslevale. It's okay, honey. He's helping us out. But come on, we need to be quick.'

She glowers in the direction of the bedroom where my boyfriend – my *ex*-boyfriend – is still sleeping. 'Is he working today?'

'No, I don't think so. He doesn't have much on at the

moment.' Not *work*, anyhow. In other ways, he's been remarkably busy.

'So he'll be lying in for ages, Mum. You know what he's like . . .'

'Yes, but we need to go now. The taxi's meeting us at the end of the road. Come on, darling . . .'

She needs no more cajoling, and doesn't even pause to rake a brush through her dark hair as she grabs more clothes and underwear from her drawers and packs them too, plus her schoolbooks, two pairs of trainers and a beanie toy rabbit she's never grown out of.

The morning is still cool, and she shudders visibly, pulling her jacket around herself, as we step outside the cottage I have hated since the day we moved in. I glare at the yellow van – specifically, at that stupid lion logo with Gary's face on. He got his mate Davy to paint it for him. Davy, who knew Gary was shagging around – as everyone did.

'I hate that van,' Kayla murmurs, clutching Wolfie's lead.

'Me too, love.' I pause, knowing it's pathetic – vandalism, really – but I can't resist picking up a rough-edged stone, and rubbing it harshly all over the picture, over his stupid beaming face. The metallic sound it makes is oddly satisfying, and when I glance at Kayla she is grinning at me. Then I crouch down and fiddle with the valve on a tyre, but of course it's not as simple as it looks in the films. There's no satisfying hiss. In fact, nothing happens. But then, in an act of solidarity, Wolfie cocks his leg and pees against the tyre.

'Are you okay?' I ask Kayla, taking her hand as we start to walk briskly along the unmade road. I can't remember the last time she let me hold it.

'I am if you are,' she says with a weak smile.

'Yes, I am, I *definitely* am.' We trudge on, each of us with a bulging canvas bag slung over our shoulders; we're bringing just the bare minimum. I can fetch the rest some other time, and anyway, it's only stuff.

'Morning, love.' The taxi driver jumps out to help us, loading our bags into the boot.

'Morning,' I say brightly, as if this were just an ordinary day, and we're going on an excursion.

'Nice dog you've got there,' he adds as we settle into the back seat with Wolfie sprawled across our laps.

I smile, resting my hand on the soft, warm fur of his back. I checked when I booked that the driver would be okay about us having a dog with us. 'As long as there's no accidents,' came the controller's reply.

'He's a good boy,' I say. 'Silly, but good. We love him to bits, don't we, Kayla?'

'Yeah,' she says, smiling now, all traces of tiredness gone.

'So, looks like it's going to be a lovely day,' the driver adds.

I glance out of the window and see that the sky is brightening, the sun shining now. 'Yes,' I say, my gaze fixed upon the lush green sweep of the hills, 'I think it is.'

Chapter Thirty-Eight

Sinead

This time, there's no slugging of lady petrol, no manically writing a note at the kitchen table. It comes out one bright Sunday afternoon when we're walking Scout, just the two of us.

Nate has seemed distracted lately, perpetually on edge, as if trying his utmost to be on best behaviour. He has reassured me over and over that the miscarriage wasn't anyone's fault, and the logical part of me knows he's right.

We have been for a coffee in a dog-friendly cafe down by the river, and now, as we make our way along the high street, he grabs at my arm: 'Look! That's him!'

I scan the vicinity, wondering who he's talking about.

'In there,' he hisses. 'Can you see him?' He points into the noodle bar – 'Canoodles' – where a stocky man with cropped red hair is handing a stack of white cartons to a customer. 'Nate, what *are* you talking about?' I ask.

'That's him. Angus Pew!'

I shake my head in confusion. 'Angus Pew?'

'The guy who said he'd do something to my food if he saw me in his restaurant. So *that's* where he works . . .'

'Oh,' I say, realisation flooding through me. 'Well, you can rest easy now, can't you? You're not likely to ever go in there.'

He nods, and we fall into silence as we walk on. Every so often, Scout stops to sniff at a lamp post or bin. When he does his business on the patch of grass in front of the petrol station, Nate has it bagged up with remarkable swiftness.

'So,' he says, dropping a deposit into a bin, 'where to now?'

'Just home, I guess,' I reply.

We pass the burger place with its garish orange and black logo, and turn down the road that leads to Little Owl.

'How are things going in there?' he asks, as we pause to glance into the window.

'Oh – you know. It's all right.' A sense of unease washes over me. 'Erm, I'm thinking of cutting back on my hours, actually. Not straight away, but once I've got things up and running, jewellery-wise.'

'Really? Well, that's great,' he says, in a strained voice. I know what he's thinking: *you haven't shared this with me*. Despite the bright smile, there's a trace of hurt on his face.

'Nate,' I add, as we turn away from the shop, 'I've also decided I'm not going to see Rachel anymore.'

'Okay, if you think that's best.'

'I do.' In fact, I have seen her several times since I came back home, and since the miscarriage; perhaps our sessions have helped after all, as I no longer feel the need to rake over the inner workings of my mind. I just want to move on now, with my life.

Nate takes my hand as Scout trots along at his side.

353

'Well, you've been seeing her for, what, six months? You've given it a good shot . . .'

I nod as my eyes blur with unexpected tears. It's been three weeks since the miscarriage. We have carried on, getting on with our lives. I returned to work after a couple of weeks off, and Flynn has found himself a summer job at the kids' holiday club, teaching the little ones guitar. I could not be more proud of him.

I turn, aware of Nate glancing at me, his dark eyes filled with concern.

'Are you okay, darling?'

I swallow and nod wordlessly as we walk. He's wearing his typical weekend attire of dark jeans and a navy blue T-shirt with a silhouetted flock of birds on the front. 'Yes, but . . .' I pause. 'Nate,' I add, 'I have to tell you something. Please believe me that this isn't about you, or anything you've done or haven't done . . .'

I glance to gauge his reaction. The colour seems to drain from his face.

'I'm sorry I wrote that list,' I go on. 'Really I am. But this time – look, I've really tried. And I know you have, taking such good care of me, being so kind. You even did up the baby's room. You sanded the floor, put up those shelves, just because I wanted it. You're a *great* husband, Nate . . .' I try to blink away the tears, hating losing it like this in public.

'But not for you,' he murmurs. 'Is that what you're saying?'

We stop at the end of the street, and I rub my face on my sleeve. 'Yes, I suppose I am. Since I came back, even before we lost the baby . . .'

Nate nods. 'I know it's been difficult.' A strained silence descends as we resume walking. 'I should have gone to counselling with you,' he adds, 'when you asked me.'

354

'Never mind that,' I murmur, even though I did mind, very much, at the time.

How would you feel about us going to talk to someone? I asked, the first time I raised it. Nate looked at me in confusion, clutching a charred oven glove that neither of us had got around to throwing away. *Talk to someone?* he asked. *What d'you mean?* Well, I didn't mean just anyone. Not the lollipop man or that new lady with the weird mustard-coloured hair in Londis. *I don't think we need to,* he said eventually, *do you?*

'It was important, though,' he says now. 'I think that's what happened. I'd become a bit blinkered. I'd stopped seeing the things that really mattered—'

'Don't blame yourself,' I say quickly. 'It was both of us. It happens to people, and I honestly think we've done our best.' I glance at him as we start to walk on, Nate clutching Scout's lead, head lowered. 'Can I ask you something?' I add.

'Yes, of course.'

I pause as we arrive at the end of our street. Flynn will be out, thankfully. 'If you were to list all my faults, what would you put?'

Nate swaps Scout's lead to his other hand. 'I can't think of any,' he replies.

'Oh, Nate.' My insides seem to crush. Nate looks at me with a sort of stoical smile, and he takes my hand again as we make our way back home. It feels warm and comforting, and I should feel happy that we've got this far; we've raised a wonderful son, and grown up together. But a long time ago, I knew our time together was running out. I think perhaps Nate did too, and I also think he knows now what I am going to say.

And so, over more coffee, this time in our kitchen, I

tell him about the vacant cottage I went to view, in a village just outside Hesslevale.

'I said I'd take it,' I explain. 'It's tiny, but it's just been renovated, and there's a small garden with a river at the bottom.' I pause, willing myself to explain things calmly. 'I think Flynn should stay with you for the time being, if that's okay.'

I see him swallow, and he nods. 'Yes, I think so too,' he says, rubbing at his face.

'He's . . . well, he's happy here, Nate.' My husband nods, unable to look at me now. I'd sensed that today wouldn't be a repeat of my dramatic shock exit a few months ago, and I was right; I'm sure Nate knew it was coming.

'So, is this place furnished?' he asks distractedly.

'In a basic way, yes. It's pretty nice. You should come over.'

'Can I help with anything? I mean, is there any DIY you need doing?' He reaches across the table and squeezes my hand. 'I mean that. I'm not being shitty, I promise . . .'

I smile awkwardly. 'Erm, I don't think I need—'

'I'd just like to come over and help you sort things out, if that's okay,' he adds quickly, taking off his spectacles and rubbing at his eyes. 'You've got loads of things here. I can pack them up for you and bring them over, if you like . . .'

'That'd be great,' I murmur. 'Actually, I think there's still some of my jewellery stuff in the attic. Would you mind getting that down for me?'

'Of course – no problem . . .'

'It's just, there's an outhouse in the garden,' I add. 'It's kind of why I decided to take the place. It was an old workshop, the guy fixed farm machinery and stuff, bit of blacksmithing, that kind of thing. And it'd be perfect to turn into a studio.'

'A studio? So, you really are ready to start over.' He musters a smile.

I nod. 'I've been thinking about some designs. It's about time, Nate . . .'

'I'm really pleased for you,' he says, looking down. 'I mean, not about you moving out. Of course I'm not. But, you know, I always felt you were wasted in the gift shop . . .'

'You once called it a "little job",' I remark with a small smile.

His cheeks flush. 'Did I really say that? God, I'm sorry. How condescending . . .'

'You were right, though,' I insist. 'I mean, basically, I've been selling chakra-balancing hot-water-bottle covers that are supposed to heal you while you sleep—'

'Is there really such a thing?' Nate asks.

'I'm sorry to tell you, but there is.'

We are nursing our coffee mugs now, knowing that Flynn will be home soon, and then we'll have to tell him all over again. I'm aware, too, that Nate doesn't really want to discuss hot-water-bottle covers. There's another issue, hanging above us.

His gaze rests upon mine across the table. 'You would tell me if there was someone else, wouldn't you?'

'You mean Brett, don't you?'

'Well, yeah, I suppose I do.'

'Um, he has been in touch,' I say hesitantly, 'and we're going to meet for a drink. But please believe me, we're just friends—'

'For *now*,' Nate says, arching a brow.

'Yes.' I clear my throat. 'That's all I'm looking for – for

357

now. I don't want anyone else, truly. I just want us to carry on doing what we do, being friends and helping and supporting each other, and being Mum and Dad to Flynn.'

Nate nods and adjusts his specs. 'I just want you to be happy, Sinead,' he murmurs.

I get up and put my arms around him. 'I want you to be happy too. You're such a good person and I'm always going to love you. But right now, and I hope you can understand this . . .' I break off at the sound of the front door opening.

Our gainfully employed son is home; the boy who has his dad to thank for making him believe he could be a guitarist, never mind his condition; why should *that* hold him back? It was a gift Nate gave to him, and I hope Flynn will realise that one day.

'You do understand, don't you?' I whisper to Nate.

'Yes, I think I do.'

'I suppose,' I add, stepping away from him now, 'I just need to be *me* again.'

Chapter Thirty-Nine

Flynn

So, my parents think, because I have a disability, that they need to worry about me all the time. Or maybe it's not that, and all parents act that way. I don't think so, though. Max and Luke are allowed to do pretty much what they want without anyone worrying madly. I mean, if they stay over at ours, or at a party or whatever, they just get a text from their mums saying something like, *Hello stranger, what do you look like again?*

It's jokey and light. My parents have never been jokey and light. Actually, that's probably not fair. We had loads of good times when I was younger, and if things got trickier as I grew up – well, I suppose that's normal. When I was little it was fine to have Mum there at every medical appointment, chipping in, praising me in from of the doctor or physio or whoever. 'That's great, Flynn!' she'd say, looking all proud. There were tears, too, when I had to have something like an operation, and Dad would step in then – not because he doesn't get emotional (he does, he just tries to hide it). I guess he felt that was his job, to be the strong one. I just wish they'd realise they don't need to be so protective anymore – Mum especially.

I mean, I'm virtually an adult. A lot's happened to my family this year, and we've got through it okay. Mum and Dad split up for a while, which was pretty shocking, but then, loads of people I know have parents who aren't together, and I decided it was probably best if Mum wasn't happy. I hoped it was just a temporary thing, though – Mum living at Abby's, I mean. And it was. Then there was the baby, and they seemed happy again, for a little while – and then they weren't.

And they worry about *me* not knowing what I want to do with the rest of my life?

I'm thinking about that as I get off the bus in Solworth and check my phone for directions. *Stan's Records*. It's down some back street, behind a garage and a broken-down building. At first, it doesn't seem like it's the right road, as the only other shops down here are a tiny news-agent's and a charity shop that looks like it's closed down. When I find the place, down the end of the road, I'm amazed the guy can make a living out of it.

It was actually Kayla's idea for me to do this. At least, she sparked things off. We became friends after the thing at school with the spray paint; then *she* was the victim, so she knew exactly how I'd felt. 'Spastic' and 'slag'. Nice, huh? We started hanging out at lunch-times, going into town to get a sandwich or chips together, and more recently, now it's the holidays, we've just been meeting up in the park. I told Dad, but only because his friend Paolo said he'd seen 'your Flynn and a girl, laughing away outside the chippie the other day'. You can't do anything around here without someone noticing.

'I'm allowed to have friends, aren't I?' I asked, not minding really.

'Sure!' Dad said with a smile. I told him who the girl was, thinking he might be weird about it. Although everyone knows Kayla didn't do the graffiti, I thought Dad might not like it all being stirred up again. I also knew about her mum's twenty-five driving tests or however many it was, and we worked out that Dad must have failed her on at least some of them. So maybe it's awkward for him. I'd hate to be a driving examiner. I'd rather do something that makes people feel happy, like give guitar lessons or play in a band, than have a job that everyone associates with stress and failure. But then, I guess *somebody* has to do it.

Anyway, me and Kayla were talking about music, and I told her about Dad selling his records (which has to count as the weirdest thing he has ever done). She suggested buying some back to surprise him. Well, Dad's birthday's coming up. He'll be forty-four or forty-five, something like that. He's started playing in a band again – with this Stan guy, who I can see now, through the window of his scruffy little shop. I'm not going to buy the whole lot, obviously. The holiday club doesn't pay that well. In fact, after my bus fare, I'm thinking: maybe just one.

'Pick something that meant a real lot to him,' Kayla had said. Now, as I push open the glass door, I'm hoping it won't seem like I'm giving him something that was already his. Like that time he gave Mum that massive clump of flowers – in the old bucket from our shed.

In fact, I know which album to buy as Stan looks up from behind the cluttered counter. 'Hey,' he says with a smile. 'You're the one who phoned, yeah?'

'Uh-huh.' I'd thought I'd better check he'd be open, as there wasn't a website or anything like that. I couldn't even find a Facebook page. I just had to google record shops in the area and finally I managed to find Stan.

'So, what can I do for you?' He pauses, checking me out. Of course he remembers me. Everyone does when there's something different about you. 'You're Nate's son, right? We met when I came to pick up his records?'

'That's right,' I murmur. 'Erm, I'm looking for something for him, actually.'

'Can I help at all?'

'No, I'm good, thanks.'

He nods, and I start to flick through randomly, even though I've decided now what I'm looking for. But I want to make it look like I'm checking everything out. That's what Dad would do. He'd browse the contents of the whole shop before making his choice.

'So, are you coming to see us play next week, then?' Stan asks. 'Your dad's not bad, you know.' He chuckles. 'Quite an addition to the band. He's shaken us up . . .'

I look up from the records and smile. 'Not sure. I'll try and make it.'

'Busy schedule?' Stan teases.

'Yeah.' I make my way round to the rock section and flick through the albums, the way I've seen Dad do so many times, when he's snuck into record shops on holidays.

And here it is: exactly what I'm looking for. I examine the sleeve and carry it over to Stan at the counter.

'Just the one?' he asks.

'Yes please.'

He looks at it closely and frowns. 'Aw, I can't take your money for this, son. Just have it . . .'

'No, honestly – I want to pay for it. Please.' I fish out the cash from my pocket, and Stan shrugs and thanks me.

'So, you think he'll like it?' he asks with a ridiculous wink.

'Yeah, I reckon.' I smile at this weird-looking man with white stitching all over the collar of his black shirt, and I leave his shop, clutching my Stan's Records carrier bag. Inside the bag, with 'Nate Turner' neatly written in Biro on the back of the sleeve, is Dad's very own copy of *Born in the USA*.

Chapter Forty

Nate

It's funny how things pan out sometimes. I mean, Flynn hasn't made me a birthday card for years. He used to draw loads when he was little, the kitchen table perpetually scattered with pens and crayons and his wild pictures. I thought he'd lost interest or grown out of it. However, today, over a late Saturday breakfast, I am presented with a card bearing a rather wonky illustration of me, in T-shirt and jeans, playing guitar on a stage.

'This is brilliant,' I exclaim. 'I wasn't expecting a home-made card . . .' Or any, in fact, as I suspect Sinead always bought them for him to give to me.

'There's something else,' Flynn says, reaching down and reappearing with a flat, square parcel wrapped in checked paper. Proper wrapping paper! Impressive. I look at my son, with his hair all messy, still in trackie bottoms and the T-shirt he slept in, and smile. I have no plans for today really; Sinead and Abby have gone to a holiday house on the coast for a week – her birthday card to me arrived by post first thing – and I ducked out of Paolo's invitation for dinner at their place.

And it's fine. I mean, I am forty-four years old, not nine: I neither expect nor want a big fuss.

'Aren't you going to open it then?' Flynn prompts me.

'Okay. Thanks.' I take it from him, sensing his impatience. He has a new sort of energy about him these days; a sign that life is good right now. Perhaps a certain girl is involved? I wouldn't dream of asking about his friendship with Kayla . . . but I suspect something is happening there.

I examine the parcel, deciding to tease him by spinning it out. Clearly, it's an album – or something that feels exactly like one. It's that satisfying size and weight. I remove the paper carefully as he shuffles on his chair, no doubt wishing I'd just rip it off, the way he does.

I stare at the album in my hands and look at him. 'Flynn! My God. Thank you so much.' I beam at him. 'This is . . . well, this is fantastic. Have I ever told you it's the first record I ever bought?'

'Yeah, only about a hundred times,' he chuckles, adding, 'It's the actual one, Dad.' He is grinning now, cheeks flushed, barely able to contain himself.

'What? How can it be *the* one?' I turn the record over, and there's my juvenile Biro'd handwriting. I used to write my name on all of my records, even the singles; they never felt mine until I had.

'See?' Flynn says. 'I went to the shop and got it back for you.'

'You went to Stan's and bought this?' I ask incredulously.

'Yeah.' He nods.

'But, I don't want you spending money on me—' I stop and try to bat the tears from my eyes.

Flynn gets up and smiles. 'Hey, I'm working now.'

'Well, thank you,' I say, getting up too. 'I'm very proud of you, Flynn.'

'Hmm.' He shrugs bashfully, hovering for a moment. 'There's something else I wanted to mention.'

I frown and look at him. 'Is everything okay?'

'Oh, yeah,' he says quickly. 'It's just . . . I want to learn to drive, Dad—'

'Really? But you're not seventeen till . . .'

'It's only four weeks away.'

I smile. Of course I know when my son's birthday is.

'I've been looking into it,' he continues. 'I know there's extra stuff I'll have to do, like declare my CP and get letters from the doctor and stuff. So I phoned Dr Kadow—'

'You *phoned* him?'

'Yeah, it wasn't a big deal.' He shrugs.

'But . . . I could've done that for you,' I say, astounded that he's done this.

'It was fine,' he says breezily, already making for the door. 'He said they'll need to know when I last had a seizure, stuff like that—'

'That was *years* ago . . .'

'Yeah.' Flynn thrusts his hands into his pockets. 'Anyway, he said he can sort all that out for me.'

I pause for a moment, taking all of this in. 'So then you can apply for your provisional licence . . .'

'Yeah, that's the plan,' he says, a trace of impatience in his voice now. 'You will give me driving lessons, won't you?'

I open my mouth to speak, momentarily stunned. Our last attempted guitar lesson flashes into my mind: *those old dead guys. Chuck-fucking-Berry.* 'Are you sure you want me to?'

My son shakes his head, and laughs at my idiocy. 'Of course I want you to. I mean, why would I want anyone else?'

And then he's eager to rush off out, but not before I've hugged him; a proper hug, that is. It's not like trying to embrace an ironing board this time. It's warm and real, and it makes my heart soar. It's like another birthday present, really. In fact, I'm already imagining the two of us in my car, with him turning on the ignition and pulling away. I have to try to calm myself, because there's something else I need to do today.

After he's gone, I while away the afternoon in the garden, and do some shopping, including a stop-off at the proper florists where they do hand-tied bouquets of all kinds of blowsy flowers: 'The cottage garden look,' the woman says approvingly, as she arranges them into a bunch.

'That's what I was after,' I say, trying to sound knowledgeable. No garage forecourt flowers today. I've learnt a lot over the past few months: choose presents with care; avoid booze-infused fruit. And, as Tanzie wisely pointed out, there never is 'just one mouse'.

Tanzie Miles. She sat her driving test last week, at a different centre; one closer to York, which I thought odd when news filtered through from the manager I know there (driving examiners might have the reputation of being a dry old bunch, but we're human beings; we're not averse to a bit of gossip). Perhaps Tanzie had thought a different environment might give her the fresh start she needed. I hope it wasn't to avoid seeing me. I couldn't have done her test anyway, as we know each other personally now.

'Are we friends now, then?' she asked, that day she talked me through Burger Bill's menu.

Well, I hope so, I reflect, as I shower and change into a fresh T-shirt and clean jeans. Not that I've been a terribly good one. I know from Flynn that Tanzie finally left Gary, and that she and Kayla live in Hesslevale now, close to

367

the high school; apart from the hug, that's something else he gave me before he dashed out today. Their address, I mean. Okay, not their *precise* address, because teenagers don't deal with addresses (I mean, why would they? They never post anything). In fact, all I managed to glean was a rather confusing description of 'the road one back – no, I think *two* back from school. Near some trees. Top flat on the end.'

Granted it would have been nice to have a *bit* more to go on.

Of course, there's the strong possibility that Tanzie might not even be in on a Saturday evening, and even if she is . . . well, she might not want to see me, as I never contacted her about the incident with Flynn. My stomach swills with something like anticipation, or sheer nerves, as I stand at the back door while Scout potters about on the grass. I call him in, apologise for leaving so abruptly, and set out into the warm August evening.

As birthdays go, it's quite an unusual one, but my hopes seem to rise as I stride across town, carrying the flowers, which I have decided to leave on her doorstep if she's not in. I have written a card and attached it to the wrapping: *Hi Tanzie. I hope you and Kayla are settling into your new flat. I'm sorry I haven't been in touch. Quite a lot on. I just thought I'd drop by with these to say thank you for finding my dad's watch. I'm amazed you did that for me. I'm also delighted to hear you passed your test! See – I KNEW you could do it. Love, Nate.*

*

I know it sounds a bit stiff, but it was the best I could do. I've never found it easy to say the right words when

368

it really matters. Maybe that's been my problem, and also why my job is ideal for me: you watch, you make notes, you don't have to say a great deal.

It takes a bit of wandering around to find Tanzie's flat. When I spot the name MILES on one of the bells, I actually blurt out, 'Yes!' in delight.

I clear my throat and look down at the flowers. Is it presumptuous to show up like this, out of the blue? But I'm here now. I try the main front door, and it opens. I trot up two flights of stairs, trying to convince myself that this is a perfectly normal thing to do on a Saturday night.

On the top landing, I realise the flowers are dripping water through their cellophane wrapping onto the floor. A small puddle has formed at my feet.

I stand there for a moment, thinking: *okay, just do it. Leave the flowers and run.* A picture forms in my mind, of Tanzie and I laughing in that bizarre shop where everything seemed to be covered in ponies and guinea pigs. And that eighties night, when she bounced out of the loos in her Bucks Fizz outfit, ready to tank a fierce cocktail like it was Coke.

She's probably not even in, I decide. She is single now. She'll be out on the town, dancing and drinking, with her friends.

But then there are sounds on the other side of the door, and I flinch as it opens. At the sight of me, Tanzie seemed to reel back. '*Nate?*' she exclaims.

'Er, Tanzie, I hope it's okay. I heard about your driving test – and the watch, my God, you actually went to Liv's garden and found it for me . . .' I tail off, realising I am babbling.

She looks down at the flowers and rakes back her

funny purplish hair. 'Wow. They're pretty special. Who are they for?'

'You, of course!' I meet her gaze.

'Really? That's sweet of you . . .' She pauses. 'I thought I heard someone at the door. I assumed it was Kayla, forgotten her key . . .'

'Well, no. It's just me.'

Then she looks at me properly and smiles that huge smile, and it brightens up not just her face, but the whole stairwell – the whole town, it seems right now. I blink, dazzled for a moment, and she laughs.

'I hope it's okay,' I add, 'to just turn up like this—'

She shakes her head and then, remarkably, she reaches not for the flowers, but my hand. 'Of course it is, Nate. So don't just stand there. Aren't you going to come in?'

The End

What happens when The One That Got Away shows up again . . . thirty years later?

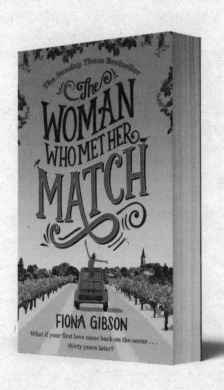

The laugh-out-loud *Sunday Times* bestseller is back – and funnier than ever!

Forget about having it all. Sometimes you just want to leave it all behind.

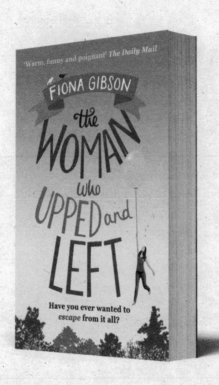

A warm, funny and honest read that's perfect for when you've just had enough.

Midlife crisis?
WHAT midlife crisis?!

A hilarious read for fans of Carole Matthews and Catherine Alliott.